ROBERT

WHAT ARE THE ODDS?

The Calculus of Coincidence

outskirts
press

Outskirts Press, Inc.
http://www.outskirtspress.com

ISBN: 978-1-9772-1759-2

Outskirts Press and the "OP" logo are trademarks belonging to Outskirts Press, Inc.

PRINTED IN THE UNITED STATES OF AMERICA

This work of fiction is dedicated to the incredible skills and tremendous personal sacrifices of thoroughbred jockeys who navigate the daily journeys of horses weighing well over half a ton, traveling at speeds upwards of 40 miles per hour, at times in tight quarters with as many as 19 fellow competitors. While jockeys ply their trade on the backs of finely tuned world-class animals, it is the thoroughbred industry whose continued success rides on the backs of these diminutive but nevertheless marvelously conditioned athletes.

I would be remiss if this novel weren't also dedicated to my loving wife and personal editor, Kim Buckey, whose role as primary breadwinner enables me to disappear for all-too-lengthy stretches of time to visit unexplored corners of my mind and commit them to paper.

Contents

Prologue

The 1970 Dodge Challenger R/T two-door convertible with a power-bulge hood came to a screeching halt in front of the Monmouth Park clubhouse. The original owner had chosen a paint job seemingly consistent with the emerging east-coast disco craze, a gaudy metallic purple (labeled Plum Crazy by the sales folks). Apparently seeking fast times in a fast car, he'd equipped the vehicle with an optional "four-on-the-floor" and a powerful RB V8 engine providing 425 B.H.P.

The muscle car's current owner, Sean Davis Jeffries, harbored few illusions about such a lifestyle. But he none-the-less had coveted his dream car for more than a decade. By his 27th birthday (March 25, 1983 to be precise), he'd finally squirreled away enough money to acquire this particular vehicle, which he spotted at a classic-car show in Freehold, NJ.

It was opening day at Monmouth Park, the thoroughbred race track nestled in the small Jersey shore town of Oceanport. Quickly emerging from his high-backed, white vinyl bucket seat, Davis searched the crew of car jockeys gathered around the valet drop-off area. He was looking for Jürgen Hauptmann, the only parking attendant he would trust with his "baby."

Sean, soon to enter his final year of evening classes at Seton Hall University's School of Law in Newark, NJ, had first met "Yor´gee" almost two years ago on the Seton Hall soccer pitch in South Orange.

Years earlier, Sean had taken a rather impromptu trip immediately following his graduation (class of '78) from Fairleigh Dickinson University in Teaneck. Rather than vacation with friends, he'd have time all to himself so he could give his brain a rest and re-charge the batteries before considering what the next phase of life might look like. He decided upon The Netherlands, Belgium, France and Germany for his two-week itinerary.

New experiences were first and foremost on Sean's list and included an "intimate" inspection of Amsterdam's red-light district, a trip to Musée du Louvre, the Grand Place in Brussels and a European soccer match in Germany's North Rhine-Westphalia region.

In Deutschland, Sean decided upon the BayArena in Leverkusen. He'd instantly become an ardent fan of the world's most popular sport, in general, and of Bayer 04 Leverkusen and Bundesliga Fußball more specifically.

So all these years later, it wasn't unusual for Sean to take time away from his legal studies to catch a soccer match at "The Hall." As he was scanning through the scorecard during his initial exposure to Pirates soccer, the town of Hückeswagen caught his eye. It was the location of an out-of-the-way boutique hotel he'd stayed at, a little more than 35 kilometers (roughly 22 miles) northwest of Leverkusen and the neighboring city of Köln (Cologne). It also happened to be Jorge's home town.

A senior midfielder, Jorge owed his stateside journey for a college education largely to happenstance, Sean had learned. Nearing completion of secondary school education in Radevormwald at Theodor-Heuss-Gymnasium, Jorge's club team had been hosting a clinic for American college soccer coaches. One of die Fußballer (the soccer players) called upon to demonstrate passing techniques, he had also been a topic of conversation between his club manager and one of the attending U.S. coaches who happened to be in charge of Seton Hall's NCAA soccer program. After an overseas telephone interview with the associate dean of academic affairs and a subsequent visit to the Seton Hall campus, Hauptmann had been offered a scholarship.

Sean further knew from their initial conversation that Jorge, who like most educated Germans was fluent in English, had spent time working at the Porsche factory in Stuttgart before heading stateside. Upon completing his bachelor's degree in business administration, Jorge ultimately wanted to return home for his M.Sc. in Automotive Engineering at RWTH Aachen University.

With Fußball and high-performance automobiles as common passions, Sean Davis Jeffries and Jorge Hauptmann developed an association that eventually extended to the track in Oceanport.

In need of a summer job to earn much-needed cash for living expenses, Jorge had asked Sean if he knew of any opportunities. As a three-year veteran of working summers in Monmouth Park's admissions department, Sean thought Fran DeSantis might be a good place to start. Known as the "matron of the Will Call window," Fran hired all the parking attendants, made sure they were well taken care of and, in her own words, "didn't screw around."

In Jorge, Fran had found not only her most reliable and hustling car jockey, but her most valuable one as well. Jumping in and out of cars while safely finding the most appropriate parking spaces for vehicles owned by some of the racetrack's wealthiest customers was the lion's share of the job. But even the most expensive automobiles sometimes arrived at the clubhouse with a problem in need of a fix.

Engine issues were most common, with overheating due to extended time in traffic jams and owner neglect in replacing engine oil the two leading culprits. Other problems ranged from the relatively simple-to-spot slow tire leak to the harder-to-diagnose transmission fluid leak. The former could be easily, if only temporarily, fixed either by one of the "spare tire in a can" products Fran stored in her office or with a compact spare many models carried in the trunk. Fran also kept a few cans of transmission fluid for the less common tranny fluid leak.

If a car jockey could diagnose and solve a problem, it would preclude the need for calling the local towing service and save the customer delays, a change in weekend plans and, quite possibly, an unanticipated expense. At a minimum, some advice for the owner before his vehicle was placed in the "care" of a repair shop could minimize the potential for a less-than-satisfactory (i.e., price-gouging) outcome.

Given his automotive experience back home, Jorge was well suited to play off the perception of German automotive engineering expertise a customer was likely to apply to him. His good looks, which included blonde hair and blue eyes set on a solid six-foot, two-inch frame and was accompanied by a slightly Anglo-German accent, certainly lent credence to this perception. In this particular instance, that pre-conceived notion was accurate.

Jorge's personal choice for transportation was a recently acquired Ford Mustang that celebrated the Official Pace Car of the '79 Indianapolis 500. He wanted a "ride" consistent with his position at the posh Jersey shore thoroughbred venue. Finished in two-tone pewter and black with orange and red graphics, the Mustang sported a unique front air dam with fog lights and a full-length cowl type hood scoop. The black interior featured Recaro seats with patterned black and white inserts. The 2.3 L (140 cu in) four-cylinder Turbo came with a four-speed manual transmission.

Now, finally spotting Jorge on the run from the valet parking lot to the clubhouse drop-off area, Sean shouted out: "Jorge! Is 'the man' here?"

"Ja, Sean. He came in about an hour ago. Herr Cutter should be upstairs in the clubhouse dining room."

Sean reflected on how his reliance on Jorge extended well beyond taking care of his automobile to gathering intelligence related to his dealings at the racetrack.

Indeed, Jorge's job as a car jockey was the arms-and-legs part of what he did at Monmouth Park. Functioning as Sean's eyes and ears filled an informal and cerebral role. It was in this latter capacity that he'd earned far more than the minimum hourly wage plus tips offered by his employer and the racetrack's clubhouse patrons.

***

Thomas Jefferson Cutter III had been a legacy student at the University of Virginia, having begun his time in Charlottesville in September of 1970. That was the year the University changed its admissions policy to allow 450 first-year co-ed undergraduate students on Grounds and offered its first scholarships to students of African-American ethnicity. TJ, as everyone called him, majored in History and earned his bachelor's degree from the College of Arts & Sciences in May of 1974.

The Cutter family had seen its share of hard times. His mother, Hannah Gordon-Cutter, had been paralyzed from the neck down when TJ was a senior in high school. The horse she was riding had spooked at a horrific head-on collision of a car and pick-up truck on a rural country road around the bend from a popular trail crossing. The horse threw Hannah to the pavement at the crossing, fracturing her neck.

Less than two months after TJ's college graduation, his father, Thomas Jefferson, Jr., had suffered a massive stroke and passed away at the ripe old age of 56. TJ was left to care for the family's massive farm where his father and grandfather, Thomas Jefferson, Sr., had bred and trained thoroughbreds, readying some for sale at auction, preparing others for racing and eventually retiring the best competitors as breeding stock. The 1,000+ -acre Cutter Farms and homestead lay north of Leesburg off of U.S. Hwy. 15, not far from the Potomac River.

An older sister, Judith, had married a fellow Texas A&M graduate, Rex Reston, who bred quarter horses at his family's ranch in Ardmore, Texas, just below the Oklahoma border. From the beginning of July through the Labor Day weekend, the couple raced their best performers at The Downs at Albuquerque and at Ruidoso Downs, about 3½ hours to the south.

Another sister, Jasmine, nine years younger than TJ, experienced hard times after the death of their dad. An unwanted pregnancy and abortion at 16, anorexia and bouts with alcohol and drugs had marked her troubled teenage years. Now 21, she was living in a bungalow in Seaside Heights, New Jersey, bought and maintained by TJ. She had supposedly straightened herself out after a temporary relapse and was working in one of the arcades on the boardwalk.

The plight of the Cutter clan aside, TJ had done wonders with Cutter Farms. He took a far more aggressive approach than his father and grandfather to the racing and breeding aspects of the thoroughbred industry while choosing to place far fewer yearlings up for auction. Honoring both family and UVA traditions, TJ had made a habit of using a derivative of his surname for all colts filed with the Jockcy Club Registry. The names of all fillies offered some connection to the University of Virginia or the Charlottesville/ Albemarle County area, honoring that first class of co-eds from 1970.

Now 30, TJ had been racing thoroughbreds under the Cutting Edge Stables moniker for not quite six years. Known within the close-knit racing community as somewhat of a wunderkind, he'd had more than his fair share of early breeding success. More than that, he was the only major industry figure personally handling the breeding, ownership and training roles for his thoroughbreds.

Patience hadn't been one of his virtues, however. Still a relative "youngster" in the business, he longed to experience the thrill of victory in one of the jewels of thoroughbred racing's Triple Crown – The Kentucky Derby, The Preakness or The Belmont.

That's not to say his stable hadn't seen the winner's circle in some of the nation's more prestigious stakes races. On the distaff side, the 3-year-old filly *She's On Grounds* captured The Kentucky

Oaks at Churchill Downs on the day before the Derby. At Monmouth Park, *TJ's Mistress* had entered the winner's circle as a 4-year-old filly in the Molly Pitcher Handicap.

As broodmares, both had been very successful, thanks in large part to Cutter's policy of paying liberal stud fees for some of the industry's most compatible stallions. Subsequent racing successes had come from his 3-year-old colt, *Fish Or Cut Bait*, who won the Grade I Travers Stakes at Saratoga, and from his 5-year-old gelding, *Cut Above The Rest*, who only last year captured the Grade II Suburban Handicap at Belmont while carrying 128 lbs.

TJ's impatience manifested itself in his inability to give trainers the time needed to develop consistency in managing his stable of horses, which is why he recently took on the role himself – at least for his top-tier thoroughbreds. The Cutter name had yet to appear atop the owner standings at any of the meets across the country at which his horses raced regularly, including Monmouth, Gulfstream in Florida and Keeneland in Kentucky. Put simply, he didn't want to spend too much time on the merry-go-round before capturing the brass ring.

Cutter's continued presence at Monmouth Park's summer meet was all about keeping an eye on his sister, Jasmine, who lived just over 35 miles south of Oceanport. During the Jersey shore track's meet, which typically ran from Memorial Day weekend through the Labor Day weekend, Cutter took up residence at a beach-side home in the posh town of Deal, essentially house sitting for Dan Steffan, a fellow UVA alum who spent summers in Europe. The arrangement had worked out quite well for both parties.

While TJ may have fared better stabling his horses with the industry's most highly regarded competitors at Belmont Park in New York, his sense of family loyalty required him to stay as close to his sister as possible. Both the reason for his presence at Monmouth Park as well as the nature of his younger sister's problems were the Cutter family's two most closely guarded secrets.

***

While Thomas Jefferson Cutter III had no idea he was about to meet Sean Davis Jeffries, Sean had been planning the precise date, time and location of their get-acquainted session as well as the substance of the conversation to take place, for several weeks.

Sean found himself in a rather precarious position. He could help Cutter avoid a catastrophic financial loss and a very public humiliation. But revealing details surrounding the who, what, when, where, how and why behind the events about to unfold could very well endanger all that he, Sean, had worked so hard to achieve over the past six years.

Heading through the clubhouse pass gate, Sean stopped for the day's program and *The Daily Racing Form* at the seller's stand and started up the escalator to the main floor. As he shortened his ride by bounding up the moving stairs, he raced through the past six years of his life. Relationships had been cultivated and events had transpired, often with unanticipated consequences. All led up to this pivotal moment. How he handled his conversation with Cutter would have a tremendous impact on many lives, not the least of which was his own.

Part One:
Coincidence, Circumstance
& Consequence

Chapter 1 – Monmouth Park

Monmouth Park, the thoroughbred racetrack in the north Jersey shore hamlet of Oceanport, was abuzz with activity as dozens upon dozens of employees scurried about preparing for opening day of the 1983 summer meet. It was Friday, May 27th.

From the main grandstand parking lot sprawled on the western portion of the property, racetrack goers walked east to the main entrance where they were greeted by a row of admissions windows and turnstiles. Fronting the entrance was a circular drop-off area, the center beautifully landscaped with an array of flowers.

Housed just inside the main gate in a pillbox-sized hut was the admissions department. Here each seller brought his or her tape to balance the turnstile count with cash receipts and passes. At the end of the day, the number on the tape was supposed to equal the tally form completed by the seller. The small structure doubled as the track's customer service department.

Upon entering the racetrack grounds, customers were confronted by several touts barking the virtues of the tip sheets they were charged with selling. With a far gentler approach, owing to the non-competitive nature of their products, were the sellers offering programs with the day's racing card and *The Daily Racing Form*. For the serious handicapper, the "industry bible" provided a wealth of historical information on all the horses entered in the day's races, including performance charts for up to 10 previous races for each thoroughbred, the latest morning workouts, as well as lifetime and current-year starts with top-four or "in-the-money" finishes. The horse's owner and trainer were included as well as its breeding (the sire, dam and dam's sire), gender, age and color. Like any other newspaper, there were hard-news items and in-depth feature stories for readers to peruse.

Having been accosted by the touts, customers now found themselves with about a hundred-foot walk before coming to the steps of a massive, three-storied white structure. Handsomely trimmed in forest green, the grandstand building contained never-ending rows of windows that allowed daylight in while affording occupants a view outward to the grounds.

Stairs and a pair of escalators carrying patrons to and from the second and third floors of the grandstand were located just inside the entrance. Two elevators – one to transport supplies and the other for handicapped and senior customers – were situated about midway between the front and side entrances. On Saturdays, two specially scheduled racetrack trains departed from midtown Manhattan and Jersey City, arriving at their terminus at Monmouth Park and dropping their passengers a few dozen footsteps from the train gate and side entrance.

Apart from the grandstand's obligatory food and beverage stations, restrooms and a no-frills dining area, all three floors of the closed-in portion of the building were dominated by several dozen pari-mutuel windows. Cashiers staffing the payout windows faced west. Sellers staffing the wagering windows faced east and, for the most obvious of reasons, were closer to the grandstand seats and racing oval. Betting windows were apportioned according to the size of the wager required. There were more $2 windows than any other. The larger the minimum bet, the fewer the number of windows. Denominations were set at $5, $10, $20 and $50. Finally, two $100 windows were set up in a small, partitioned alcove, ostensibly to offer privacy to the largest bettors. Closed-circuit television monitors carried minute-by-minute odds reflecting wagers at the track. With under a minute to post time, all monitors switched to the starting gate so customers could watch the race.

The eastern end of the building was open, with football stadium-style seating on the second and third floors accommodating some 8,000 racing fans. Toward the very front of the second floor, reserved boxes offered families and small groups something more than the standard, straight-across seating.

On the ground floor, row upon row of concrete-legged green park benches were lined up on a slight downward angle to allow customers a sightline to the "deep stretch" and finish line. Finally, there was a wide patch of concrete leading to the fence separating the grandstand from the main race course. Here's where hard-core racing fans, known as railbirds, staked out territory.

If the Monmouth Park grandstand was the pedestrian setting for "run-of-the-mill" spectators, the clubhouse was an opulent playground for the Jersey shore's well-heeled, politically connected and social in-crowd. The path horses and their jockeys took from paddock to the race course provided a natural divide between the grandstand and clubhouse sections. A break in that path allowed patrons and employees to pass from one section to the other. There was an upcharge for those customers going from grandstand to clubhouse, and men were required to wear jackets – although attire ranging from a three-piece suit to a ratty windbreaker was deemed acceptable.

The Monmouth Park Jockey Club made every effort to cater to the needs of its clientele. Second-hand jackets and ties were available at the employee gate for forgetful male patrons who found themselves in need of an attire fix in order to enter the clubhouse. Men's room attendants were equipped with a full complement of products to provide head-to-toe grooming, from shining shoes and removing food stains on clothing...to combing hair, brushing teeth, freshening breath, shaving five-o'clock shadows, manicuring cuticles and trimming nails. Female attendants carried everything from hair spray, eye shadow, lipstick, nail polish and emery boards to replacement hosiery for ripped stockings and glue to repair broken heels.

Clubhouse amenities catered to a clientele used to having the very best life had to offer. Under the corporate banner of Harry M. Stevens, Monmouth Park provided the finest in continental cuisine along with some of the Jersey shore's best seafood from its third-floor Dining Terrace. Customers ate in air-conditioned comfort or dined al fresco and watched the races from the convenience of their tables. On the third floor as well were the Salvator Bar & Grill, which afforded customers a more casual setting with a view of the Paddock, and the Garden Room, overlooking the English walking ring.

Then, of course, there were picnic areas sprinkled throughout the clubhouse side of the track where families could sit at umbrellaed patio tables lined with high-backed plastic benches.

A cigar bar catered to those who fancied themselves aficionados of some of the world's best stogies. A visitor could roam from one corner of the room to the other and experience olfactory overload as plumes of smoke – from Diamond Crowns, Fonsecas and Gurkhas to Hoyo de Monterreys, Olivas and Perdomos – invaded the nostrils.

Monmouth Park was often referred to within racing circles as "the graveyard of champions" because of its penchant for delivering big upsets in major stakes races. It was more likely that the "upsets" had as much to do with the relative naivety of the trackside betting public compared to their counterparts at the NYRA (New York Racing Authority) circuit's major tracks – Aqueduct, Belmont and Saratoga. Sure, there were "regulars" at the Oceanport racing oval, but they paled both in numbers and intensity to their urban peers.

Chapter 2 – The Seaside to A.C. Shuttle

Jasmine Cutter reached across her body for the all-too-loudly ringing alarm clock on the night stand before connecting with the button after two failed attempts. Ready to blissfully welcome the silence, Jasmine groaned at the realization that her forehead was throbbing with pain. Was it four Jim Beams on the rocks – or maybe more – that she'd downed while plying her last "date" of the night with booze until the wee hours of the Atlantic City morning? Drunken johns always seemed to tip more, so she'd established the practice of active participation.

With the middle-aged, bald-headed stranger passed out, Jasmine's night ended mercifully with her regular limo driver picking her up at the motel and taking her back to the Bay Terrace bungalow in Seaside Heights she now called home.

It was 1 p.m. as Jasmine wearily trudged her way to the bathroom to shower and otherwise get ready for her day job as a boardwalk arcade attendant. She frowned at another unpleasant but slightly more mundane thought: the neighborhood peace so characteristic of Seaside Heights on a mid-May Wednesday would soon be replaced by the crush of humanity brought about by the fast-approaching Memorial Day weekend, which this year came late (May 27-30).

"Well," she thought to herself, "At the ripe old age of 21, at least I can't be arrested for underage drinking or not being old enough to frequent the casinos."

New Jersey's drinking age had been raised from 18 to 19 in 1980, creating an under-age situation for her. Then Governor Keane convinced the State legislature to make yet another increase to 21 effective Jan. 1, 1983, which would have continued to make Jasmine's "second job" a whole lot more challenging. Fortunately, she'd celebrated her 21st birthday on November 11th of the previous year. Finally outracing "the fucking Trenton airheads," Jasmine's preferred term of endearment, she no longer had to sweat using a fake I.D. in order to gain entrance to the gambling houses or to purchase and consume liquor.

6

As hot water streamed from the spout, drenched her long brown hair and washed over her 5-ft., 10-in., 125-lb. frame, Jasmine reflected on her childhood and the situation in which she currently found herself.

Her mother's paralysis when she was eight and the sudden death of her father four years later left her alone and emotionally distraught. Despite the presence of a maid, a home-care provider for her mom and a nanny to tend to her basic daily needs, Jasmine sorely missed the nurturing she'd been accustomed to in the years before the family's tragedies. Her sister was married and living in Texas, while her brother was attending school in Charlottesville. For better or worse, she'd been left to make her own choices.

From her early teens, she'd always been curious and willing to experiment – first with sex, then with alcohol and finally with drugs. What began as a series of exciting and exotic adventures ended with pregnancy and abortion at age 16, drunkenness leading to school expulsion shortly thereafter, and addiction followed by rehab and a stint in a halfway house at age 17.

Through it all, Jasmine's brother, TJ, was there to help. In fact, he'd tabled all thoughts of graduate school and aspirations of a diplomatic career in order to return home, run the family farm and thoroughbred business, and care for his mom and sister.

When TJ learned Jasmine was pregnant, he took her to an out-of-state clinic for an abortion. Time after time when Jasmine came home late from a drinking binge, he cleaned her up and put her to bed. When Jasmine succumbed to mescaline and cocaine, he entered her into an inpatient rehab facility and then arranged for her admission to a halfway house.

Ultimately, TJ purchased a bungalow in Seaside Heights, arranged a job at a boardwalk arcade owned by a retired cop from Brooklyn, Irving Katzman, whose nephew, Sammy Eisenstat, had been TJ's classmate at UVA, and provided her with a monthly allowance to supplement her arcade paychecks.

One of Jasmine's only passions was music, and she soon found herself heading to rock concerts at Asbury Park's Convention Hall and Atlantic City's Steel Pier. Unfortunately, her curiosity soon took her to the casinos, where she began to gamble with her brother's monthly support check. Her new habit left her in need of cash. Unwilling to confide in TJ, she sought another way to generate replacement income.

Despite the wear and tear her body had endured for someone so young, Jasmine remained very attractive by most people's standards. With sin permeating A.C.'s salty air, she soon turned to "the world's oldest profession." Over several months, her work took many forms as she worked her way up what some in the business called the "meat chain" – from streetwalker to brothel prostitute to call-girl.

In fairly short order, vice became an "all-too-essential" part of her life. This much Jasmine recognized. But the notion that trouble couldn't be far behind was lost on her, as were the increasing financial exigencies of her situation. The bottom line?... Jasmine loved to gamble, enjoyed the power-sex trip that came with her call-girl gig and seemed to crave living on the edge.

Slipping on a satin white push-up bra with matching panties, skin-tight blue jeans and scoop-necked pink sweater that revealed more of her 36-C breasts than young male customers playing Skiball, Pokerino and pinball machines had a right to expect (Jasmine was turned on by comments within earshot like "nice rack" and "great set"), she began to comb her long strands of hair when the telephone rang. She headed into the kitchen and lifted the receiver from the bungalow's wall-mounted and only telephone.

It was June, her evening employer, calling to discuss the previous evening's three dates she'd arranged between Jasmine and clients of the escort service known as A.C-D.C. Reflecting the local presence of the Atlantic City Race Course, its slogan was "Our fillies are world-class thoroughbreds." Diligently, if with a tad too much impatience for June's taste, the latest addition to her "stable" ran through answers to all the usual post-mortem questions:

Yes, the johns were all respectful. No, none of them insisted on sex without protection. Yes, they all paid fees that met the time and specific services requested. Yes, she'd have the cash less her own cut ready for pick-up by the A.C.-D.C. carrier at the designated time and location. And, of course she'd be available for work on Friday of Memorial Day weekend.

As June had explained during Jasmine's job interview, it would be a grave mistake to be anything less than 100 percent truthful when it came to the basics of the business. Customer satisfaction was the most critical element of customer retention. If Jasmine tried to skim cash by under-reporting the time spent with clients or by not reporting specific services for which clients paid additional money, June would eventually find out when those clients called to request A.C.-D.C. services once again. Any discrepancies would eventually emerge from such conversations, particularly if they requested the same filly. June was quite clear that offenders would not appreciate the tactics of her "HR department." The unmistakable impression was that violence – to one's property and/or to one's person – was a trusted and effective implement in the tool box.

June paused for a moment after running through the obligatories. Jasmine sensed some hesitation in her voice as she laid out the specifics of Friday's client:

"We have a young and very successful businesswoman who'd like to spend an evening with a youthful female companion. Your looks and personality closely match her request. Dinner and an evening of gambling at Bally's Park Place Casino are on the agenda. If things go well, you'll likely wind up at the Dennis Hotel. This 'mount' is a big step up in class. You'll be stretching out in terms of distance. And the assignment, quite obviously, is a change from dirt to turf."

Jasmine couldn't help but smile when it came to her boss's use of horse-racing lingo, from the tag line of her business right down to descriptions of the dates. June would find it somewhat ironic that her newest employee had quite the background and knowledge of the thoroughbred industry. While she'd never been with a woman before, Jasmine's curiosity and penchant for new adventures made her decision a relatively easy one.

"Sounds like fun. Any dress requests?" Jasmine asked. Listening to June's response, she mouthed one simple word…Wow! "I might have to do some shopping. Any chance for reimbursement?" she quipped and then laughed. Clothes shopping – or laughing for that matter – were two things Jasmine hadn't done very often of late.

Chapter 3 – Following an American Dream?

Consuela Parks Pettiford was born and raised in the Washington Heights section of New York City's upper Manhattan, the only child of a mother who'd come to Miami from the Dominican Republic as a teenager and a father whose family had roots in New Orleans since the early 18th century.

As young adults, Concesa Parks and Elton Pettiford had both moved to Harlem in the years immediately after World War II. They met as co-workers – one a waitress, the other a cook – in a small, hole-in-the-wall restaurant called *A.M. Bagels/P.M. Burgers* on the ground floor of an aging apartment building on Broadway close to the George Washington Bridge.

Concesa and Elton spent time together, eventually sharing tight living quarters in an apartment building just north and west of Broadway a few blocks from the restaurant, as much to make ends meet financially as to share a relationship that was more than companionship but fell short of love.

Their economic situation and the nature of their relationship explained both the birth of a daughter and their decision (rooted in reality as they both had their tubes tied) to make sure another child wouldn't be born to either of them. At the same time, Concesa and Elton committed to do whatever they could to give their newborn daughter the best possible shot at "the American dream," the seed for which they both believed would be the finest education they could afford. They asked a priest in the hospital to marry them, with their newborn daughter, Consuela Parks Pettiford, in attendance.

Concesa the waitress eventually became Concesa the cashier while Elton the cook was promoted to shift manager. The two saved diligently for their daughter's schooling, led a spartan life and made sure Consuela hit the books every night. When it came time for high school, mom and dad sent their daughter to the Columbia Grammar & Preparatory School on a partial scholarship. Excelling at one of the nation's oldest nonsectarian private schools, Consuela graduated magna cum laude and earned a full scholarship to Columbia.

Four years later, the daughter of a Dominican waitress/cashier and Creole short-order cook/shift manager had earned a bachelor's degree with honors from Columbia's School of Journalism and gained admission to Fordham University's School of Law. Consuela deferred entry for a year in order to earn a second bachelor's degree in business administration. Incredibly devoted to her parents and having marveled for years at Concesa's and Elton's dogged determination to give her a far better life than they'd experienced, Consuela decided to pursue a legal career focused on immigration law.

After she'd passed bar exams in the State of New York and in Washington, D.C., Consuela accepted a position as an associate at Stratton-Oakes, one of the nation's preeminent immigration and international business law firms. Having climbed the proverbial mountain, Consuela abruptly had her American dream shattered within months of joining Stratton-Oakes.

The telephone was ringing as Consuela opened the door to the one-bedroom apartment she'd recently leased at the corner of West End Avenue and 79th Street. It was a Thursday evening at about 10:30. She was "running on empty" as a result of her fourth consecutive 12-hour work day.

Consuela's research involved a case the federal government had brought against one of Stratton-Oakes's clients, a Manhattan-based conglomerate with agri-businesses in Texas. She was fascinated in reviewing applicable case law as it might apply to the current litigation that had wound its way up the judicial ladder from the court of original jurisdiction to a federal appeals court. The senior partner she was assisting, Charles Janovsky, had been very impressed with her timely and thorough work.

As Consuela answered the phone, her fatigue abruptly vanished as she heard the words: "This is Detective Mark Makowski of the 34th precinct. Are you Consuela Parks Pettiford?" The balance of the conversation dropped away into the realm of the surreal as she listened to the detective describe a late-afternoon armed robbery at the *A.M. Bagels/P.M. Burgers* restaurant in which three employees, including the shift manager and the cashier, had been shot multiple times. All three were pronounced D.O.A. at Columbia Presbyterian Hospital.

Finding Consuela's business card with a phone number written on the back in the pants pocket of the deceased male, the NYPD had been calling for a couple of hours. Required to come to the city morgue, Consuela needed to confirm the identities of the deceased shift manager and cashier. They'd send a car to pick her up and take her back home.

Chapter 4 – The Future of the Business

It was very early on Saturday morning of Memorial Day weekend. For the third time in a week, Jorge awoke with a start, his pillow again soaked with perspiration. He glanced at the digital clock-radio on his nightstand, which read 2:10 a.m. Ordinarily it would be another four hours before he'd go for his morning run, have breakfast, shower and dress for the drive to his summer job at Monmouth Park.

Although Jorge hadn't seen his father, Fabian, since the elder Hauptmann left his wife, Gretchen, and five-year-old son, he'd only recently begun to experience a recurring dream – one he found hard to fathom.

Despite his questions, his mom never fully explained the reason for his dad's departure other than saying: "Wir beide konnten die Dinge einfach nicht auf Augenhöhe sehen." ("The two of us just didn't see eye to eye on things.") For many years, Jorge would daydream of his father reappearing, either at the door to their home in Hückeswagen or during one of his fußball matches in Radevormwald. Eventually these thoughts faded as he resigned himself to the certainty that he'd seen the last of his father.

As to the recent dream, it was disconcerting – particularly since he hadn't thought much about his dad in such a long time. In it, Fabian had come home from a fishing trip and knocked on the back door of the family's winter retreat in Cuxhaven, where the mouth of the Elbe River empties into the North Sea. Except apparently the log cabin wasn't in its proper geographic location.

As Jorge opened the door, his father asked: "Warum sind wir in Nürnberg?" ("Why are we in Nuremberg?") Stunned and clueless about how to respond, he watched in horror as his dad pulled a Luger from the inner left-side pocket of his lumber jacket, placed the gun to the side of his head and pulled the trigger.

So disturbed by this latest and now recurring nightmare, Jorge again checked the digital clock, added six to local eastern time and reached for the phone. He figured that 8:15 a.m. in Hückeswagen might be early enough to catch his mom before she started her day.

***

Gretchen Weiß Hauptmann was preoccupied with an important board meeting that afternoon – a meeting at which a decision was to be made about the future of die Sinterformteile (the Powder Metal parts manufacturer) she'd founded some 25 years earlier in Wuppertal. As chair of the Advisory Board of GWH GmbH, she had floated the idea of a change from her company's current limited liability legal structure to one whose shares would be publicly traded. On this point, the seven-person board was divided. Proponents of the switch argued that funds were needed to invest in both pre-production (tool & die manufacturing) and post-production (machining) operations as well as to upgrade the firm's physical plant. Those opposed believed the sale of shares to the general public would add an untimely and ill-advised degree of regulatory complexity to managing the company. Technological innovation, facility modernization and expanding to a soup-to-nuts, full-service operation could be achieved by hiring a new generation of Jungen Löwen (young lions) to the Board of Management to oversee daily operations.

Gretchen had always been held in the utmost respect by members of the Board. After all, she was a "self-made" business woman, having begun as an hourly employee working at Pulver-Metall Lüdenscheid, another P/M parts manufacturer, and rising to manager of its nearby connecting rod production line.

It didn't hurt her standing that she'd experienced a particularly painful Second World War. The youngest of three siblings, Gretchen alone had survived. Harald, the older of two brothers, was a sergeant killed in January of 1943 during the Battle of Stalingrad. Wolfgang died in early January of '45 while commanding a King Tiger tank in the final German offensive the Nazis termed Unternehmen Wacht am Rhein (Operation Watch on the Rhine), but was more commonly known as the Battle of the Bulge.

Meanwhile their parents, Helmut and Gertrude Weiß, were both killed in an early March bombing raid on the Dresden railway marshalling yard where they worked. Among the residents to have survived the massive firebombing of Dresden that took an estimated 25,000 lives in mid-February of 1945, Helmut and Gertrude had the misfortune to be in the wrong place at the wrong time during a narrowly focused but highly strategic British & American mission a few weeks later.

Now Gretchen Weiß Hauptmann was gathering from the desk of her home office several index cards upon which she'd written key talking points. She placed the cards in an inside compartment of her briefcase and then turned to the kitchen to leave food for Pulver (in English, Powder), her 11-year-old Deutscher Schäferhund (German Shepherd).

Pulver had been trained as a guide dog and was originally in service to Anna Bregmann, a legally blind and elderly widow who lived less than a kilometer down the road from the Hauptmann home. Periodically, the owner of Wuppertal's powder metal parts business visited her neighbor, which is how Frau Bregmann came to name the dog Pulver.

When Anna passed, Gretchen was surprised to learn Pulver had been left to her in the will. With Jürgen off to America, Pulver offered Hauptmann companionship and security as he transitioned from guide dog to *guard* dog. Though somewhat long in the tooth and not in the best of health, Pulver was intelligent, loyal and a comfort to Gretchen, whose home was nestled in the woods on the outskirts of Hückeswagen.

Heading down the hallway to the front door, Gretchen heard the phone ring. Ordinarily she wouldn't have stopped to answer it. But on the outside chance it was a call related to the afternoon meeting, she dropped her brief case to pick up the receiver.

***

"Jorge! I haven't spoken to you in weeks. How are things going at the race track? You must love working so close to the ocean. I'm so sorry I couldn't be there for your graduation, but you know what the company is going through. In fact, I was just heading over to Wuppertal. We have that important board meeting I told you about. I'm hoping you'll be able to spend a week or two with me in Cuxhaven toward the end of August. We can discuss your future plans and do some fishing."

It was so like his mom to launch into a one-sided conversation,

Jorge thought, replete with introductory comments and her own status report on matters big and small before he had a chance to say anything more than hello.

But now he simply wanted to tell his mom about the "encounter" with his dad. Not that he expected her to shed any light on the meaning of his recurring dream. But he needed to share it with his "other" parent – the one who raised him, the one who offered guidance on everything from academic preparation and athletic training to developing friendships and considering courtships ... the one who always had his back no matter the circumstances ... the one who loved him completely and unconditionally.

When Jorge finished explaining this suddenly recurring nightmare, he was somewhat taken aback by his mom's response. For someone who never had difficulty weighing in on a range of issues – whether it be of a business nature, family-related or dealing with the politics of the day – her words seemed, well ... measured.

After several moments, Gretchen finally said: "In all my years knowing your father, he never seemed like the kind of person who would consider doing such a thing."

"Well, you'd be in a far better position to know," Jorge said.

Way more than his act of suicide, the words from his dad's mouth – "Warum sind wir in Nürnberg?" ("Why are we in Nuremberg?") – defied explanation. He was well aware of the historical relevance of the town. Die Nürnberger Prozesse (the Nuremberg trials) had been post-World War II military tribunals run by the Allied forces under international law. The trials had been most notable for the prosecution of prominent members of the political, military, judicial and economic leadership of Nazi Germany – those who planned, carried out, or otherwise participated in the Holocaust and other war crimes.

On Nuremberg, Gretchen remained without words. After several more moments of silence, more awkward than the earlier ones, she said: "Well, we're certainly not going to solve this mystery right now. And I have a big day ahead. I'll let you know how things turn out at GWH. Talk to you soon!"

Said Jorge quite wistfully, "Du bedeutest mir sehr viel... Tschüs," ("You mean so much to me... Bye.") And with those words, he heard the phone click back in Hückeswagen.

Through the wee hours of the morning until the sun came up,

the phrase seemed to take on a life of its own: "Warum sind wir in Nürnberg?...*Warum sind wir in Nürnberg?*...**WARUM SIND WIR IN NÜRNBERG?!?**" Jürgen Hauptmann couldn't get those five words out of his head. As his Saturday unfolded, Jorge thought he might very well begin to solve the mystery.

Chapter 5 – From 18th Infantry to the Mossad

Growing up in Brooklyn, David Katzman never imagined his parents living anywhere else. But when Irving Katzman cashed in his early-retirement chips after 25 years of service to the New York City Police Department, he purchased a boardwalk arcade in Seaside Heights and a year-round home in nearby Point Pleasant Beach down the Jersey shore, deciding he and his wife, Rebecca, would prefer life at the beach to the city streets of Brooklyn.

David's younger brother, Nathan, was currently living in the North Druid Hills section of Atlanta while completing his residency at the Grady Hospital. Having earned his B.S. degree in Biology at the University of Georgia in Athens while on scholarship as a member of the Bulldogs basketball team, he'd then completed his medical degree at Atlanta's Emory School of Medicine.

As far as the Katzman family could tell, Nathan would be perfectly happy to settle down for the next several years in his current neighborhood. He'd been dating a young woman who was both gorgeous (long, dark brown hair, almond-shaped hazel eyes, standing 5 ft. 8 in. at about 120 lbs.) and brilliant (ranked near the top of her class at Georgia Tech's Stewart School of Industrial and Systems Engineering and having just been chosen for a much-sought-after internship at GM's Doraville plant). Better yet, her family lived nearby in upscale and fashionable Buckhead. The fact that Beth Feingold was very close to her parents certainly didn't hurt the prospect of geographic stability one bit. Other than bickering over Dawgs vs. Jackets football, Nathan and Beth seemed a perfect match.

On the other hand, David's far-flung adult life had been determined by the relationship between one number and his date of birth. On Dec. 1, 1969, the U.S. Selective Service System conducted two lotteries to determine the order of call to military service for the Viet Nam War for men born from Jan. 1, 1944 to Dec. 31, 1950. Born on Nov. 1, 1950, David Katzman's date of birth had been drawn as #19.

As a result, the elder son of Irving and Rebecca Katzman served two tours of duty in Viet Nam in the 18th Infantry Division, rose to the rank of sergeant, received the Purple Heart and Bronze Star as a wounded soldier who'd displayed courage under fire during the Battle of Xuan Loc, and returned to the United States a far different person than when he first left home for basic training.

Growing up as the son of a New York City cop who'd eventually earned his detective's badge, David learned to live with the daily prospect of an uncertain future. Would he come home from school one day to learn that his dad was in the hospital or worse yet that he, David, was now head of the household? While that moment thankfully never arrived, the constant awareness of that possibility served him well. Death was not something to be feared; it came to everyone sooner or later. Mental preparation was the key. It helped him live through his darkest of hours in the jungles of southeast Asia.

As a practicing member of the Jewish faith, David was also thankful for his mere existence. At the age of 19 his father had been sent to live with his Uncle Samuel Katzman in Brooklyn, only months before Hitler's Blitzkrieg overran Poland in September 1939. Shortly after his arrival in America, Irving enlisted in the Army Air Corps and rose to the rank of staff sergeant. After his honorable discharge following V-J Day, Irv submitted his application to become a New York City policeman.

Irv's parents, Isaac and Sylvia, hadn't been as fortunate. Still living in Krakow, they were imprisoned and eventually gassed at the Auschwitz-Birkenau extermination and labor camp in Poland.

His family story aside, David had been profoundly affected by the 1967 Six-Day War in which the State of Israel fought for its very survival against Egypt, Jordan and Syria. He remembered television coverage that week in June, when almost all of American Jewry had been transfixed by the continuous status reports coming in from the Middle East. To be sure, it seemed like a modern-day David vs. Goliath.

Back home following his time in Viet Nam, Katzman felt his calling moving forward should be for a cause in which he strongly believed – as opposed to a conflict he'd questioned. He had fought long and hard, not so much for his country as for his comrades in arms.

David was now equipped with the physical skills and mental fortitude to do battle in virtually any theatre on Earth. With his father's blessing and the name of a contact Irving knew from his time as a member of Brooklyn's finest, he boarded an El-Al flight from JFK to Tel-Aviv. Following an extensive background check, he began his service in the Israeli Army.

Now years later, וְבוּאר זְב דוד (Phonetically spelled in English: Da VID ben Reuven. Translated: David son of Reuben ... Irving Katzman's given Hebrew name.) was an agent of the Mossad, Israel's National Intelligence Agency. During his lengthy and intense training program, he added martial arts skills, expertise in state-of-the-art communications technology and fluency in Hebrew, German and Dutch.

Recently, David's unit had been alerted to a Nazi war criminal in hiding who was thought to be involved in gassing and cremating some 8,000 Dutch and Hungarian Jews at the Mauthausen-Gusen concentration camp complex roughly 12 miles east of Linz in Upper Austria. It was time to go to work.

Chapter 6 – Angel in the Morning

Seated in the jockey clubhouse in the morning's pre-dawn hours, Angel Barrera was studying *The Daily Racing Form*. The 34-year-old Dominican wanted to make sure he reviewed the past performances of all the horses that might present challenges for the five mounts he'd be riding on opening day that afternoon. Angel was looking forward to the 1983 meet at his favorite track, Monmouth Park. Having won three riders' championships in the past four seasons, he had his mind set on regaining the title he'd lost at last year's meet.

Leading by seven first-place finishes heading into August, Barrera had taken a mount his agent seriously questioned. It was the 9th race, last on the day's program. A $10,000 claiming sprint for 2-year-old maiden fillies to be run at 5 furlongs, the race featured a crowded field of 12 and included Trifecta wagering. To maximize the size of the exotic pari-mutuel pool, the racing secretary did his very best to put in place conditions that would ensure large fields.

The particular conditions of this race had deeply concerned Barrera's agent, Chris McCardle, himself a former jockey and winner of three Haskell Handicaps, Monmouth's most prestigious race. First, it was a cheap race with the potential for entries changing ownership for $10,000. Second, it was for 2-year-old *maiden* fillies – that is, very young horses who'd never won a race and typically included horses "dropping in company" (i.e., facing lesser competition), horses with very little racing experience and several jockeys who were relatively inexperienced as well. Third, the five-furlong distance meant the starting gate provided a shortened backstretch, resulting in a "cavalry charge" for forward positioning heading into the turn.

But Barrera had overruled his agent, seeking every opportunity to expand his lead in the jockey standings. Almost immediately out of the gate, his filly – ironically named *Dance Partner* – took a misstep as horses jostled for position. Coming from the number-three post position, she swerved sharply to the left, lurched and threw Barrera to the dirt. Landing awkwardly, he cracked two vertebrae in his spinal column and was done for the meet. Fortunately, his mount's post position close to the rail and the collapse of the filly's front-left hoof minimized the potential for other horses trampling the fallen jockey. Rehab fixed Barrera, but *Dance Partner* had to be put down.

The best news for Barrera heading into the new meet had been a contract McCardle negotiated with the rapidly rising superstar breeder/ owner and now trainer TJ Cutter III. Under terms of the agreement, Barrera would get "first call" on any Cutting Edge Stables horse based at Monmouth Park. Further, Angel could refuse a ride in any stakes race in which a Cutter horse was entered if the jockey thought he had a better opportunity with another entry. On the flip side, Cutter could lock in Barrera's services in all allowance and claiming races at the meet regardless of the other horses in those races.

Barrera had been the "rider up" for Cutter's *TJ's Mistress* in the '82 Molly Pitcher Handicap at Monmouth and *Fish Or Cut Bait* in the '80 Traverse Stakes at Saratoga. Clearly, Angel was a jockey whose services Cutter valued. As with any business transaction, the best deals were those in which "give and take" had come from both parties. McCardle had done a good bit of "horse trading" to come up with an arrangement that pleased both Cutter and Barrera.

Chapter 7 – Change of Pace

For Jasmine, the hours between Wednesday and Friday afternoons felt like an eternity despite her Big Apple shopping spree on Thursday. It would be several additional hours before the rendezvous with her date at Bally's Park Place Casino in Atlantic City.

She stared at herself in the full-length bedroom mirror. Sleek, mustard yellow Lycra hipster panties with a matching push-up bra and thigh-high tights. "So much for the bare essentials," Jasmine thought. "Now for the items designed to form that not-at-all-subtle hint of what's to come."

Jasmine slipped on a wet-looking, black Lycra Spandex micro-mini skirt and a ribbed, mustard-yellow Rayon/Spandex zip-front crop top. She finished her wardrobe preview with mustard-yellow thigh-high leather boots. All she could say (this time aloud) was ... "Wow!"

But when all was said and done, she reminded herself of the evening's key question: When the package is unwrapped and the gift is revealed, will forbidden fruit taste as good as it looks? "Well," Jasmine concluded, "that's what this adventure is all about."

***

Consuela Parks Pettiford's descent into the abyss had been swift. What began as two weeks' leave from work to mourn and straighten out affairs turned into total immersion in a world of physical and psychological self-abuse. The mood swings had come and gone in rapid succession ... from anger and self-loathing to self-pity and eventually apathy. What emerged was a person well-acquainted with "the bottle" and a tendency to extreme behaviors antithetical to all she'd been as a human being during her quarter century on the planet.

Not much had changed in her world the past couple of weeks – save, of course, for the murder of her parents. Her job at Stratton-Oakes was secure and...what else? The sudden realization that she'd spent virtually every waking minute of her life in pursuit of two objectives – achieving her current status in the legal profession and making sure the lives of Concesa and Elton Pettiford were as comfortable as possible – left her with a hopelessly overwhelming feeling of emptiness.

But starting down the road to a *healthy* recovery would take months and require her to seek positive experiences like joining a yoga or fitness club, becoming involved in Columbia's alumni group, exploring civic activism at the neighborhood level. At this juncture, knowing that everything she – and her parents, for that matter – had accomplished in life came with extraordinary challenges, Consuela was set on filling the void by the quickest, most aimless means possible ... and hang the consequences.

It was Thursday, May 26th. Awaking in her West End apartment at about 11:00 a.m., Consuela moved from king bed to en suite. She'd contacted one of the city's private car services, careful not to use the one employed by Stratton-Oakes. She wanted a stress-free ride down to Atlantic City for her weekend at the Dennis Hotel, so Friday's Memorial Day weekend crush of traffic on the New Jersey Turnpike and Garden State Parkway was to be avoided at all costs. Consuela wanted a completely relaxing day before embarking upon a first-time sexual experience that evening.

Emerging from her floor-level shower stall decorated with deep chocolate brown, warm beige, orange and yellow gold tiles (part of a remodeled en suite in which she took great pride), Consuela dried off and paused to examine herself in the mirror.

At 5 ft. 4 in. and 115 lbs., she'd never stood out in a crowd. A few male observers who'd commented on her attractiveness over the years focused on her mouth (pearl-white teeth, perfectly framed by a compact mouth with pert lips), eyes (deep brown and saucer-like), skin (smooth and fawn-colored) and hair (long and jet-black, but typically pulled back in a tight bun as one might expect from a young legal associate). Consuela looked at her breasts which, when in a good mood, she described as "perky." At 34B for at least the last few years, she'd long given up her pet phrase, "a work in progress."

For the day before the big evening, Consuela opted for comfy-casual: a button-down white cotton blouse; stretchy black travel pants and ink-black mocs.

Always a minimalist when it came to make-up, Consuela was

just about ready to leave. Moving back into the bedroom, she picked up the business card. Well-worn not from use but because it had competed for space in an overstuffed purse since her college days, the white card with lavender script bore the name, A.C.-D.C. with the slogan "Our fillies are world-class thoroughbreds" beneath it. At the bottom right was a first name, June, and a telephone number.

The card had been given to her by a classmate whose name Consuela had long-ago forgotten. From a lower-middle class family, the fellow first-year student fit into that unfortunate category of coming from a family with too much income to secure financial aid but not sufficient monetary resources to afford an Ivy League tuition, room & board. Weekend call-girl work in Atlantic City had made all the difference in gaining a world-class education.

A week ago, Consuela had found the card during one of her alcohol-induced flights of fancy and decided to call June – not for employment, but as a client. All her life, she'd been a conformist, keeping with societal norms. For once, she was not simply going to cross a line of social demarcation; she was going to clear the guardrails with a running triple jump.

Several days ago, a neighbor in her mid-30s who worked as a sales rep at Bloomingdale's invited Consuela to have coffee and cake in her apartment down the hall. Hearing from the apartment building's doorman about the unfortunate turn of events, Bonnie Dubinski had offered her grieving neighbor some company and a few words of consolation. As Consuela was leaving, she noticed a *Frederick's of Hollywood* catalog among a stack of magazines. Asking if she could borrow some reading material, Consuela grabbed the catalog and quickly placed it underneath recent editions of *Vogue* and *Harper's Bazaar* as the woman turned to open the door. Thanking Bonnie, Consuela said she would return the magazines after the weekend.

Setting the magazines on the kitchen counter, Consuela opened her pantry and reached for a bottle of Mamajuana. Only last month, her now departed mother had given her a case that she'd received from a close friend of hers back in the D.R.

Long the most popular drink indigenous to the Dominican Republic, Mamajuana is made of cured tree bark, various herbs and rum. Allowed to ferment, it turns a deep red and is likened to Port. A branded version of the drink had been introduced back in the 1950s.

Whether it be legend, fact or a combination thereof, Concesa also imparted some words of wisdom when she gave her daughter the supply. "I'll have you know that Mamajuana can cure ovarian, prostate and digestive disorders as well as influenza. But the best thing is that it can help deal with sexual impotency. So, drink to enjoy, and drink for good health!"

Well into her second bottle of the day, Consuela was now on the phone with June. The more she drank, the more she became enamored with the set-ups in the *Victoria's Secret* catalog – not for her to wear but, to her own surprise, for a partner. Arranging for a female client to go on a date with one of A.C.-D.C.'s fillies came under the category of "exotic" sex and would come at a greater cost than the standard date. "Connie Pett," the alias she decided upon for her Memorial Day weekend activities, had determined that cost was not going to be a factor.

When Connie asked about the possibility of her date arriving in specific apparel, June said it wouldn't be a problem: "Just tell me what you'd like your date to wear and we'll make sure to deliver. Receipts will be provided to you. We'll be adding a 10 percent surcharge to cover the cost of acquisition.

Connie thought about it for a minute and then placed her detailed order:

- mustard-yellow Lycra hipster panties

- matching push-up bra

- matching thigh-high tights

- wet-looking, black Lycra Spandex micro-mini skirt

- stretchy-ribbed, mustard-yellow Rayon/Spandex zip-front crop top

- mustard-yellow thigh-high leather boots

Thinking back on that conversation with A.C.-D.C., she actually began to get excited – so much so that Connie was wondering if she had time to..."Oh, what the hell," she said to herself. "The driver can always wait a few minutes."

Chapter 8 – Brooding About Breeding

TJ Cutter sat at his regular table tucked away in the far corner of the clubhouse's third-floor Dining Terrace. He was anticipating, somewhat impatiently at this point, the arrival of Beauregard Wellington, patriarch-in-waiting of the Lexington, KY, Wellingtons, long regarded as Kentucky's first family.

Steeped in all things of, by and for the Blue Grass State, Beau's grandfather, Buford "Buff" Wellington, had been a member of the U.S. Senate for nearly three decades before retiring from political life and pivoting to the family's thoroughbred business. A bout with pancreatic cancer led to his passing in 1978. Beau's daddy, Bentley, after serving a second four-year term as Governor, had founded one of the Commonwealth's newer distilleries, Bourbonesque LLC. An untimely accident and related stroke during a quail hunt in East Tennessee three years ago had left the former Governor paralyzed from hip to toes, confined to a wheelchair and incapable of running the day-to-day operations of the business. His wife, Abigail Prescott Wellington, was now COO and nominal head of Bourbonesque.

For his part, Beau was now principal owner of the Thoroughbred Bs Farm, one of the premier breeding operations in the nation. The Wellingtons' slogan? "We breed, broker and breathe thoroughbreds." The family raced them as well under the recently branded Triple-B Racing Stables. In a move whose rationale would soon become clear both within and outside the thoroughbred industry, the Wellingtons had recently formally segregated their breeding and racing businesses.

Working on his third Maker's Mark on the rocks, TJ glanced up to see Beau Wellington talking with the maître d', who pointed to where he was sitting. Tall at 6 ft. 2 in. and a slender 185 lbs., Beau was clean-shaven and greased back a full head of blonde hair. He came as if he were going to Churchill Downs on Derby Day, dressed in a blue Seersucker suit with powder blue Buckskin shoes. A white shirt with sapphire cufflinks, matching dark blue tie with white horseheads and powder-blue suspenders matching his shoes completed his attire. He strode to the table, gave TJ a hearty slap on the back and took a seat directly across from his dining partner.

TJ was wearing stone-colored khakis, an orange golf shirt with the University of Virginia logo at the top left and a navy blazer with gold buttons sporting Mr. Jefferson's Rotunda on the jacket sleeves and down the front. He offered a stark contrast in fashion to Wellington but certainly not in physical stature, as the native Virginian stood at 6 ft. 4 in. and weighed in at an even 200 lbs.

After some idle chit-chat that had little to do with the anticipated topic for today's discussion, Beau got down to business:

"I've admired what your fillies have done at the races," Beau started. "And one certainly can't argue with the success of *She's On Grounds* and *TJ's Mistress* as broodmares. We know you're early into your makeover of Cutting Edge Stables as a more aggressive operation," he continued. "Notwithstanding where you are in this process, we'd like to talk with you about a unique opportunity for us to do something together before the calendar year is over."

As Beau described the business proposition, TJ did his best to maintain a poker face while both his brain and stomach were churning. The Wellingtons were asking Cutter to combine the breeding portion of his thoroughbred business with Thoroughbred Bs Farm, creating arguably the largest and most prestigious breeding operation not named Florida's Ocala Stud Farm. Unlike Ocala, however, both parties would continue to race – the Wellingtons under the recently formed Triple-B Racing Stables and Cutter presumably by transferring the breeding assets of his thoroughbred business and maintaining Cutting Edge Stables as his racing-only entity.

But even a highly disciplined businessman like Thomas Jefferson Cutter III couldn't help but react with a very un-business-like "You'd really consider doing that?!?" as Beauregard Wellington suggested capitalizing the hypothetically conceived business combination he'd just outlined through a $200 million initial public offering of stock.

"The capital realized from a successful IPO would enable us to purchase a generation of the best stallions and broodmares," explained the young and animated Wellington. "For a colt or filly owned by either of our *racing* entities, we can structure an agreement providing an option to acquire at a hometown discount, so to speak."

There were so many aspects of this proposal that required further scrutiny, Cutter thought to himself, not the least of which were issues surrounding ownership structure, controlling interest and what a decision tree might look like.

As if reading TJ's mind, Beau broke an awkward silence by suggesting Cutter "take some time to think about it." The brash Kentuckian concluded his pitch: "If our proposal is something you'd like to *seriously* consider we'll bring the lawyers and accountants into our discussions."

Having done most of the talking, Beau indicated he'd finished the pitch by abruptly changing the subject to lunch, "Whew! I've worked up quite the appetite. What do you recommend, TJ?"

"If you like shellfish, I'd suggest Jersey blue crab. Otherwise, I'd go with blackened swordfish. All seafood is brought in fresh each day, so you really can't go wrong," Cutter offered.

"Oooh ... I'm gonna take a pass on the crab. My daddy almost died from a reaction to some Maryland blue crab at a Governors' Conference in Baltimore. Had to rush him to the hospital," explained Beauregard. "I've always been a bit leery of heading down the same culinary path. I think I'll go with blackened swordfish and a Caesar salad to start," concluded Beau.

TJ ordered Manhattan clam chowder and filet of flounder.

Over lunch, talk turned to the day's racing card. One of Cutting Edge Stables' 2-year-old colts, *Cut To The Chase*, was running in the co-featured 7th race, the ungraded Nijinsky II Stakes. A 5½ furlong sprint run on the turf, it honored the career of the Canadian-bred, Irish-trained *Nijinsky II*, who captured 1970 European Horse of the Year honors by winning the English Triple Crown – the Grade I 2000 Guineas run over Newmarket's straight mile in early May; the Grade I Derby over Epsom's switchback at 1½ miles in June, and the Grade I St. Leger Stakes over Doncaster's sweeping extended 1¾ miles in September.

It all made sense for Cutting Edge Stables, since its entry was sired by *Nijinsky II* out of the TJ Cutter-owned *Lawn Girl*.

Chapter 9 – Kentucky's Two-Time Governor

Democrat Bentley Wellington, age 43, became the 46th Governor of the Commonwealth of Kentucky on December 7, 1943. He served an initial four-year term that came to an end on December 9, 1947. Perhaps owing to the fact that he occupied the Governor's Mansion in Frankfort during what arguably had been two of the most joyous days in the lives of a majority of the Commonwealth's citizens – VE Day (May 8, 1945) and VJ Day (August 14 of the same year) – Wellington would be elected to a second term, which spanned December 11, 1951 to December 13, 1955.

Those aspiring to the State's highest office were not eligible to run for *consecutive* terms, so Bentley – sitting on the political sidelines for four years – used the time to focus on family life. On April 30, 1950, his young bride of two years, Abigail, gave birth to the Wellingtons' first child, a son they named Beauregard. Unfortunately, there were medical complications for Mrs. Wellington following the happy event. It was soon learned she couldn't bear any more children.

Abigail, devastated by the news, was determined to put all her energy into being the best parent possible to Beau. Bentley, on the other hand, seemed to distance himself from both his newborn son and the new mother. For the first time in his adult life. he lacked direction. He began to spend time at a local hunt club and eventually found himself in a small group of business execs who hunted deer, elk and black bear.

When Bentley wasn't hunting, he was drinking – at first socially but increasingly as an end-of-day habit. He soon developed a particular fondness for bourbon, the Kentuckians' alcohol of choice – so much so that he immersed himself in the history of the drink, the business operations of distilleries and what went into the process of making a first-class bourbon whiskey. He'd rapidly become a connoisseur of everything bourbon.

At the time, Bentley's dad, Buford, was serving as Kentucky's senior-ranking U.S. Senator. He'd considered a run for the gubernatorial office to succeed his son. But Democratic Party officials in Washington, D.C. persuaded Buford that his duties as chairman of the upper house's foreign relations committee were far more important than having another Wellington in Frankfort, particularly given the role the country was expected to play in the post-War international arena.

Seeing the turn of events in the younger Wellington's life, Buford and some political cronies had spent a weekend with Bentley and convinced him to prepare for a second run for governor. There'd be ample time to resume his newfound "hobbies" after a second stint as leader of the Commonwealth.

The gubernatorial race in the fall of 1951 wasn't much of a contest and Bentley Wellington was installed as the 48th governor of the Blue Grass State. By mutual agreement, Abigail remained at the family estate in Lexington while her husband took up residence in the Governor's Mansion in Frankfort. While just 29 miles separated the state capital and Lexington, the distance could not have created more of a chasm between the governor and first lady. To those closest to the couple, it wasn't a question of *whether* their relationship would deteriorate, but under what particular circumstances.

Those circumstances began to materialize shortly after Bentley arrived at his Frankfort residence in December. Wellington's chief of staff, Hugh Delaney, had been interviewing candidates for administrative staff across the various cabinets of the governor's office. The Governor had let it be known his preferences leaned in the direction of graduates from his alma mater, the University of Kentucky, with an emphasis on hiring young, attractive and intelligent female candidates.

While UK had been a co-educational institution since 1904, African Americans were not admitted to the University until 1949. At that time, UK's graduate and professional programs were finally opened to African Americans when Lyman T. Johnson won a lawsuit challenging the State of Kentucky's 1904 Day Law that prohibited students of color from attending the same school as white students. It would be another five years before African Americans would be admitted as undergraduates following the U.S. Supreme Court's landmark decision in Brown v. Board of Education.

One of the first African American women to earn her graduate degree in business administration from the University was Marci Davis, a Louisville native who'd earned a bachelor's degree in political science from the University of Cincinnati. As Delaney reviewed Davis's resume, he was noting the qualifications his boss had established as criteria for employment in the governor's office – UK alumna?...check. Young?...check. Intelligent?...clearly. Female?...obviously. He told his secretary to escort Ms. Davis into the office.

Delaney had been taken aback and wasn't quite sure whether the woman walking toward him noticed any change in his facial expression. He, himself, couldn't determine whether it was her ethnicity...or her sheer beauty that was responsible for his reaction.

A white blouse and medium beige pencil skirt complemented Ms. Davis's skin tone, while deep brown leather pumps decorated with bows made it a challenge to determine where ankles ended and shoes began. She carried leather gloves that matched her shoes and wore a medium beige round cloche hat with a dark brown silk band. Ms. Davis's Italian cut hairstyle was a knock-off of the style made popular by African American actress/dancer/singer Dorothy Dandridge who, a few years later, would be nominated for an Academy Award for her performance in the 1954 film *Carmen Jones*.

At a model's height of 5 ft. 10 in., Marci Davis would have been incredibly shapely even without the girdle that cinched her waist. Her makeup was understated in a way that suggested she knew exactly how to look for a business interview.

If Delaney hadn't already decided to add her to Wellington's staff, he would have had a fight on his hands. The good governor happened to enter Delaney's outer reception area and caught a glimpse of Ms. Davis as she sat on a high-backed arm chair to the right of the chief of staff's desk. Marci was the perfect picture of professionalism. Bentley interrupted, introduced himself and essentially took over the interview from Delaney. Some 25 minutes later, Marci Davis became the administrative assistant to the 48th governor of the Commonwealth of Kentucky.

Chapter 10 – Of Politics and Other Matters

In the ensuing weeks and months, Marci Davis cemented her role as a key aide to Governor Wellington. She came to the job with a thorough knowledge of the Commonwealth's socio-economic, legislative and judicial history; quickly acquired a practical understanding of how to get things done on behalf of the Governor's office, and cultivated relationships with key influencers who often had competing agendas.

Perhaps most important was Marci's perspective on Kentuckians working in the Commonwealth's coal-mining, whiskey-producing and thoroughbred industries. The position paper she'd prepared for Bentley on the intermediate and long-term impact of oil and gas on the future of coal was as valuable as it was prescient.

Bentley's ever-increasing reliance upon Marci's general organizational skills, political insights and growing relationships with industry lobbyists and other political hacks had them spending more and more time together. Their discussions often spilled into the evening hours. Dinner for two became the rule rather than the exception from Monday thru Thursday evenings. Bentley kept things strictly professional, though alcohol stirred temptations he'd thus far been able to suppress. For her part, Marci Davis seemed completely oblivious to whatever lascivious thoughts Bentley might have been entertaining.

Fast-forward to the spring of 1955. Hugh Delaney was making plans for his boss's attendance at the National Governors Association meeting in mid-July. With the end of his gubernatorial term approaching in December, Bentley Wellington would be heading to his final NGA summer gathering. This year's event was slated for San Francisco.

As more and more "last times" came and went, an increasing share of Bentley's mental energy was given over to what life would be like after leaving the Governor's Mansion. It was at this time Bentley began serious planning to launch Bourbonesque LLC.

The more he thought about it, the more he came to one conclusion: his new company's prospects for success would be greatly enhanced with the presence of a key right-hand executive

... and that exec should be Marci Davis. But further thought on the matter would have to be tabled until after the gathering of the nation's governors.

The Governor's *official* travel party to San Francisco included the Governor, Chief of Staff Hugh Delaney and Marci Davis. Going along for the ride – that is, at their own expense – were Bentley Wellington's wife, Abigail; their son, Beau, now five years old; and Hugh Delaney's wife, Shirley. Despite their eroding marital situation, Abigail was not about to miss a trip to San Francisco. She'd become friendly with Shirley Delaney over the past few years and could always spend time touring, shopping and dining with her – particularly if Bentley, Hugh and "that colored staffer" (as Marci had come to be known within Abigail's circle of friends) were busy with "political stuff." The Wellingtons and Delaneys would combine the three-day NGA business meeting with a long weekend vacation in and around "the City by the Bay" before returning to Kentucky.

For Marci Davis, it would be three days of meeting her senior-staff counterparts in other states and identifying very specific opportunities that had economic promise for Kentucky. She'd also have a platform in a key committee meeting to elaborate on her position paper dealing on the future of coal in light of major advances in the oil & gas industry.

The travel itinerary called for the Governor's party of six to travel from Frankfort to Cincinnati via a 1954 Packard limousine. At the Cincinnati/Northern Kentucky Airport, the group boarded a private plane bound for Chicago's Midway Airport, where another limo whisked them to Chicago's Union Station. The 11-mile-drive into the heart of the city took about an hour to negotiate.

The next-to-last leg of the party's journey involved a 2½-day trek of some 2,555 miles via a recent addition to transcontinental rail service, the Santa Fe Railroad's *San Francisco Chief*. The train's western terminus was actually Oakland, across the Bay from 'Frisco. Their third limo of the trip brought them to the NGA's host Fairmont Hotel, located atop Nob Hill.

Rich in U.S. business and political history, the hotel had been named after silver-mining magnate, real estate investor, railroad builder and former U.S. Senator James Graham Fair (D-Nev.). Almost completed in 1906, the hotel sustained heavy damage in the San Francisco Earthquake and didn't open until the following year. It was built in Senator Fair's honor by daughters Theresa Fair Oelrichs and Virginia Fair Vanderbilt.

Bentley arrived at the Fairmont utterly exhausted, having devoted more time to his son during the four-day trip to California than he'd probably spent with him since the beginning of his second term as governor. Abigail, happy to have Bentley take on the somewhat unfamiliar role of daddy, invested the bulk of her outbound adventure in conversation with Shirley, who thankfully shared many of her interests. Topics ranged from cooking, gardening, sewing and horseback riding to craft-fair rummaging, jewelry-making, ink and watercolor painting, scrapbooking and, oh yes, singing in the church choir. The pairings of talkative spouses and re-introduced father and son left Hugh Delaney and Marci Davis to devise the Kentucky contingent's meeting strategy.

Check-in took place on Wednesday, July 20th, at about 3:00 p.m. The Wellingtons occupied an upper-floor suite with a bedroom toward the back that offered a king bed, bureau and clothes closet. Night stands at each side of the bed held a telephone on one stand, an alarm clock on the other, and twin lamps. A separate living area in the front part of the suite included a Castro Convertible sofa bed and second bureau with room on top for a small black & white television set. A large bathroom off the living area completed the guest arrangements.

Once settled, Abigail said what Bentley had already anticipated: "I'll have Beau sleep with me in here. You can have the sofa bed. That way you can work as late as needed and not disturb us."

"Would you like to go downstairs for dinner?" Bentley asked. With Beau already tucked in, Abigail yawned and said she would wait until Beau finished his nap before deciding when and where to eat. "Besides, I'm feeling a bit under the weather. Might be better to get a good night's sleep and wake up to a big breakfast in the morning," she added.

"Tell you what," offered Bentley. "I'll bring you up a couple of sandwiches right now and leave them on the night stand by your side of the bed. That way, you'll be able to eat or sleep."

"Thanks Bentley. That would be grand." She then leaned toward the lamp, turned off the light and effectively ended her day. Abigail and Beau had four full days before the NGA meeting kicked off on Monday morning. How much time Bentley would spend with them she didn't know. She was hoping for a bit more than civility when it came to exchanges with her husband. Now that his time as a politician was drawing to a close, maybe he'd look to rekindle his roles as a father *and* husband.

***

Gently closing the hotel-room door behind him, Bentley felt a huge burden lifted from his shoulders. Not that he hadn't enjoyed the time with his son. But he'd essentially gone from absentee dad to marathon sitter, a situation he hadn't been prepared for either mentally or physically.

Now 4:00 p.m. locally, it was well into prime dinner hours according to his stomach, which was still stubbornly functioning on Eastern time. He took the elevator down to the lobby, planning to call Marci to see if she wanted to join him for dinner. When the elevator door opened at the third floor several guests stepped in, including Marci. They exchanged smiles. Bentley explained he'd be ordering sandwiches and bringing them up to the suite and suggested Marci ask the concierge for a couple of restaurant recommendations.

Back in the lobby after the sandwich drop-off, Bentley saw Marci heading toward him from the concierge's desk. "Fisherman's Grotto," she said in a matter-of-fact tone. "The gentleman at the desk said it was the first restaurant opened on Fisherman's Wharf back in 1935. Great lobster rolls and Dungeness crab. It's about a mile from here and we can catch a cable car outside."

All Bentley could think about was the impact this young woman could have as a key member of his start-up's management team. He'd dropped a few hints regarding his post-gubernatorial ambitions, hoping they would draw a response from Ms. Davis. All to no avail. Having no clue as to what career path she might choose, Bentley figured this evening would be the right time to flat-out offer her what he considered to be the opportunity of a lifetime.

Although several people were waiting for tables, a Commonwealth of Kentucky business card slipped to the maître d´ with a folded 50-dollar bill underneath earned Bentley the next open table. He and Marci were going to be dining al fresco. From their vantage point off to a corner, they could do a fair share of people-watching as summer crowds made their way to and from The Embarcadero along Taylor Street. Bentley was actually pleased with the ambient sounds of a busy summer evening at the wharf. While it may have intruded a bit on their dinner, it also allowed him to talk without neighboring diners overhearing their conversation.

Marci ordered Pacific sole. While Dungeness Crab was a local specialty, Bentley remembered his life-threatening reaction to the Maryland Blue Crab he'd eaten in Baltimore a couple of years back and settled on Blackened Pacific Rock Cod. Looking over the wine list, Bentley ordered a '51 sauvignon blanc in honor of the year Ms. Davis joined the Wellington administration. Marci said she was flattered although Bentley, thinking to himself, couldn't tell if she'd ... well, what would it be?... blushed? What a strange, unique advantage when folks couldn't tell if you were caught in an awkward moment, at least by a change in skin color. Thinking about his own, chalk-white pigmentation, Bentley knew when other people could observe sudden embarrassment in the Governor. He always felt that warm "from-the-neck-up" sensation that was accompanied by a reddening of his cheeks.

For dessert, Marci decided upon black forest chocolate mousse, a decadent combination of chocolate, brandied cherries, toasted pecans and chocolate tuille. Bentley could never turn down New York cheese cake. The Grotto's offering came with a mixed berry sauce. Finishing dessert as well as their second bottle of wine, most of which he'd consumed, the Governor contemplated adjourning to the Fairmont's lounge before "popping the question." As Bentley took the napkin from his lap to wipe his mouth, he thought to himself: "Hmmm. That seemed to be an odd way of putting it – popping the question."

Back on the cable car, Bentley told Marci he wanted to "go over something with her" before calling it a night. Interpreting his words as somewhere between a request and a demand, Marci decided to table her exhaustion for a little while longer to hear what her boss had to say.

It took Bentley two bourbons on the rocks before getting to the crux of the matter. After about a half-hour's worth of detailed explanation of his plans for Bourbonesque LLC, during which he'd had a third Maker's Mark, Bentley Wellington, he of the Commonwealth's first family and part of Lexington, Kentucky's landed gentry, confided to Marci Davis that his master plan included an unparalleled opportunity for the administrative assistant sitting across the table to advance her career and be rewarded with a lucrative compensation package loaded with financial incentives – "for someone who has earned the right to be called the Governor's top aide."

Considering the amount of wine and bourbon he consumed, Bentley Wellington was quite pleased with how he'd presented his offer.

Marci Davis, however, sat there nonplussed while thoughts about the life she'd lived flashed through her mind – her childhood in Louisville during which she'd been raised by her Uncle Lou (Marci's parents perished in a horrific, weather-related bus accident in December of 1930 en route from Louisville to Birmingham, Alabama to visit relatives); Lou's insistence on Marci adopting education, organization and cultivating relationships as foundations for a successful life; the lengths to which her high school guidance counselor and teachers had gone to recommend her admission to the University of Cincinnati; her desire to excel in political science and to understand the endless civil rights plight and fight of Negroes across the United States; the role the NAACP had played in pushing her to apply to the University of Kentucky for graduate work in business.

"This is all so sudden, Governor," she said after a pause that seemed to last an eternity. "May I take some time to think about it?"

Now it was Bentley's turn to be flummoxed. Under ordinary circumstances, his response might have gone along the lines of: "I know this is sudden, there's a lot to consider and you may already have decided what you'll be doing after my term is up." But Bentley Wellington had ingested close to two bottles of wine and three bourbons, and he was in no position to think rationally or respond reasonably. All he'd heard in Marci's response was rejection. And with that, he snapped.

"I'm giving you the chance of a lifetime and all you do is ask for time to think about it!?! Who hires someone with no professional experience to become the personal assistant to the Governor? Who gives a person with your background the assignment to develop a position paper on one of the most important issues confronting the citizens of our great Commonwealth? Who the hell do you think you are, you ungrateful black bitch!?!"

And there it was, Marci Davis thought, out in the open from a closet bigot now sitting across from her and in a drunken rage because this proud and accomplished "Negro" wouldn't fall all over him with gratitude and simply reply, "Where do I sign?" She rose from her chair, turned her back on him and strode to the elevator outside the lounge, stating firmly and surely loud enough for him to hear, "You'll have my letter of resignation in the morning!"

Then, of course, Bentley felt immediate remorse, calling out "Marci!" Then louder ..."Marci!!!" He saw the elevator door close with his soon-to-be former aide behind it.

If that had been the end of what was turning into a dreadful evening for both of them, the relationship might have survived with an early morning apology from Bentley. But the verbal exchange in the lounge was just the opening act of a three-act tragedy.

Now after 11:00 p.m., Bentley – transitioning from drunken rage to drunken stupor – weaved his way to the elevator, boarded and, recalling Marci's room number from the information sheet Hugh had given him at check-in, pressed the button marked 3.

Staggering down the hallway and making a left turn, Bentley made his way toward room 348 at the end of the corridor. He knocked softly on the door, waited several seconds and then knocked again. With the Governor about to bang loudly in total disregard for occupants of neighboring rooms, Marci Davis opened the door and said perfunctorily: "I figured it would be you."

"Marci...Miss Davis, I'm terribly sorry. Can you possibly accept my most humble apologies?" At first she thought ... and thought hard, finally answering, "Clearly, your drinking was responsible for your rude behavior which, given time, I would be willing to overlook." The Governor was about to thank her, but Marci hadn't finished.

"But what I can't get past is your bigotry as well as your belief that I couldn't possibly do anything but accept your offer – almost as if I were an indentured servant obligated to accept passage from the Wellington administration to your 'New World!'"

The brilliance of her analogy was overshadowed by Bentley Wellington's sudden realization that her value as a key executive in his yet-to-be-founded bourbon business paled by comparison to the underlying feeling that...yes, *he loved her.* Clarity in his mind was followed by an actual utterance – "I love you, Marci."

The disaster about to unfold even then might have been avoided by some words of consolation from Marci. But somewhat naive in dealing with the romantic dalliances of rich and drunk white southerners, she unwisely chose words of condescension: "Come now, Governor. It's been a long night and you're clearly not thinking straight. Go upstairs to your wife and son."

That was the final straw. He'd just confessed his love for Marci and her response was one of disdain? By God, if she won't accept my affection, maybe she'll understand *this*!...And with that, he pushed into the room, grabbed Marci around the waist and threw her on the bed. It all happened so fast, Marci was unable to react.

Bentley covered Marci's mouth with his left hand and with the other untied the white terrycloth hotel robe she was wearing, revealing a completely naked body underneath. The 48th Governor of Kentucky then buried his face between her breasts and reached for her crotch. As tears welled up in Marci's eyes, she remembered something one of her co-ed college friends had advised in any such confrontation: "Don't resist. It'll only bring on more physical abuse." Already thinking of how all this would go down afterward, she couldn't fathom any outcome other than being on the short end of a "he said/she said" situation. That would be particularly true when the 'he' was who *he* was and the 'she' was who *she* was.

Bentley, at a mere 5 ft. 9 in. and evidently short-changed, coming from a long line of men appreciably taller than six feet, had no difficulty in meshing his body with hers. His weight, now at 225, allowed him to easily keep Marci pinned in place while he struggled with his right hand to pull down his pants.

Given the amount he'd drunk, Bentley was surprised at his ability to "function." Eventually he was able to force his way inside her and began pumping. There was virtually no resistance from Marci at this point. Sooner than he'd wanted, he climaxed. For a couple of minutes, he lay there while catching his breath. Not fearing any after-the-deed noise from Marci, he removed his hand from her mouth, sat up, pulled on his trousers and left the room.

***

Despite telling Bentley she would resign the next morning, Marci instead remained in her position as an aide to Governor Wellington. Neither mentioned the incident to the other (or to anyone else). With the exception of an occasional knowing glance, business proceeded as usual. One aspect of the relationship *did* change: there were no more after-hours dinners or meetings. This did not seem particularly unusual to folks like Hugh Delaney, given the Governor's term of office would soon be over.

The mutual silence on the matter abruptly changed in early October, some three months after Bentley had forced himself on Marci. Knowing she was pregnant and would soon begin to show, the Governor's top aide retained the services of an attorney in Louisville to help extract a financial settlement from Bentley.

There was no question about who fathered the baby, as Marci hadn't been involved in a relationship during her entire time in Frankfort. A devout Catholic, Marci was committed to keeping the unborn child. She wanted terms that would secure not only her future but the future of the baby conceived with the Governor. Once Bentley knew about the pregnancy, he was quite amenable to a settlement very favorable to Marci – particularly considering her loyalty in the face of his abhorrent actions and, as his lawyer pointed out, what was at stake for his personal as well as his family's wealth and reputation.

At a private, all-day meeting in November attended by Bentley, his personal attorney, Marci and her attorney, the parties worked out an agreement in which Marci would receive an immediate, lump-sum payment of $100,000. A trust would be established for the child, with $500 monthly payments to continue until the child reached the age of 18. Funds were to be used for either a college education or for technical training.

Further, Bentley would use his Wall Street connections to arrange for a suitable position with Steinberg Stavros Rogers & Co., Inc., a global asset management firm specializing in the energy and transportation industries, both areas of expertise for Marci.

Finally, Bentley would purchase a home in Marci's name somewhere that would allow for an easy commute to Manhattan, allotting up to $200,000 for the property of her choice.

All, of course, was subject to a non-disclosure agreement regarding the events that took place in San Francisco and terms of the settlement. Any evidence indicating such information had been shared with a third party were grounds for a suit that could be brought against Marci by Bentley and/or his heirs and family members.

Marci Davis took the final month of Bentley Wellington's term in accrued vacation pay, chose her new residence in Jersey City (a pastel yellow brick Tudor on Bentley Avenue between Hudson Boulevard and West Side Avenue), started the new job with Steinberg Stavros in midtown Manhattan in January 1956, and cut off all ties with the Commonwealth of Kentucky.

As an extra hedge against discovery, soon after arriving in New Jersey Marci legally changed her name to Marci Davis Jeffries.

On March 25, 1956, evidently anxious to get on with life "on the outside," Sean Davis Jeffries arrived roughly 3½ weeks early at the Margaret Hague Maternity Hospital of the Jersey City Medical Center. Mom and baby son, born at 4 lb. 7 oz., were doing fine.

Chapter 11 – A Looming Board Decision

To be sure, her just completed phone conversation with Jorge had been unsettling. But Gretchen Weiß Hauptmann quickly shook off any maternal-related thoughts as she hopped into her 1983 metallic-red Porsche 930 Turbo coupe for the drive over to Wuppertal.

Although the meeting of GWH GmbH's seven-person Advisory Board wasn't until that afternoon, she felt compelled as the chairperson to arrive early at the meeting's location. Her administrative assistant, Hanna Schröder, had scoured the community for suitable venues and ultimately decided upon the Park Villa. Located outside Wuppertal Zentrum (center city), the hotel was a family-run boutique constructed in the early 1900s.

Gretchen's agenda called for the meeting to get underway at 1400 Stunden (2:00 p.m.). and go until 1900 Stunden. During the initial five-hour session, detailed plans and forecasts would be laid out for operating as either a public or private company. After a break for dinner, the meeting would reconvene for debate that would end no later than 2300 Stunden. Rooms had been reserved to give Board members a night to "sleep on it," to use an American expression. Nach dem Frühstück (after breakfast), die Vorsitzende (the chairperson) would call for final statements from each member. Hauptmann would be the last to speak and then call for a final vote.

There were two routes Gretchen used interchangeably for her trips to Wuppertal. Today, she chose to stay away from the quicker route that would have taken her ever so briefly on the Bundesautobahn 1, part of Germany's federal motorway. There was road construction at Remscheid and she didn't want to chance a major delay.

Her alternative was shorter by about 3.1 km (or 2 miles), but would take about five minutes longer – maybe less if she put the Porsche through its paces. For Gretchen, the daily trip back and forth had become a game to see how quickly she could get from point A to point B. "What was the point in owning a Porsche 930?" she reasoned.

Der Rückweg ("the back way") started Hauptmann on Bachstraße heading in the direction of Bahnhofstraße at the northeast end of Hückeswagen. Working through three roundabouts left her on L414, a road full of twists and turns that eventually took her to Berliner Straße. A left at that junction and a right onto K14 enabled her to arrive in Wuppertal.

As Gretchen backed her Porsche from the driveway, a light mist began to fall.

Chapter 12 – S. Davis Jeffries: Turf Consultant

While spending three summers working at Monmouth Race Track, Sean Davis Jeffries had gradually become immersed in just about every aspect of thoroughbred racing. From his dual vantage points as an admissions seller at the clubhouse pass gate and as assistant to the director of admissions in the attendance office, he'd soon developed relationships with an array of industry figures – from trainers, jockeys, agents and horse owners to race track personnel, New Jersey Racing Commission officials and executives of the Thoroughbred Breeders' Association of New Jersey. He'd also become acquainted with some of the seedier characters involved in the underbelly of the thoroughbred industry: bookies, touts, confidence men and members of various "families."

There was money to be made with the general knowledge and inside information that came to his attention on almost a daily basis. The trick was separating fact from rumor, good info from bad, relevant knowledge from that which should be discarded. There was seldom time or the ability to corroborate information, so good instincts, understanding the relative merits of various information sources...and plain old experience were critical. It was great to learn as a result of success. But there were lessons, albeit painful at times, to be learned from failure.

For his second summer at the Oceanport venue, Sean had business cards printed: *S. Davis Jeffries, Turf Consultant at Monmouth Park*. The card included his home telephone number, but no address. At this early stage of his "avocation," he needed to be careful not to cross a line of impropriety. There were about a half-dozen tip sheets sold to patrons each day by "barkers" located at long counters near the main gate, train gate and clubhouse entrance. The owners of these tip sheets, many of whom operated at multiple tracks, literally had license to be there. While they knew touting was a race track fact of life, none of them would be happy with an unofficial tipster "setting up shop" and providing competition – particularly without the necessary paperwork or paying the requisite fees for doing so.

While hundreds of well-to-do Monmouth Park patrons passed

through the turnstile of his clubhouse booth each day, only a half dozen or so fit the profile of prospective repeat customers. He focused on two types: older, wealthy women who clearly had nothing better to do with their money and time than fritter both away gambling, and middle-aged men who happened to be small business owners.

Just short of 6 feet tall ("I'm six feet in my 'Cons,'" he used to say while playing high school basketball) and tipping the scales at 175 lbs., Sean's caramel skin and handsome face certainly appealed to the female side of the Jersey Shore's "senior circuit." For male owners of small businesses, the touch point appeared to be entrepreneurship. In Sean's hustling, these guys saw a younger version of themselves.

A race track patron's loyalty was never a guarantee, but Sean figured customer retention required a reasonably high degree of consistency between his pre-race prognostications and the way races were actually run. In some instances, Sean named one horse as his winning choice. These picks more often came as a result of inside information. There were other races where his handicapping set up an either/or scenario, depending upon the strategies of competing horses' connections and the relative strengths and weaknesses of the horses themselves. Regardless of the *source* of information, continuing success depended upon the ability to make customers believe S. Davis Jeffries knew what the hell he was talking about.

Compensation for successful selections came in various forms. There was the cash gratuity, sometimes a percentage of the winnings but more often an amount (e.g., $20, $50 or $100) bearing no relationship to the winnings but more a function of the size of the customer's wager.

Then there was the pari-mutuel ticket purchased by a customer for Sean, typically the same wager (e.g., #4 in the eighth race) for either the same amount for small bettors (e.g., a $2 or $5 wager) or, in the case of larger bettors, a smaller amount (e.g., customer places a $100 wager on #4 in the eighth race and makes a $5 or $10 wager for Sean).

Finally, there was the periodic next-day gift, most often a bottle of wine or hard liquor. Such gifts always reflected the "good taste" of the patron (e.g., a vintage bottle of Baron de Rothschild Bordeaux or a fifth of 12-year-old Glenlivit).

Regardless of how compensation was received, Sean's most important rule was "never request it." There was no law against offering an opinion to a race track patron. But *asking* for something in exchange – the quid pro quo, if you will – would be considered a contract and was most definitely a "no-no." Accepting a gift for his hospitable manners and overall helpfulness in making a customer's race-track experience the best it could be left him just short of crossing that line, at least in Sean's mind. And regulars of the Monmouth Park clubhouse were always gracious to the staff – on the last day of the meet and, in particular, on the evening of the Monmouth Park Charity Ball, when alcohol and money flowed rather freely.

***

Now years removed from his employee days at Monmouth Park, Sean was no longer distributing business cards to patrons, although there were many familiar faces who recognized him and asked if he had any info to share. He was at the track on opening day for one reason ... to have a conversation with one Thomas Jefferson Cutter III.

Reaching the top of the escalator, Sean worked his way toward the third-floor clubhouse dining room for his well-planned "chance" encounter. But as he came to the entrance, he noticed Cutter had company...and someone he recognized at that!

What was Beauregard Wellington doing at Monmouth Park today? Was it a chance encounter with Cutter or a planned meeting? Taken aback, Sean retreated to a nearby men's room and chose a stall at the far end to think through what he'd just seen and what were the implications.

While contemplating his next move, he halfheartedly scanned the pages of the race-card program. Suddenly, there it was: the 6th race at one mile on the turf course along the hedge, a handicap for 3- and 4-year-old colts. The #4 entry was *Dance To The Music*, a 3-year-old colt sired by *Nijinsky II* out of *It Was Meant To B*. Sean knew what the letter 'B' likely meant in a thoroughbred's name and he confirmed it by going to *The Daily Racing Form*, which listed the broodmare's owner as Thoroughbred Bs Farm of Lexington,

KY. And *Dance To The Music* was racing under the Royal Blue and White colors of Beauregard Wellington's Triple-B Racing Stables.

With all of his race track experience, how ironic his plans had hit a snag because he hadn't done his homework thoroughly enough. Sean wouldn't make that mistake again. He'd spend some time thinking about how, when and where to meet with TJ Cutter, but knew it needed to be sooner rather than later.

Chapter 13 – Coming to Grips with the Truth

Growing up in Jersey City, Sean accepted without much lasting curiosity his status as an only child along with Marci's concocted version of events surrounding his dad's disappearance. As far as he knew, his mom's husband, Lee, had deserted her shortly after his birth. When Sean asked his mom if she knew his dad's whereabouts, she said he'd disappeared one night and left no answers – or clues, for that matter – as to why he left and where he went.

Sean had been told the truth about his grandparents losing their lives in a bus crash and Uncle Lou raising Marci in Louisville since the age of three. While Marci had been able to provide Sean with all of life's "basics," she wanted Sean to learn the value of a dollar, to earn his way, and to appreciate what he had rather than to long for what he didn't have. By all indications, she'd done a pretty decent job.

Mother and son had come to enjoy Jersey City, which offered the conveniences of an urban setting with easy access to the Big Apple just across the Hudson River. As Marci progressed in her career at Steinberg Stavros, she decided to join the thousands of city dwellers who spent anywhere from a week to the entire summer in rental properties "down the Jersey shore." The month of August soon became the Jeffries' annual time to relax and re-charge the batteries. Marci regularly rented a couple of rooms at a boarding house in Belmar, just a couple of blocks from the boardwalk and beach.

The decision turned out to be quite fortuitous. For years Sean had honed his basketball skills, taking time off only to play Little League and Babe Ruth baseball. He spent countless hours shooting hoops in the backyard of his Jersey City home and played CYO Biddy Basketball for St. Aloysius parish and the Jersey City All-Stars. Finding himself in Belmar each August, he was introduced to the Spring Lake Heights Summer Basketball League, where some of the Garden State's best high school and prep players competed in front of college scouts.

Among the friends Sean had made on those summer league teams was Nathan Katzman. "Kat Man," a 5-9 point guard who was a tenacious defender and brilliant floor general, lived in Point Pleasant Beach and played for Point Pleasant Borough High School. An older brother, David, was in the military.

Sean soon met Nate's dad, Irving, a now-retired New York City cop who lived in Point Pleasant Beach and owned and operated a boardwalk arcade in Seaside Heights.

Sean, playing basketball at Lincoln High School, became a bona fide D1 prospect. Keeping up with his studies, he was a member of the Honor Society and was elected class president. Never into the sciences (he actually had his female biology lab partner dissect a crayfish due to his squeamishness), he excelled in English, History and, in particular, Mathematics.

Sean's academic work and athletic prowess earned him a full scholarship offer from Fairleigh Dickinson University, where he played hoops for the Division I Independent Knights. It was in the spring of '75 following an 11-13 season that he applied to Monmouth Race Track for a summer job to earn some "carrying around" cash.

It was then that Marci chose to talk with her son to more accurately fill in a piece or two of his life. Like most anything of potentially significant consequence, she thought through her decision with great care.

She'd seen that Bentley's son, Beauregard, had become steward of the Wellington family's Thoroughbred Bs Farm. It wasn't terribly difficult to keep tabs on one of Kentucky's most prominent families. She also knew the thoroughbred business was an incredibly close-knit community in which well-kept secrets were few and far between.

What Marci *didn't* know was whether Bentley had ever discussed with Beau his "indiscretion" with a senior aide that had resulted in a child. Or might Beau have somehow found out on his own? Taking all the variables into account, Marci decided full disclosure from her would be far better than risking the possibility of Sean discovering the identity of his "father" and, by extension, learning he had a half-brother.

Marci chose the date, time and venue for her conversation with Sean: Sunday, May 11th, Mother's Day, at Ilvento's, a neighborhood Italian restaurant. Sean loved the al dente spaghetti with meat balls, which he rated the best he'd ever tasted. Marci was partial to the baked ziti. Both started their meals with a cup of minestrone. She waited until they'd finished their meal and half their bottle of Chianti.

"Sean, I want to talk with you about your father." And so began an hour-long monologue encompassing the period from Marci's December 1951 interview at the Governor's Mansion with Chief of Staff Hugh Delaney and Governor-elect Bentley Wellington...to the November 1955 meeting in the office of her attorney in Louisville. (The only interruption came when Marci described, understandably with some degree of difficulty since she'd worked very hard to purge the specifics from her memory, the "evening of conception" at the Fairmont Hotel in San Francisco.) Marci paused to take a deep breath while Sean reached across the table to finish off his mom's half-full glass of Chianti.

After what seemed to be an eternity, Sean spoke: "Mom, I've never been prouder of you, for what you've accomplished and for how you stood up to the Governor. And I've never been prouder to be an African-American."

With a mountainous burden lifted from her shoulders and greatly relieved at her son's response, she exhaled slowly and said, "Now how about some of that New York cheese cake with raspberry sauce? I think I'll have mine with a cup of espresso."

***

Some four years had passed since Sean learned about the rape of his mom by Governor Bentley Wellington. In the days and weeks immediately following that momentous Mother's Day revelation, he'd spent much time wrestling with a burning anger at what Wellington had done as well as the knowledge that he owed his existence to the Governor's abhorrent, criminal behavior.

Of one thing Sean was certain: this new knowledge of what had transpired between his mom and Bentley Wellington would guide much of his subsequent decision-making.

It was no coincidence then, that Sean had chosen history as his major with an emphasis on post-Civil War Reconstruction of the South; had spent an inordinate amount of time reading about the political history of the Commonwealth of Kentucky; had found himself in Louisville on Derby Day in 1976 and 1977; had used his summers at Monmouth Park to accumulate an intimate working knowledge of the thoroughbred racing industry; had taken a guided tour of Bourbonesque LLC, a business founded by Bentley Wellington shortly after concluding his second four-year stint in Frankfort; and finally, that he, Sean, had applied to Seton Hall University School of Law in Newark, NJ.

Through it all, five words uttered by Lincoln High School baseball and basketball teammate Bruce Willett played over and over like an echo chamber in Sean's mind: "Don't get mad, get even."

Sean had committed to Seton Hall's four-year evening program, preferring to have maximum flexibility during daytime hours. Now back home with his mom in their Bentley Avenue Tudor in Jersey City, they were having their favorite Sunday morning breakfast, Aunt Jemima buttermilk pancakes and Jimmy Dean sausages. The ironic cultural juxtaposition of the two was not lost on either of them.

Passing sections of *The Sunday Times* between them, it was Marci who came across a feature story on Beauregard Wellington's efforts to reverse his family's recent run of bad luck. It appeared in the section devoted to sports rather than politics. So while the article mentioned the passing of longtime U.S. Senator Buford Wellington the previous year and the recent hunting accident and stroke suffered by former two-term governor and current head of Bardstown, Kentucky-based Bourbonesque Bentley Wellington, the focus was actually on the future of the Thoroughbred Bs Farm, now under the guidance of Bentley's son, Beau.

Marci, of course, already knew about Bentley's misfortune through the connection between the Wellington family and her now long-time employer. She hadn't mentioned it to Sean because, well ... she diligently avoided any unnecessary discussion of the Wellingtons in the aftermath of her 1975 Mother's Day revelations.

It was Sean who kept his mom "in the dark" about the pivotal role that conversation had been playing in his life. Reading *The Sunday Times* piece with more than passing interest, he made a mental note to purchase another copy of the newspaper later that morning so he could include the article in his "Wellington" three-ringed binder. The last thing he wanted his mom to know was the degree to which he'd been gathering intel on Kentucky's first family. His binder now had four sections labeled *Politics*, *Bourbonesque*, *Thoroughbred Bs Farm* and *Family Ties*.

Chapter 14 – Deep Cover

He'd been living in Hamilton, Ontario, ever since leaving Hückeswagen roughly 17 years ago during the summer of 1966. Brian Harper, a.k.a. Fabian Hauptman (spelled with one 'n' not two, as he had used during World War II and in the years immediately thereafter), had left his wife, Gretchen, and five-year-old son, Jürgen, in the middle of the night.

An only child, Fabian had endured an incredibly dangerous Second World War inside Germany, not only hiding his Jewish identity but aiding both his fellow Jews and the Allied cause. In the early stages of the war, Fabian sheltered several Jews in a secret basement at his Dresden home as they were making their way across the German border into Czechoslovakia, through the Balkans, and eventually by sea to Palestine. His parents, Ludwig and Sarah Hauptman, had been among the first to escape. Rather than join them, Fabian chose to remain to help others. That's when he added a second 'n' to his surname.

Later, Fabian was quietly asked to table this particular clandestine activity because of his day job as scheduler in Dresden's railway marshalling yard. In this capacity, Fabian had access to planned movements of artillery- and munitions-laden trains – information he passed along to one of the few British SOE (Special Operations Executive) contacts within this region of Germany. His value in this latter capacity was so consequential that it simply couldn't be risked by discovery of his *underground* railway activities. He was also asked to abandon his family's home and move to an apartment, in case the Nazis somehow connected the dots between the Jewish family that had previously owned the single-family dwelling and its current occupant.

Shortly after the fall of the Third Reich, he met Gretchen Weiß in a Dresden pub. Both were exhausted – Fabian because he'd been living under such a heavy shroud of secrecy during the war; Gretchen because she'd lost her entire family. While hardly the basis for a lasting relationship, their shared experience certainly made for short-term companionship. One night turned into two, two became four and ultimately their joint desire to get as far away as possible from Dresden governed their willingness to relocate together.

They decided to head across country to the Rhineland, settling on the small village of Hückeswagen. Fabian took a job in Wuppertal with the *Reichsbahn-Generaldirektion*, that part of the former *Deutsche Reichsbahn* (German National Railway) operating in the British Zone of occupation. Unbeknownst to Gretchen, the British had arranged for Fabian's appointment and the couple's passage from Dresden. Gretchen interviewed for a line position with Pulver-Metall Lüdenscheid, a P/M parts manufacturer with a plant in nearby Radevormwald. With a new residence and decent-paying post-War jobs, Fabian and Gretchen married. But it was several years before they decided upon a family, both of them still bearing the deep psychological wounds inflicted by war.

Working hard, Gretchen rose quickly through Pulver-Metall Lüdenscheid's ranks to the position of shift manager. A half-dozen years later, she took the entrepreneurial plunge and formed her own firm, GWH GmbH, based in Wuppertal.

On June 3, 1961 Gretchen gave birth to Jürgen after assuring Fabian a year earlier that she'd be able to accommodate motherhood along with her nascent business. With both parents having flexibility in their work lives, Fabian and Gretchen managed to bring their son successfully through his first five years of life.

Then came the note, imperceptibly placed in Fabian's hand by a passerby as he walked from his Oberbarmen office at the eastern terminal of the *Wuppertal Schwebebahn* (Wuppertal Suspension Railway) to a nearby public parking lot. The note was short and to the point:

> Arrive tomorrow evening by 2000 Stunden (8:00 p.m.) at Brauerei Zum Schlüssel, a Düsseldorf brewpub located at Bolkerstraße 43-47. Enter the front entrance and move past the main bar and standing tap room to sections in the rear where meals are served. At a corner table for two, look for a thin, pale and balding middle-aged man sitting alone. He'll motion for you to join him.

That was it. No explanation as to why, although given his wartime activities and the British government's role in arranging his railroading position, Fabian had expected some sort of contact sooner or later. Ever since the 1964 founding of *die Nationaldemokratische Partei Deutschlands* (the National Democratic Party of Germany), billed as the far-right successor to *die Deutsche Reichspartei* (the German Reich Party), Fabian had felt increasingly uneasy.

After his meeting, he faced a life-altering choice ... not only for himself, but for Gretchen and Jürgen as well. Fabian learned from this German-based operative of the Mossad, Israel's National Intelligence Agency, that a small group of the NDP would soon be ready to launch a rogue "seek-and-destroy" mission aimed at removing those Germans who'd sympathized with Jews during the war. He offered Fabian's family – likely targets of such a mission – an opportunity to leave Germany and relocate to Israel.

Fabian Hauptman(n) asked his dining companion, "How much time do I have?"

The Mossad agent, who never provided his name, was quite candid in his response: "Given your war history, I wouldn't want your family to be here come next fall. Call this number when you decide. We'll need to hear within the next four weeks in order to make the appropriate arrangements." With that, he handed Fabian a piece of paper with a number on it, stood up from his chair and walked away. He never looked back.

Chapter 15 – The Day Before...

Connie Pett had absolutely zero interest in spending time in the back seat of a town car taking the New Jersey Turnpike and Garden State Parkway south to Atlantic City. She had very specific instructions for the driver: "I want to hug the ocean as much as possible. Once we hit the north Jersey shore, open the roof so I can smell the salty air. In terms of food, I'll know it when I see it. Your meal is on me."

Getting into the car, Connie couldn't help but notice that Calvin Thomas was "easy on the eyes." A well-built African-American man who looked to be in his early 40s, he came with a well-groomed mustache, close-cropped black curly hair and an engaging smile that showed off his near-perfect pearly whites.

Having driven the casino circuit countless times over the past couple of years, Calvin headed downtown toward the Brooklyn Battery Tunnel, eventually taking the Verrazano Narrows Bridge to Staten Island. From there, he picked up the Outerbridge Crossing that spanned the Arthur Kill, which separates New York and New Jersey.

In fairly short order, Calvin went from U.S. Route 9 South in the small city of South Amboy; crossed the Raritan River where he switched to N.J. Route 35 South in Laurence Harbor, and moved through Keyport and Hazlet onto N.J. Route 36 East. Heading toward Sandy Hook State Park, he passed through Union Beach, Keansburg and Atlantic Highlands before hitting Highlands and the Atlantic Ocean.

"I'm opening the roof now," he notified his passenger. And with that, Calvin turned his town car southward on Ocean Avenue, the Atlantic on their left, the Navesink River on their right and the town of Sea Bright a little less than three miles ahead.

Eventually passing Monmouth Beach, Route 36 branched off to the west. Connie, now intoxicated with the salt air, was pleased Calvin remained on Ocean Avenue. Her jaw dropped as they continued south through the decidedly upscale town of Deal, with block after block of multi-million-dollar estate homes. The town of Allenhurst, with houses not quite as exquisite as those of its neighbor to the north, was next. Moving onto Deal Lake Drive in a westerly direction, the main road – now N.J. Route 71 – curved south again.

This was Asbury Park and Convention Hall, site of dozens of rock concerts during the '60s and '70s. Calvin, who assumed the role of tour guide when his passengers seemed interested, did the obligatory left turn on Cookman Avenue at the south end of Asbury Park so Connie could see the famous indoor Palace Amusements and Merry Go Round.

Cookman ended at the intersection of Asbury Avenue. A quick right and then left put the town car back on Ocean Avenue, where Connie could see the Salt Water Taffy store, miniature golf courses, kiddie rides and other boardwalk features. Ocean Avenue, a northbound multi-lane one-way street, afforded her an up-front look at the Convention Hall/Paramount Theatre/indoor arcade complex to the right, along with the Planters Peanuts Store, Monte Carlo Salt Water Pool and Kingsley Arms Hotel to the left.

Now heading down Main Street/Route 71 for the second time, Calvin told Connie about Ocean Grove and its founding by Methodist clergymen back in 1869 as a summer camp meeting site. He noted that "until a couple of years ago," local law banned vehicular traffic as well as street parking on Sundays. "So every Saturday, you'd see a mass exodus of cars leaving the town limits in search of parking spots," chuckled Calvin. "Now don't that beat all!?!"

They continued down Main Street through Bradley Beach, Neptune City and Avon-by-the-Sea. It was a minute or two before 2:00 p.m. when Connie became startled by the loud clanging of a bell. Looking out the front window, she saw a black and white striped gate blocking the road...which was rising at an ever-steeper angle into the sky.

"Every hour on the hour the bridge opens to allow boats through the inlet," Calvin informed her. "The next town is Belmar, which has a sizable marina in the Shark River Inlet." He pointed to the right. As Connie looked that way, she noticed the railroad tracks raised as well.

Anticipating her question, he explained that "trains operating on these tracks take passengers from New York City and Hoboken to towns along the Jersey shore as far south as Bay Head Junction."

With the bridge now down, Calvin continued along Route 71,

quickly leaving Belmar, Spring Lake Heights, Spring Lake, Sea Girt and Manasquan in his rear-view mirror. At Brielle, he made a left-hand turn onto Route 35 South which spanned the Manasquan River. Immediately after crossing, Calvin made another left onto Broadway and then a third left onto Channel Drive. At 83 Channel Drive he pulled into the parking lot of one of the Jersey shore's best seafood restaurants – The Lobster Shanty.

"Understand you said 'I'll know it when I see it,' but afraid I'm gonna have to overrule you on this one," said Calvin as he turned to look back at his passenger with a big grin.

After a meal that started with lobster bisque and never-to-be-forgotten corn fritters, then featured twin lobster tails accompanied by Jersey Silver Queen corn on the cob and concluded with freshly brewed coffee (Calvin would not partake of any alcoholic beverage while working, so Connie abstained as well), driver and passenger returned to the town car. What conversation they had was confined to a casual discussion of life growing up in New York City and the beauty and charm of the Jersey shore. Connie learned that Calvin had been raised in the Washington Heights section of upper Manhattan, not far from the neighborhood she called home as a youth. He'd recently purchased a small, two-bedroom house in Oceanport, about a mile up the road from Monmouth Park Racetrack.

Heading east on Broadway, it was only a few, short blocks before the town car again hit Ocean Avenue, where Calvin once more headed south. They passed Bay Head and the Metedeconk River as the land on which they drove became ever narrower until Ocean Avenue was the only road running north and south. In Mantoloking, land widened sufficiently to allow for gorgeous seaside homes and private docks with access to Silver Bay. Connie was amazed at the willingness of people to invest in homes in such close proximity to the "inland" coves on the left and the Atlantic Ocean on the right, imagining the residents must watch the weather with heightened interest as hurricane season approached each year.

They drove through Normandy Beach, Silver Beach, Ocean Beach and Chadwick Beach, which all benefitted from a wider land mass on this incredibly long peninsula. Switching to Bay Boulevard at Lavalette, Calvin passed through Ortley Beach and one of the more well-known boardwalk towns, Seaside Heights. He finally turned west onto N.J. Route 37 and the bridge spanning Toms River.

"We're far enough south to take the Garden State Parkway for the balance of our trip," explained Calvin. "Hope you enjoyed the tour."

Connie was lost in thought, as the afternoon's drive had opened a whole new world, one that might just fit nicely into a future lifestyle she envisioned for herself.

Ordinarily it took 3½ hours in heavy traffic for the 126-mile trip from midtown Manhattan to A.C. using the New Jersey Turnpike and Garden State Parkway. Calvin had delivered his passenger to the front entrance of the Dennis Hotel – located at Michigan and the Boardwalk – at a little after 5:30 p.m. "Roughly 6½ hours, taking the scenic route and stopping for a leisurely lunch," said Calvin. "Not bad...not bad at all."

Connie and Calvin confirmed the pick-up time, which they agreed would be at 9:00 a.m. on Monday. A bit on the early side, she thought to herself, but worth heading home before the really heavy traffic made the Memorial Day return trip a royal pain. "What will you be doing over the holiday weekend, Calvin?" Connie asked, wondering how he'd be spending Friday, Saturday and Sunday.

"Oh, don't you worry about me none," he answered. "I have a half-dozen gigs lined up, including two runs between here and Philly and several late-night/early-morning pick-ups for high-rollers who want a trusted ride between their last social stop and local hotel room. Sometimes," Calvin added with his infectious grin, "that means back-seat to hotel-room delivery."

Calvin handed off Connie to the bell hop and returned to his car. Pulling into a parking area reserved for limos, cabs and town cars, he tuned in an FM station with an easy-listening format, placed his seat in a much more relaxing position and proceeded to "saw off some z's."

59

Chapter 16 – Opening Day's Mounts

While some casual racetrack goers might believe the work of a jockey begins with his first mount of the day's race card, regulars know better. Particularly when it comes to a higher-class thoroughbred preparing for an added-money, handicap or stakes race, a trainer likely has the jockey on first call also handling a key morning workout leading up to the big race.

On this opening day of the 1983 Monmouth Park meet, Angel Barrera and his agent, Chris McCardle, were at trackside waiting for TJ Cutter to bring his unraced 2-year-old colt, *Cut Me A Break*, from the stables behind the backstretch. It was 6:00 in the morning. No matter how routine early-morning works had become, some jockeys simply didn't take kindly to the practice. Barrera was one of those jocks. But for the sake of his new contract with owner/trainer TJ Cutter, and particularly because in this instance he'd be aboard a young and unraced horse, he'd grin and bear it. Angel knew it was important to establish a degree of familiarity – some would say rapport – with his mounts.

"Buenos días señor Cutter," Angel said while reaching out to shake TJ's hand. Then the Dominican jockey patted the forehead of the horse Cutter had brought from the barn for Barrera to work. "¿Hasta dónde quieres que lo lleve" ("How far do you want me to take him?")

Cutter answered Barrera's question: "Let's see what he can give us over four furlongs and ride him out the distance. As a final prep, we'll likely breeze him over three next week."

By "the distance," the owner/trainer of *Cut Me A Break* was referring to the upcoming Tremont Stakes to be held at Belmont Park and run at six furlongs. Cutter wanted to see what the colt would give him over four furlongs and then let the unraced 2-year-old get a feel for the distance he'd be asked to run in New York.

The track was rated *fast*, thanks to a week without rain. Cutter held a stopwatch as Angel Barrera put the 2-year-old colt through his paces. At four furlongs, TJ clicked his stopwatch, showed it to McCardle and stated the obvious: "Looks like we might have ourselves a runner!" *Cut Me A Break* had just run four furlongs in a razor sharp 0:44.4, a morning best among horses working the same distance. The effort would earn the workout bold-type status in the next day's edition of *The Racing Form*.

With Barrera breezing his mount the remaining two furlongs, Cutter again clicked the stopwatch and noted with satisfaction a final time of 1:10.3. More importantly, a breakdown by quarter showed times of 0:22.1, 0:22.3 and 0:25.4.

When Barrera returned to Cutter and McCardle, he dismounted and, with an excitement that even surprised himself, told Cutter "the colt glides so effortlessly."

"He'll only get better with experience," TJ responded. "He'll get better as you become more and more familiar with him." The latter comment was a not-so-subtle reminder to Barrera that a thoroughbred's success was a function of the horse's talent and heart along with the jockey's skills, knowledge of his mount and the ability to anticipate and adapt to rapidly changing circumstances as a race unfolds.

Back at the jockey clubhouse, Barrera showered, dressed and met McCardle on one of the benches ringing the outside of the paddock area. "How's your weight?" his agent asked, knowing that staying at 110 lbs. would enable Barrera to meet the weight conditions assigned to most thoroughbreds entering a mid- to high-level claiming or allowance race at the current meet. Replied Angel: "Nunca en major forma" ("Never in better shape").

On Monmouth's main track, a one-mile dirt oval, sprints were typically 5, 6 or 7 furlongs. Longer, route-going races were most often held at distances of a mile and an eighth (9 furlongs) or a mile and a quarter (10 furlongs). Then there were intermediate routes of one mile (8 furlongs) or a mile and a sixteenth (8½ furlongs). Races of 6 furlongs and 1¼ miles started from chutes.

The turf course, inside of the main track, was 7 furlongs in circumference. A diagonal chute was used for races between one mile and a mile and an eighth. Turf races were run along the hedge or with a portable rail out 12 feet (dubbed the "Haskell Course") or 24 feet (known as the "Monmouth Course").

For Monmouth Park's opening-day card, Angel Barrera had mounts in three sprints over the main track at 6 furlongs, which were scheduled as the 1st, 3rd and 5th races: a Maiden Special Weight race for 3-year-old fillies; a $15,000 Claiming race for fillies and mares 3-years-old and up, and an Allowance race for 3-year-old colts.

His fourth mount was in the 6th race, at one mile on the turf course along the hedge. A handicap for 3- and 4-year-old colts with lifetime earnings "on the grass" of at least $40,000, assigned weights started at 118 lbs. for 3-year-olds and 121 lbs. for 4-year-olds. Two lbs. were added for each $10,000 earned over $40,000. As a general rule, a horse carrying two pounds more than another over a distance of one mile was generally thought to be at a one-length disadvantage.

Angel's mount, *Dance To The Music*, was a 3-year-old colt sired by Nijinsky II out of *It Was Meant To B*. The broodmare was owned by Thoroughbred Bs Farm of Lexington, KY. *Dance To The Music* was racing under the royal blue and white colors of Beauregard Wellington's Triple-B Racing Stables. Having earned $72,000 on the turf over his racing career, the colt would be asked to carry 124 lbs., 110 of which would be Barrera.

The day's final mount for Angel, a 1¼ mile Claiming race over the dirt for Jersey-bred horses 4-years-old and up, was a handicapper's nightmare. A full field of 12 had been entered, as one would expect for a race with Trifecta wagering. The conditions were as follows: *All entries assigned 117 lbs. Claiming price of $5,000 with a 1 lb. allowance for each $250 deducted from the claiming price down to $3,000.*

In other words, an entry could carry up to 8 lbs. less than the initially assigned weight if the horse's connections decided to risk a claim of $2,000 less than the race's original claiming price. Over the distance, that disparity could mean as much as a 4½ length advantage. Of course, some railbirds were likely to argue that one might as well take numbers from a Chinese fortune cookie, because a couple of these nags may have been at the front of a milk wagon in northwest Jersey or a tourist carriage in Central Park only a few days earlier.

To make matters even more interesting, trainers would often use apprentice jockeys – referred to as "bug boys" because of the asterisk appearing after their names – to gain additional weight advantage for their entries. Until they served a specified time or won a certain number of races, apprentices came with as much as a seven-pound weight reduction for their mounts.

As McCardle and Barrera analyzed the last of the jockey's assignments for the day, McCardle looked at the low-end claiming race and noted that the horse breaking from the rail, *Immigration Sensation*, a 6-year-old Jersey bred, was entered for the minimum claiming price of $3,000. His 8-lb. allowance, due to the reduced claiming price, would be coupled with another 5 lb. allowance because trainer Joe O'Dowd had Australian apprentice Stevie Thorn in the saddle. The big question was whether Thorn would be able to get down to a weight of 104 in order for the horse's connections to take full advantage.

All of this told McCardle and Barrera that O'Dowd and Thorn represented an entry likely to be "all out" to win the race. Given the horse's decent past performances at this level of competition and at distances of a mile and a sixteenth or longer, his return to "favorable conditions" signaled a serious attempt to capture the winner's share of the purse. And because this race was for Jersey-breds, the purse had been supplemented by funds from the Thoroughbred Breeders' Association of New Jersey.

The casual race fan, McCardle reflected, couldn't begin to fathom what jockeys might have to endure to successfully negotiate the conflicting challenges of their job. A jock had to maintain sufficient strength to handle a 1000 lb. to 1250 lb. animal traveling in heavy traffic at about 40 miles per hour while carrying dangerously low weight and watching every morsel of food he or she ate.

He thought back to his racing days and how often he had to throw up before weigh-in. And he was one of the "fortunate" ones who didn't have to starve himself, spend large amounts of time in the steam box or take purgatives.

At its visible tip of the iceberg, thoroughbred racing was well deserving of the title, "sport of kings," Chris McCardle concluded. But beneath the surface, well...he wasn't so sure.

Chapter 17 – Arranging a Reunion

Fabian Hauptman had been living under the name of Brian Harper in Hamilton, Ontario, a port city located on the western shore of Lake Ontario about 40 miles south of Toronto and 55 miles west/northwest of Niagara Falls. Hamilton's lifeblood for decades had been steel, with Dofasco and Stelco the area's two major employers.

Having picked up enough knowledge of the steel industry from his years listening to Gretchen talk about the powder metal business, Brian was able to land a position as a steel structural supervisor with Dofasco upon his arrival in Canada in 1966. When an opportunity presented itself to work in a setting better suited to his declining health (he'd been a chain smoker during the years immediately after the war), Harper became head of maintenance at Ivor Wynne Stadium, home of the Canadian Football League's Hamilton Tiger Cats. The hours and seasonality of his job with the TiCats enabled him to work part time as a tour guide for the Canadian Football Hall of Fame, which opened in downtown Hamilton in 1972.

For the 17 years since he last saw Gretchen and Jürgen, Fabian had become accustomed to life as a loner. Thinking back to his meeting with the Mossad agent in Düsseldorf, Fabian knew he couldn't take his wife and son to Israel. But he couldn't very well tell his Jewish brethren the reason for turning down the offer. He couldn't tell them what he'd learned as a result of his spouse talking in her sleep. No, Fabian couldn't bring himself to explain to the Mossad that Gretchen Weiß worked as a records keeper for the Nazis in the Terezin holding and transport center in Czechoslovakia.

At first, he simply didn't trust what his ears were hearing. But several more early-morning episodes convinced Fabian that Gretchen had been a tortured soul who felt trapped and helpless in her war-time duties. It all made sense. Terezin, just 20 miles inside the Czechoslovakian border, was a scant 60 miles south of her family's residence in Dresden. And the Reichstag's narrative about Terezin meshed with what he desperately wanted to believe about seine Frau die Mutter seines Kindes (his wife, the mother of his child).

Hitler had ostensibly constructed a city for the Jews to shield them from the stresses of war. In fact, a film was produced to show the world at-large this idyllic city that was to be a destination – a safe haven – for musicians, writers, artists and social leaders.

Unfortunately, this story was yet another Nazi obfuscation – one that worked largely because to believe otherwise would be to admit the unthinkable was happening unchecked by political leaders of the civilized world. Nearly 200,000 men, women and children passed through Terezin, which functioned as a war-time ghetto – but only until the more infamous labor and death camp, Auschwitz-Birkenau, was operational and ready to accept them.

The question Fabian desperately wanted answered with absolute certainty was: "Did Gretchen realize what was happening to those Jews who'd been transported east during the war years?" And then, "But how *couldn't* she know?!?"

All of these long-held anxieties resurfaced as Fabian waited for David Katzman, the Mossad agent who'd contacted him a couple of days ago. Katzman wanted to discuss his son, Jürgen. The two were to meet at a Tim Horton's on King Street East, not terribly far from the Canadian Football Hall of Fame.

It was early Friday morning, May 27th, when Katzman entered the donut shop. The Mossad agent reminded himself there would be no heavy exodus from Hamilton to celebrate a long holiday weekend. Unlike its neighbor to the south, Canada didn't celebrate Memorial Day. If the conversation he was about to have with Fabian went as planned, however, they both would be dealing with plenty of traffic later in the day during their trip through the State of New York.

As requested, Fabian found a table in the corner opposite the counter where customers "doctored" their coffee. "Morning Brian (Katzman naturally used Fabian's assumed name). Thanks for agreeing to meet with me on this personnel matter," said David, with the vaguest of references to the reason for getting together.

After chatting for several minutes about the TiCats' prospects for the upcoming CFL season, the latest news on the city's two biggest employers, and goings on within the local and provincial political scenes, Katzman suggested they take their coffee outside. Before doing so, he stopped at the counter and bought a dozen Timbits to go with the coffee.

Once outside and away from the storefront, David got down to cases: "As you know, the 1980 Oktoberfest Bombing in Munich killed 13 people and injured more than 200. The investigation concluded that Gundolf Köhler, a university student from Donaueschingen, had made the bomb, taken it to Munich and placed it at the scene of the crime. Although Köhler had been technically adept and knowledgeable about explosives, he was said to have died when the explosive detonated prematurely.

"Was Köhler a suicide bomber who'd acted alone or did he have help?...Or might a co-conspirator have tampered with the explosives to ensure Köhler would never be captured and made to talk?"

The Mossad was reasonably certain that *Wehrsportgruppe Hoffmann*, a banned neo-Nazi terrorist militia to which Köhler had ties, was involved in the planning – particularly since the bombing had taken place just nine days before parliamentary elections. And this same group was now targeting Jewish sympathizers and supporters.

"And this is why," Katzman added, "our organization has had your former home under electronic surveillance since the early part of January 1981."

Fabian paused while munching on his third Timbit, took a slug of coffee to wash it down, and asked pointedly: "But what does this have to do with Gretchen...or Jürgen for that matter?"

"You underestimate us, Brian. We've suspected for quite some time the role Gretchen Weiß played at Terezin. Our surveillance provided us with corroboration. She still talks in her sleep, you know ... and quite often at that."

The two men walked over to a nearby street bench and sat in silence for an eternity, or so it seemed to Fabian. Katzman added: "We figured you had discovered Gretchen's secret, and that drove your decision to leave your wife and son, head to Canada and disappear from their lives. Maybe you thought both would be better off without you. But more to the point, as a German Jew who worked so hard to help your fellow Jews escape the death camps, you likely felt you couldn't be a good husband to a wife who'd been a part of Nazi Germany's efforts toward die Endlösung (the final solution)."

Try as he might, Fabian couldn't hold back the tears. Years of living in solitude with this internal conflict had at last caught up to him. He was overwhelmed by the knowledge that an empathetic comrade – a fellow Jew – understood.

***

Several hours later, David and Brian found themselves on New York Route 17, rolling along the Southern Tier in the Mossad agent's rented 1982 Chevy Impala. First Corning, then Elmira and finally Binghamton passed into the rear-view mirror as they sped toward their final destination.

Once over the initial shock, the day had been quite cathartic for Fabian. Now, however, he was consumed by the Mossad's threat analysis, which saw Gretchen Weiß Hauptmann exposed to potentially compromising scenarios on multiple fronts:

First, there was the very real possibility that more radical elements of *Wehrsportgruppe Hoffmann* might harm her because of who she'd married.

Second, there was the more sophisticated component of the neo-Nazi group that could take advantage of Frau Hauptmann's position as head of a growing business – one that, according to the Mossad agent, had recently begun to contemplate going public. If the leadership of *Wehrsportgruppe Hoffmann* knew of her wartime role, Gretchen could be blackmailed into committing white-collar illegalities that could benefit certain shareholders of a newly formed public company. Her situation would be akin to slowly sinking in corporate quicksand, with ever-increasing negative consequences until she'd be completely submerged in a web of criminality.

Third, there was always the potential for compromising Frau Hauptmann by threatening her son, Jorge. As a college student in a densely populated metropolitan area, he was an easily accessible target in a setting that could provide cover for a terrorist team bent on abduction or worse.

The last piece of information offered by Katzman had been the most unnerving. The Mossad's surveillance had picked up an international call between Jorge and his mom, one in which Jorge described the dream about his dad blowing his brains out after asking: "Warum sind wir in Nürnburg?"

Katzman recounted that part of the call where Jorge indicated he might be able to interpret the suicide as an act of someone who thought he'd failed as a dad and husband. But he couldn't begin to comprehend the words, "Warum sind wir in Nürnberg?"

Knowing the secret Gretchen had kept from her husband and son...and surmising that Jorge also might have heard his mom talking in her sleep, Fabian felt there was a good possibility his son may already have begun to make sense of his recurring dream.

One thing Fabian knew: It was urgent that Jorge learn the entire truth behind the lives his parents had led during World War II. His own life could very well depend on it.

Chapter 18 – Surprise at the Smithville Inn

Consuela Parks Pettiford (Connie Pett for her weekend adventure) had an insatiable appetite to explore as much of the Jersey Shore as time and distance would allow. So when Connie asked the Dennis Hotel concierge to recommend area restaurants that "aren't necessarily within Atlantic City itself," the Historic Smithville Inn in nearby Galloway Township became her destination.

Taking a cab for the 12-mile drive inland across the Atlantic City Expressway and north on U.S. Route 9, Consuela arrived at not simply a restaurant but a colonial village, replete with cobblestone paths, a picturesque lake, at least a few dozen "shoppes" and boutiques and the Colonial Inn Bed & Breakfast, which had its origins back in 1787.

Not interested in another heavy meal or a formal dining area (that had been taken care of thanks to Calvin and the Lobster Shanty), Consuela simply wanted to have a relaxing evening. The Inn's Baremore Tavern offered a cozy bar and lighter fare along with an array of local-themed cocktails and the usual lineup of hard liquor. Everything lined up perfectly with her mood.

Taking a seat at one of the swivel bar stools, Consuela asked the bartender for his recommendation on a Jersey-based white wine. Introducing himself as Nick (Consuela gave him her first name in exchange), his wine of choice was a 1980 Shamong White from the Garden State's Valenzano Winery:

"The wine is produced in the outer coastal plain region located in the southeastern corner of our state. The terroir, or grape-influencing conditions, include proximity to the Atlantic Ocean and the area's flat sandy hills. This particular white is tropical and balanced with a touch of oak. The aromas of ripe citrus, nectarine and passionfruit are unmistakable. Would you like to try?"

The detailed description he provided belied his age which, judging by his baby face, Consuela mistakenly gauged to be no more than 24. As it happened, Nick had graduated from the American Bartenders School in Little Falls. Established in 1969, it was the state's oldest licensed bartending school. A framed certificate behind the counter indicated Nicholas Esposito had completed his training in 1978.

Nick then asked: "So what brings you here?" Opting for the short answer, Consuela explained she was an overworked New York City attorney who lived in Manhattan and had simply looked for someplace "different but close" to get away for the long holiday weekend.

The bartender responded by saying: "Well, you've certainly found it here." Detecting his customer's seeming need to do a major mental detox, he dropped any notion of a follow-up question, unscrewed the cork, poured a tasting sample and waited for the verdict. With her one-word response to the selection, "Marvelous!" Nick poured her a glass and went down to the other end of the bar where an elderly couple was seated.

With that, the overworked Big Apple attorney took a healthy swig more associated with consuming a shot of hard liquor and began thinking about Connie Pett's date the next evening.

***

It was about 7:45 p.m. as Consuela was finishing an order of fried calamari which had been preceded by corn & crab fritters. The elderly couple had departed about five minutes ago, leaving her as Nick's only customer until a face familiar to the bartender appeared at the front of the tavern.

"Hey, Jasmine! How ya' doin' tonight?" asked Nick, his tone as well as his words indicating to Consuela – the only person within earshot – that this young lady was a regular.

"Doin' just fine, Nick. Heading down to the Sands for the weekend and thought I'd stop by for a bite to eat and something to take the edge off," she replied. Only when she didn't have "work" did she drive her own car, a 10-year-old red Mercury Montego with a black vinyl top.

"The usual?" Nick didn't even wait for an answer. He grabbed a glass, filled it with five ice cubes, reached for the Jim Beam and poured a double. He then called the kitchen to place an order of steamed P.E.I blue mussels au naturel with melted butter and a loaf of freshly baked garlic bread.

Jasmine took a seat to the right of Consuela and asked Nick, "So who's your friend?"

"Not a friend...at least not yet. She's a first-timer. Consuela, this is Jasmine. Jasmine...Consuela." With that brief introduction, the two shook hands and began what turned out to be a get-acquainted conversation that lasted the better part of two hours. It included a full bottle of wine for Consuela and three more "visits" with Jim Beam for Jasmine, along with a second order of mussels.

If only the two young women could have read each other's minds. Prior to their conversation, the next evening's adventure was all each could think about. In just a few hours, both had learned enough about the other to believe they could very well be at the start of a long-term friendship. What they couldn't possibly know is that they'd meet again the next evening – as call girl and client.

Consuela was the first to leave. She'd asked Nick to call for a taxi while Jasmine had retreated to the ladies' restroom. Before heading back to the Dennis Hotel, she handed Jasmine her business card. "Give me a call next week. I've fallen in love with the Jersey shore and wouldn't mind spending some time in your neck of the woods."

Jasmine had been candid about her daytime job, explaining it was "just temporary" until she could find something better suited to her talents. She mentioned the possibility of going to work for her older brother, who owned and trained thoroughbreds. All of which was to say she didn't have a business card of her own. "But I'll definitely give you a call," she said as they gave each other a brief hug.

"Well," said Nick. "It looks as though you two might become best buds." Jasmine looked up from her drink, smiled and answered: "Could be, Nick. I think it's time for me to have a cup of coffee ... black." She paused for a second and changed her mind. "No make that espresso."

Jasmine wanted to sober up a bit before driving the short distance to the Sands Casino Hotel on Indiana Avenue, her weekend base of operations. A night without a client, she decided to spend a couple of hours playing some black jack. Nothing heavy, she'd confine herself to a $2 table and sip on a club soda. Jasmine wanted to look *and feel* her best for tomorrow evening.

Chapter 19 – Pre-Meeting Prep

By mid-morning, Gretchen Weiß Hauptmann had arrived at the Park Villa outside Wuppertal Zentrum. Her administrative assistant, Hanna Schröder, was there to meet her. They expected members of the Advisory Board of GWH GmbH to arrive about an hour before the scheduled start of the meeting at 1400 Stunden, using the time to exchange pleasantries before getting down to business.

As far as die Vorsitzende (the chairperson) could tell, the Board was evenly divided on whether to become a publicly held corporation or remain private. After walking up a flight of stairs to her second-floor suite and setting down a small overnight suitcase, Gretchen removed a binder from her briefcase and turned to the section containing die Geschäftsbiografien (the business biographies) of the company's board members. She took out a notepad, drew a line down the center of the blank front page and wrote Jawhol *in favor of going public* on the left side and Nein *opposed to going public* on the right side. Gretchen then read through each bio before placing the name on one side or the other.

Dieter Hartmann – Age: 68. Born: Bonn, Germany. Current residence: Wuppertal. Current position: Retired as VP Business Development Pulver-Metall Lüdenscheid GmbH. Education: Technische Universität Darmstadt/Materials & Earth Sciences. Personal: Widower, two sons (deceased).

Elina Lang-Haas – Age: 46. Born: Köln, Germany. Current residence: Köln. Current position: Direktor REWE Group – Deutsche diversifizierte Genossenschaft für Einzelhandel und Tourismus (German diversified retail and tourism co-operative group). Education: Rheinische Friedrich-Wilhelms-Universität Bonn. Personal: Married to Helmut Haas; one son, Anton (age 12), one daughter, Lena (age 10).

Mia Mangels – Age: 36. Born: Hannover, Germany. Current residence: Leverkusen. Current position: VP Kommunikation Bayer

AG. Education: Humboldt Universität zu Berlin/Albrecht Daniel Thaer Institute of Agricultural & Horticultural Sciences. Personal: Single.

Harald Schneider – Age: 40. Born: Köln, Germany. Current residence: Milan, Italy. Current position: SVP Deutsche Bank/ Milan. Education: Universität Heidelberg/Alfred-Weber-Inst. for Economics. Personal: Married to Renee Neubert-Schneider; two daughters, Emma (age 6) and Luisa (age 4).

Barnard Scholz – Age: 68. Born: Berlin, Germany. Current residence: DuBois, Pennsylvania. Current position: Associate Professor of Applied Materials, PSU-DuBois. Education: Technische Universität Darmstadt/ Materials and Earth Sciences. Personal: Single.

Eckhardt Vogt – Age: 51. Born: Aachen, Germany. Current residence: Whitley, Coventry, England. Current position: Sr. Design Engineer Jaguar Cars. Education: RWTH (Rheinisch-Westfälische Technische Hochschule) Aachen. Personal: Married to Anwen Driscoll-Vogt; three sons – Emil (age 14), Maximilian (age 12) and Oskar (age 10).

Gretchen considered her past discussions with each Board member; input she'd received about the person from fellow Board members and from those within the GWH GmbH community; and intel from other contacts within her business, political, academic and social circles. She'd pulled from her memory bank public speaking engagements, position papers and published materials, only then deciding on which side of the ledger to place each name.

For Gretchen, this pre-meeting assessment was important, as it would serve both as a check against each person's contribution to the upcoming debate and as a basis for follow-up questions probing any departure from previously expressed ideas. Die Vorsitzende fully intended to challenge her fellow members of the Board in order to arrive at a thoroughly thought-out decision.

Concluding her analysis, she expected Mangels, Schneider and Vogt to be in favor of taking public the company she'd founded a quarter century ago. The remaining three – Hartmann, Lang-Haas and Scholz – were likely to prefer GWH remain a private firm. She was certainly prepared to cast a deciding vote if after the meeting's discussions and subsequent overnight soul-searching the Board was deadlocked. But it was just as likely that one or more members would be persuaded by the debate, thus precluding die Vorsitzende from deciding with her vote the direction of the company.

Over the years, Gretchen had played her cards quite close to the vest, a practice she'd long ago learned as a result of guarding her wartime secret. One of her greatest assets was the ability to listen. She was quite certain none of her fellow members of the Advisory Board knew for sure auf welcher Seite der Frage Ihre Vorsitzende stand (on which side of the issue their chairperson stood).

Gretchen was still lost in thought when she was interrupted with a knock on the half-opened door to her suite. As Gretchen looked up, Hanna said: "Das erste Auto ist angekommen." ("The first car has arrived.")

In response, Gretchen simply said: "Lasst die Spiele beginnen." ("Let the games begin.")

Chapter 20 – Loving Mom, "Estranged" Wife

Any notion Abigail Wellington had entertained about her marriage to Bentley returning to some semblance of normalcy disappeared entirely after the events in San Francisco. A "return to normalcy," the phrase made famous by Republican presidential candidate Warren G. Harding in describing his campaign objective to return the country to life as it existed before the Great World War, had been used quite often as an expressed desire by Abigail at the Wellington's Lexington estate during her husband's second term in Frankfort.

She'd heard the whispers and rumors that the close working relationship between the governor and his young, college-educated Negro aide had been evolving into something more. If it hadn't satisfied her woman's intuition enough while watching Bentley interact with Marci Davis during their cross-country rail excursion, then the rumpus that took place in Marci's room had erased any doubt in her mind – at least as far as Bentley's desire for Marci was concerned. While none of the hotel guests could confirm exactly what had occurred on the third floor of the Fairmont that night, there was a certain buzz in the lobby and sidelong looks that seemed to follow Abigail during the remainder of their stay.

For his part, Bentley desperately wanted to put his life in politics and the inexcusable behavior he'd exhibited while in San Francisco behind him. Shortly after the Louisville meeting at which he and Marci quickly reached a settlement, the outgoing Governor of the Commonwealth of Kentucky confessed all to his wife and pleaded for forgiveness. But Abigail, whose suspicions had been fueled by the rumor mill and fanned into a full-blown conflagration by Bentley's now admitted "passing attraction" to Marci, was in no mood to accept her husband's sudden contrition.

But divorce was not a path Abigail Prescott Wellington would consider.

First and foremost was her unqualified love for and devotion to Beauregard, the only child she'd ever bear. She'd more or less raised Beau as a single mother while her husband played politics in the Governor's Mansion in Frankfort. Despite the short distance between Kentucky's capital and Lexington, "daddy" was rarely seen during his second stint as governor. Yet his mother strongly believed that Beau, now five, deserved to have love and guidance from *both* of his parents.

Second was the social status the Wellingtons enjoyed as Kentucky's first family and the access to influence and financial resources that came with it. These benefits would redound not simply to Abigail but to Beauregard as well. While she was clearly the "wronged" party, a messy and public separation could have negative consequences for her and her son. At this point, Beau had a clear path to eventually running the family's thoroughbred breeding and racing operations. She would do nothing to jeopardize his future.

Third was Bentley's strong desire to start a bourbon distillery, a business in which she had every intention of playing a major role. If need be, she was prepared to use the "Marci situation" as leverage.

The Wellingtons' 740-acre estate included both a plantation home and a second residence that had been used to house guests when hosting gala celebrations. Abigail could always suggest that Bentley spend time there if the relationship proved to be more contemptuous than she could stand.

Ever the pragmatist, Abigail Prescott Wellington pressed on as the family matriarch. Over the next quarter of a century, she made sure her marriage survived while her political, social and financial power grew.

***

On this day, Abigail was anxious to hear from Beau about his trip to the New York area, where he'd met with TJ Cutter at Monmouth Park in New Jersey to discuss his thoroughbred proposal and also had opened talks on Wall Street with Silverstein-Gladstone, an investment house well-versed in IPOs.

Now 58, Abigail had done quite well for herself and her son. Running Bourbonesque LLC since Bentley's hunting accident, Abigail had overseen a major refurbishing of the distillery's equipment, implemented a new profit-sharing program for employees and retained a consulting firm to work on a plan to broaden the company's distribution network and expand its retail marketing efforts.

Abigail had brought Bourbonesque back from the brink of financial disaster as a result of her actions. She'd tried to persuade Bentley that his sagging business fortunes required still further investments on multiple fronts, but he had become increasingly resistant to change. Abigail supposed it had something to do with his career in politics and the inability of government bureaucrats to accomplish anything significant without mind-numbing and time-consuming analysis paralysis. The bottom line was that without Bentley's authorization for an infusion of capital – Abigail and the company's CFO, Blake Tinsdale, had been in favor of floating a bond issue – the company was likely to lose the operational momentum it had gained over the past couple of years.

Disdain for her husband had steadily grown over the years; she often found herself daydreaming about Bentley meeting an untimely end. What was it the post-accident investigation had concluded?... The wrong ammo was loaded into the "right" chamber? A careless mistake made by a hunter using his rifle "under the influence." She wasn't terribly clear on the technical details. "I've never handled a gun of any kind," Abigail offered when questioned by Lexington detectives. And that was that....

Part Two:
Confliction, Conflation
& Consternation

Chapter 21 – Shock and Relief

It was Friday and Jasmine had slept into the early afternoon in her room at the Sands Casino Hotel. Yesterday had been exhausting, starting with her morning shopping spree in Manhattan followed by the tedious drive to Atlantic City and concluding with a lengthy, unanticipated (but surprisingly pleasant) stop at the Baremore Tavern.

After checking the clock radio on the nightstand, she stared once again at the business card left by her new acquaintance. The name and address on the card read: Consuela Pettiford, Esq., Stratton-Oakes, P.C., 1251 Avenue of the Americas, New York, NY 10020...same as it had been when she turned off the bedside lamp late last night. Judging by the telephone number that ended in a pair of zeros, Jasmine believed it to be a general number as opposed to a direct dial. While she was really looking forward to the evening's "work," she found herself anticipating next Tuesday and the invitation she would extend to Consuela Pettiford to join her for a weekend in Seaside Heights.

After taking a hot shower, Jasmine slipped on a pair of black jeans and a loose-fitting white blouse, pausing for a quick look in the bathroom mirror to be sure she was marginally presentable. Making her way to the restaurant downstairs, she wolfed down a three-egg swiss cheese omelet, hash browns and a side of bacon. A big glass of OJ and a pot of coffee rounded out a meal that would last until dinner at a time and place to be determined by this evening's date.

Per June's instructions, Jasmine was to arrive at the Dennis Hotel on the Boardwalk and Michigan Avenue by 7:30 p.m., taking a seat at the bar. Due to her date's very specific apparel request, the onus would be on the A.C.-D.C. client to introduce herself. Jasmine was completely in the dark regarding her date's physical appearance or any other information for that matter, apart from June describing the client as "a successful business woman in her early 30s."

***

When it came to a 'look' she'd wanted to create for herself, "Connie Pett" opted for sultry and tawdry Latin. She judged herself off to a good start with her makeup. Pairing smoky eyes with strong brows and bold cherry red lips took care of *sultry*. A black leather mini skirt with a side slit and a ribbed canyon rose tank top added *tawdry* to the equation. A black satin bomber jacket provided a relaxed fit. Capezio black leather flats would ensure comfy feet for the evening.

Now moving toward half past six and just an hour before her scheduled rendezvous, Consuela began to experience a weird feeling in the pit of her stomach. She couldn't decide whether it was a nervous but largely positive anticipation of her pending date ... or anxiety brought on by growing second thoughts about the evening about to unfold.

One way or another, Consuela knew a sure way to take the edge off. She reached into a tote bag for her portable cassette player, loaded one of her favorite tapes, "Louis Armstrong Meets Oscar Peterson," and pressed the "play" button. She then grabbed a bottle of Mamajuana and started a full pour into one of the hotel room's wine glasses.

After finishing off her third full pour, a far more relaxed and somewhat blitzed Connie suddenly realized it was 7:45. She stood up abruptly, steadied herself, left the room and headed downstairs to the bar.

Jasmine arrived at the Hotel Dennis bar 15 minutes early, was exceedingly nervous when the grandfather clock by the far wall chimed once signaling the bottom of the hour and ordered a double Jim Beam on the rocks. She'd quickly downed her initial drink and had just about finished her second double when she did a double-*take* as a familiar face came toward her.

Although Connie was a bit bleary-eyed, there was no mistaking the black micro-mini skirt, ribbed mustard-yellow crop top, mustard-yellow thigh-high leather boots ... and the face that went along with the outfit. Approaching the bar stool at which her date was seated, Consuela reached out to embrace Jasmine while imagining her date stripped to what surely must be her mustard-yellow Lycra hipster panties with matching thigh-high tights and push-up bra.

"Oh my God!" exclaimed Consuela.

All Jasmine could manage was "Holy shit!"

Shock...followed by immense relief were shared emotions.

81

Chapter 22 – Sean's "Hotlanta" Connection

Having returned to live in his mom's Bentley Avenue home in Jersey City for his Seton Hall Law School years, Sean Davis Jeffries had been quite comfortable commuting between Journal Square and Newark's Penn Station via PATH trains each weekday afternoon for evening classes. He'd just completed moot court competition and was once again turning his attention to Abigail Prescott Wellington and her growing role in guiding the financial fortunes of Bourbonesque. Having made a few trips to the Commonwealth over the past couple of years, he still was in need of the kind of intelligence one could gain only from the inside.

With that in mind, he placed a call from his upstairs phone to Atlanta. He was reaching out to a friend he believed would be uniquely positioned to assist – one Nate "Kat Man" Katzman. The person answering on the other end of the line, however, was not Nate, although Sean recognized the voice from previous conversations. "Hi, Beth. It's Sean. Is Nate around?"

"Well, right now my fiancé is in the shower," answered Beth Feingold, who was quickly interrupted by Sean.

"Why that SOB! I can't believe he didn't let me know," responded Sean.

"Maybe it's because he just popped the question tonight," laughed Beth, clearly enjoying how she'd dropped the news on one of Nate's old buddies.

Sean proceeded to pepper Beth with all the typical questions: "Have you set a date?" "Where are you getting married?" "What about your honeymoon?"

After answering "No"…"I don't know" and "Who has the time?" Beth groaned and said in mock frustration, "Here's Nate…still a bit wet, but ready to talk."

The two briefly exchanged pleasantries, talked hoops at some length and asked each other about the direction their careers – one in the legal field and the other in the medical profession – were likely to take once finished with "all the preliminaries," as Sean had put it.

"So, what's *really* on your mind, Sean?" Nate finally asked.

"Nothing in particular, except I'd like to visit a former Seton Hall law professor who's hung out his shingle in Sandy Springs," offered Sean, adding that he'd also want to use the trip to visit friends, "particularly since you and Beth have agreed to tie the knot."

In reality, Sean had no current plans to visit Denton Dandridge but he was prepared to arrange a visit to one of his favorite law school professors simply as an excuse to see Nate and Beth. A Richmond, Virginia native who'd spent 15 years teaching Contracts at Seton Hall Law School, Dandridge attended the University of Richmond as an undergraduate, earned his Juris Doctor at the Dean Rusk International Law Center at the University of Georgia, and after passing the Bar exams in Georgia and Virginia worked for an Atlanta law firm for the better part of two decades. When he realized a partnership wasn't in the offing, he decided to try the academic side of the legal profession and headed to Seton Hall.

At this point, Sean wasn't prepared to tell Nate the actual reason for his trip. Naturally, he'd be glad to see them. But this would be a recruiting expedition that ideally would result in retaining an experienced gum shoe and some expertise in electronic surveillance. Nate's dad, Irving, and older brother, David, could very well help with the former. Beth, with a background in systems engineering, likely had the connections to assist with the latter.

Chapter 23 – Harper's Ferry

The plain white #10 envelope with no return address had arrived in the mailbox of the Bradley Beach boarding house where he'd rented a room for the summer. The 20-cent stamp commemorating the 100th anniversary of the Brooklyn Bridge bore a cancellation mark indicating the point of origin had been Brooklyn, NY, ironically enough, and the mail date had been the previous day.

While the envelope was nondescript, the note inside was anything but: "Go to the Binghamton Restaurant located on a ferry moored in the Hudson River in Edgewater just south of the George Washington Bridge. Be there at 12:00 noon sharp on Saturday, May 28th. Wear a Seton Hall soccer jersey. Shred or burn this note and the accompanying photo. Tell absolutely no one about this communication. The man in the photograph will be there to meet you only if you precisely follow these instructions."

A black-and-white wallet-sized photo showed a man wearing a double-breasted wool peacoat. Although much older looking than Jürgen Hauptmann remembered, the man in the photo was unmistakably his father.

Stunned, Jorge stumbled upstairs to his room and sat on the bed, alternately re-reading the note and staring at the photo. His initial reaction was to reach out to his mom. But upon further thought he realized it would accomplish nothing and needlessly upset her when she was focused on the upcoming board meeting. Besides, he reasoned, what assurances were there that this communication was legit?

Jorge decided to go to Edgewater at the designated time on Saturday. But he would hold onto the note, photo and envelope in case he needed them should the meeting be something other than what was implied. He could always destroy them afterwards. Meanwhile, he'd need to tell Fran DeSantis he would be unable to work on Saturday. As it was one of the busiest days of the summer at Monmouth Park, he'd not only miss out on a great day's tips, but would let down his boss as well.

***

Fabian, along with his escort, ex-U.S. Army sergeant and now Mossad agent David Katzman, arrived at the Binghamton Restaurant an hour ahead of schedule. They'd stayed overnight at one of the several "no-tell motels" located on Tonnelle Avenue/U.S. Route 9 just north of the Pulaski Skyway in Jersey City. It was about a half-hour drive from there to the ferry-turned-restaurant in Edgewater.

Regardless of how the discussion would be framed, the explosive revelations surrounding how Fabian Hauptman and Gretchen Weiß had spent their war years were going to be incredibly challenging for Jorge to digest. After all the time that lapsed since the father's desertion, there was the very real possibility of Jorge turning a deaf ear to whatever explanation his father might offer. Jorge's response could also be a combustible mixture of pent-up anger, irrational defiance and uncontrollable rage.

Apart from wanting father and son to repair their long-lost relationship, Katzman was well aware of the critical need for Jorge to realize the potential dangers that lay ahead for both of them, dangers exacerbated by the perilous situation to which Gretchen Weiß Hauptmann was exposed. For both reasons, the Mossad agent insisted Fabian leave the initial stages of the conversation to him.

What David Katzman had not covered in his discussions with Fabian was the Mossad's indifference toward Gretchen's well-being. Ensuring her safety mattered only insofar as it would prevent harm to Jews and the Israeli State. To the Israeli intelligence agency, Gretchen Weiß Hauptmann was just another open-and-shut case – she was guilty of war crimes against the Jewish people.

Arriving a few minutes early, Jorge left his precious Mustang with one of the attendants. It wasn't terribly surprising when he suggested the attendant "take it easy" driving his wheels to a parking spot and added: "Don't place my vehicle between two other cars."

As he walked up the gang plank to the main deck of the ferry, Jorge took a quick look back to check on his car before searching the dining room and spotting his dad with another man at a table for four. Located on the port side of the ferry, the table offered a spectacular view of the river traffic, the George Washington Bridge and Upper Manhattan on the other side of the Hudson. But that view would likely be wasted given the gravity of the discussion to take place.

While he wasn't certain, Jorge hoped today's conversation might also allow him to make sense of his recently recurring dream, something his mom had been either unable or unwilling to do over the phone. Of course, Jorge hadn't mentioned a word about his rendezvous later in the day. Instructions from the anonymous source had been clear about keeping the matter to himself. Common sense told him not to utter a word to his mother. He'd simply wished her good luck with the company meeting in Wuppertal.

Chapter 24 – Present, Debate...and Sleep on It

From what Die Vorsitzende could gather, the welcome hour for GWH GmbH's Advisory Board at the Park Villa had gone well enough. Initial pleasantries had been exchanged among members and conversations then morphed into opinions on the current business landscape for the powder metal industry and prospects for GWH in particular. For the most part, discussions had been one-on-one affairs with the occasional threesome mixed in for good measure. Gretchen had been far less interested in the conversations themselves than how members paired off, figuring (correctly) that individuals were far more likely than not to seek like-minded thinking at this early juncture. For that reason, Gretchen had been off to the side going over details of the meeting's agenda with Hanna Schröder, her administrative assistant.

One of Gretchen's observations was a decided *absence* of contact between two individuals she would have expected to be fully engaged in conversation: Dieter Hartmann and Barnard Scholz, his former classmate at Technische Universität Darmstadt. Hartmann had spent most of his business career at Pulver-Metall Lüdenscheid GmbH and recently retired. He was a long-time resident of Wuppertal. Scholz, on the other hand, had moved to the United States soon after completing his degree and technical training. He wound up working for several mom & pop P/M operations in the Midwest and north-central Pennsylvania before leaving the private sector to take a position as Associate Professor of Applied Materials at Penn State-DuBois.

Gretchen knew Dieter and Barnard to be long-time friends from their days at Darmstadt. At least from their years on the GWH Board the two seemed to be on the same page from a business philosophy standpoint. Was their lack of contact a mere coincidence? Or did they have a pre-meeting discussion and, being of the same mind, agree to use the hour to articulate to fellow members their shared preference for growth through the firm's current, privately owned limited liability form?

Approaching 1400 Stunden, Hanna Schröder went around the reception area asking individuals to move to the meeting room.

Members found their name placards at a long rectangular table with room enough for seven, the seats facing a podium with a mic. Die Vorsitzende sat at the center of the table with three members to each side.

Toward the back of the room was a table on which an overhead projector had been placed. Hanna, seated behind the projector, was given transparencies for each presentation a member of GWH GmbH's Board of Management would be making. It was her job to change transparencies so they coincided with specific information provided by each speaker.

After formally recognizing each member of the Advisory Board, then welcoming the Board as a whole, and finally reminding them of their specific charge at the conclusion of their business agenda, Gretchen introduced members of the company's Board of Management, who were responsible for the daily operation of GWH GmbH. Dedrick Walter would be making a presentation on *finance* (past performance and future projections); Engel Fischer on *operations* (current and proposed expansion of the physical plant and an assessment of the skills needed to meet business objectives); Garrick Imhoff on *technology development* (impact of recently completed R&D programs and newly proposed projects); and Dr. Wilhelm Fuchs on a *SWOT analysis* (strengths, weaknesses, opportunities and threats vis-a-vis other P/M parts manufacturers as well as competing parts-producing technologies).

The final hour would be given over to Wolfgang Becker, der Hauptgeschäftsführer (the chief executive officer), whose presentation would compare five-year operational assumptions and financial projections for a publicly held GWH AG in the aftermath of equity financing through an IPO to those of a still privately owned GWH GmbH following debt financing via the bond market.

Gretchen devoted most of her time with the company in her capacity as head of the company's Advisory Board for two reasons. First, she found objective, outside perspectives of individuals with no appreciable stake in the company to be invaluable in fulfilling her primary legal position as Vorsitzende der Geschäftsführung (chairperson of the Management Board). Second, her son Jorge had reached an age where he needed the guidance only a parent could provide.

And so eight years earlier she had handpicked Becker, a colleague of hers at Pulver-Metall Lüdenscheid, to run the daily operation. As incentive for him to leave his current top management position, she wrote into his contract a clause that would give him up to a 15 percent stake in the firm should certain revenue objectives be met. To date, Becker had earned roughly half of the shares available through his contract with GWH GmbH.

For the most part Gretchen had been pleased with his performance. As majority owner of the now privately held GWH GmbH, Gretchen had the authority to extend Becker's term of service or replace him. If she decided GWH *AG* was the way to go, her unilateral decision-making authority would then be a thing of the past.

Gretchen listened intently to each presentation. While on intimate terms with all of the data points, quantitative analyses and qualitative assessments provided during the five-hour info dump, she knew well that a second or even third pass at intel could provide new insights and a different perspective on business matters big or small.

Questions from members of the Advisory Board had been on point and reflected a deep dive into the core issue they'd have to resolve for the company's founder the next morning. Gretchen was particularly proud of Herr Becker's management team, which had accumulated, distilled and organized mountains of information into presentations offering a rich picture of GWH's past, present and future. Furthermore, their answers to questions showed Sie kannten ihre Sachen (they knew their stuff).

A leisurely dinner of asparagus soup, braised rabbit with pan fried potatoes and red cabbage, and apple strudel followed the afternoon's presentations. The dining room seating configuration consisted of three round tables of three – one table at which Gretchen and Hanna were joined by Wolfgang, who'd been invited to stay for the evening meal, and the other two tables for the six members of the Advisory Board.

With all having been seated, Gretchen couldn't help but notice that Dieter Hartmann and Barnard Scholz were not at the same table. Again, she wondered: Was it planned or just a coincidence?... Or was it something else? It wasn't simply a matter of not engaging in conversation. Dieter and Barnard seemed to be avoiding each other. Had there been a falling out? Given the longevity of their friendship, it would seem unlikely.

***

Much was going through the mind of Barnard Scholz during the meeting, not all of which pertained to the momentous vote to take place at the conclusion of their business agenda. He was deeply distracted by the apparent end to his relationship with long-time friend and business colleague Dieter Hartmann.

Earlier, in the Park Villa parking lot, Dieter had pointedly told Barnard he was severing ties with his former classmate. When Barnard asked why, Dieter simply stated: "I find your attitudes on business, politics and social mores Unvereinbar mit meiner (incompatible with mine). I want nothing more to do with you."

Late into a day of information overload, Barnard was still shocked at the abruptness of Dieter's rebuke and naked disdain for him. During dinner he reflected on his relationship with Dieter, attempting to trace the origins of its decline. As far as he could tell, nothing discernible had changed in Dieter's behavior until, what – about 15 to 18 months ago? The only remarkable event common to both of them had been the first rumblings that GWH was approaching a major financial crossroads and the future direction of the company would soon need to be decided.

Barnard remembered the earliest conversations with Dieter about the choice the company faced between debt financing as a private firm and equity financing through a public stock offering. At the time they seemed to be on the same page, agreeing that the added administrative and regulatory headaches of a publicly traded company, the fiduciary responsibility to shareholders along with their tendency to look at stock price and quarter-to-quarter performance as opposed to intermediate- to long-range growth, and the added scrutiny on the work of the Advisory Board with the accompanying pressures that would bring – all seemed to argue in favor of remaining a private firm.

But Dieter's point of view seemed to abruptly change about a year ago. Suddenly, his friend became enamored with the ability to raise a vast amount of capital without increasing debt and the potential

90

to sell additional shares further down the road in a second offering. Gone were concerns about scrutiny from outside stakeholders or fiduciary responsibilities. It was almost as if company access to the capital markets would somehow redound to his personal benefit.

"And what do my politics and social mores have to do with anything?" Barnard asked himself, believing his political ideology to be centrist and his social standards to be in the mainstream. Neither had been a topic of conversation between the two over recent years. He was more perplexed than ever.

***

For Barnard to understand what had been behind Dieter's changed behavior towards him, he would have needed to look back to World War II and the incredible anguish Hartmann had been carrying within himself over the past 38 years.

The seeds of Dieter Hartmann's tragedy had been sewn in the early 1930s amidst the backdrop of Germany's economic depression and Hitler's rise to power. It was April 1933 and Dieter, then 18, had been with a local girl from his home town of Bonn for almost a year. Out of wedlock, Monika Ludwig, 17, gave birth to their first son, Luka. In December, Dieter and Monika, now 18, were married. Shortly thereafter, they had their second son, Emil, in February 1934.

Fast forward to the war years when Dieter served as a seaman on the Scharnhorst-class battlecruiser Gneisenau, which had been scuttled in Gotenhafen in 1945. After VE-Day he'd been one of the "fortunate" Germans to survive the post-war trip home.

Once back in Bonn and reunited with Monika, however, he learned the fate of Luka, 12, and Emil, 11. Both had been pressed into service by Der Volkssturm (The People's Army) which was formed late in 1944 to prepare for the Allied invasion. The boys had been arming artillery units when they were captured early in 1945 by American troops advancing across Germany. Luka and Emil had been among thousands herded into cages along the Rhine. With no shelter and very little food, they perished days before Dieter and Monika learned of their whereabouts.

The Hartmanns had been inconsolable. Within two years

Monika, just 31, died of "unknown causes," according to doctors at the hospital. But Dieter knew better ... his love had perished due to a broken heart.

Dieter found the British and in particular the Americans so hypocritical and sanctimonious, speaking of Nazi atrocities when they'd thrown women and children in cages and allowed them to die slow deaths from lack of food and sickness. He had learned to live – no, not really live, but survive – with the recurring nightmares and with an abject hatred for all things Anglo-American, the Jewish people and the steps Germany, itself, had taken to purge Nazism from the country and its culture.

After close to two decades of life without purpose, Dieter finally found a mission for which life would be worth *living* and not merely *surviving*. He had read with great interest the birth of die Nationaldemokratische Partei Deutschlands (NDP) and soon found himself closely following its activities.

Shortly after retiring from Pulver-Metall Lüdenscheid, Dieter had been invited by GWH GmbH founder Gretchen Weiß Hauptmann to join the Advisory Board. He'd happily accepted, both because he respected Gretchen from her days at Pulver-Metall Lüdenscheid and to avoid the sheer boredom of retirement. But when he learned of the possibility of the company turning to an IPO for funding future growth, he began to mull over the prospect of melding his new fascination with the NDP and his Board membership with GWH.

At first pleased that his friend Barnard Scholz was also a member of the Advisory Board, Dieter soon found Barnard at odds with his thinking on many levels. First, he'd been brainwashed by all those years spent in the United States, to the point where he believed in the "inherent good" of the American people and their precious "democracy" with its adherence to "the rule of law." Second, he clearly didn't understand the financial freedom equity financing could provide to a company like GWH and the financial power it could use to influence government policy.

In recent months, Dieter had found the very thought of associating with Barnard distasteful. That morning outside the Park Villa he decided to tell him, Fest und unmissverständlich (firmly and in no uncertain terms), that they were done.

Chapter 25 – What a Mess at Bourbonesque

Abigail Prescott Wellington had issues with the two men in her life. Setting aside his Marci Davis indiscretion while serving a second term as Kentucky's governor, husband Bentley had shown himself to be a significantly flawed businessman. While able to take Bourbonesque LLC from concept to reality and successfully negotiate the distillery's path in its formative years, he'd been sorely lacking in two key skill sets necessary to move his business through the next phase of its development: the ability to delegate and the ability to recognize talent in others. How ironic, thought Mrs. Wellington, that Bentley's best hire, Marci Davis, had helped him succeed as head of the Commonwealth's government while ultimately becoming the instrument by which he destroyed his family life.

On the other hand, Beauregard had a brilliant business mind, taking the Wellington family's Thoroughbred Bs Farm from a mid-sized concern to one of the premier breeding operations in the nation. Operating under the same business umbrella, Triple-B Racing Stables had likewise experienced a hugely successful growth phase, with an increasing number of colts and fillies winning graded stakes races at major tracks across the country. "We breed, broker and breathe thoroughbreds" was not simply a slogan; it captured the business plan Beau was implementing.

But Beau exhibited his own major flaw. He had become addicted to gambling, a particularly damaging trait for someone whose business was predicated on wagering. And because he'd become a recognizable personality in racing circles, Beau's gambling didn't take place at the $100 pari-mutuel windows of race tracks at which his thoroughbreds were competing. No, he'd developed contacts with bookies – in New Jersey, Florida, Chicago and Los Angeles. And once these relationships had been cemented, the bookies wasted little time in cultivating Beau as a customer by encouraging him to expand his gambling interests into other sports, in particular college and pro football and basketball.

That Abigail had been able to maintain the good reputation of the Wellingtons as "Kentucky's first family" was no small feat. Of course, she'd come to her partnership with Bentley carrying the Prescott family imprimatur as a leader in the Commonwealth's coal industry.

Abigail's daddy, Ezekiel Prescott, a native of Cumberland born in 1905, had moved to Lynch, a coal camp community built in 1917 by the U.S. Coal & Coke Company, a subsidiary of U.S. Steel. At the age of 16, he started working as a miner in the #30 and #31 mines. Three years later, he took on a bride, Mary Barrett, from the town of Grundy in Buchanan County, Virginia. On August 22, 1925, Zeke and Mary had their only child, Abigail. The young family remained in Lynch through the Great Depression of the 1930s.

By the start of World War II, however, Zeke and three long-time associates decided to take advantage of the war economy and started a small business. Under the name Bowling, Claywell, Prescott & Trivette Coal Co., the partners' union-free surface mining operation was based in Pike County near the convergence of the Kentucky, West Virginia and Virginia borders.

Moving to the county seat of Pikeville (host to part of the famous Hatfield-McCoy feud), Mary had enthusiastically embraced her new life, not only because her family still lived in nearby Grundy but also because life in Lynch had become somewhat strained under the thumb of the U.S. Coal & Coke Company.

Shortly thereafter, Zeke found himself one of the early activists helping to organize the Kentucky Coal Association (KCA). He'd gained notoriety in business and political circles as one of the original signatories to the KCA's 1947 by-laws. On one of his business trips to Frankfort, Zeke and the two Prescott women, Mary and now 22-year-old Abigail, had been invited by outgoing Governor Bentley Wellington to attend a Governor's Mansion reception for coal industry execs. Introductions made, Bentley Wellington had become instantly smitten with Abigail.

Despite the 25-year age difference between Bentley and Abigail, the Kentucky coal exec saw an incredible opportunity – politically, socially and of course financially. Zeke's daughter, who was nothing if not pragmatic, did little to discourage the Governor's overtures. They were married less than a year later.

Now 58, Abigail reflected on her current situation, which had changed dramatically over the past few years. Bentley was now confined to a wheelchair as a result of his 1978 hunting incident in

Tennessee. Her daddy's passing in 1980 left her with a 25 percent share in a southeast Kentucky surface-mining business. Abigail was sole heir, as her mama had lost a five-year battle with breast cancer in 1976.

Believing the coal industry's best years were in the past – a view whole-heartedly shared by her son, Beau – she sold her Prescott share of the enterprise back to the company. In failing health, Bentley was still a thorn in her side. She could make decisions that benefitted Bourbonesque as long as they didn't require significant capital "expenditures" (his word) or "investments" (her word).

At least Abigail now had some discretionary income earning money in an aggressive growth fund managed by Steinberg Stavros Rogers & Co., Inc., the firm handling the Wellington family's liquid assets. If Beau couldn't keep his gambling habit in check, and if her low-cost investments (i.e., stop-gap expenditures) weren't enough to stem the financial bleeding at Bourbonesque, she'd need access to those funds sooner rather than later.

Chapter 26 – Operation Bluegrass

It was the time of year when business routines were slowing to a halt, the period between Christmas Eve and New Year's Day. The end of 1982 and beginning of 1983, however, had conspired to give everyone an extra day's respite as the 24th fell on a Friday and the 1st arrived on a Saturday. Pleased to see January 2nd shown as a Sunday on his desk calendar, Sean started to go over plans to head down to Atlanta.

Although Sean had always made a special effort to be home on both Christmas *and* New Year's Day, this year Marci had to settle for just Christmas with her son. He'd booked a round-trip flight on Delta, departing Newark on Sunday morning, the 26th, for Atlanta and returning the following Sunday afternoon, Jan. 2nd. In between, he'd have an opportunity to visit with Professor Dandridge in Athens and do a tour of the Dean Rusk International Law Center.

But the primary purpose for Sean's trip was to sit down with Nate Katzman and Beth Feingold for a discussion on his information needs in Kentucky. He was particularly pleased to learn that Nate's father, Irving, the retired Brooklyn cop, was visiting for the holidays as well.

Sean booked at the Hyatt Regency in downtown Atlanta and invited Nate, Beth and Irving to dine at the Hyatt's Polaris rotating restaurant. On Sunday evening, the party of four met in the lobby and traveled up the hotel's glass elevator some 22 floors, where they were treated to panoramic views of the Atlanta skyline.

This wasn't the first time Sean and Irving Katzman had met. After one of their summer league basketball games years ago in Spring Lake Heights, Sean and "Kat Man" had ventured to Seaside Heights, where they enjoyed an evening on the boardwalk. They devoured hot dogs, french fries and root beer snow cones before heading to the amusement park, where Sean almost "gave back" his meal more than once while on the Wild Mouse and Tilt-A-Whirl. After an aggressive one-on-one bout with Nate in the electric Bumper Cars, Sean was ready for the relative calm of pin ball. It was there that Sean had been introduced to Irv.

Seated at a window table, Sean patiently allowed the conversation to proceed through Irv's questions on progress with wedding plans, where Beth's parents had visited during their recent 10-day Hanukkah trip to Israel, and how Nate and Beth were doing with their job searches now that his son was nearing completion of his residency and Beth would be graduating in May.

Halfway through the main course, Sean finally became the object of his guests' inquiries. After updating them on his progress at Seton Hall Law School and his intention to pursue a career as a sports agent, he turned to Nate and said, in a matter-of-fact tone, "I need some help, Nathan, and I believe the folks sitting here tonight may be in a position to provide it."

Sean spent the next 20 minutes detailing the relationship between then-Governor Bentley Wellington and his senior aide, Marci Davis – the events in San Francisco and the subsequent agreement that resulted in Marci relocating to Jersey City and starting work at Steinberg Stavros Rogers & Co. Finally, there was Marci legally adding "Jeffries" to her name and Sean's birth.

He then offered a half-hour brain dump on what he knew of the Wellington family's business dealings – Bentley's hunting accident and his wife's increasing role in Bourbonesque LLC; Beauregard's stewardship of Thoroughbred Bs Farm and Triple-B Racing Stables; and Ezekiel Prescott's involvement in the Kentucky coal industry, with Abigail eventually inheriting Zeke's share of the surface mining business upon her dad's passing.

Indeed, Sean had been quite busy over the past few years gathering information from publicly available documents and gaining insights during tours of the Wellington family's businesses. He'd gone the extra mile, engaging in casual and seemingly innocuous conversations with folks in and around Kentucky's close-knit racing, distilling and coal industries.

Based on the accumulated intel and revealing gossip now contained in his Wellington dossier, Sean had theorized that (a) the Wellington businesses were on shaky financial grounds, (b) Abigail, with increasing difficulty, had been keeping said businesses from collapsing like a house of cards, (c) Beauregard, apparently in league with his mother, was in the midst of hatching a plan to rescue their business holdings and (d) the Wellington plan was likely to run afoul of the law.

"But I need proof...corroboration straight from the horses' mouths, so to speak. Can you help?" Sean said when he'd finished, more pleading than asking.

Two Katzmans and a Katzman-to-be looked at each other, then at Sean, and uniformly nodded in the affirmative. Irv then spoke: "I know a guy who can do what's needed. I'd estimate 15K will do the trick, plus travel and lodging in Kentucky. That okay with you, Sean?"

Acknowledgement had come in the form of a handshake between Irv and Sean, after which the retired cop proclaimed, "We'll call it Operation Bluegrass!"

Chapter 27 – Oh What a Night!

After a warm and prolonged embrace, a buzzed Connie Pett stepped back from Jasmine and exclaimed: "Wow...Eres caliente!" ("Wow...Are you hot!") Surprised, but clearly pleased, Jasmine blushed.

The first several minutes of their conversation centered on what each of the young women had learned – and liked – about the other as a result of their chance meeting the previous evening at the Baremore Tavern. Having consumed appreciably more alcohol than they'd intended, taking a walk on the boardwalk sounded mutually appealing. Afterwards, they'd go to the Sands for dinner and some action at the black jack tables. From there, well ... it would be up to Connie. After all, she was the client.

Before rising from their seats, Connie could sense some hesitance in Jasmine. The young attorney opened her purse, removed a plain, white envelope containing five crisp $100 bills and handed it over to Jasmine. "Is this what you were looking for?"

Peeking inside ever so quickly, Jasmine blushed for the second time in the young evening. "Well, given the unusual situation, I was having a bit of difficulty spitting out the words," she confessed. "Thanks so much for recognizing the awkwardness!" Business behind them, the ladies departed the Dennis Hotel arm in arm and made their way to the Atlantic City boardwalk.

Consuela commented on the pleasant smell of the salt air, which was blowing in from the ocean. Jasmine explained the air was actually a mix of decomposing organisms and seaweed that had been deposited on the beach. She recounted the circumstances under which she'd been informed of this somewhat obscure fact and how it had been an unforgettable moment during a *mostly* forgettable date. "It sort of took romance out of the equation," she said and added: "Just consider it part of your Jersey shore education." Both of them laughed heartily.

Their heads beginning to clear after a stroll that periodically required course corrections due to the Memorial Day weekend's heavy pedestrian traffic, the pair finally decided it was time to have dinner. Sticking with the seafood theme she'd established the day before at the Lobster Shanty, Consuela started with local Top Neck Oysters iced and served on the half shell with cocktail sauce and moved on to crab-stuffed flounder. Jasmine, true to her light eating habit, followed her Maryland crab cocktail with a Mediterranean salad of sweet crabmeat, chunks of shrimp and fresh lobster served on a bed of fresh Romaine and red onions tossed with a house dressing.

The two engaged in light conversation and managed to keep alcoholic consumption to sharing a bottle of Sauvignon Blanc. By 10 p.m., they shifted the evening's activities to the casino. Consuela, experiencing her first visit to a gambling establishment, was content to play quarter slots and then try her luck at a $2 black jack table. Jasmine, more familiar with waging war at the dollar one-armed bandits and plying her card skills at the $10 black jack tables, nevertheless followed her date's lead. Despite their unique meeting the previous night, she was still feeling a bit more comfortable following the rules of the call girl-client arrangement.

At about 11 o'clock, Jasmine excused herself and retreated to the powder room. Touching up her makeup, Jasmine stared at herself and started to think. Creeping into her consciousness had been a growing admiration for Consuela Parks Pettiford, now knowing the story of her immigrant parents and how they'd sacrificed to give their daughter an education only to meet a horrific end to their lives. And here was Consuela, a young attorney at a prestigious New York City law firm alone in the big city with no family, coming out of her shell to take on new adventures. What exactly was Jasmine feeling? Respect?... compassion?... Or was it something more serious? And if so, was it about her date?... or about herself?

Shaking this train of thought from her head, she moved over to the full-length mirror. What was it Connie had exclaimed when they first came face to face? Something uttered in Spanish. Jasmine didn't know the language, but she certainly understood the tone of voice and facial expression. "Well," she said to herself out loud, "Let's see how Connie likes unwrapping *this* package."

***

It was close to midnight and the two women had retreated to Jasmine's room at the Sands. Connie had already removed her black satin bomber jacket and black leather-woven flats. A single candle provided a flickering light to an otherwise darkened room. The lavender-scented aroma from the candle was accentuated by the lavender perfume worn by Jasmine.

Emerging from the shadows with two wine glasses and the evening's second bottle of Sauvignon Blanc, the A.C.-D.C. call girl had prepared well for the evening's final act. Milt Jackson's 1973 *Sunflower* album had recently been produced on CD, a new format, and she had the music playing softly in the background on her newly purchased CD player.

She set down the glasses on the bureau, poured generously for her date and then for herself, placed the bottle in a marble wine chiller and handed a glass to Connie. "Here's to tonight," toasted Jasmine. The two clinked glasses and took a sip from each other's wine. Assertively, Jasmine took the glass from Connie and along with her own, set them on the bureau next to the chiller.

She moved toward her date and planted a warm wet kiss on her lips, soon parting them by gently slipping her tongue inside Connie's mouth. Jasmine then spread her partner's legs wide enough to stand between them, using her right thigh to part the side slit of Connie's black leather mini-skirt. She placed her kneecap firmly against Connie's crotch and slowly moved it from side to side. Finally, Jasmine bent over to stretch the opening of her date's tank top and began slowly licking between her breasts.

By now Connie had been aroused as she'd never been before, as much by the fact that Jasmine had taken complete control of the situation as by her actual actions that had dampened her and hardened her nipples. Jasmine took Connie's right hand, placed it on the zipper to her yellow crop top and gently brought both hand and zipper down. She slipped off her top and then, stepping back, removed her micro-mini skirt. Jasmine was left wearing her thigh-high leather boots, push-up bra, thigh-high tights and skin-tight Lycra hipster panties.

Gazing at Connie, Jasmine asked in a coy voice: "Would you like to take off my boots?" Connie knelt down, unzipped each boot and removed them. As she did so, Jasmine slid off Connie's tank top, providing a closer look at a perfectly proportioned set of 34Bs.

Before she could reach to cup them in her hands, she felt a wet warmth through her Lycra panties courtesy of Connie's tongue. Now it was Jasmine's turn to experience the tingling sensation of clitoral stimulation which...if Connie kept it up much longer...she would...*SHE...WOULD..."OH MY GOD!"* Jasmine squealed as she felt a gush of liquid from her vagina and an orgasm that left her convulsing.

Before long they were both completely naked, groping, grinding and probing every crevice, every orifice, every erogenous zone of their bodies as seconds morphed into minutes which ultimately became hours of newfound pleasures.

***

It was 10 in the morning before Jasmine awoke. She didn't remember getting under the covers ... or turning on the A/C for that matter. Connie must have done that. She also noted that the alluring scent of last night's lavender had been replaced by the welcome smell of "the morning after" coffee. But where was Connie? She trudged into the bathroom, turned on the shower and saw the note Connie had left by the sink. It wasn't long, but it certainly gave Jasmine a whole lot to think about:

> "Dear Jasmine. I can't tell you how much our time together over the past couple of days has meant to me, coming so soon after the death of my parents. Given the strange circumstances leading up to last night, I truly hope our 'date' became more than the financial arrangement initially intended. I don't know if anything will come of this. But I would like for us to get together again ... as friends. You have my firm's business number in the City. But if you'd like to talk today, I'll be doing a slow recovery this morning. Brunch at the Dennis would be great! Yours, Consuela."

Chapter 28 – The Road to Perdition

Abigail and Beauregard Wellington had an extremely close mother-and-son relationship. By virtue of his only-child status, Beau had been destined to run the family's thoroughbred business since his parents learned they wouldn't be able to add offspring – at least in the traditional manner. That he'd be asked to take over the business at such a young age was due to his father's single-minded pursuit of a distillery venture during his post-political years.

With Bentley's incapacitation and soon followed by her father's passing, Abigail found herself quickly thrust into a significant role in Kentucky business circles. She'd leaned heavily on her son for counsel in those first days and weeks.

For his part, Beau had done a good job preparing for the work to come. Not shy about breaking with family tradition, he pursued an education outside the Commonwealth and earned a business degree with a major in Finance from the University of Miami in Coral Gables.

Understanding that his future would be directly tied to his family's thoroughbred business, Beau headed to the northern part of the Sunshine State to intern with the Ocala Stud Farm. A family-run business in its own right, Ocala had been at the forefront of creating the 2-year-old auction market in the 1950s and '60s, pioneering an approach to marketing young thoroughbreds by emphasizing training and physical ability over pedigree.

Upon his return to Lexington, Beau had gone to work at Thoroughbred Bs Farm as the business's "number-two" under the supervision of his granddaddy, Buford "Buff" Wellington. When doctors had discovered aggressive pancreatic cancer, Buff hastened transition of the farm to Beau. Almost immediately after Buff had passed in 1978, the 28-year-old Beau began the operational and financial separation of the breeding and racing aspects of the business. Thus Triple-B Racing Stables was born, with both the new entity and breeding farm experiencing much-improved bottom lines.

It was Beau's insight into all things financial – projections, company forecasts and the economic impact of marketplace and other external forces on the family businesses – that often left Abigail in a state of bewilderment. How could someone so in touch with the world of business finance be so lax with his *own* finances? In her more lucid moments, her thoughts were a bit more concise: *How could my son piss away so much money by gambling?!?*

All of which had brought Abigail and Beau to a critical meeting on the Saturday (April 2nd) of the 1983 Easter weekend.

Bourbonesque LLC had been hemorrhaging money due to Bentley's unwillingness to invest either in improvements to the company's physical plant or in upgrades to its aging information systems. And in the increasingly crowded marketplace for bourbon whiskey, if a company's management hadn't been investing in marketing, it wasn't just treading water, it was falling behind.

"Beau, honey. I can't get your daddy to invest the funds needed to keep Bourbonesque competitive. And you know my coal money won't do much more than serve as a temporary Band-Aid," Abigail complained. "I'm trying really hard to keep that money in reserve in case we need it for some unforeseen situation."

Beau knew quite well his mom had been referring to his gambling habit: "I've got that under control, Abby. You won't have to worry about it anymore." When mother and son discussed business, Beau tended to call his mom Abby. She thought it was both patronizing *and* cute at the same time and trotted out a facial expression that somehow conveyed that mixed-bag sentiment to her son.

Actually, Beau's habit had long ago spun out of control. He owed well over a quarter-million dollars to bookies from Atlantic City, Miami and Chicago to Las Vegas and Los Angeles. Because of his family's considerable wealth and debt-free status, he'd been able to establish lines of credit from those willing to feed his habit. But if one bookmaker learned of his obligations to others, Beau could well anticipate certain of his "associates" operating "in the shadows" to "call in" what he owed. And if he didn't "make himself whole" soon, the likelihood of discovery would grow.

What had given Beau a false sense of security was knowledge that his debts would be so much chump change compared to the pending $200 million IPO New York-based Silverstein-Gladstone had recently agreed to underwrite on behalf of Thoroughbred Bs Farm, Inc. (TBF).

Today, Beau was meeting with Abby to review the scope of

information required in the Registration Statement to be filed with the U.S. Securities & Exchange Commission (SEC).

Sections of Form S-1 included (1) a *business summary* describing the general nature of business to be conducted by TBF, which included the breeding, public auction and private sale of thoroughbred horses; (2) a *financial summary* providing a 10-K for the most recently completed fiscal year (a document that included a comprehensive company analysis with audited financial statements) along with a "fresh" but unaudited income statement and balance sheet covering the most recent quarter (a truncated version of the 10-K, the 10Q, would need to be completed within 45 days of the end of the latest quarter of TBF's fiscal year); (3) an exhaustive list of *risk factors* describing the potential pitfalls facing prospective investors in TBF, including risks specific to the company (e.g., lack of depth in executive talent), industry-wide challenges (e.g., the trend toward further regulation of the thoroughbred breeding business, competition from overseas operations, long-term uncertainties in market demand for breeding services) and general economic trends that could have an adverse impact; (4) details surrounding TBF's plans for *management and compensation* including identifying officers and directors; putting in place a compensation and benefits plan; and once in place, material transactions between the company and these individuals, as well as material legal proceedings involving the company and/or its officers and directors.

The meat & potatoes of the filing, however, were to be found in the final three sections:

(5) Details of the *stock offering*, itself, were a product of discussions between Beau and TBF's underwriter, Silverstein-Gladstone. A preliminary understanding called for [a] 20 million shares of TBF common outstanding, tentatively to be set at an opening price of $10 per share and [b] an additional 20 million shares of TBF, Inc. common issued, to be earmarked for potential use in stock option plans, executive compensation and/or for barter for goods and services. Silverstein-Gladstone had recommended *authorizing* a total of 50 million shares to avoid the necessity of reapplying to the SEC and other regulatory bodies should additional shares be required. This would save on associated costs in time and money.

(6) TBF would be required to list the intended *uses of the*

proceeds from the initial public offering (e.g., for broodmare and stallion acquisition, public auctions and private sales marketing, and "for general corporate purposes"). In one of his more aggressive IPO scenarios, Beau envisioned the acquisition of TJ Cutter's Virginia-based Cutter Farms to form what could become the nation's leading thoroughbred breeding operation. He would make it his business to arrange a sit-down with Cutter in New Jersey once the Monmouth Park meet was underway at the end of next month.

(7) Under the critical MD&A section (*management discussion and analysis of financial condition and results of operations*), TBF would be required to provide financial statements from the three most recent fiscal years (f.y. 1980, 1981 and 1982), focusing on material changes or nonrecurring items that may make the comparison of results misleading. Among the specifics to be mentioned were the change in leadership at TBF due to Buff Wellington's passing and Beau's initial steps in segregating the racing activities from the breeding activities of TBF.

When Beau finished going over the Registration Statement, Abby asked her son to clarify the difference between issued shares and outstanding shares.

Beau explained: "Issued shares would include shares in the treasury that TBF holds for future sale. We may want to use issued shares in the treasury to barter for goods and services. Outstanding shares are those actively owned by people within or outside the company as well as those held by institutions."

Beau went on to state that the number of *issued* shares would help determine the value of TBF stock and play a role in setting the price at market. The number of *outstanding* shares would be used to determine what percentage of TBF a particular shareholder owned as well as how much voting power he, she or it (in the case of an institution or other legal entity) would hold.

The next part of Beau's agenda had been a bit touchy, as Abby and Bentley owned not insignificant minority interests in Thoroughbred Bs Farm. Those areas of the SEC filing that involved selection of the executive team and members of the TBF Board of Directors, executive compensation, distribution of "restricted" shares to insiders (who couldn't sell their interest for a specified period following a stock offering to the general public), stock options and, in particular, use of proceeds all required a deft approach.

Finally, there'd be the small matter of agreeing upon a "poison pill" strategy, a tactic used by companies to prevent or discourage hostile takeovers. Beau would leave the specifics to Silverstein-Gladstone.

For his part, Beau would be concentrating on two areas: *executive compensation* (his best option for acquiring money to get out from under his growing debt) and *use of proceeds*, which might include investments in other companies' bond issues, purchase of foreign currencies or precious metals, and even private loans on terms favorable to TBF to businesses like, say...Bourbonesque LLC.

Boiled down to its simplest terms, Beau was looking at the prospect of siphoning from the treasury of a publicly traded company (i.e., TBF, Inc.) enough cash to place a private business (i.e., Bourbonesque LLC) owned by members of his immediate family (Bentley and Abigail Wellington) on firm financial footing.

That he'd been considering such actions while working on a draft of an SEC filing for Thoroughbred Bs Farm was indicative of just how far down the road to perdition he'd already traveled.

Chapter 29 – A Man of Many Talents

It was just after New Year's Day 1983 when Irv returned from visiting his son, Nate, and his fiancée, Beth, in Atlanta. He immediately called Calvin Thomas. Asked by his former N.Y.P.D. colleague to consider a gig that would take him to Kentucky, Calvin had only to check his appointment book before responding in the affirmative. The story Irv had recounted – about Sean Davis Jeffries and his mission – was straight out of a paperback novel.

Calvin had agreed wholeheartedly with Irv's assessment. And the "gig" was exactly the kind of freelance assignment he'd relish after 20 years with New York's finest. Retired from his position as detective in Brooklyn's 76th Precinct, which served south Brooklyn including the neighborhoods of Carroll Gardens, Red Hook, Cobble Hill, parts of Gowanus and the Columbia Street Waterfront District, Calvin wasn't about to spend his days watching TV and playing poker Thursday evenings with the neighborhood guys.

Calvin loved to meet new people and enjoyed driving. His second career as a chauffeur for a limousine service enabled him to do both. The New York metropolitan area arguably boasted the nation's most diverse resident population and was visited each year by thousands of tourists and business people from around the world. More times than not, a simple question or casual observation from Calvin spurred a full-blown discussion with his passenger.

Calvin Thomas was a survivor. Born in 1940 as the youngest of three boys raised by Elijah and Maxine Thomas, he'd been raised in the Washington Heights section of upper Manhattan. As a youth, he was the constant beneficiary of playground rescues by his older siblings, Noah and Isaac. As a young teen Calvin survived a bullet to the abdomen, a by-product of a gang-related drive-by shooting that riddled his family's home with gunfire. That incident had everything to do with the career path he would choose as a young adult.

As a junior at George Washington High School, Calvin enrolled in the U.S. Army National Guard. He graduated from GWHS in 1957 and fulfilled the minimum three-year Guard obligation, after which he gained admission to the New York City Police Academy.

Calvin had been assigned to the 76th Precinct in Brooklyn

following completion of his training and rose through the ranks. On the beat, he'd survived everything from police chases and domestic disputes turned violent to drug busts and armed robberies. Decorated multiple times, he eventually earned a promotion to detective.

With pension in hand, Calvin Thomas had purchased his current home in Oceanport, strategically positioned to service limo clients traveling to and from the Big Apple and north Jersey to the Jersey shore as far south as A.C. and over to Philly. Keeping his hand in the sleuthing he'd come to enjoy as a detective, Calvin had struck an arrangement with his employer that gave him the flexibility to take time during the year to accept intriguing projects requiring the services of an experienced gumshoe. This Sean Jeffries case was just such an assignment.

For the occasion, Calvin shaved his mustache as well as his closely cropped, curly black hair.

***

Booking a room at the historic Boone Tavern Hotel in Berea, Calvin had situated himself roughly 45 miles south of Lexington and Thoroughbred Bs Farm and 80 miles east of Bardstown and Bourbonesque LLC's distillery. He wanted to be a reasonable drive to each, but far enough removed from the locales he needed to reconnoiter to avoid running into the wrong people in the wrong place at the wrong time. The drive to Lexington was less than an hour north on I-75 while the trip west to Bardstown would take him 1½ to 2 hours depending upon traffic via secondary routes.

His initial objective was to seek employment with either of the Wellington family's two businesses. Part-time manual labor was the strong preference. The more menial the job Calvin might secure, the less likely he'd come in contact with Abigail, Beau or Bentley Wellington. As it turned out, Calvin struck gold as both Bourbonesque *and* Thoroughbred Bs Farm had need for a part-time security guard. One resumé with a slightly altered name, two interviews (one with a shift manager at Bourbonesque who quickly referred Calvin to the stable manager at Thoroughbred Bs Farm) and one well-placed recommendation from long-time N.Y.P.D.

policeman Irving Katzman, and a pair of Wellington-owned-and-operated businesses had filled their need for a security guard.

On Monday, January 31st, "Carson Tobias" began work as a security guard for Bourbonesque, filling the 11 p.m. to 7 a.m. shift on Mondays, Wednesdays and Fridays, and as an overnight watchman for Thoroughbred Bs Farm on Tuesdays, Thursdays and Saturdays from nine at night until five the next morning.

"Nothing like killing two birds with one stone," Calvin had chuckled to Irv after spending his first day at each location.

Chapter 30 – "Brakes" of the Game

While the contentious post-dinner discussion among Board members in Wuppertal had surprised Gretchen Weiß Hauptmann, the instigator, Dieter Hartmann, was no shock at all. It wasn't enough for Herr Hartmann to disagree with those on the Board who seemed to lean towards remaining a private firm; his responses to their concerns over transitioning to a public company were filled with contempt.

Gretchen's original plan was to head back home after the meeting to check on the aging Pulver, then return in the morning in time for Frühstück (breakfast) and the final vote. But now, witnessing how the debate had unfolded, she began to rethink this course of action. Preferring to remain at the Park Villa should anyone want to continue discussion with her on a one-to-one basis, Gretchen decided to turn over to Hanna Schröder the task of checking on Pulver and letting him outside to tend to his needs.

With the roads damp from the light, misty rain that had been falling all day and patchy fog reducing visibility, Gretchen insisted Hanna use her Porsche for the drive to Hückeswagen rather than the administrative assistant's 10-year-old Mercedes Benz 200D that showed some 150,000 kilometers worth of wear and tear. She handed over keys to the house and coupe, telling Hanna: "Fahren Sie sicher und rufen Sie mein Zimmer an, wenn Sie ankommen." (Drive safely and call my room when you arrive.")

Hanna left shortly after midnight for the half-hour drive. By 1:15, Gretchen began to worry. All of her guests had turned in for the night. She telephoned the house in case Hanna forgot to call. There was no answer. Deeply concerned, she then rang Die Polizei (the police). Explaining the reason for her call, she mentioned there were two possible routes to her house (both of which the officer at the other end of the phone line was quite familiar), and provided her home address as well as the Park Villa number to call if there'd been any accidents between Wuppertal and Hückeswagen involving her vehicle. At that point, all Gretchen could do was wait.

The call Gretchen had been dreading finally came at three in the morning. A vehicle matching the description she provided had been found in a gully at the bottom of an embankment off the L414. It appeared the vehicle had failed to negotiate a sharp right curve. The driver, whose wallet contained a license in the name of Hanna Schröder, had been found dead just outside the vehicle. According to der Rettungssanitäter am Unfallort (the paramedic at the scene), she died instantly from a broken neck as a result of the impact. It would be at least a couple of days before an autopsy was performed to determine whether there were circumstances related to her physical and/or medical condition that contributed to the accident. Investigators would also inspect the vehicle to see if there were any mechanical flaws that might have been a contributing factor.

At the morning's meal, Gretchen informed her stunned fellow Board members of the accident, immediately suspended a final vote until further notice and announced services would be held at Basilika St. Laurentius in Wuppertal on that Wednesday. She declared a company-wide period of mourning and indicated there would be a formal communiqué sent via special delivery as to the timing and manner in which a final vote was to be taken. No action would occur pending answers from authorities on the cause of the early morning accident.

***

On Sunday, Hanna Schröder's body was transported to a Radevormwald morgue for an autopsy. Meanwhile police had called in a wrecker and flatbed to retrieve the badly damaged Porsche from the gully and transport it to the North Rhine-Westphalia (NRW) Police Force in Düsseldorf for inspection.

Although a formal report wouldn't be completed for 10 days, the first team of inspectors quickly discovered the likely cause of the accident – a severed brake line that left the driver with little ability to stop the vehicle at speeds of 25 km/h or greater. The team estimated the Porsche had been traveling at a speed of 40 km/h when it approached the road's sharp right curve. Given the newness of the Porsche, it was unlikely to have been caused by either a poorly installed line or mechanical defect.

Around the same time, the morgue's forensic pathologist found the deceased's blood alcohol content at the time of the crash was

0.01 to 0.02 mg of alcohol/100 ml ... within the range of alcohol produced constantly by the human body. There also was no evidence of stroke, heart failure or other medical conditions that might have contributed to loss of control of the vehicle.

Given these preliminary reports and the high-profile executive who owned the vehicle, the officer in charge of the inspection team in Düsseldorf, Gustav Zimmermann, contacted his counterpart in the Nordrhein-Westfalen Landeskriminalamt in Düsseldorf (LKA NRW), the State Investigation Bureau. A recommendation was made to open a case file on the incident.

The LKA NRW officer, Bertram Krieger, did just that. He also placed an international call to the Tel Aviv headquarters of the Mossad and asked for one David Katzman. Informed Katzman was "out of the country," Krieger left a coded message: "Code Yellow for Terezin scheduler."

Within minutes, another international call was made from Tel Aviv to the Israeli Consulate in New York City. The coded message was relayed to a dispatcher at the midtown Manhattan building that housed officials conducting Israel's business in the New York metropolitan region. From there, a communiqué was sent via telex to a machine installed at a penny arcade in Seaside Heights, NJ ... an arcade owned and operated by Irv Katzman.

It took exactly 15 minutes for the critical coded message to travel from Düsseldorf to Tel Aviv to New York City to Seaside Heights, where David Katzman, napping on a cot in the back office of his dad's arcade, awoke at the sound of the telex machine printing. Wiping the sleep from his eyes, he tore the sheet of paper from the machine and read the coded message.

It was urgent he immediately reconnect with Jorge and Fabian. He quickly showered, dressed, reminded himself to get ahold of his dad, bolted down the boardwalk ramp to his car and headed to Jorge Hauptmann's Bradley Beach boarding house. Thankfully, the reunion he'd arranged had gone better than expected. David had been able to sit at the bar of the Binghamton Restaurant while Jorge and Fabian spent the better part of two hours rekindling their relationship.

Now Katzman would be checking in on the Hauptmann boys. Until he could speak with NRW authorities, he couldn't tell them anything more than Gretchen Weiß Hauptmann was safe.

Chapter 31 – A Day at the Track

By 9:45 Saturday morning, Jasmine Cutter had accepted Consuela's invitation for brunch and was heading to the Dennis Hotel. She'd already gone through her mandatory post-mortem with her A.C.-D.C. boss, June, during which Jasmine committed a cardinal sin by telling her there was no sex involved. "I set the stage in my room at the Sands. Music, perfume, wine...the works. Evidently, she got cold feet." When June asked if there would be any follow-up date, she answered: "I doubt it, but you never know. Maybe she's kicking herself for not taking advantage of the situation."

Jasmine was careful not to dismiss out-of-hand a client who might be a source of repeat business. With her young call girl indicating she'd remain available should the client have second thoughts during the Memorial Day weekend, June agreed to leave Jasmine's schedule open just in case. The usual cash pick-up arrangement would take place on Tuesday rather than Monday due to the holiday.

Jasmine would have to explain the morning-after business routine to Consuela so she'd be able to corroborate her version of events with June. Jasmine simply didn't have it in her to take additional money for sex, probably because what transpired between the two seemed to have been the beginnings of a relationship of substance. Time would tell.

Today's weather was unseasonably cool and not a particularly good beach day for sun lovers. Consuela was already seated in the dining room when Jasmine arrived. Both had dressed casually in form-fitting designer blue jeans, Consuela wearing a powder blue, scoop-neck Spandex top and Jasmine sporting a sheer, white mesh see-through blouse with long sleeves. Windbreakers had been a wise decision given the spring-like temperature. Eddie Bauer hiking boots were the preferred footwear of the day.

Approaching the table, Jasmine leaned over to kiss Consuela on the cheek. But the young attorney quickly moved her face a bit in order to give her new friend a full and lingering kiss on the mouth. Aroused, Jasmine flicked out her tongue as an indication of approval.

The ladies decided on freshly toasted water bagels with all the accompaniments – cream cheese and nova smoked salmon; sliced tomato and sliced cucumber; diced red onion and capers, and black olives on the side. Mimosas were the late-morning drink. They fell into a comfortable silence as their food came. If each could read the other's mind, Consuela and Jasmine would know that was an indication of good chemistry.

Finishing up, Jasmine spoke first. "Do you have anything planned for the day? If not, we can drive up to Oceanport and take in a day at the races."

Consuela, visibly pleased with the offer, quickly agreed. "Great! This will be another first for me. I've never been to a race track before. Are we dressed appropriately?"

"Absolutely," said Jasmine. "I'm pretty sure my brother, TJ, has a horse running in one of the stakes races today. We can probably hook up with him at some point. If we can head upstairs to your room, I'll give Fran DeSantis a call at the clubhouse Will Call window. She'll have a couple of comp passes waiting when we get there and see if there's room for us in TJ's box." A glance at her wristwatch indicated it was 10:45. "If we hurry, we can make it there for post time of the first race. We don't wanna miss betting on the daily double."

"What's a daily double?" asked Consuela.

Jasmine rolled her eyes and answered with a laugh: "I can see my role for the day is gonna be teaching 'Thoroughbred Racing 101.'"

"Ready, willing and able to learn," said Consuela, happier than she'd been in quite some time.

***

For jockey Angel Barrera, Friday's opening-day card had been a mixed bag. He'd been kept out of the winner's circle in four of five races. The exception had been in the 6th race at one mile on the turf course along the hedge. A handicap for 3- and 4-year-old colts. Angel's mount, *Dance To The Music*, was a 3-year-old sired by *Nijinsky II* out of *It Was Meant To B*. The broodmare was owned by Thoroughbred Bs Farm of Lexington, KY. *Dance To The Music* was racing under the royal blue and white colors of Beauregard Wellington's Triple-B Racing Stables.

Stalking the leader at the three-quarters pole, which had been covered in a decent 1:11.3, *Dance To The Music* took the lead and won going away in a fast time of 1:35 flat. The $50,000 purse eased an otherwise forgettable afternoon capped by a half-length defeat to *Immigration Sensation*, ridden by Stevie Thorn, that "maldito (damned) Aussie bug boy." In Angel's mind, the result had little to do with the jockeys' comparative skills and everything to do with all the weight his mount had to cede to Thorn's.

Worse yet, Thorn was off to a fast start, crossing the finish line first with five of his six mounts and giving him a lead of four wins only nine races into the meet. Today they'd do it all again with Barrera listed on five mounts, all having a reasonable chance of winning. With Saturday cards typically stocked with larger purses and better thoroughbreds, his opportunity to appreciably increase his money earnings was all there in front of him.

Most important, Angel had first call on the 2-year-old colt *Cut To The Chase* under his new contract with TJ Cutter. The son of *Nijinsky II* out of the Cutter-owned *Lawn Girl* was running in the co-featured 7th race on today's card, ironically named the Nijinsky II Stakes, a 5½ furlong race on the turf. The purse was $75,000.

A solid second choice according to Monmouth Park's program handicapper, *Cut To The Chase* would be facing *B Kind To Your Enemies*, the morning-line favorite owned by Beauregard Wellington. Angel Barrera had ridden Wellington's charge in its most recent win on Derby Weekend at Churchill Downs in Louisville. Under the new contract negotiated by Chris McCardle, Barrera had the option in any stakes race to accept a mount other than TJ Cutter's entry.

Barrera and McCardle faced a dilemma most good jockeys might encounter from time to time in stakes races – which of two assignments to take. While there was little to choose between the 2-year-olds from a pure handicapping standpoint, there was another consideration: Should Angel show a good-faith choice in a new relationship by honoring first call on *Cut To The Chase*? ... Or should he go with Wellington's *B Kind To Your Enemies*, a connection with whom he'd experienced recent success?

McCardle, taking the long-range view, leaned towards getting

Angel's relationship with Cutter off to a solid start. Barrera, possibly with the sting of Stevie Thorn's opening-day salvo of successes in his mind, chose Wellington's morning-line favorite.

***

The Saturday of Memorial Day weekend was traditionally one of the busiest days of the Monmouth Park meet. So Fran DeSantis was not at all pleased Jorge Hauptmann had called in sick. With Sundays dark in New Jersey racing circles, Jorge promised he'd "get out of my deathbed, if that's what it takes" to be back for the anticipated packed house on Memorial Day.

Meanwhile, Fran put together the complimentary passes for Jasmine Cutter and her guest, along with a pair of pins indicating they were entitled to seats in the Cutter private box in the clubhouse section. Two programs, Saturday's edition of *The Racing Form* and a couple of tip sheets – *Lawton's* and *Riley's* – rounded out the guest package.

At 12:50 p.m., Jasmine's Mercury Montego pulled into the clubhouse valet area. Driver and passenger emerged quickly, with Jasmine grabbing Consuela's hand and rushing toward the Will Call window. Fran, used to last-minute arrivals before the first race, spotted Jasmine and her guest and had their passes, pins, programs and "thoroughbred bible" ready for pick-up. Scurrying to the nearby clubhouse pass gate, Jasmine virtually threw the passes at the young attendant behind the admission booth's glass window and nearly doubled over when the turnstile wasn't released in time to let her through. Not letting go of a trailing Consuela, she led her up the escalator and to one of the $2 windows.

"What are your two favorite numbers?" asked Jasmine.

"Well, uh...4 and 24," answered an out-of-breath Consuela.

"Four's okay, but the other number can't be greater than 12!" laughed Jasmine. "There are only 12 horses in each of the first two races."

"Okay, then. Let's do 7 in the first race and 4 in the second race," Consuela answered, now understanding what her friend was getting at.

The voice on the loud speaker announced: "Three minutes to

post time. Three minutes to post."

Jasmine didn't bother asking Consuela to reach into her purse and come up with a couple of bucks. She dug into the right front pocket of her designer jeans and managed to pull out a wrinkled twenty. Third in line, she started muttering in a progressively louder voice: "Come on ... *Come on ...* COME ON!"

Hitting the front of the line with the overhead signs indicating one minute to post, Jasmine placed the bill on the counter, said "four dollars on the daily double, 7 in the first race, 4 in the second race." The seller calmly punched in the numbers and two pari-mutuel tickets emerged from the slot of the steel box. He quickly counted $16 in change. With the transaction just completed a bell rang indicating no more bets could be taken.

A couple of seconds later, the starting gate opened at the top of the backstretch for the six-furlong sprint as 12 horses sprang forward looking to gain early favorable positioning. At the same time, an announcer calling the race loudly proclaimed through his microphone: "And they're off!" Jasmine again reached for Consuela's hand and rushed her down to the rail where they could get a better view of the homestretch and finish line. Ever prepared, Jasmine had taken binoculars from the back seat of her car so they could get a better look as the races unfolded down the backstretch.

The #7 entry in this Maiden Special Weight race for 3-year-old fillies had been 10-1 on the morning line but closed at odds that dropped precipitously during the last five minutes before post time to 4-1, often an indication that late – and possibly "smart" – money had been wagered on that entry.

Ridden by Stevie Thorn, *Wise Beyond Her Years* settled in the middle of the pack after an opening quarter of :22.3 and the half in :45.4. Jasmine, keeping one eye on the race time posted on the infield tote board and the other on the green & yellow silks of the #7 horse, poked Consuela in the side and said, "The race is setting up for a closer. We have a shot!"

Completing the race's only turn and heading down the stretch, *Wise Beyond Her Years* began to pick off horses as Thorn changed his whip hand from left to right in order to force his charge to switch leads and move to the rail. With an eighth of a mile to go, it was going to be close between the #7 horse and the #2 filly who held the lead from the start. At the wire, it was too close to call. The PHOTO sign flashed in red.

Fans who wagered on horses finishing "up the track" ripped up or otherwise discarded their tickets, while others who bet on either the #2 or #7 horse waited with baited breath for posting of the vertically placed yellow numbers indicating the 1st through 4th place finishers. Another red sign would then flash OFFICIAL, at which point the payoff prices would be posted.

A last hope for fans who bet on the second-place finisher were two red signs, one that would flash OBJECTION if one jockey lodged a complaint against another, and a second that would flash INQUIRY if the racing stewards had seen some activity on the track that might be a foul (e.g., one horse bumping another or one horse impeding the progress of another). This would require the stewards to review a replay of the race.

After what seemed like an eternity, the yellow lights appeared in quick succession starting at the top: 7 – 2 – 12 – 5. The payoffs followed. The #7 entry, having gone off at 4-1 odds, paid $10.80 to win. The place (2nd place) and show (3rd place) payoffs for the # 7 and #2 entries were posted, as was the show payoff for the #12 entry. Time of the race was 1:12.1, indicating that a fast half mile had cooked the horse making the fractions and enabled another horse to come from off the pace and win with a final quarter in a snail-like :26.2.

Consuela screamed when her number had flashed on the infield tote board. Jasmine quickly tempered her enthusiasm. Now that they had approximately 20 some-odd minutes until the second race, she turned to *The Daily Racing Form* page containing past performances and other data on the 2nd race entries at Monmouth Park.

The second half of the daily double was 1¼ miles on the dirt and was a claiming race for fillies and mares 3-years-old and up. Noting the claiming price was the meet's minimum at $3,000, Jasmine said rather caustically: "This is gonna be one helluva boat race! The big question is how many of these nags will be able to make it to the finish line." On the good-news side of things, she added that no horse deserved short odds. "Yeah, our horse is 20-1, but has as good a chance as any."

Consuela had experienced a wild roller-coaster ride of emotion crammed into less than 10 minutes, commencing with her exit from Jasmine's car at clubhouse valet parking. "How often do you come here?" she asked Jasmine, and followed it with an interesting observation: "Do you always take on a Jersey accent when you go to the track?"

Jasmine looked up from the tip sheets she was now reading and with a deadpan expression replied, "Why yes, I do. And I take that as a compliment." She stared at Consuela for a few more seconds and then burst out laughing. The afternoon had just begun, but the native Virginian from horse country north of Leesburg and her companion, a lifelong resident of New York City, were clearly experiencing an enchanting day.

The young women's excitement grew as the tote board showed the payoff for each of the 12 daily double possibilities. Each of them stood to win $942.80 if their #4 horse won. With odds to win the race at 40-1 approaching 12 minutes to post, Consuela had a wild idea: "How about we each bet two dollars to win on 'Nuff Said," the #4 horse's name. "If it's our day, let's make it a big one." Interestingly enough, the 5-year-old mare was to be ridden by Stevie Thorn, the apprentice who'd just captured the first half of the daily double.

Who was Jasmine to disagree? As a veteran of the thoroughbred business, she was all too familiar with the good fortune often bestowed upon first-time track goers by the gods of horse racing. "I've got it this time," added Consuela, who disappeared amid the banks of pari-mutuel windows to place the bet.

It was nine minutes 'til post as Consuela made her way back to watch the second race with Jasmine and other railbirds. Out of the corner of her eye, she spotted a gentleman in tan riding breeches, a red huntsman's jacket, black top hat and black boots striding to where thoroughbreds completed their walk from the paddock to the dirt race course. He stopped, hoisted a long coach horn straight into the air, then lowered it to a position parallel to the ground. Placing the mouthpiece to his lips, he played the tune all racing fans recognize as the announced entry of the horses onto the track.

Jasmine inspected 'Nuff Said, a big 5-year-old bay mare who appeared quite calm entering the track. She pointed out to Consuela the blinkers the trainer had added for the race "which hopefully prevents our horse from being distracted and keeps her attention on the job at hand."

Jasmine also explained how the race track's outriders help

horses in the post parade and, in particular, when approaching the starting gate. She was of the opinion that keeping horses calm in the post parade and entering the starting gate enabled them to conserve energy and focus on responding promptly to a jockey's commands during a race.

Consuela was amazed at just how much her new friend knew about thoroughbreds and racing. She wondered why Jasmine hadn't gone to work for TJ but sensed today wasn't the day to go there.

At a mile-and-a-quarter, the second race gave folks in the grandstand and clubhouse seating areas two up-close looks at the action – the first coming in the initial run from the chute at the one-mile oval's northwest corner down the entire length of the track toward the first turn, and the second coming in the final turn and stretch drive to the finish line. Although the only body of water was a man-made lake behind the turf courses and tote board on the infield, jockeys aboard all the horses seemed to be piloting boats (as Jasmine had quipped) as opposed to riding thoroughbreds.

After passing the grandstand the first time and turning toward the backstretch, Stevie Thorn had 'Nuff Said in fourth about five lengths off the lead. But the horse was running easily and Thorn had tight hold of the reins. As the bay mare headed into the final turn, Consuela could see through the binoculars that Thorn had loosened his grip and showed his charge the whip. Almost instantly, 'Nuff Said began to move steadily on the three horses ahead of her. Straightening into the home stretch, the apprentice jockey took his horse to the outside and gave one crack on the mare's left flank. 'Nuff Said may not have been moving very fast, but she passed the other horses like they were standing still and won going away. Consuela was so dizzy from the excitement that she had to sit at one of the benches located about 60 feet behind her.

Minutes later, horse and jockey entered the winner's circle where the owner, trainer and representative from the sponsor of the race posed for photos and a trophy presentation. Jumping off, Stevie Thorn carried his saddle to a nearby box containing a scale where the assigned weight the horse is supposed to have carried was confirmed. (Jasmine explained to Consuela that the jockey's weight plus his saddle weights for the race are supposed to equal the weight assigned to the horse by the track's handicapper.)

A winning ticket paid $94.00, meaning the final odds at post time had been 46-1. Consuela, who'd been pretty good at math for as long as she could remember, asked Jasmine why the tote board's final calculation ("turn" in racing parlance) showed odds of 40-1. "Once the odds reach a certain point, the board starts calculating at increments of 10," offered Jasmine. "I can't remember if that starts at 20-1 or 30-1."

In any event, the women scurried over to the cashier side of the pari-mutuel banks and would soon have a little more carrying cash in their possession. "Let's see.... $942.80 for the double and another $94.00 for the second race. That's $1,036.80! Wahoowa!" shouted Jasmine.

"Is that a race track expression?" asked Consuela.

"Nah," explained Jasmine. "It's something I picked up from TJ during his time at UVA. A nickname for the school's sports teams is 'Wahoos.' When one of their teams wins or when something really good happens, you often hear students, alumni and other fans shouting 'Wahoowa.' Speaking of TJ, why don't we head up to his box? Hopefully, he'll be around so I can introduce you."

***

After taking the escalator to the second floor, Jasmine paused to show Consuela the Monmouth Park paddock and walking ring. With a great aerial view from gigantic open windows, they could see horses for the third race along with their trainers, grooms and jockeys slowly circling the ring. It was typically where trainers and jockeys went over last-minute race strategy and where horses were saddled and jockeys heard the call, "Riders up!"

The paddock and walking ring were a particular source of pride for those who kept Monmouth Park in great shape. The paddock was comprised of a series of stalls running north to south and open facing east. It was here that groom, trainer, jockey and thoroughbred convened in the time leading up to horse and jockey entering the race course. Horses were saddled and any necessary equipment added (e.g., bit, blinkers, shadow rolls or bandages) before they were led across a short path to the walking ring. Surrounded by wood fencing, the walking ring was an opportunity for fans to come within a few feet of the thoroughbreds and their connections. At the center of the walking ring were a pair of majestic beech trees – one a European fern leaf and the other an American purple leaf – which offered shade to those using the ring. Above the paddock, of course, was yet another strategically placed tote board (short for totalizator) so fans could check the latest odds of the horses they were "giving the once-over."

"Let's head over to the box," urged Jasmine. "I suspect TJ will be using it today. He may have some guests to see our horse, *Cut To The Chase*, run in the stakes race." She also suggested they order from one of the food & beverage wait staffers serving the private boxes. "All this excitement has given me an appetite. What about you?"

Consuela couldn't agree more, while silently mulling over her compadre's use of the word "our" in referring to the horse her brother had entered in today's stakes race. Was she making too much of one, three-letter word? She was becoming increasingly interested in the relationship between brother and sister and intrigued by the Cutter family overall.

Chapter 32 – Bluegrass Sleuthing

"Amazing what people will share with a virtual stranger given an appropriate time and place," Calvin explained, as he presented initial findings to Sean.

The "place" had been The Old Talbott Tavern in Bardstown, not too far from the Wellingtons' Bourbonesque distillery. The "time" had been a succession of mid-week early evenings when locals needed to unwind before heading home from the day's work.

The Old Talbott had been built in 1779 and was considered within the Commonwealth the oldest western stagecoach stop in America. During the latter part of the 18th century, this tavern had been the Western terminus of the stagecoach road from Pennsylvania and Virginia. Architecturally, the thick Flemish bond stone walls, deep window casings, heavy ceiling timbers and built-in-cupboards were reminiscent of the Warwickshire Inns in England.

With his eight-hour shift at Bourbonesque starting at 11:00 p.m., "Carson Tobias" had found it easy enough to head over from Berea each Wednesday (patronage was sparse on Mondays and the crowd on Fridays was more the out-of-town variety) in time to grab dinner and a sarsaparilla, a sweetened carbonated beverage flavored with sassafras and oil distilled from a European birch. Soon after Carson arrived, the "regulars" – a combination of hourly workers at Bourbonesque, employees of small retail shops and area businesses, and local retirees – filtered in for some good drink, idle chat and perhaps a bite to eat.

After a month of Wednesdays, Carson was on a first-name basis with several members of the Bourbonesque clique, a teller at the local bank, and a long-time clerk at the U.S. Post Office in town. It was by schmoozing with these new connections that he'd learned of serious operational issues at Bourbonesque.

Carson ran through a few specifics he'd learned from company employees that ranged from poor equipment maintenance that caused faulty seals and cracks in the still which, in turn, led to premature replacement and higher than normal operational shutdowns...to poor ventilation where the still was located, leading to overheating and additional operational shutdowns...to failure to monitor critical readings in the distilling process. Further, he'd heard from multiple inside sources that the company seemed unable to effectively evaluate whether employees actually knew what they were doing.

The bank teller had let slip the sizable withdrawals from Bourbonesque's reserve savings account; multiple business checks written from Abigail Prescott Wellington, COO, to various suppliers of equipment required for the distillery, and three substantial transfers from Abigail's personal checking account to Bourbonesque LLC's primary business checking account.

The postal clerk had mentioned the arrival of a certified/ return-receipt-requested envelope sent from Steinberg Stavros Rogers & Co., Inc., to Bourbonesque LLC CFO Blake Tinsdale.

Of course, Carson Tobias hadn't asked outright about Bourbonesque. He did little more than what others had done: Wednesday after Wednesday *he filtered in for some good drink, idle chat and perhaps a bite to eat...AND LISTENED* – until he'd gathered enough intelligence to report back to his client.

After Irv Katzman had recruited Calvin Thomas to take on the sleuthing assignment. Irv, Calvin and Sean met to iron out deliverables, reporting methodology and payment details. This mid-March long-distance phone call had been the first of these deliverables.

Gathering intel at Thoroughbred Bs Farm was proving to be more challenging. In addition to the risk of being in close proximity to his targets (i.e., Abigail and Bentley Wellington), there was the sheer size of the Wellington estate itself.

Although Carson's position as part-time night watchman placed him on the Wellington family's property three times each week, the hours – 9 p.m. until 5 a.m. – were hardly conducive to accessing the plantation home, let alone sifting through files. So Calvin placed a call to Beth Feingold, asking her to deliver on what she'd indicated was a highly specialized vocational activity.

Covert surveillance had started as a part-time gig to make some pocket change during her years at Georgia Tech. Her dad had put Beth in touch with an attorney friend who'd developed a substantial practice representing women who wanted to divorce their cheating husbands. From time to time the attorney needed visual and/or audio surveillance of a residence for "evidentiary" purposes, be it the client's home or that of the husband's mistress. Through a connection with one of her professors, she'd been able to latch onto equipment appropriate for any number of situations.

Within a week, Calvin had received a small box from UPS at the Boone Tavern Hotel in Berea. In it were three items: a lighter with a voice-activated audio recorder that could lay dormant for up to 25 days using standby power until it heard audio to record…a digital voice-recording pen with the capability of recording close to 150 hours for up to 25 days…and an ultra-high-frequency (UHF) transmitter housed in a functional pocket calculator which could wirelessly transmit voice or other sound to a receiver.

New to the role of ensuring the security of an estate the size of the Wellington family's spread, Carson naturally had questions. He'd made an appointment three hours in advance of his first shift and engaged Abigail in an extended conversation that moved from her home office to the library and finally to the kitchen where hot cocoa in advance of a cold overnight was welcomed. Suggesting he get "the nickel tour" of the mansion so he could assess potential points of vulnerability, Abigail readily obliged. When they'd completed their tour of each room, it was 8:45 and time for Carson to start his shift.

Calvin Thomas had judged the evening a success. His photographic memory recorded details of each room, the locations of the four telephones in the home, and an assessment of the relative likelihood one Wellington (i.e., Abigail) would be talking to another (i.e., Bentley or Beauregard) in any particular room. He'd need an excuse for a second visit to place the covert bugs.

***

For the past few years, Easter Sunday had been a very special occasion at the Jeffries home. On April 3, 1983, Marci and her son, Sean, once again were sitting down to a baked Virginia ham dinner in her beautifully furnished Bentley Avenue Tudor home in Jersey City. Like a fine wine, Marci – now 55 – had aged well. Although she'd been asked on dates by numerous businessmen with whom she came in contact, Marci always found reason to turn away from social overtures. She'd been perfectly happy with her singular family role as a mother, watching her only son grow into a fine young man with a life full of opportunities in front of him now that he was close to completing his legal education.

Sean had always found Easter suppers for two as an occasion on which he fretted about his mom's future. She deserved companionship and he'd always been disappointed to learn about his mom refusing yet another chance to get to know a gentleman on a social basis.

So Sean had been both shocked and elated when his mom gave the go-ahead for her son to invite Denton Dandridge to dinner. Sean's favorite law professor at Seton Hall was representing the University of Georgia's Rusk Law Center at an international symposium in New York City under the auspices of the United Nations. Denton had accepted and even called Marci to tell her how gracious she'd been to have him to her home on Easter Sunday.

It was during dessert, Marci's home-made peach cobbler with vanilla ice cream, that the call had come from Berea, Kentucky. "It's for me, mom!" Sean called into the dining room from the wall-mounted phone in the kitchen. "I'm gonna take it upstairs."

It had been a little more than two weeks since Calvin's first report to Sean, one focusing almost exclusively on Bourbonesque LLC and based largely on hearsay.

In the interim, Carson had been able to gain access to the Wellington home, ostensibly to report some suspicious activity at the back of the main barn very early one morning. He'd chosen a time when Abigail was scheduled to be at a business meeting in Bardstown. Only Bentley, confined to a wheelchair and in the care of a home nurse, along with a butler and maid, were around.

Carson had placed the pen in the desk of Abigail's office, the pocket calculator between two books on ancient Greek and Roman history in the library, and the lighter at the bottom of a large plastic basket of odds and ends in the kitchen.

The timing was fortuitous because Calvin Thomas had been able to listen to the entirety of the Saturday, April 2nd meeting between Abigail and Beau, during which he'd learned of Abigail's growing frustration with her husband's unwillingness to spend the capital necessary to maintain Bourbonesque's physical plant, and Beau's recent meeting with Silverstein-Gladstone about plans to take Thoroughbred Bs Farm public with a $200 million IPO.

Of particular interest, Calvin noted, was Beau's focus on executive compensation, which he saw "as the best option for personally acquiring money to get out from under his growing debt." Calvin told Sean he could place those last words in quotes.

He then added: "Between that and Beau's earlier but seemingly cryptic remark: 'I've got that under control, Abby. You won't have to worry about it anymore,' I decided to do a little homework because we're likely talkin' two possibilities – gambling or drugs. I didn't have to go any further than reconnecting with a bookie who owes me a favor. He confirmed what I suspected."

Then Calvin quickly summarized other details captured by his transmitters, including Beau's questionable plans to use TBF funds to solve Bourbonesque's financial issues as well as his own personal debts, and Abigail's heightened concerns over the prospect of having to use her inheritance to keep Bourbonesque afloat.

"That's about it," Calvin concluded. You need me for anything else down here? Seems like you might have enough dirt to at least make some informed decisions on what to do next."

Calvin's report had Sean's mind racing. Clearly, he knew *where* he could avail himself of further details and updates on the Wellington situation. The question of *how* to come up with the goods without posing any danger to his mom and her career at Steinberg Stavros Rogers & Co. was another matter. "Let's consider this gig a wrap," was Sean's response. "Job really well done."

Carson Tobias now had to come up with a reason for suddenly severing ties with the Wellingtons. He'd probably use the tried-and-true line about "a new opportunity I just couldn't pass up."

Finally, Calvin Thomas would reacquaint himself with the mustache and curly hair he had abandoned for his assignment in the Commonwealth.

Chapter 33 – JFK to Düsseldorf

In Germany, the establishment and supervision of stock exchanges fall within the jurisdiction of the respective Bundesländer (federal states) in which particular stock exchanges are located. Typically, eine Börsenaufsichtsbehörde (an Exchange Supervisory Authority) is part of the Ministry of Economics in each federal state.

The North Rhine-Westphalia (NRW) Exchange Supervisory Authority oversees the Düsseldorf Wertpapierbörse (Düsseldorf Stock Exchange) or DWB. Specific areas of supervision include the DWB's internal organization, the admission of banks and other financial institutions, the listing of securities, and the proper conduct of trading and settlement of securities transactions. Under this last area is supervision of market price fixing, approval of the DWB's Börsenordnungen (rules of the Exchange), development of preventive measures and supervision of proper trading.

By virtue of its location in Wuppertal, GWH GmbH – along with any company plans to issue publicly traded securities – would fall under the oversight of the NRW Exchange Supervisory Authority.

On Memorial Day Monday, May 30, 1983 (not a holiday in Germany), David Katzman's first waking moments were spent on an international call to Bertram Krieger for a thorough briefing. Based on what the Mossad agent and the LKA NRW Police Force Investigation Bureau officer both knew regarding the Hauptmann situation, Krieger had called a case officer in the NRW Exchange Supervisory Authority, Jakob Seidel, to discuss temporarily blocking any GWH GmbH action related to the company's potential application for a public offering through the DWB.

Concluding their conversation, Katzman next booked a Lufthansa flight from JFK to Düsseldorf to meet with Krieger and Seidel. Before grabbing his "go bag" (he always had a week's worth of clothes and other travel necessities appropriate to his line of work at the ready), he made one more call, to Jorge Hauptmann. Rather than head over to his Bradley Beach summer residence, the Mossad agent opted for the immediacy of informing the young German of the situation by phone. He prefaced the news by emphasizing that his mom was safe and under the watchful eye of the LKA NRW.

While Katzman didn't believe Jorge or his dad were in imminent danger (Fabian had joined his son for a couple of days so they could catch up), he wanted to make sure neither of them had any notion of heading overseas to be with Gretchen.

Assured by Jorge that he'd solemnly promised his boss to be at work that day and that his dad "knows better than to head back to Hückeswagen," David then made his way from the makeshift living space he'd affectionately called "the shack" to Point Pleasant Beach to check in and let his dad know he'd be heading across the Atlantic.

***

Fran DeSantis was relieved to see Jorge's car pulling into the clubhouse parking lot that morning. Memorial Day was now much more likely to go smoothly when it came to "herding" the well-heeled among the day's customers from valet parking to the Will Call window and through the clubhouse admission turnstiles.

But Jorge's thoughts were far from Monmouth Park. He was still trying to digest what had happened to Hanna Schröder. If his mom hadn't asked her long-time assistant to tend to Pulver back at their home in Hückeswagen, it could well have been Gretchen's body found beside the Porsche coupe.

Jorge's knee-jerk reaction to the news had been to hop on the first jet to Düsseldorf to be with his mother. But he knew injecting himself into the situation would only complicate the investigation. David Katzman told him he'd be going to Düsseldorf that evening to meet with the lead police investigator, who now considered Hanna's death Ein schuldhafter Mord (a culpable homicide).

The Mossad agent also told Jorge the NRW Exchange Supervisory Authority had been brought into the rapidly expanding investigation.

Yet these revelations paled in comparison to what he'd been told about the wartime activities of both parents at the Binghamton Restaurant in Edgewater just two days ago.

"Brian Harper" agreed to allow David Katzman to tell his son about Fabian's war years, and so the Mossad agent had recapped the experiences of Herr Hauptman (spelled with one 'n'): hiding his Jewish identity while sheltering his fellow Jews in a secret basement at his Dresden home as they were making their way across the German border into Czechoslovakia, through the Balkans and eventually by sea to Palestine. This took place during World War II's early years. Later, because of his work as scheduler in Dresden's railway marshalling yard, Fabian (his last name now spelled with two 'n's) had access to planned movements of artillery- and munitions-laden trains – information he passed along to one of the few British SOE (Special Operations Executive) contacts within this region of Germany.

The Mossad agent yielded to Fabian when it came to telling Jorge about how Gretchen Weiß found herself working as a records keeper for the Nazis in the Terezin holding and transport center in Czechoslovakia. Jorge had listened to his father's rationale for giving Gretchen the benefit of the doubt, but that explanation was largely lost amidst the shock of the initial reveal.

***

Now headed to the airport, David Katzman reflected on the day's events: After all was said and done, he believed it best for Jorge to stay behind and continue working at Monmouth Park as if nothing of consequence had occurred in his life. He'd strongly suggested that Fabian return to Canada for the time being and resume his life as Brian Harper even though he wanted to remain to watch over his son. Until the North Rhine-Westphalian authorities could *definitively* assess the cause of the auto accident, and more to the point who'd been behind it, David would enlist the help of someone to do just that.

Before boarding his Lufthansa flight to Düsseldorf, David dialed a New Jersey number from the pay phone at JFK. After five rings, a recorded message began: "You've reached the home of Calvin Thomas. I'll be returning on Monday evening at about 8:00 p.m. Please leave a name, number and detailed message. I'll get back to you as soon as I can."

Chapter 34 –Ilvento's, Part Deux

One of the highly useful skills Marci Davis had honed during her time as an aide to Kentucky Governor Bentley Wellington was the ability to eavesdrop – whether it be overhearing a conversation between a journalist and his source a couple of tables away at a noisy restaurant, picking up a whispered discussion between two political hacks in a crowded meeting room, or listening in on a highly sensitive phone call taking place behind a closed door.

The advancing years had not diminished this skill, although a particular trait of her son, Sean, did not make it terribly difficult in this instance. Marci often chided Sean about his loud voice, reminding him he wasn't "addressing Congress" when engaging in one-to-one communication. This habit carried over to Sean's decibel level during phone conversations.

Marci's skill and Sean's trait came together on the evening of April 3, 1983, Easter Sunday. The telephone rang at the Jeffries home in Jersey City, with Sean quickly leaving the dinner table to answer the call from the kitchen wall phone. Hearing Calvin Thomas on the other end, he'd shouted in the direction of the dining room: "It's for me, mom. I'm gonna take it upstairs."

Sean bounded up the stairs to the family study, picked up the phone receiver, waited for the click indicating his mom had hung up the kitchen phone and swung the door shut, although it remained slightly ajar.

After 10 minutes Marci began to feel a bit uncomfortable, not because she was alone with Professor Dandridge but because it was certainly not good etiquette for Sean to leave the table for so long. "Would you excuse me, professor? I'm going to see what's taking Sean so long. It's not like him to be so ill-mannered."

"It's Denton, Marci. Please call me Denton."

Marci smiled and headed upstairs to the study. Given Sean's telephone voice, however, she heard him before setting foot on the second-floor landing. With the door open a crack, Marci stopped at the end of the hallway. Apparently in mid-discussion, Sean had been talking with...whom? Within a few minutes, she'd learned the person at the other end of the line was an individual named Calvin.

While the name meant nothing to her, the topic of conversation left her reeling. When it seemed as though Sean and Calvin were finishing up, Marci crept back downstairs to the dining room.

"He'll be down in another minute, Denton," Marci informed her guest. "So how do you enjoy teaching at the Rusk Center while getting back into client work in Sandy Springs," she asked while trying very hard to set aside all that was spinning around in her head.

***

The conversation Marci had overheard prompted some serious and perhaps long-overdue reflection on her feelings about the Wellingtons, that infamous trip to San Francisco, and how radically her life had changed since. The rapid pace of events in the weeks after that meeting in Louisville – her move to Jersey City, changing her name, taking on a new job in New York City and the birth of her son – hadn't really given her an opportunity to consider just how much she had loved her career in Kentucky politics.

Instead, motherly instincts kicked into high gear and dominated her life. Sure, she'd turned the job given to her into a successful business career at Steinberg Stavros Rogers & Co. Because the firm's focus was on the energy and transportation sectors, Marci's transition from governor's aide in Kentucky to industry analyst in Manhattan had been made that much easier. Marci had also been able to make the two-story Tudor house on Bentley Avenue into a *home*, spiritually as well as decoratively. She owed that success to Uncle Lou, who'd done everything in his power to provide a warm and loving home life after the death of Marci's parents.

As her thoughts turned to Uncle Lou, she felt a deep sadness. What had been an extremely close relationship was forever changed with her sudden relocation. No longer living within a couple of hours of the home in which she was raised, Marci had lost the ability to see him whenever she wanted. One of her most memorable weekends occurred when Sean, then a sophomore guard at FDU, had traveled to play the University of Louisville Cardinals. Marci made the trip and stayed with Lou over the weekend. He'd been so proud as the two of them watched Sean play at Freedom Hall.

When Lou passed a few years back, Marci had allowed herself only the briefest time to grieve. But now she felt an emptiness, and it wasn't simply because of the loss of family. No, it was more than that. Marci had stayed away from social entanglements. The fact that only last week Denton Dandridge was the first man to be a guest in Marci's home underscored the point. What she'd begun to feel now was a slowly emerging anger. She was angry at herself for allowing a horrific personal experience – nightmarish in its unfolding and immediate aftermath – to crush the life out of her.

But even more, Marci now found herself increasingly furious – albeit some 27 years after the fact – that a wealthy, prominent individual could perpetrate such an egregious assault on her, then "kick things under a rug" by buying her silence with a roof over her head, a respectable job with plenty of miles between them, and enough cash for her to raise their unborn baby.

Ever since the article on the Wellingtons appeared in *The Sunday Times*, Marci had been keenly aware of events transpiring in Kentucky. And in her role at Steinberg Stavros, she was now in a position to corroborate information Sean had obtained from this Calvin person.

As if jolted from a Rip Van Winkle trance, Marci felt a great need to help her son. In fact, her sudden call to action actually was as much to help herself. She'd help Sean on two conditions: First, whatever his plans were, it couldn't involve personal legal jeopardy. He'd accomplished too much and had come too far both in his law school education and his overall development as a young man to risk his future. Hopefully, he hadn't yet done anything to cross that line. Second, in assisting Sean she would not jeopardize her own career or reputation.

Meanwhile, Marci found herself unexpectedly attracted to Professor Dandridge...uh, Denton.

***

Marci took not one, but two nights to "sleep on it," finally asking Sean if they could talk over dinner at Ilvento's on Thursday. Not on a Friday or Saturday, which could ruin the weekend, but on the penultimate weekday which would leave 24 hours to reflect, regroup and move on before heading into a couple of days without the trials and tribulations of work.

Sean, remembering their last mother-to-son conversation at their favorite neighborhood restaurant, suspected the discussion would be of the "heavy" variety. He drove from Bentley Avenue to Journal Square where he'd pick up his mother who called from the PATH station.

Sean was still contemplating his next move based on the information Calvin Thomas had provided as he turned in yet another virtuoso parallel-parking performance by squeezing his Dodge Challenger between a 1982 Cadillac Seville and a 1981 Lincoln Continental on his first attempt. He chuckled to himself, surmising that "Nick and Tony" would be pleased he hadn't so much as touched either the rear bumper of the Caddy or the front bumper of the Lincoln. Always polite, Sean rushed around the front of the Caddy (there wasn't enough room for him to fit between his car and the Cadillac's rear bumper) to open the door for his mother. Closing it, he escorted her behind the Lincoln and across the street to Ilvento's dining-room entrance.

No matter the situation and regardless of who she was speaking to, Marci knew of no other way than to be direct and to the point. So immediately after mother and son placed their dinner orders with the waitress, Marci opened with a simple statement followed by an even simpler question: "The other night I overheard part of your conversation about the Wellingtons' business situation. How can I help?"

Sean sat across the table a bit stunned. For all the world, he thought his mom was going to tell him she'd become interested in Denton Dandridge. While he was correct in this particular assessment, he'd missed badly in terms of what was on his mom's mind. What followed from Sean was part confession, part status report in what had been an hour-long brain dump that left Marci nonplussed.

From Marci's perspective, Sean's reaction to her "tell-all" story the first time they sat at Ilvento's for a" heart-to-heart" seemed to have been one of acceptance and pride in how she'd handled the situation with no discernible impact on Sean's psyche. Now Marci was learning about her son's slow burn – evidently eight years' worth of slow burn – over the horrific actions of Bentley Wellington more than a quarter century ago.

Straying from her lifelong habit of providing counsel and offering an opinion only when asked, Marci demanded that Sean stay within the legal guardrails in his efforts to right what he perceived to be a grave injustice perpetrated against his mother. "You've worked so hard...you've come so far...you've lived the right way. *Do not* run afoul of the law."

Marci then laid her cards on the table:

"Whatever you decide to do, know that *any* ill will we might harbor toward the Wellington family should be confined to the former Governor. Whatever his faults, Beau is your half-brother and may not even know you exist. I was not the only victim of Bentley's behavior. Whatever his marital relationship had been with Abigail before San Francisco, it surely had to be damaged afterwards.

"I am sure Abigail knows there was a child born as a result of her husband's behavior. And she may even hold a grudge against me because of some misguided notion that I had encouraged the Governor's advances.

"I, for one, long ago decided to move on and make the best of the situation presented to me. I don't think we've done too bad for ourselves. I've built a successful career at a first-rate firm in the world's financial center, have a beautiful home to be proud of...and I have a wonderful son who seems to have limitless opportunities just ahead of him. It's also quite possible that after all these years, I may have found someone in whom I am interested socially.

"You know my firm handles the Wellington family's assets. Beau is working with Silverstein-Gladstone on his IPO, but our firm clearly has a role in providing information and documents related to SEC filing requirements. I'll tell you straight away that I have no reason to deal with that area of the firm and have no intention of doing so. I am willing to offer opinion, however. From what I overheard of your conversation with Calvin, Beau may be on the precipice of jeopardizing *all* of his family's business holdings.

"Beau's actions could well be an attempt at a money grab dressed as an IPO, with his personal need for cash – and lots of it – creating the very real potential for turning his operation into a white-collar criminal enterprise. The key question would appear to be: Is this pending IPO the result of a genuine business plan? Or is his growing need for cash governing his decision to use the IPO as a means of doing so?"

Then came a stunning final assessment from Marci, one that surprised her as much as it did Sean. "If what I overheard – and I apologize for being in the wrong place at the wrong time, but I've told you so many times about how loud you talk...If what I overheard had come from a stranger, I'd already have reported this information to the appropriate people at my firm. As it is, I'm uncomfortable just knowing what I now know."

Sean sat in silence for several minutes. Marci shared his silence, knowing her son was taking his time to digest what she'd said. For that matter Marci was processing her words as well, having come as an atypical stream of consciousness.

Close to finishing his formal legal education and with a bar exam not far off on the horizon, Sean's legal mind had taken over. There were unknown future shareholders who would be placing their trust and money in those managing the new public enterprise. Then there were the dozens upon dozens of employees at Thoroughbred Bs Farm, Triple-B Racing Stables, Bourbonesque LLC and the Wellington family estate who would bear the brunt of any misdeeds affecting the daily operations of their employers.

But Silverstein-Gladstone had a battery of attorneys to do background checks on its clientele and to help draft and review the content of Securities & Exchange Commission filing documents, not to mention attorneys at the SEC itself along with state regulatory authorities and stock exchange officials from the NYSE, AMEX or NASDAQ, depending on which exchange public shares would be traded.

Sean wasn't looking to be a "whistle blower," particularly given how he'd come by some of the juicier aspects of the intelligence (i.e., via some highly illegal "bugs" planted by a gumshoe for hire). There was another person...another family...and dozens of other individuals whose lives could be damaged if current events were left to run their course.

If nothing else, it seemed to Sean that he'd need to alert TJ Cutter, an increasingly prominent young figure in thoroughbred industry circles and a person with whom he had become familiar if not directly acquainted during his years working at Monmouth Park.

Finally breaking his silence, Sean responded to his mother's pleas. His response reflected the quick but deep impact his mom's words had on his thinking: "I hear what you're saying and I understand where you're coming from," Sean began. He continued by going over his thought process, indicating he would let the checks and balances put in place by the various federal and state bodies regulating the capital markets as well as Silverstein-Gladstone's own due diligence process run their course.

"There's one exception," Sean concluded. "I need to have a very private conversation with TJ Cutter. His business and family don't deserve to be blindsided by this situation." Marci nodded in agreement. Remembering that opening day of Monmouth Park's meet this season was May 27th, less than two months away, he began planning for an impromptu get-together with Mr. Cutter on that Friday.

Chapter 35 – Change in Riders

There was a very business-like conversation going on just outside the Monmouth Park jockeys' clubhouse between TJ Cutter, owner and trainer of *Cut To The Chase*, and Chris McCardle, agent for jockey Angel Barrera. It was only recently that McCardle had negotiated an arrangement between his client and Cutter.

Cutter, who based a modest number of horses from his family's Cutting Edge Stables at Monmouth Park, had predicated his decision to secure the services of Barrera on the Dominican jockey's record of success at the Oceanport, NJ track over the past several years. For his part, McCardle had certainly been amenable to offering conditional exclusivity for Barrera's services to Cutter given Cutting Edge Stables' high success rate at Monmouth. During last year's meeting, in fact, Cutter had saddled 12 winners in 23 mounts for a gaudy 52 per cent success rate.

The discussion taking place had been about the difference of opinion between McCardle and Barrera as to which riding assignment for the Nijinsky II Stakes they should accept. In addition to Cutter's thoroughbred, installed as the second choice by the Monmouth Park handicapper, Barrera had "first call" on the morning-line favorite, the Beau Wellington-owned-and-trained *B Kind To Your Enemies*. Unbeknownst to Cutter, that decision had already been made by Angel Barrera, who told his agent he'd be riding Wellington's entry.

But before Chris McCardle could tell Cutter, Angel Barrera emerged from the clubhouse as if on cue and asked his agent, "¿le dijiste" ("Did you tell him?")

Cutter, well-versed in Spanish backstretch talk, turned to Angel and replied: "¿Dime lo que estás montando caballo de Wellington" ("Tell me what? You're riding Wellington's horse?") Cutter understood Angel's dilemma and had anticipated the possibility of Barrera choosing to go with Wellington's horse. After all, Barrera had ridden *B Kind To Your Enemies* to victory in the colt's previous start at Churchill Downs on Derby weekend. He'd never been aboard the Cutting Edge Stables 2-year-old.

Just because TJ Cutter *understood* didn't necessarily mean

he'd give Angel a free pass on abandoning his first opportunity to be productive for his new connection. "Tanto para acuerdos contractuales." ("So much for contractual arrangements.") Cutter feigned taking offense to the Dominican jockey's decision. Turning back to McCardle, he patted the agent on the shoulder and said, "We'll talk later." With that, the boss of Cutting Edge Stables headed off to another morning meeting in hopes of landing his preferred jockey alternative for *Cut To The Chase*.

***

It was rare for a jockey to win a thoroughbred race with anything other than a "live" mount – that is, a horse whose trainer had the entry prepped to give a top effort. The past performance charts and workouts published in *The Daily Racing Form* offered a wealth of data handicappers could apply to a specific race. But it didn't reveal the long-range plans and short-term strategies a horse's connections (i.e., trainer and owner) might employ and how they fit into that same race.

A current race might be used to prepare a thoroughbred for an upcoming competition...whether to assess the horse's affinity for a particular surface and/or distance, to meet the conditions of a future race (e.g., non-winners of two races), or to come back from a long layoff rather than using a series of workouts to prep for a top effort. All of which explains, at least in part, why some thoroughbreds whose data points might suggest success nevertheless came up with "disappointing" performances (at least in the eyes and wallets of the betting public), while other entries whose data points would seemingly require bettors to take a pass wound up with "surprising" winning efforts.

It's not as if trainers had been unaware of Stevie Thorn's considerable riding skills as Monmouth Park's 1983 meet opened. With the added advantage of an apprentice's weight allowance, Thorn and his agent, Jean Archambault, had been the beneficiaries of "live" mounts from trainers eager to use the young jockey's services. The sample size had been incredibly small, but in his six opening-day mounts Thorn had entered the winner's circle five times! The bug-boy's tour de force included victorious races on dirt and turf, in a sprint and route-going distance, as well as under claiming and allowance conditions.

So it didn't take a crystal ball to predict TJ Cutter's first conversation upon learning of Angel Barrera's choice of mount in the ungraded Nijinsky II Stakes would be with Frenchman Jean Archambault. The former jockey had carved out a well-deserved reputation as a hardnosed competitor in European thoroughbred racing circles, and now served as an agent to some of the leading stateside jockeys including Australian apprentice Stevie Thorn.

Cutter spotted Archambault just inside the main building. He was inspecting the day's program changes which had been posted in a glass-encased bulletin board. Included were the day's scratches, overweight entries (i.e., a rider couldn't make the assigned weight), equipment changes and updated jockey assignments. Under race #7, the jockey now listed for *B Kind To Your Enemies* was Angel Barrera. *Cut To The Chase* was currently listed as having "no rider."

Archambault finished reading and turned to face Cutter: "Bonjour, Monsieur Cutter. I see you are in need of Monsieur Thorn's services, yes?"

"As a matter of fact, I am," answered TJ. "Stevie was quite impressive yesterday. I may not have much available here at Monmouth because of my arrangement with Angel Barrera. But I've been known to ship a few of my better horses over to Belmont and up to the Spa. Let's see what Stevie can do this afternoon."

A few moments later, TJ Cutter was on his way up to the stewards' office to submit a "change in riders" form, replacing "no rider" with Stevie Thorn on *Cut To The Chase*.

Chapter 36 – "Persons of Interest"

The Lufthansa overnight flight had been uneventful, but David Katzman wasn't looking forward to a workday without at least a few hours' shuteye, a shave and a shower. Fortunately, he'd been able to arrange for early check-in at the recently opened Hotel Haus Rheinblick, roughly eight kilometers from the airport. He'd be in decent shape for the meeting with NRW officials at 1400 Stunden.

Unaccustomed to dressing in business attire, Katzman forced himself into a navy pinstriped suit, white buttoned-down shirt with a solid burgundy tie, black nylon socks and black wing-tipped shoes. Soon after hailing a taxi, he found himself at the front entrance of the LKA NRW, North Rhine-Westphalia's State Investigation Bureau.

At the Rezeption (front desk), Katzman gave his full name to the security officer, offered his Israeli Intelligence credentials for inspection and provided the name of the person with whom he had an appointment. Today's quickly arranged meeting involved Bertram Krieger, his initial point of contact with the LKA NRW; Gustav Zimmermann, the officer-in-charge of the NRW Police Force inspection team investigating the circumstances under which Hanna Schröder lost her life; and Jakob Seidel, case officer for the NRW Exchange Supervisory Authority and the individual who'd be determining whether the events surrounding the death of Vorsitzende Hauptmann's administrative assistant warranted any action with respect to the possible initial public offering of securities by GWH GmbH to the investing public.

Katzman was escorted by another uniformed officer down a lengthy hallway until they reached a double-doored entrance to a conference room. Her knock was quickly answered by a male voice: "Bitte kommen Sie herein." (Please come in.) The doors opened to a simple wood table with several empty wood chairs running the length of the room.

Seated at the far end were two individuals, one in uniform and the other in a gray pinstriped suit. The Mossad agent assumed the uniformed person was Zimmermann and the "suit" was Seidel. Extending a hand was Bertram Krieger: "Ich freue mich, dass Sie so bald kommen könnten." (I am pleased you could come so soon.")

Confirming Katzman's assumption on the identity of the two individuals, Krieger made the introductions and motioned for his guest to take the first open seat opposite Seidel and Zimmermann. Before sitting in the chair at the head of the table, Krieger removed four thick manila folders from a credenza behind him. He handed one to each person, keeping one for himself.

Each folder contained 13 dossiers, one on each member of GWH GmbH's Advisory Board (Dieter Hartmann, Elina Lang-Haas, Mia Mangels, Harald Schneider, Barnard Scholz, Eckhardt Vogt and Vorsitzende Gretchen Weiß Hauptmann); one on each member of the firm's Management team (Wolfgang Becker, the chief exec; Engel Fischer, head of operations; Garrick Imhoff, R&D director; Dr. Wilhelm Fuchs, head of strategic planning, and Dedrick Walter, CFO) and one on Hanna Schröder. At the top of the dossiers for Wolfgang Becker, Dr. Wilhelm Fuchs and Dieter Hartmann were red asterisks, marks that caused the Mossad agent to raise his eyebrows.

Krieger caught Katzman's reaction and answered the question: "Becker, Fuchs and Hartmann are members of the Nationaldemokratische Partei Deutschlands" (National Democratic Party of Germany).

Katzman's next thought had more to do with whether they'd be bringing in some form of sustenance or taking a break to eat at an area restaurant. He guessed the exigencies of the matter at hand would outweigh the need for temporary relief from the four walls of the LKA NRW conference room.

Chapter 37 – Consuela Meets TJ and "Guests"

The digital clock on the infield tote board hadn't yet reached 2:00, but Consuela was already mentally drained and physically exhausted. Jasmine was close behind, although more from witnessing her companion's emotional gyrations than from her own excitement with the first two races. "Beginner's luck" had struck in a big way, with both women winning more than a thousand dollars while wagering all of four bucks.

From the area near the escalator landing, Jasmine led Consuela to the top of the first of three aisles from which customers could descend steps to several rows of private boxes. "Hi Sam, long time no see," said Jasmine while reaching out to give the clubhouse's senior-most usher a warm hug. Sam Goodman was smartly dressed in the official usher's uniform: white pants and white buttoned-down collar oxford shirt, a navy tie patterned with white horse heads, navy blazer with gold buttons and a Monmouth Park insignia on the left pocket, a captain's cap and white buckskin shoes. Like a fine wine, Sam Goodman seemed to improve with age.

"Good to see you, Jasmine," answered Sam. Anticipating her question, the usher let her know of her brother's whereabouts: "TJ's upstairs in the Dining Terrace meeting with someone. He has only one guest today, so there's plenty of room for you and your friend."

Blushing slightly, Jasmine quickly added: "Where are my manners? Sam, this is Consuela Parks Pettiford. Consuela, this is Sam Goodman, a living legend here in the Monmouth Park clubhouse."

Sam and Consuela exchanged greetings, after which Sam led the women down to the first row, wiped clean a pair of green wooden chairs with his fluffy gray dusting mitt and stepped to the side. "Your hostess is Chandra. She'll be along in a couple of minutes to see if you'd like something to eat or drink," he said as he retreated to the top of the stairs.

But before the hostess appeared, another person made his way toward the box. "So this is where you're spending the long holiday weekend?" a familiar voice asked. It was her arcade boss, Irv Katzman. "Well, it's good to see you're not getting into any trouble," he quipped. "Does your brother know you're here?" As a long-time acquaintance of TJ Cutter, Irv was quite familiar with the circumstances under which TJ had asked him to give his sister a job at the arcade.

"Still trouble-free. And no, my brother doesn't know I'm here yet. By the way, who's minding the store while you're here gambling away the profits?" Jasmine had always been able to give as good as she got.

"The Mrs. has things covered, don't you worry," said Irv. "Your brother and I haven't spoken in quite a while and we thought today would be a good time to catch-up."

Making sure to not repeat her earlier mistake, Jasmine quickly introduced Consuela to Irv, describing her as a successful attorney living on the West side and working for a prestigious Manhattan law firm. "Jasmine seems particularly proud of her friend," Irv observed to himself, leading him to wonder just how they'd met and what (if anything) might be brewing between the two.

Native New Yorkers, Irv and Consuela immediately began chatting about events taking place over the past few years in their city, a discussion that encompassed everything from current Mayor Ed Koch, the opening of the *Trump Tower's* pink marble atrium at 721-725 Fifth Avenue, the press conference at which Billie Jean King had revealed her lesbian relationship and the N.Y.P.D.'s raid on *Blues*, a Times Square gay bar frequented by black and Latino men.

Jasmine listened with rapt attention, fascinated by animated exchanges as the young lawyer of Latino and African-American background butted heads with the retired Jewish New York City cop. She found herself increasingly drawn to Consuela, thinking her emerging relationship with this woman might be – what?... something much more than a passing fancy?

In the meantime, Chandra had come to the box for food & drink requests. There was unanimity in their preferences: three jumbo kosher franks with fries and large Cokes with plenty of ice. As they ate, the conversation shifted to the Jersey shore. Jasmine was grateful for the opportunity to participate. Engrossed in their discussion, the three didn't notice the third, fourth and fifth races had come and gone.

Now closing in on the four o'clock hour, Jasmine looked up

to see her older brother briskly heading down the steps to the box. TJ Cutter's face broadened into a big smile at the sight of a seemingly happy and well-rested Jasmine there at the track to visit. Immediately in front of her brother was someone she didn't know – a young and attractive African-American man she guessed was the person with whom TJ had been meeting.

Jasmine stood up and first leaned past the stranger to give her brother a big hug. She then extended her hand. "Hi, I'm Jasmine, TJ's sister. This is my friend, Consuela Parks Pettiford, and Irv Katzman, who I work for in Seaside Heights." Then looking at her brother, "TJ, Consuela Parks Pettiford, an attorney from New York I met over the weekend."

If TJ was surprised at the background of his sister's friend, he didn't show it. Meanwhile, Sean was certainly taken aback at running into Irv Katzman here at the track. He wondered how Cutter's sister had come to work for Irv. Maybe he'd find out at some point today.

"Nice to meet you. I'm Sean Jeffries." The private boxes at Monmouth Park were configured in two rows of four seats. The ladies, who'd been sitting in the second row with Irv, now relocated themselves to the front row. Sean took the far seat in the back row, allowing Irv to sit next to him and giving TJ the aisle seat.

"Hey Jasmine." TJ said, "Things are about to get busy for me with the 7th race coming up. If you and your friend don't have plans, how about joining Irv, Sean and me for dinner. I have reservations at The Molly Pitcher Inn in Red Bank. We can all have a leisurely meal and catch up."

Jasmine looked at Consuela, whose smile was all the answer she needed. Sounding a bit more excited than she'd planned, she quickly answered: "We'd love to!"

With that, TJ Cutter left the box to tend to the primary business of the day – preparing *Cut To The Chase* for the Nijinsky II Stakes. Looking back as he bounded up the stairs, he added: "If our guy happens to win, how about getting your butts downstairs for a presentation in the winner's circle."

Upon TJ's departure, Irv and Sean exchanged looks at each other as if to say: "What the hell are you doing here?" Each wondered who was more surprised by the chance encounter. They hadn't been face-to-face since their December dinner at the Hyatt in Atlanta. Both had to be thinking the upcoming dinner at the Molly Pitcher

Inn would be interesting to say the least.

Before heading down to the paddock, TJ paid an unscheduled visit to Fran DeSantis's clubhouse Will Call office, one of the few locations at Monmouth Park from which outside telephone calls could be placed. He felt obligated to inform two other members of his dinner party that his sister, her friend and Sean Davis Jeffries would be joining him at the Molly Pitcher Inn.

Chapter 38 – Bug Boy on a Tear

Following each race, grooms walked entries for the next event from the barn area behind the backstretch through a gated opening to the dirt course. From there, they guided the horses around the far turn, through the home stretch in front of the grandstand, and then turned right onto the path separating grandstand from clubhouse that led to the walking ring and paddock.

It was here that trainers and jockeys came together to go over strategy and to make sure their charges were properly saddled. A walk around the ring was followed by the announcement, "Riders up!" Jockeys were helped onto their mounts and began the procession from walking ring to the track for pre-race warm-ups. Even for races scheduled to be run on the turf, pre-race warm-ups at Monmouth Park took place on the dirt course.

There were 10 horses entered in the 7th race, which in all likelihood meant a free-for-all out of the starting gate to establish position. For any frontrunners in post positions 8, 9 and 10, the trick would be quickly moving across the width of the course before the bulk of the field blocked their path. Much depended upon how horses to the inside broke at the bell. For those on the inside (post positions 1 through 3), the challenge was not to get buried on the rail and be trapped behind a wall of horses in what would be a very short sprint.

This early-season stakes race appeared to be a two-horse battle between Triple-B Racing Stables' morning-line favorite, *B Kind To Your Enemies*, and Cutting Edge Stables' *Cut To The Chase*, the Monmouth Park handicapper's second choice. The former had drawn post-position 4; the latter would break from the number-10 slot.

For Beau Wellington the draw had been kind, enabling jockey Angel Barrera either to move to the front without tremendous exertion or to lay just off the pace until his charge was ready to dig in for a run to the finish. For TJ Cutter, the draw offered far less flexibility. Against Wellington's horse, attempting to take the lead from the far outside would be suicidal. And laying back with the task of picking up nine horses in less than three-quarters of a mile offered equally poor prospects. For this race, the ability of Stevie Thorn to negotiate a position toward the back end of the first group of horses (Cutter estimated laying fourth or fifth) would be critical.

Knowing *B Kind To Your Enemies* and his connections, TJ believed his primary competition would move to the lead if nobody else was interested in setting a reasonable opening quarter (say 22.1 to 22.4). A faster pace and Angel Barrera would have his charge laying second or third. Thorn's task after the break was to stay just outside the favorite, stalk him through the half and overtake him in deep stretch. The key question in Cutter's mind was: "Would there be enough real estate to do the job?"

TJ Cutter's assessment after meeting with Stevie Thorn was that the jockey conveyed a quiet confidence yet wasn't hesitant about asking all the right questions about his 2-year-old colt's tendencies. (Did he have a preferred lead? How did he react to the whip?)

But what made the most lasting impression was Thorn's observation on weather conditions: "I'm not so sure we should lay outside of Barrera's horse – at least not for the first quarter. There's been a stiff breeze blowing in the face of the first couple of horses down the backstretch today and it's a factor. If we tuck in more *behind* the pace, we can benefit from a drafting effect. Let Barrera face the wind. Whatever it takes out of him might spell the difference."

Having digested this bit of information, TJ Cutter simply responded: "Do what you feel is best."

In another paddock stall, Beau Wellington and Angel Barrera were having their own pre-race strategy session. But if calm, rational discussion ruled the Cutter/Thorn camp, anxiety appeared to be the overarching theme of the Wellington/Barrera connection. For Barrera, anxiety had come in the form of Stevie Thorn's white-hot start to the meet. For Wellington, anxiety had more to do with a rather sizable five-figure wager he'd placed on his colt with one of his bookmaking connections.

"Our colt hasn't raced since you wired the field three weeks ago at Churchill Downs," Beau began. "This is an eighth of a mile shorter and we breezed him 5 furlongs on Belmont's turf course at 58 and change. He's ready for a winning effort," he continued. "Watch your fractions for the quarter and half. If we're at 45, we should be home," Beau concluded ... well almost. "And whatever you do, *"don't give up the lead to Cutter's horse."* With that, Wellington smacked a folded program in the palm of his hand.

***

Back at Cutter's private box, Jasmine suggested Consuela, Irv and Sean join her in watching the horses enter the track from the path between the clubhouse and grandstand. "Then we'll be close to the winner's circle in case we're needed for a presentation."

Before heading downstairs, Jasmine and Consuela made their third wagers of the day – this one a tad more than their previous two bets. Sauntering over to the $100 window, each took a C-note from their winnings and asked the teller for "one hundred to win on number 10." Irv, whose retirement business dealt in nickels, dimes and quarters, had never been a betting man while Sean, not wanting to jinx the ladies, simply said: "I'll take a pass."

Nine minutes after entering the dirt track for the race, 10 2-year-old colts were loaded into the starting gate for the 5½ furlong turf sprint. While Jasmine and company became clubhouse railbirds for the race, TJ Cutter took up a more strategic position along the finish line on the grandstand side.

With the last on-track wagers placed, the totalizator board showed odds for the favorite, *B Kind To Your Enemies*, at 8-5 while *Cut To The Chase* remained the close second choice at 2-1. In choosing the former as the number-one choice, the general betting public seemed to be focusing on Angel Barrera's choice of the Triple-B Racing Stables entry as his mount and the poor post position of Cutting Edge Stables' charge in a speed-favoring sprint.

The bell rang, the mechanical starting gates opened and 10 thoroughbreds took their first strides. *B Kind To Your Enemies* broke from the number-four post position and went directly to the front without much effort. At the same time, *Cut To The Chase* took three strides straight ahead. As his charge cleared several horses to the left, Stevie Thorn tapped his right flank to move the colt toward what now was a lead group of four. Per the pre-race observation Thorn shared with Cutter, he made sure *Cut To The Chase* tucked in behind (as opposed to outside) the leaders.

At the same time, Thorn's internal stopwatch told him his

primary adversary had likely gone the first quarter in 21 and change. Three horses in the lead group began to fade as they approached the sole turn in the race. Thorn now took his charge three wide to allow the tired horses to drop back. The half was run in 44.4.

Then something unfolded in front of him that he hadn't anticipated. *B Kind To Your Enemies* began to drift and was taking the turn too wide. Was it possibly due to the turf workout the colt had at Belmont, where the turns weren't nearly as pronounced? Rather than move on Barrera's charge immediately, Thorn waited a couple of seconds longer. Then he asked *Cut To The Chase* to change leads and accelerate, allowing his colt to pass Barrera on the inside.

At the wire *Cut To The Chase* was 1½ lengths the better horse, finishing the 5½ furlongs in a crisp 1:01.3, less than a second off the track record. The tote board showed fractions of 21.3 for the quarter and 44.4 for the half. The final three-sixteenths of a mile had been run in 16.4.

***

The winner's circle at Monmouth Park was crowded for the post-race presentation. Groom Dudley Buchanan held the reins with Stevie Thorn still aboard. TJ Cutter, flanked on the left by Irv Katzman and Sean Davis Jeffries and on the right by his sister Jasmine and Consuela Parks Pettiford, stood in the foreground as the track photographer memorialized the occasion. A silver plate, to be inscribed at a later date with the names of the winning entry, owner, trainer and jockey, was presented to Cutter by a senior member of Canada's United Nations delegation, a nod to the fact that Nijinsky II was Canadian bred. In its current state, the plate was saved from complete emptiness only by the name (Nijinsky II Stakes) and date (May 28, 1983) of the race.

Thorn jumped off the colt and took his saddle into the weight room as per post-race protocol. Meanwhile, Buchanan threw a blanket over the colt and began the long walk back to the space reserved for Cutting Edge Stables' thoroughbreds behind the Monmouth Park backstretch.

Not more than 30 paces from the winner's circle, a rather heated discussion was taking place between the trainer and jockey of *B Kind To Your Enemies*.

For Angel Barrera, anxiety had been replaced by frustration at once again losing to Stevie Thorn.

For Beauregard Wellington, anger and panic were emotions of the moment. First, the anger. He'd seen his horse take a wide turn and couldn't help but think back to the Belmont workout he'd arranged on a turf course radically different from that of the Oceanport track. And he rued his last words to Barrera, emphatically demanding he not give up the lead to TJ Cutter's horse under any circumstances. Damaging fractions of 21.3 and 44.4 had been a result of that demand.

Second was the panic. Beau had fallen even deeper into the gambler's abyss and would have to head back to Lexington in a world of hurt. He honestly didn't know which would be worse, facing his mother...or dealing with his father.

The exchange between Beau and Angel went largely unnoticed by those close by who were heading to cashier windows to collect on winning tickets...or burying their heads in *The Daily Racing Form* to handicap the next race...or finishing off their third or fourth beer and were too far gone to care. But three individuals did in fact take note – TJ Cutter, Irv Katzman and Sean Davis Jeffries.

Chapter 39 – Sean's Second Shot

After his earlier meeting with Jean Archambault to secure the services of Stevie Thorn for the Nijinsky II Stakes that afternoon, TJ had returned to his customary Dining Terrace table on the third floor of the clubhouse for lunch. He'd invited Irv Katzman to be his guest, but the retired New York City cop would not be arriving until later in the day. Irv had done TJ a big-time favor by giving his sister Jasmine a part-time job at his Seaside Heights arcade. Not hearing much from Jasmine in recent days, Cutter was hoping Irv could give him an update on how his sister was handling things now that activity was on the upswing at the Jersey shore resort town.

TJ was set to enjoy a jumbo shrimp cocktail when he spotted a well-dressed, good-looking African-American man walking purposefully toward his table. TJ judged him to be in his mid- to late-20s.

"Fran DeSantis said you'd likely be at your usual table," said Sean. "My name is Sean Davis Jeffries. I spent three summers working here in clubhouse admissions while attending FDU. Currently, I'm completing my law degree at Seton Hall. I was hoping to talk with you yesterday, but you were occupied with Mr. Wellington. My family has had what you might call an 'interesting' relationship with the Wellingtons over the years and we're in a position to know of their business plans moving forward. That's why I need to speak with you."

Cutter was not in the habit of taking meetings with strangers. But given Wellington's surprising proposal the day before, he wasn't about to ignore the young man standing in front of him. "Have a seat, Sean. You have me at a distinct disadvantage. You obviously know me and are at least somewhat familiar with the Wellingtons." Looking at his watch, he continued: "I have some time. First, tell me more about yourself. Then tell me what you know about the Wellingtons."

Until now, Sean hadn't decided on exactly how much information to share with TJ Cutter. But he felt strangely comfortable in the man's presence, particularly as he had asked first about his own story before considering any info he had to offer about the Wellington family. His gut told him Cutter was someone he could trust with "the whole enchilada."

***

"That's a powerful narrative, Sean," TJ concluded after listening to the story of Marci Davis and the Kentucky governor. "While I can understand your strong desire to right a family wrong," Cutter continued, "I'm not sure the time and effort you've expended in pursuit of balancing the scales of justice are worth the return on your investment. Your mother appears to have moved on, although it seems as if some scar tissue remains. But it sounds like the two of you have a close relationship and a wonderful home. And with the passage of time, your mom is apparently emerging from her social cocoon. Might Denton Dandridge turn out to be a keeper?"

TJ and Sean both chuckled with those last words. Although Sean was having his first conversation with Cutter, it felt as if he'd been listening to advice from an older brother. He'd echoed many of the sentiments his mom had expressed just a couple of months earlier. But somehow the words came through with far more clarity. Indeed, Sean felt he was "falling in like" with this horseman from Leesburg, Virginia who was all of four years his senior.

"I appreciate your candor, particularly with respect to your mother-son dinners at Ilvento's. You should know that Beau floated the idea of a business combination between our thoroughbred businesses during yesterday's lunch. A lesson I've learned fairly early in life is that one should never dismiss an idea without giving it some consideration, no matter how outlandish it might seem at first. But *Cutting Edge Stables* would be hard pressed to do business with the Wellingtons given their family's current state of affairs. So I'm grateful to you for the heads-up."

"Well, sir. I've taken up a lot of your time," said Sean as he rose from the table and extended his hand in friendship.

"Wait a minute, Sean. Do you have anything on your agenda for the rest of the day? If not, why don't you join me for the last few races. We have a 2-year-old colt..."

Sean interrupted. "Nothing on my plate, Mr. Cutter. And I know all about *Cut To The Chase*. I think you have the right boy in the saddle. I'd love to join you."

"Alright, then. Let's go downstairs. I have another guest in my box who must be wondering where the hell I've been. You'll be interested to meet him."

Chapter 40 – Mulling Things Over at Molly's

Leaving the winner's circle, TJ suggested they all head over to the clubhouse valet parking area to pick up their cars. "We can head over to Red Bank for dinner and beat the racetrack crowd." In all, there would be four vehicles in the caravan – TJ's metallic blue Chrysler LeBaron convertible, Jasmine's '73 Mercury Montego, Sean's '70 Dodge Challenger and Irv's '77 light-brown Chevy Impala, a car that reminded him of his days as a detective driving through the streets of Brooklyn.

Jasmine shouted back: "I'll catch up. Consuela and I have to cash our winning tickets." *Cut To The Chase* returned $6.20 as the 2-1 second choice, meaning the ladies would each receive $310. "Quite the day, Ms. Pettiford!" beamed Jasmine.

"Increíble!" (Unbelievable!) is all Consuela could manage in response.

As the party of five waited for the car jocks to retrieve their vehicles, Sean wandered over to the Will Call window to ask Fran DeSantis about his good buddy Jürgen Hauptmann. "I was in such a hurry coming in, I neglected to ask about Jorge. Is he sick?"

"I don't think so," said Fran. "Jorge said he'd be back bright and early Monday morning. He didn't say *why* he couldn't make it. But knowing how reliable he's been for so long, I'd have to imagine it was important."

Just to make sure he was okay, Sean decided he'd call Jorge at some point after leaving the Molly Pitcher Inn. He would also take him to task for causing Sean to leave his precious Dodge Challenger in someone else's care while he tended to business with TJ Cutter.

***

Despite the holiday traffic, the Cutter caravan managed to keep together for the duration of the drive from Oceanport to Red Bank. Having turned their vehicles over to a new set of valets, the party of five now stood at the entrance to the Molly Pitcher Inn just off the Navesink River.

A gentleman in a handsome black suit, yellow and black striped tie with matching pocket square and black wing-tipped shoes approached TJ. In a voice too low for others to hear, he informed him: "Your room is ready, Mr. Cutter."

TJ turned to his guests and simply said, "Follow us." Heading away from the main dining room and through the inn's lobby, the gentleman led Cutter's party toward a richly carpeted winding staircase on the left. Ascending to a mezzanine-level series of rooms, he stopped at the far end of a hallway. Opening double doors, the gentleman said to everyone there: "This is the Tea Room. There's a telephone on the table next to the window. Should you require anything, please dial nine and ask for me, Geoffrey. Specially prepared menus are on your plates. Candace will be along in a few minutes to take your orders." Geoffrey then left the room and closed the double doors behind him.

Sean spoke first: "This couldn't possibly have been a spur-of-the-moment arrangement." But instead of hearing from TJ, two individuals entered from the double doors Geoffrey had just closed.

"No, it wasn't, Sean. Actually, this meeting was originally supposed to include TJ, Irv and the two of us." Speaking was a well-sculpted young man wearing a navy blazer, open-collared blue-and-white plaid shirt, off-white khaki pants and penny loafers. Sporting a crew cut of sandy-brown hair and blessed with crystal blue eyes and a straight nose, he could have been delivered directly from central casting.

Cutter interrupted to introduce one of the two new persons in the room: "This is Sammy Eisenstat, a classmate of mine at the University of Virginia, a graduate of Georgetown University Law Center and a field agent with the Federal Bureau of Investigation."

Eisenstat continued: "Our meeting has its roots in your effort this past December to enlist the aid of others in order to do a deep dive into your 'friends' in Kentucky. I'm pleased you're here. It saves me the trouble of a separate meeting with you."

TJ's afternoon call from the track had been to Eisenstat, letting him know of his encounter with Sean Davis Jeffries. With Jasmine and her attorney friend as unanticipated visitors to his box, he'd asked Sammy if they might come along.

Sean's head was spinning, but his legal training began to kick in. Jasmine, her jaw having dropped when the two men first opened the double doors, was frozen in place. An attorney but having no idea of the relationships among and between Jeffries, his Kentucky friends and Cutter, Consuela was at a complete loss.

"My first instinct is to ask the two ladies to head downstairs for dinner while we have our meeting," Eisenstat said. "But since you all know one another, I'm inclined to have you remain with the understanding that everything discussed this evening is to be held in strictest confidence. It beats wondering when and if you'd be asking questions of the others."

The other new arrival then chimed in: "Connie. I had absolutely no idea you'd be here today. I didn't even know you were getting together with Jasmine." Calvin Thomas and Connie Pett – the name by which Calvin had known Consuela Parks Pettiford – had locked eyes from the moment he entered the room.

"Didn't realize you'd be meeting me this early for the return trip to Manhattan," Connie answered sarcastically.

Now it was Irv Katzman's turn to speak: "It just so happens, Sean, that your desire to exact payback on Bentley Wellington ran smack dab into an ongoing investigation into business entities owned by Bentley, Beauregard and Abigail Prescott Wellington."

Needless to say, all thoughts of a celebratory dinner among new acquaintances had gone by the wayside with the appearance of Sammy Eisenstat and Calvin Thomas. The challenge for Eisenstat had been twofold – *first*, he needed to determine the extent to which information about the investigation should be shared with any of the folks assembled before him, and *second*, he had to decide if any of them had a role to play moving forward.

Before getting together at the Molly Pitcher Inn, Eisenstat and his associates at the FBI field office in Trenton had agreed on the information to be conveyed to his UVA classmate's guests.

Sammy explained that Calvin Thomas had been an independent, part-time contractor to the FBI for several years. He'd already been cleared by the Bureau before agreeing to investigate the Wellington family operations at Sean's request, with the understanding that all information obtained as a result would be provided first to the Bureau and only after said information had been "scrubbed" would the remaining intel be given to Mr. Jeffries.

The FBI had alerted both the Criminal and Civil Divisions of the Circuit Court in Fayette County, Kentucky, of the need for electronic surveillance of the Wellington estate in Lexington, related to investigations into suspected illegal activities by members of the Wellington family, the specifics of which remained confidential. Said surveillance had been approved for a period not to exceed 180 days but could be renewed by petitioning the court. Only last week, a renewal was granted.

Looking directly at Jasmine, Consuela and Sean, Eisenstat reiterated that information imparted today was to be kept in strictest confidence and not to be shared or discussed with anyone, including family members, and "except as specifically directed by the Bureau, none of you should take further actions related to the investigations now underway."

He added to the final point one additional comment: "One of you is a practicing attorney. Another is close to completing a legal education and taking a Bar exam. Two others have spent their careers in law enforcement and have taken oaths of service. You have ethical and, in all likelihood, legal obligations to follow these directives. We will periodically check on each of you to ask whether you are complying. I needn't remind you that it is a crime to lie to the FBI."

Dinner was a muted affair, with the four men talking quietly by the window overlooking the Navasink. The women engaged in small talk and kept their distance.

Jasmine and Consuela were the first to leave. They returned to the Dennis Hotel in Atlantic City, whereupon they shared a bottle of Mamajuana and soon lapsed into a second night of sexual intimacy.

Calvin was next to leave, telling Sammy he'd be available if needed on this or any other matter. He had a short drive back to his Oceanport home and made a mental note to call Connie at the Dennis Hotel to see if she still needed a ride back to the City on Monday.

Irv Katzman called his wife, Rebecca, in Seaside Heights and asked her to close the arcade by 11:00 p.m. but not to do the end-of-day bookkeeping. He'd take care of that in the morning before opening. As he headed for the door, Sammy asked him to remain.

The FBI field operative wanted to hear from his Uncle Irv about his relationship with Calvin Thomas. More specifically, whether Calvin ever mentioned his own work for the FBI. Satisfied that Irv had just that day learned of Calvin's relationship with the Bureau (and that he'd turned to Thomas simply by virtue of their shared history at the N.Y.P.D.), he then inquired as to the role his son, David – Sammy's cousin – had played thus far in the Wellington situation and whether he knew of David's current whereabouts.

Concluding that David had done nothing to jeopardize the legality of an FBI investigation, Eisenstat ended the meeting. "Okay Irv. We'll stay in touch. We may require your assistance and that of David." Sammy made it a point never to refer to Irv as his uncle in the presence of others. Then turning to TJ, "And I suspect we'll get in touch with you as well."

Part Three: Friends, Foes, Fate & Finality?

Chapter 41 – Discussion with Daddy

Following Saturday's Nijinsky II Stakes loss, Beauregard Wellington was in no mood to spend any more time than absolutely necessary in or around the Garden State. But the departure of a near-record crowd from Monmouth Park and the difficulties of negotiating traffic patterns in northern New Jersey during the holiday weekend conspired against leaving that evening. Beau called ahead to his pilot at north Jersey's Teterboro Airport, asking him to file a flight plan to Blue Grass Field for a return home as early as possible the next morning. Beau would reserve a motel room near the airport in order to be ready at zero-dark-thirty.

Since the late '50s, the Wellington family had staged a huge shindig at its Lexington estate on Memorial Day. This year would be no exception, with dignitaries from across Kentucky's business and political spectrums attending. The event had been Bentley's brainchild. Wellington saw the need to press the flesh with movers and shakers of the Commonwealth in the aftermath of holding the state's highest political office. It was one of the few issues on which he and his wife, Abigail Prescott-Wellington, had agreed. After all, what would the Commonwealth be if not for the bourbon, coal and thoroughbred industries – not to mention University of Kentucky basketball?

With as many as 500 luminaries coming to Thoroughbred Bs Farm, conversation ranged from fact-based discussions on issues of the day to rumor-mongering about the most trivial affairs of businesses and individuals. The Wellington gathering had often given birth to unintended as well as intended consequences affecting public policy and private people. It was Abigail who'd first realized their family's annual event needed to be managed. To this end, she demanded a pre-party meeting during which she, her husband and son would devise a plan on how to best leverage their Memorial Day extravaganza.

Since Beau had taken the reins of the family's thoroughbred business, these meetings had become somewhat complicated. It was made so because of Beau's gambling addiction and Bentley's willingness to "help" his son financially. Of course, daddy's continued assistance was predicated on the clear understanding that any and all transfers of money from father to son be kept between the male members of the family.

Scheduled this year as part of their Sunday supper, the meeting would begin at four o'clock. Abigail had insisted on an accompanying meal, wryly joking that "it will allow us to more easily digest our thoughts if food is consumed at the same time."

After the pilot confirmed a 7:30 a.m. departure from Teterboro, Beau called his father and asked for a two-thirty meeting.

***

It was a gorgeous Sunday afternoon in Lexington, although storm clouds of a man-made nature had been building over the Wellington estate. After a smooth flight and limo ride from Blue Grass Field, Beau was on time for what promised to be a bumpy discussion with daddy.

"This is breaking new ground, Beau buddy," a concerned Bentley concluded after listening to his son's recap of *B Kind To Your Enemies'* loss. Beau's explanation included throwing jockey Angel Barrera under the bus for a poor tactical ride while conveniently neglecting to add his own demand to not surrender the lead to the eventual winner, and a questionable training move in working the 2-year-old colt at Belmont's turf course.

But Bentley's annoyance had less to do with the outcome of the race itself. Rather, it lay in his son placing a sizable wager on a race involving one of the Wellington family's own thoroughbreds. "There's enough pressure in this business and far too many variables without the added factor of placing an unseemly amount of money at risk with that kind of wager."

Aside from his great distaste when his daddy referred to him as "Beau buddy," Beau knew from previous one-on-ones that his father was about to embark upon his favorite "beat a dead horse" lecture. And here it came.

"You know about the Black Sox Scandal, Beau buddy. Shoeless Joe Jackson hit .375 for the White Sox against Cincinnati in the 1919 World Series. Did it matter? Hell no! Along with seven of his teammates, he was banned from baseball for life for fixing the Series."

"Oh boy, here we go again," Beau thought to himself. He'd heard this story at least a few times before, but in a much different context. The Wellington family had been ardent baseball fans for generations, dating all the way back to the original Cincinnati Red Stockings. Founded in 1866, the Red Stockings had become the nation's first fully professional team in 1869 and won 130 straight games before losing to the Brooklyn Atlantics in 1870. At one point, Brett Wellington, Beau's *great* granddaddy, had considered offering to purchase the franchise. But until the appointment of Judge Kennesaw Mountain Landis as baseball's first commissioner in the aftermath of the Black Sox Scandal, the family elders thought the sport was a bit too shady to mix with the Wellingtons' emerging political aspirations.

"That damned kike Rothstein had to stick his greedy mitts and oversized Jew nose into baseball," lamented the former two-time governor of Kentucky. He was referring to Arnold Rothstein, an American racketeer, businessman and gambler who had become a kingpin of the Jewish mob in New York City. Nicknamed "the Brain," Rothstein was reputed to have organized corruption practices in the world of professional sports, including conspiracy to fix the 1919 World Series.

"I know why you do your betting away from the track. You don't want to attract attention from people who may see you at the windows. But that's nothing compared to those individuals you *don't* know who are behind these illegal gambling operations. This has to stop...*and now*, Beau buddy. Or I'll have to cut you off... before *they* do!"

With that having been said, Bentley reached into his left vest pocket to pull out an old brass-plated steel skeleton key. Opening the center drawer, he removed a checkbook and asked his son, "Now how much do you need?"

Beau hesitated while beginning to rise from the chair on the other side of the library desk and then answered: "Uh...Seventy-five thousand."

Bentley looked up, reached for the reading glasses that were affixed to what he referred to as his "old-man's necklace" and asked again before putting them in place: "I won't ask again, Beau buddy. How much do you *really* need?

Sitting back down he said quickly and with far more conviction,

"One hundred-fifty grand, sir."

"At this rate, you're not going to have much of an inheritance. Don't matter to me much. Once they fit me for a box, I won't know the diff!" Bentley said in plain-folk lingo spoken in a matter-of-fact tone that told Beau his daddy was reaching the end of his patience. "Course at this rate, Beau buddy, you may be in the market for a casket before me!"

Beau rose to his feet and extended his hand for the check. In one more not-so-subtle warning, Bentley held firm on the check as Beau pulled at it. Father and son locked eyes. "Thank you, sir! I have to get ready for our meeting with mom." With that, Bentley released his fingers so Beau could take his money as he turned to leave.

"God damned Hebe! 'Cause of him, we have an asterisk by our team's 1919 Series win," Bentley muttered as Beau exited the library.

Chapter 42 – Investigation Underway

After the case team reviewed all 13 dossiers in their folders, Gustav Zimmermann, the officer-in-charge of the NRW Police Force inspection team, began the meeting:

"Our inspectors have firmly established the cause of death of Hanna Schröder as a broken neck. The victim died when the 1983 metallic red Porsche Turbo 930 coupe she was driving failed to negotiate a sharp right curve on the L414 and toppled down an embankment to the bottom of a gully.

"The cause of the accident has also been determined – a severed brake line that left the driver unable to stop the vehicle at speeds of 25 km/h or greater. We estimated the Porsche had been traveling at a speed of 40 km/h when it approached the road's sharp right curve. Given the newness of the vehicle, it was unlikely to have been caused by either a poorly installed line or mechanical defect.

"We have confirmed the forensic pathologist's report, indicating the deceased's blood alcohol content BAC at the time of the crash was 0.01 to 0.02 mg of alcohol/100 m …in other words, within the range of alcohol produced constantly by the human body. There also was no evidence of stroke, heart failure or other medical conditions that might have contributed to loss of control of the vehicle.

"While these reports will not formally be recognized by the NRW for another eight days, we are making them available because of the extraordinary circumstances surrounding the incident."

As Herr Zimmermann returned to his seat, LKA NRW Investigation Bureau Officer Bertram Krieger now stood: "Thank you for your inspectors' quick and thorough work, Officer Zimmermann. We continue:

"Having referred to the notes from our initial interview with Gretchen Weiß Hauptmann following the incident, we know die Vorsitzende offered her vehicle as transportation. Frau Hauptmann explained the deceased's car was a 10-year-old Mercedes Benz 200D that showed some 150,000 kilometers of wear and tear and she was concerned for her administrative assistant's safety. Frau Hauptmann indicated there'd been a light mist falling all day long with patches of dense fog and told us it wasn't the first time she'd loaned Hanna Schröder her vehicle. We have corroborated each element of her story. Reviewing GWH GmbH's personnel file on Hanna Schröder and learning of her lengthy and excellent service to die Vorsitzende and the company, we have no reason to believe Hauptmann was in any way involved in Frau Schröder's demise.

"Based on the information and assessments we've made thus far, we are looking for ein *Triebfeder* (a *motive*) for the attempted murder of Gretchen Weiß Hauptmann. We know das *Bedeutet* (the *means*) by which the perpetrator, working alone or in concert with others, intended to carry out the objective. And we know die *Möglichkeit* (the *opportunity*) or circumstance under which the perpetrator or perpetrators intended to carry out the objective."

Krieger now turned to Jakob Seidel, case officer for the NRW Exchange Supervisory Authority, who spoke next:

"I have a working theory on that aspect of our analysis. Turn to the meeting agenda prepared by Frau Schröder. You'll find it in her dossier.

"Note the final vote on whether to remain a private business entity or file for a public offering was to be taken the morning following presentations and debate, after which the meeting was to be adjourned with participants going their separate ways. There was *no* reason to believe anyone's vehicle would be used prior to the final vote. And there was *every* reason to believe the next person driving Frau Hauptmann's car would be the owner herself.

"Also note the hand-written scorecard compiled by die Vorsitzende, which you'll find in Hauptmann's dossier. The scorecard reveals a projected 3-3 split which, if it came to fruition, would leave the deciding vote with Frau Hauptmann. An unforeseen change in one Board member's vote could well be decisive in determining the company's future direction.

"While it is somewhat premature, our office posits the following: (1) Frau Hauptmann's death was to take place after the vote of GWH GmbH's Advisory Board; (2) this plot was not the work of one person, but a coordinated effort by multiple individuals; (3) every effort was to have been made to tilt the vote in favor of a public offering; and (4) the plan to remove die Vorsitzende from the corporate equation was in order to clear the decks for future white-collar crimes undertaken within a newly minted GWH AG.

"One line of questioning for members of both the advisory board and management team should be developed with this hypothesis in mind," Seidel concluded.

Finally, David Katzman rose to address the others. Herr Seidel's working theory seemed to have dovetailed perfectly into the Mossad's perspective:

"In 1966, one of our German-based Mossad agents contacted Fabian Hauptman – our organization spells his surname with one 'n' – regarding the activities of the far-right Nationaldemokratische Partei Deutschlands (National Democratic Party of Germany). Specifically, a small group of the NDP was launching a rogue 'seek-and-destroy' mission aimed at removing those Germans who'd sympathized with Jews during the war. Given Fabian's wartime activities, our people assessed his family was in imminent danger and offered Fabian an opportunity to leave Germany and relocate to Israel with his wife and son. Herr Hauptman declined the offer.

"Fast forward to the deadly 1980 Oktoberfest Bombing in Munich. The German government's investigation had concluded that Gundolf Köhler, a university student from the Swabian town of Donaueschingen, made the bomb, took it to Munich and deposited it at the scene of the crime. Köhler was thought to have died when the explosive detonated prematurely. Our people assessed with a high degree of probability that Wehrsportgruppe Hoffmann, a banned neo-Nazi terrorist militia to which bomber Gundolf Köhler had ties, was involved in the planning.

The North Rhine-Westphalian authorities had been well aware of the facts covered in this initial part of Katzman's intelligence. But their ears perked up as the Mossad agent continued:

"Because the October 1980 bombing marked a heightened level of terrorist activity and knowing that elements of the NDP had knowledge of Fabian Hauptman's wartime activities as well as his subsequent marriage to Gretchen Weiß, our organization believed Frau Hauptmann could be a target. Given these circumstances, we placed her home under electronic surveillance as of the early part of January 1981. We'd suspected for quite some time the role Gretchen Weiß played at Terezin during the war. Our surveillance provided us with corroboration. She still talks frequently in her sleep."

Katzman went on to reveal he'd been in recent contact with Fabian to check on his safety, but did not disclose when the contact took place, where he was residing or the alias under which he was currently living. He also explained the Mossad had developed classifications of Nazis based on the severity of their crimes. While the Israeli security agency placed a high priority on gathering evidence, capturing, extraditing to Israel and ultimately prosecuting those guilty of the worst transgressions, it found ample reason to continue to observe those who participated in lesser crimes in hopes they would provide leads on locating "bigger fish to fry."

"One final point," added Katzman. "While Fabian Hauptman is under deep cover, Jorge Hauptmann has been living a normal life as a student at an American university in the New York metropolitan area and participates in a major NCAA soccer program. It wouldn't be difficult for the wrong people to locate him. I'm taking steps to ensure his safety. But we need to move forward on this investigation as expeditiously as possible."

Having already left a phone message at the home of Calvin Thomas before he'd boarded the flight to Düsseldorf, Katzman nevertheless decided to place an overseas call to the senior Katzman and ask him to get in touch with Calvin. He wanted to make doubly sure Jorge would be under Calvin's watchful eye.

Chapter 43 – "Take a Powder"

There was no denying the future of the Wellingtons' business holdings would be best served by the leadership of the family matriarch. But with her decision-making authority hamstrung as long as Bentley remained chief executive of the distillery and Beau continued to run the thoroughbred operation, Abigail had been forced to resort to psychological gymnastics in order to get things done. At times she felt like the proverbial little Dutch boy – or girl, in this case – who plugged the dyke with her finger to prevent the great flood that would destroy Holland.

Although the annual Thoroughbred Bs Farm Memorial Day affair was by invitation only, it nevertheless topped the Kentucky Chamber of Commerce's statewide list of major weekend events. With close to 500 guests expected to descend upon their Lexington estate, Abigail, Bentley and Beauregard were meeting over Sunday supper to review the next day's agenda.

Abigail had met two weeks ago to sign off on the details with a local business, *Bluegrass Gas,* that specialized in organizing large events. Working on its sixth consecutive annual shindig for the Wellingtons, the firm's lead team, headed by Laurie Van Zant, had developed a theme, hired entertainment, would provide catering and wait staff, and had arranged the evening's fireworks finale. This last-minute review with Bentley and Beauregard was to get the men in the room up to speed with what would be taking place the next day.

Abigail was particularly excited about this year's entertainment. For young children, two acres had been fenced in for a skit and sing-along featuring actors and actresses costumed as the characters of *Fraggle Rock*, which had premiered in January on HBO. Adults would be treated to a replay of the series finale of *M*A*S*H* (sans commercials), which aired at the end of February. For "children of all ages," a Michael Jackson look-alike and his cover band were set to open with "Billie Jean" and a reprise of MJ's famous "moonwalk" dance move.

Of greatest importance was that portion of the meeting in which Abigail, Beau and Bentley went over a short list of guests with whom they wanted to curry favor, transact business or otherwise grease the skids. The Wellington trio shared the same thought heading into their family gathering: With a financially tumultuous year behind them and perhaps a more challenging year moving forward, there'd be some "heavy lifting" to do during their holiday event.

***

For years Dieter Hartmann and Barnard Scholz, one-time classmates in the Materials and Earth Sciences program at Technische Universität Darmstadt, had been close colleagues as they built their careers in the powder metal industry. Though on opposite sides of the Atlantic – Scholz at a couple of "mom & pop" P/M operations in north-central Pennsylvania and Hartmann at Pulver-Metall Lüdenscheid GmbH in the homeland's North Rhine-Westphalia region – they'd seen each other at least once a year in June at the Metal Powder Industry Federation (MPIF) annual convention. With attendees from across North America and around the globe, the MPIF changed the site of its gathering each year.

In 1982, the MPIF chose Cincinnati for its three-day convention. It had been something of a coup for the Cincinnati U.S.A. Regional Chamber. Anxious to bring attention to its redevelopment efforts, the organization was focusing on its Over-the-Rhine (über den Rhein) neighborhood. An epicenter of German immigration in the mid-19th century, the neighborhood acquired its distinctive name from early residents, many of whom walked to work across bridges over the Miami and Erie Canal that separated the area from downtown. Known for its ornate brick buildings built in the two decades following the Civil War, Over-the-Rhine had long been reputed to be one of the largest, most intact urban historic districts in the country.

It was at the manufacturers' exhibit – a typical business-to-business event designed to bring together prospective users of P/M components and companies with the capability of producing such components less expensively than (and just as reliable as) more traditional processes like casting or forging – that Blake Tinsdale, chief financial officer at Bourbonesque LLC, had met Dieter and Barnard.

Tinsdale had been under fairly heavy pressure from Bentley to bring down costs while maintaining the distillery's operating efficiency. That in mind, he was quick to comprehend the basic P/M process and anxious to have Barnard and Dieter visit Bourbonesque in Bardstown. For Scholz, Bourbonesque represented a referral and possible sales commission – handy given his teaching position at Penn State-DuBois. For Hartmann, learning about applications for manufacturing components for breweries and distilleries could certainly open opportunities for GWH domestically and elsewhere in Europe.

Pleased with discovering a potential source of savings, Tinsdale reached out to Hartmann and Scholz to arrange a tour the day after the convention. Abigail wanted to hear more from the German businessmen before she'd be convinced. Bentley, confined to his wheelchair and increasingly missing his daily involvement in Bourbonesque, simply wanted the pleasure of a couple of visitors and a reason to flex his diminishing corporate muscle.

After the tour had been completed, the Wellingtons dispatched their private helicopter to pick up Barnard and Dieter. Naturally, Bentley invited them for a late lunch and offered to have their limo take them to the Cincinnati airport afterwards.

Over a down-home country meal featuring ginger-ale & brown sugar-glazed smoked ham, cream cheese biscuits with figgy port chutney and blue cheese butter, Abigail had grilled her guests on details of the powder metal process and, in particular, on P/M filters, which seemed better suited to the low-volume applications Bourbonesque might find useful. Lunch was accompanied by bottles of Wiedemann's Bohemian Special Brew, a Cincinnati staple. The Germans nodded in approval upon their first taste, both of them thankful bourbon hadn't been the hosts' choice as a liquid refreshment.

Inevitably conversation turned to sports. Seeking common ground from basic "How to Sell 101," Hartmann spoke of his fondness for the Köln-Weidenpesch Racecourse. He recounted his last visit to the track the previous October for his country's most prestigious race, the Grade I Preis von Europa.

"I had the privilege of watching the 3-year-old colt *Glint of Gold* capture the mile-and-a-half race by 3½ lengths," recounted Dieter. "As I recall, there'd been a torrential downpour and the turf was very heavy. His victory still stands as the slowest winning time since the stakes race was first run back in 1963."

Bentley's eyes lit up as he listened to Hartmann: "That's a right-handed track, right? Ya' know, I remember meeting Paul Mellon several years ago at Saratoga. He owned and bred thoroughbreds including that horse, I do believe. Quite the sportsman...and quite the philanthropist as well. Paul's daddy, Andrew, was U.S. Secretary of the Treasury back in the '20s. 'Course his granddaddy started the Mellon Bank."

Bentley was on a roll now. The former Governor paused to take the last swig of his brew: "Our families have a lot in common. My daddy, Buford – most everyone called him 'Buff' – had been a member of the U.S. Senate for nearly three decades. He died a few years back. Pancreatic cancer. Now our son Beauregard handles the thoroughbred business. Maybe you'll get to meet him some day."

For octogenarian Bentley Wellington, the mere mention of Beau and thoroughbred in the same sentence had seemed to trigger an automated recitation mechanism in his brain as he began to describe his granddaddy Brett's long-ago consideration of buying the Cincinnati Red Stockings. As always, the story was accompanied by a vivid account of the 1919 Black Sox Scandal, the role played by Arnold Rothstein and Bentley's crude, anti-Semitic diatribe.

Noticing his wife's raised left eyebrow, a visual cue to end his monologue, Bentley concluded: "Well, I know your game is soccer, but maybe we'll have to get you over to Riverfront Stadium to see the Reds play next time you're in town."

Chiming in, Barnard said it would be a wonderful experience. "Maybe we could have you, Frau Wellington and Beauregard to dinner afterwards at a German restaurant in Over-the-Rhine."

Dieter added: "Ja, Ja...Wir hoffen, mit Ihnen Geschäfte zu machen. (Yes, Yes...We hope to do business with you.) Clearly, Dieter had been deep in thought since the end of Bentley Wellington's baseball story.

***

Customer 'A' has a specific need that, for a combination of cost- and performance-related reasons, can be best met by a product or service offered by Supplier 'B'. Often times, this business tautology only begins to explain the basis upon which a customer-supplier relationship is built. Such was the case in the evolving relationship between GWH GmbH and Bourbonesque LLC.

Ostensibly offered as a preferred alternative to improve one aspect of the bourbon distilling process, a high-performance porous metal filter had actually kick-started a far right-wing German political organization's cultivation of one of America's leading business and political families.

Just shy of a year since Dieter Hartmann and Barnard Scholz had toured Bourbonesque and dined with the elder Wellingtons, Hartmann and Wolfgang Becker, chairman of the GWH GmbH Management Board, were on the hosts' guest list and a subject of the Wellingtons' Memorial Day pre-event strategy session.

The topic of conversation, however, was not whether to employ GWH GmbH as a supplier of powder metal filters. That step had been taken within 60 days of last year's introductory meeting when Hartmann, Becker and the company's director of strategic planning, Dr. Wilhelm Fuchs, returned to Kentucky to go over details of Bourbonesque's initial order.

Fuchs had been brought along to underscore GWH GmbH's position as a leading supplier of high-performance porous metal filters worldwide, using stainless steel, bronze and nickel alloys for liquid or gas filtration. His appearance to reaffirm the efficacy of the technology along with that of Becker to underscore the importance of the Bourbonesque book of business in developing the U.S. market for high-performance porous metal filters, had been a winning formula for GWH.

With each and every expense-related business decision turning into a pitched battle with her husband, Abigail found herself relieved with the prospect of a temporary truce and the return to some semblance of normalcy with the P/M filters transaction.

Up for discussion for the Wellingtons prior to seeing the German contingent at their Memorial Day extravaganza was an intriguing but somewhat strange communication from an organization calling itself *German and American Business Executives for Bilateral Relations* (Deutsche und amerikanische Führungskräfte für bilaterale Beziehungen). The letter was sent to Bentley Wellington, chief executive of Bourbonesque LLC, within 30 days after the initial order for filters had been delivered.

The letter started by referencing the large German population based in the United States and the contributions made to the American economy by several German industrialists including John Bausch and Henry Lomb who created the first American optical company; Steinway, Knabe and Schnabel (pianos); John D. Rockefeller (petroleum); Peter and Clement Studebaker and Walter P. Chrysler (automobiles); H.J. Heinz (food), and Frederick Weyerhaeuser (lumber).

It went on to cite the mutual benefits to be gained by facilitating transatlantic dialogues between German and American business executives and by supporting economic and social relationships between the two countries. Finally, the letter proclaimed the organization represented German and American core values as reflected in its board and general membership.

In closing, the organization said its outreach to Bentley Wellington and Bourbonesque LLC had come at the suggestion of Wolfgang Becker who stressed "the strong leadership qualities of Herr Wellington, having served two terms as Governor of the great state of Kentucky." At the top of its letterhead was a list of the Board members, which included Becker and Dr. Fuchs.

Accompanying the letter was a membership application to be completed and forwarded, along with a check in the amount of $1,200, to Deutsche und amerikanische Führungskräfte für bilaterale Beziehungen at the organization's address in Munich. What had eluded Bentley Wellington – as well as his far more astute and business-savvy spouse – was the overarching entity housed at that same location: Die Nationaldemokratische Partei Deutschlands.

Bentley had completed the membership form, cut a personal check for $1,200 and was prepared to give both to Wolfgang Becker the next day. He was virtually certain his wife would not be pleased, if for no other reason than he'd fought her on virtually every front when it came to intermediate- to long-range investments.

Over the past few months, Bentley had received multiple calls from Becker, Hartmann and Fuchs, ostensibly to inquire about the performance of the filters Bourbonesque had purchased from GWH, but also to engage in casual conversation on contemporary social issues in Germany as well as in the United States.

With great patience and subtlety, discussions initiated by the trio of NPD sympathizers were designed to rationalize and garner sympathy for a far-right wing agenda. In Bentley Wellington, they had a willing ear. Of course, it had been no surprise to Hartmann.

After listening to Bentley's baseball "rant," Hartmann had done some digging and learned where the family's skeletons were buried – to wit: Bentley's rape of and hasty settlement with a colored member of his staff and his latent anti-Semitism, which manifested itself during periods of anger and/or intoxication; Beauregard's gambling addiction and pell-mell pursuit of an IPO, a possibly desperate attempt at a money grab that could leave him open to cutting legal corners in regulatory filings and/or subsequent uses of capital; and Abigail's suspected involvement in her husband's hunting accident and her continuing efforts to cover for her husband's and son's weaknesses when it came to their business dealings as well as their character flaws.

All represented potential vulnerabilities that could be used against the "Commonwealth's First Family" to extract support for policies and practices advantageous to the NDP's cause. That the German businessmen's modus operandi might be unlawful was of no concern to an organization whose members were willing to use blackmail, extortion and threat of bodily harm to achieve their objectives.

Dieter Hartmann figured Bentley Wellington to be the easiest mark. He expected to secure his "buy in" with membership in the German and American Business Executives for Bilateral Relations. At the appropriate time, he would make sure Bentley learned of the ties between this front organization and the neo-Nazi ambitions of the underlying movement. Hartmann would arrange it so the elderly Wellington "discovered" the relationship. Then they'd wait for a reaction.

Hartmann suspected Beau would require a bit more enticement. Knowing of the Wellington plan to take Thoroughbred Bs Farm public, he'd work on a way to involve Beau in GWH's parallel track for equity financing. It might be as easy as securing Beau's commitment to purchase shares before the GWH offering, but making sure he had in his possession company documents leading the NRW Exchange Supervisory Authority to see him as trading on insider information. Simple? Maybe...maybe not.

Abigail remained the biggest threat to their plan. She had knowledge of her husband's and son's transgressions, was an intelligent and tough-minded business woman who to this point had demonstrated an ability to think clearly and cover for the Wellington boys' shortcomings – but quite possibly had planned her husband's hunting "accident." More information about events surrounding the accident would certainly help. But how to go about securing that knowledge was another matter.

***

Although Abigail had some concerns about Bentley's growing attraction to the German executives representing Bourbonesque's filters supplier, she was far more occupied with business connections within the Commonwealth and up north in New York City. And so expected guests from a half-dozen entities dominated the Wellingtons' pre-event discussion for their Memorial Day extravaganza:

First up was *Steinberg Stavros Rogers & Co., Inc.*, the asset management firm tasked with managing the Wellington family's liquid assets. Those assets now included funds realized from the sale of Abigail's share of her father's coal company. Steinberg Stavros guests included President & CEO Nikko Stavros and Senior Vice President Robert Rogers, who was responsible for overseeing the firm's investment management group for high net-worth individuals. A third person, Sven Ericsson, managed the Wellington asset portfolio.

Abigail would spend time with Messrs. Stavros and Rogers, while Bentley and Beau would persuade Sven Ericsson to shift to a more aggressive posture with the family's investment portfolio.

Next the trio discussed what had become an annual exercise in futility – attempting to persuade lead bureaucrats at *KACo*, the *Kentucky Association of Counties* (invitees included the current Director of Public Affairs Joan Ashcraft and Director of Governmental Relations Mary Beth Colston), to push their members across the Commonwealth to streamline the state laws governing the sale and consumption of alcoholic beverages. Some 120 counties continued to present a patchwork of "dry" (prohibiting all sale of alcoholic beverages), "wet" (permitting full retail sales under state license) and "moist" (occupying a middle ground between the two) regulations which had confounded everyone – from the general citizenry, restaurateurs and their bartenders to clergy, law enforcement and the sales & marketing arms of the Commonwealth's distilleries.

John Daniels had been on the Wellington family's short list for the past several years. His title was Distilled Spirits Administrator, one of three individuals making up the *Alcohol Beverage Control (ABC) Board.* He was quite accessible, affable enough and an inveterate punster – as long as you didn't call him "Jack." If you made the mistake, Daniels would then launch into a detailed technical explanation of the difference between Tennessee whiskey and Kentucky bourbon, concluding with the statement: *"This* Jack Daniels has more to do with Kentucky bourbon."

Abigail agreed to take the lead in speaking with their KACo guests, while Bentley would see if he could be persuasive with Daniels.

Despite the difficulties of the past year, the Wellington family had reason to celebrate. Their equine enterprises had been at the forefront of a group of Kentucky's finest horsemen in forming the *Kentucky Thoroughbred Association (KTA).* The new organization was trumpeting three objectives: to unite the industry by addressing long-term challenges; to represent the Commonwealth's thoroughbred industry on the national stage; and to maintain world-class standards of racing, breeding and training within the Commonwealth.

Invited to the Wellington estate were the biggest names in Kentucky's thoroughbred industry, from such world-class farms as Calumet, Claiborne, Overbrook and Spendthrift. Beau viewed the attendance of his fellow horsemen as an opportunity to probe the best minds in the industry on the pros and cons of his plan to take the family's Thoroughbred Bs Farm public.

"It's not that we're going to change course if our fellow horsemen pan the notion of an IPO," Beau explained. "But there may be a good idea or two we can incorporate into our business plan."

Under the direction of Executive Vice President Arthur Zinstein, the international investment house of *Silverstein-Gladstone* had served as the primary underwriter for some of the largest offerings of securities on both the debt and equity sides of the capital markets over the past few years. For private sector efforts, Zinstein had steadfastly refused to involve his firm in any transaction of less than $100 million.

It was at the EVP's insistence that Beau Wellington had formally separated the breeding and racing operations, S-G's participation as primary underwriter contingent upon this step. Abigail would take Zinstein aside and explore his rationale for this precondition. Not that she disagreed with the demand, particularly with her son's "extracurricular activities" on the racing side of the Wellington family's thoroughbred equation. At times, she'd wondered whether Thoroughbred Bs Farm should focus solely on breeding. Her competitive nature had purged those thoughts from her mind.

Bentley, Beau and Abigail knew that Arthur Zinstein would also be keen to hear the opinions of their fellow Kentucky horsemen on the pending IPO, likely out of earshot of family members. Did they see Wall Street's participation in their industry as a harbinger of things to come? Would any of them take a financial position in publicly traded TBF securities? Might any of them consider taking a position on the Board? The Wellingtons would more than likely have to rely upon post-event feedback from S-G and their fellow horsemen, comparing notes from both camps to determine exactly where things stood.

Finally, there was *GWH GmbH*, the source of Bourbonesque's recent purchase of high-performance porous metal filters. Becker, Fuchs and Hartmann were, of course, on their guest list. As fate would have it, the telephone at the Wellington estate rang just as the family began strategizing its approach to the German contingent. When one of the staff entered the dining room to inform the family there was "an overseas call from Dieter Hartmann," Abigail quickly said she'd take the call before her husband could react, rose from her chair and went to the study to pick up.

"Frau Wellington. Ich danke Ihnen, dass Sie meinen Anruf in dieser geschäftigen Zeit für Sie genommen haben. Oh, pardon the German. We've been quite distracted and a bit unnerved here, Frau Wellington. Thank you for taking my call during this busy time for you," Dieter began. He then took a couple of minutes to explain why he and his colleagues would be unable to join the next day's festivities:

"We've had an unfortunate incident in the GWH family. Earlier today we learned that Hanna Schröder, long-time administrative assistant to our company founder, Gretchen Weiß Hauptmann, perished in an early-morning car accident. The police are investigating and our weekend meeting has been suspended before completing some very important business. Please accept our apologies for this last-minute cancellation."

Taking a moment to digest what she'd heard, Abigail offered a response one might expect from a seasoned business person: "I am so sorry, Herr Hartmann. Please extend the Wellington family's condolences to Hanna Schröder's family, Frau Hauptmann and your fellow Board members. We were looking forward to seeing you all. But I trust we'll be speaking with you in the weeks to come."

Returning to the dining room, Abigail relayed the news to her husband and son. With so much on their plates (figuratively and literally, as talk had made food consumption somewhat challenging) Bentley and Beauregard suggested they adjourn. After all, the GWH folks were the last on their guest-list agenda.

Bentley, who hadn't seen any reason for further delay, decided he'd send his completed membership form and check to the German and American Business Executives for Bilateral Relations in Germany via DHL on Tuesday and so informed his wife. Abigail's response – "If you *must!*" – reflected her frustration with Bentley's decision. On at least a couple of occasions, she'd expressed to Bentley her skepticism about building a relationship with "this German-American group." What's more, Abigail couldn't understand how her husband, at the same time, could be so tight with Bourbonesque's finances when it came to improving operations.

Chapter 44 – A Transatlantic Link?

When Calvin Thomas returned to New Jersey, he did so without removing the surveillance apparatus he'd placed in the Wellington family estate. His phone call to the Jeffries residence in Jersey City on April 3rd, Easter Sunday, had been placed from the FBI's resident agency in Lexington, one of seven offices that fed into the Louisville field office serving the entire Commonwealth.

Marcus McQueen, who'd been in charge of FBI operations in Kentucky for almost 20 years ("...since Cassius Clay whupped Sonny Listen in February of '64," he was fond of saying), was briefed by Sammy Eisenstat on the Wellington file. McQueen was tasked with assigning staff to pick up where Calvin Thomas left off. The bird dogging fell to field agent Madison "Matts" Meriwether, who continued to observe the activities of Abigail, Bentley and Beauregard Wellington within the Commonwealth and maintained electronic surveillance of their Lexington estate.

There hadn't been much by way of new intel since Thomas had departed Kentucky. But eight weeks later, on Sunday of the Memorial holiday weekend, Matts Meriwether listened in on both the Wellington family's strategy session ahead of the next day's holiday extravaganza as well as the father-and-son conversation earlier in the afternoon.

That earlier meeting, which revealed Beau's growing and increasingly reckless gambling habit and Bentley's continuing role as enabler, was an eye-opener and would set off alarm bells within a host of state and federal regulatory agencies, not the least of which were the newly formed Kentucky Thoroughbred Association (KTA) and the U.S. Securities & Exchange Commission. Meriwether listened to his recording of the brief meeting twice — once to make sure he understood exactly what had transpired and a second time to capture the gist of what certainly sounded like the Governor's long-held anti-Semitic feelings.

As for the family gathering, much of the discussion had been innocuous enough. The family's desire to have Steinberg Stavros Rogers & Co. shift funds into a more aggressive investment portfolio could well be a reflection of the financial challenges Bourbonesque was facing, in combination with the legal bills associated with preparing for the IPO. And then there was the drain on funds created by Beau Wellington's gambling habit.

Silverstein-Gladstone's insistence on formal separation of the breeding and racing operations as a precondition to underwriting the IPO had been an interesting stipulation. How much had their staff uncovered in conducting due diligence into the affairs of the Wellington family?

Bourbonesque's plan to lean on the ABC Board and KACo to overhaul the antiquated patchwork of laws governing the sale and consumption of alcohol from county to county was certainly in line with the distillery industry's position. And given the Wellington family's long history of leadership in Kentucky politics, one would expect them to take an aggressive position in such an effort.

Bringing in the Commonwealth's leading horsemen to opine about the pros and cons of selling securities in the family thoroughbred business to the general public had been an interesting play. Invitations to the annual shindig were a perfect "cover" for eliciting input on the pending IPO without requesting a meeting for that specific purpose. It also provided the ideal opportunity to corner each guest individually amid an informal atmosphere.

The phone call late in the Wellington family meeting, however, had received heightened attention from the FBI field agent. The call from Dieter Hartmann to inform the Wellingtons of the GWH contingent's change in plans certainly was understandable. But what exactly were the circumstances surrounding Hanna Schröder's death? And what did Bentley's comment about sending his membership form and check to Germany mean?

After reviewing his notes, Madison Meriwether reached for the phone and dialed Sammy Eisenstat. "It isn't so much the 11th-hour call from Hartmann cancelling the GWH attendance," Meriwether explained. "It's the comment from Bentley about his decision to send a completed membership form and check to Germany immediately after Abigail's conversation with Hartmann."

What the FBI didn't know was the name of the organization Bentley was joining and the amount of his membership fee.

***

After serving two tours of duty in Viet Nam, David Katzman –
like so many Viet Nam vets – had publicly questioned the conflict.
Moved by the Israeli victory in the Six Day War, he'd taken his
skills and devotion towards his fellow Jews and under Israel's Law
of Return relocated to Tel Aviv and began his service in the Israeli
Army.

Three years later, citizenship was bestowed upon David ben
Reuven (Irving Katzman's given Hebrew name). And after an
extensive period of training, he became an agent of the Mossad,
Israel's National Intelligence Agency. By this time, most of the
U.S. intelligence community – including his cousin Sammy – had
become familiar with Katzman. In fact, David had worked on a
couple of important classified operations run jointly by the CIA and
Mossad.

Having met with Irv Katzman, Calvin Thomas and Sean Davis
Jeffries the previous evening at the Molly Pitcher Inn and then
receiving Matts Meriwether's call 24 hours later about the accident
that had disrupted the GWH special meeting in Wuppertal, Sammy
Eisenstat clearly needed to speak with the younger Katzman sooner
rather than later. Still a bit unsettled about the unorthodox and
seemingly speedy manner in which the now transatlantic situation
was unfolding, he decided against tracking down David through
formal communication channels. Instead, he'd use his personal
family backchannel, Uncle Irv.

Chapter 45 – The Canadians

Following World War II, Canada had participated as one of the Allied Nations in the prosecution of war criminals at the Nuremberg Trials. Under Canada's War Trials Act, proceedings against war criminals lasted until 1948.

During the '50s, an anti-communist political climate had turned public opinion away from the atrocities of World War II and resulted in an immigration policy more permissive to former Nazis. During this period, approximately 40,000 such individuals emigrated to Canada from Germany. Among the influx of Nazis were an unknown number of suspected war criminals. Despite growing awareness and some legislative changes, Canada still had lacked the political will to prosecute the most senior war criminals.

Fast forward some two decades and the aftermath of the September 1980 Oktoberfest Bombing in Munich. Like the Israeli and American governments, Canada had taken more than a passing interest in the activities of Germany's right-wing NDP – particularly given the country's post-World War II immigration policies.

***

Under its federal mandate, the Royal Canadian Mounted Police (RCMP) was responsible for enforcing federal laws covering commercial crime, counterfeiting, drug trafficking, border integrity, organized crime and other related matters. The Mounties handled counter-terrorism cases, were charged with maintaining domestic security and provided protection services for the Canadian Monarch, Governor General, Prime Minister, their families and residences and other ministers of the Crown as well as visiting dignitaries and diplomatic missions.

The RCMP Security Service was a specialized political intelligence and counterintelligence branch with national security responsibilities and participated in various international policing efforts. Since June of 1953, the RCMP had been a full member of the International Criminal Police Organization (Interpol).

185

John Edgerton, 34, was the recently appointed head of the RCMP Security Service. The Windsor, Ontario native was well qualified to lead the organization, having earned his undergraduate degree in political science at the University of Toronto's Scarborough campus and a graduate degree in international relations from Harvard University. He'd spent four years with the Forensics Unit of the Ontario Provincial Police before joining the RCMP's Security Service, where he quickly rose through the ranks to his current position.

Sitting in Edgerton's Ottawa office was Cameron Connors, a senior field officer who reported directly to the head of the RCMP Security Service. The topic of conversation this Tuesday morning, the final day of May, was one Brian Harper, a.k.a. Fabian Hauptman, who'd been living in Hamilton since coming to Canada from Germany back in 1966.

Connors had been on the phone with Louis Andrew Boaz, an FBI officer in charge of the organization's Economic Espionage Unit and part of the Bureau's Counterintelligence Program. According to Boaz, there'd been an attempt on the life of Harper's spouse, Gretchen Weiß Hauptmann, currently the majority owner of a small powder metal parts manufacturer in Wuppertal. That attempt resulted in the death of Frau Hauptmann's administrative assistant. The Mossad, Boaz explained, was currently working on the case with the LKA NRW Police Force Investigation Bureau.

Edgerton, up until this moment sitting back in his office chair with hands clasped behind his head, quickly leaned forward when hearing this latest piece of information. Connors proceeded to recount Fabian's Jewish background, his wartime efforts assisting fellow Jews in escaping to Palestine and his clandestine work for the allies. He also went over Gretchen's wartime work as a records keeper for the Nazis in the Terezin holding and transport center in Czechoslovakia. He paused after describing just how Fabian had learned of his wife's role.

"And I'm sure you're going to tell me why all of this is relevant to us," the RCMP Security Service head said by way of urging Connors to continue.

"Of course, Edge," Connors resumed, calling his boss by the casual name all of John Edgerton's law enforcement associates – peers and staff alike – had come to know him. "The NRW and

Mossad both suspect a domestic far-right-wing political group with neo-Nazi elements, die Nationaldemokratische Partei Deutschlands (NDP), is behind the attempt on Frau Hauptmann's life – an attempt resulting in the death of Hanna Schröder. What's more, they believe individuals supporting the NDP hold positions within GWH GmbH."

Then came the kicker: "In what had seemingly been a completely unrelated case, the FBI was conducting electronic surveillance of owners of one of America's leading thoroughbred breeding farms down in Lexington, Kentucky, when a family meeting revealed a potential relationship between events in Wuppertal and a pending blockbuster IPO. And this is no ordinary family – we're talking Bentley Wellington, former two-term governor of Kentucky and current owner of Bourbonesque LLC; his wife, Abigail, current COO and a former co-owner of a Kentucky-based surface coal mining company, and their son, Beauregard, who runs the breeding farm and racing operations."

Now Edgerton was standing away from his desk and looking out the full-length window of his third-floor corner office, his right hand jingling several coins in his pants pocket.

"There's no reason to believe Brian Harper is in any danger. But he and Gretchen have a son, Jürgen Hauptmann, who's been attending Seton Hall University in New Jersey on a soccer scholarship. The FBI has someone keeping an eye on the young man." Cam Connors actually found himself breathing a bit heavily as a result of running through all of the dizzying details for his boss.

John Edgerton remained by the window, staring at the people and traffic below while continuing to work over the coins in his pocket. Not only were several individuals contemplating criminal activity, but one murder already seemed to have been committed with the prospect of other lives in danger. Then there was the small matter of protecting the money of individuals who had a right to expect their investments in companies to be used in the pursuit of honest, profit-making business objectives. Finally, he ruminated on his own government's lax immigration policy when it had come to the admittance of former German Nazis in the years following World War II.

"Better to fight terrorism overseas today than within your own borders tomorrow," he thought to himself.

There were three nation's agencies involved – Germany's NRW, America's FBI and Israel's Mossad. Now a fourth, Canada's RCMP, was about to be dragged into the complicated case unfolding in North America and Europe. Everyone needed to be on the same page with a cohesive and comprehensive plan that could be implemented quickly.

Edge pivoted to face Connors: "Cam. Let's see if we can arrange a conference call with Lou Boaz and the FBI field agent working the Stateside case. Did Boaz give us a name?"

"Yes sir. The field agent is Sammy Eisenstat," Connors said. "Knowing the level of coordination required, Mr. Boaz already suggested a 3 p.m. call. He'd have Eisenstat with him."

***

The conference call lasted less than a half hour, largely because all parties agreed that any discussion about an action plan required participation of the Mossad's David Katzman as well as officers of the North Rhine-Westphalia departments involved in the Hanna Schröder/GWH GmbH case.

Sammy Eisenstat briefed Connors and Edgerton on the individuals from German law enforcement – Bertram Krieger of the NRW Landeskriminalamt in Düsseldorf (LKA NRW); Gustav Zimmermann, the officer-in-charge of the NRW Police Force inspection team investigating events surrounding the fatal auto accident; and Jakob Seidel, case officer for the NRW Exchange Supervisory Authority and the individual who'd be determining whether the events surrounding Hanna's death warranted any action with respect to the possible initial public offering of securities by GWH GmbH to the investing public.

Eisenstat emerged from the conversation as the person charged with arranging a planning session in Düsseldorf with all interested parties – a session that would include Krieger, Zimmermann and Seidel of the NRW; the Mossad's Katzman, and Cam Connors of the RCMP.

Ultimately, a meeting was set for Friday, June 3rd, at 11:00 a.m., after the Wednesday services to be held for the late Hanna Schröder at Basilika St. Laurentius in Wuppertal. One other item upon which all participants agreed – time would be set aside late Friday afternoon for a second interview with Gretchen Weiß Hauptmann. Arranging for the GWH GmbH founder's appearance would be the joint responsibility of Bertram Krieger and Jakob Seidel.

Chapter 46 – Memorial Day Marred

Abigail couldn't have ordered better weather for the Memorial Day extravaganza. Blue skies dominated the Bluegrass State and were accompanied by a warm westerly breeze, temperatures in the low 80s and slow-moving cumulus clouds parading over Lexington and heading east toward neighboring West Virginia.

Chauffeured limousines, town cars, vintage automobiles and current luxury models began to appear at the gated entrance to the Wellington estate by mid-morning. At 10:30, several dozen vehicles started their long and winding half-mile drive over the graded and packed dirt road that led to a parking area roughly the size of four football fields laid side-by-side. Visitors emerging from their vehicles were no more than 150 to 200 feet to the left of the mansion Abigail, Bentley and Beauregard Wellington called home.

A staff of attractive young men and women from *Bluegrass Gas* was waiting to greet guests, quickly moving them to a tented dining area for their first meal of the day. Brunch, served between 11 o'clock and 12:30, included scrambled eggs, flapjacks and Belgian waffles; sausage links, maple-glazed bacon and country ham; and grits, biscuits with gravy and hash browns. All items were laid out on two long wood tables (one for adults and the other for children) in a series of stainless-steel heating trays. The tables were covered with royal blue and white checkered table cloths patterned after the Triple-B Racing Stables' jockey silks. An assortment of muffins, breakfast rolls, citrus fruits and cold cereals were available for those preferring lighter fare.

Several dozen tables, most set for four people but a number of which accommodated parties of eight to a dozen, afforded convenient and comfortable seating. Hot coffee and tea, iced sweet tea, orange juice, milk and water, as well as Bloody Marys and Mimosas were offered by female servers dressed in "Daisy Duke" blue-jean shorts, white tied blouses and matching leather boots.

A second meal, to be served between seven o'clock and eight-thirty in the evening, would be a classic Blue Grass Pig Pickin'. Laurie Van Zant of *Blue Grass Gas* had encouraged cut zucchini, asparagus, bell peppers, onions, tomatoes and eggplant as vegetable accoutrements surrounding the roasted pigs, along with grilled pineapple rings, corn on the cob and baked potatoes as additional sides. The evening's meal preparation actually had begun late Sunday afternoon.

After brunch had been served, the children were taken to the fenced-in two-acre theatre-in-the-round set up for the skit and sing-along featuring the characters of Fraggle Rock. At the same time, adults headed to one of the Wellington family's feed-storage barns to view the concluding episode of M*A*S*H on a giant screen.

Immediately thereafter, Beau Wellington took advantage of the captive audience to show a 20-minute film highlighting the breeding and racing successes of Thoroughbred Bs Farm and Triple-B Racing Stables. While Thoroughbred Bs Farm hadn't yet entered the "quiet period" (an SEC-mandated embargo on promotional publicity), Beau was careful not to include any financial elements in the piece.

Throughout the course of the day, Beau had, as planned, sought out each of the Commonwealth's leading horsemen. He was certainly disappointed in the largely negative opinions about the wisdom of a public offering. In a brief late-afternoon comment, Beau passed along his assessment to Abby: "Although they didn't come right out and say it, our peers seem to feel 'the sport of kings' should remain firmly *and wholly* in the hands of the kings. Let's face it, Abby. We're pioneers and will be judged by the success or failure of our operation in the aftermath of the public offering."

Although she didn't say it, her son's comments crystallized in her own mind the administrative and operational challenges to be faced by a publicly traded TBF, Inc. and the incredible physical and mental toll it would exact upon those trying to make things work. And given Beau's demons, she wondered whether he – no, actually whether *they* – were up to the task.

Returning to events of the day, Abigail was pleasantly surprised at the positive reception accorded the Michael Jackson cover band. Once again, kudos to Laurie Van Zant for an outside-the-box idea that placed smiles on the faces of the Wellingtons' guests.

While the evening meal was still a few hours away, food and drink were widely accessible – from a steady stream of servers heading in and out of the temporary kitchen set up in the guest house behind the family mansion as well as at three tables strategically located next to open-bar stations.

The servers had been well rehearsed in descriptions of the hors d'oeuvres they were offering to guests, many of which hid their delights under pastry. At the tables, a dozen food items were offered on a rotating basis. Flanking the hors d'oeuvres at both ends were a charcuterie board and accompanying spread of assorted cheeses, pâtés and crackers. Descriptors of the food offerings were displayed on cardboard placards so guests understood what they'd be consuming.

Both food and drink were being consumed at a record-breaking pace, judging by total server round trips to and from the kitchen; *Blue Grass Gas* food truck deliveries from the caterer's headquarters in downtown Lexington, and discarded bottles of wine, hard liquor, mixers and soda.

Laurie Van Zant had also recommended using no fewer than six high-end, 13-ft. multi-unit portable toilets – three men's suites and three women's suites with one of each located adjacent to the theatre-in-the-round, the "movie-going" barn and tented dining area. "While it might seem like overkill," she'd told Abigail, "it would virtually eliminate any waiting and enable us to clean up any mess with no inconvenience to your guests." Mrs. Wellington, sparing no expense, certainly understood the rationale.

That evening's pig pickin' was a fitting culinary climax to the day's food festivities, particularly as desserts included "home"-baked apple pie, peach cobbler, New York cheese cake, crème brûlée and vanilla and chocolate ice cream served atop old-fashioned sugar cones "for kids big and small."

Fully sated, the Wellington family's guests settled in for the fireworks scheduled to get underway at 10 p.m.

***

For Bentley Wellington, the day had been markedly unremarkable. The much-anticipated arrival of his German friends had not materialized. Abigail's perfunctory request to the Kentucky Association of Counties to push their members to streamline the laws of Kentucky governing the sale and consumption of alcoholic beverages had resulted in the equally perfunctory response from Director of Public Affairs Joan Ashcraft and Director of

Governmental Relations Mary Beth Colston: "We'll see what we can do." He hadn't fared much better with John Daniels, the ABC Board's Distilled Spirits Administrator.

Bentley had been perfectly happy to allow Beau to take the lead in discussing with Steinberg Stavros Rogers & Co's Sven Ericsson a more aggressive profile in the family's investment portfolio, particularly since he, Bentley, had zero taste for gambling on Wall Street. He'd long been an advocate of a conservative position in the capital markets.

As far as Silverstein-Gladstone was concerned, he wanted no part of Arthur Zinstein and the pending IPO. At least Zinstein had the good sense to segregate the racing part of the Wellingtons' thoroughbred business from the breeding component. It made the investment less volatile. The bottom line?...Bentley had little patience for his son's growing tendency to play fast and loose with the family fortune – whether it be on Wall Street or at the races.

As dusk descended on the Wellington estate, the patriarch of the Commonwealth's "first family" sat alone in his study. He was taking time to review Bourbonesque's first-quarter financials and to read through departmental memos from the marketing and operations departments.

Ever since his hunting accident confined him to a wheelchair, he'd found the family's massive Memorial Day event increasingly tiring. Forced conversations and the traditional Wellington pig pickin' were not on his list of preferred holiday activities. Bentley never looked forward to the business or political discourse. And for all the obligatory pig roasts he'd attended during his career in politics, Bentley's taste buds actually railed against pork in all of its permutations.

Two things he *did* like, however, were the fireworks finale and the variety of hors d'oeuvres that served as a bridge between the two main meals offered to guests. Bentley routinely made an obligatory appearance at the pig pickin' before retiring to his study to catch up on some paperwork and feast on appetizers while awaiting the evening's final activities.

Bentley Wellington was ideally positioned to view the evening-ending fireworks from the massive west-facing window. Placed on top of the 30-inch wide ledge running the length of the window about three feet from the floor were five Sterno burners. At about nine o'clock, a member of the wait staff wheeled in a serving cart with five steel trays filled with stuffed mushrooms, mini spinach and cheese pizza rolls, buttermilk fried chicken fingers, pigs-in-a-blanket and mini quiches.

"What do we have here, young lady?" Bentley asked, adding "And what's your name?"

"My name is Darci," she answered and then described each hors d'oeuvre as she set the tray atop the wire holder above each Sterno burner.

"These mushrooms are baked and stuffed with goat cheese and bread crumbs," Darci began.

Then placing the second tray in its place…"These mini spinach and cheese pizza rolls consist of pizza sauce, wilted spinach and parmesan cheese rolled into whole wheat pizza dough and then baked until golden brown and gooey." She smiled, almost blushing, as she uttered the word 'gooey'.

Moving to the third tray, Darci offered the Governor detailed preparation instructions: "These are buttermilk fried chicken fingers, which we prepare by flattening chicken breasts, slicing them into strips and placing them in a large bowl. Then we completely cover the strips with buttermilk and refrigerate for about five hours.

"Before frying, we fill pie plates with flour and season with salt and pepper. We then heat skillets with about a half inch of oil and simultaneously coat the chicken fingers with the seasoned flour. It takes 10 to 12 minutes to fry each batch."

Darci showed Bentley the fourth tray which contained about a dozen mini quiches. "These are incredibly sumptuous," she explained while using her tongue in a circular motion to wet her lips. "The insides have salmon with spinach and mild cheddar cheese that will melt in your mouth."

Moving on to the last tray, Darci turned Bentley's wheelchair so that it faced her. "You know what these are, Governor…Pigs in a blanket. Remind you of anything?" She leaned towards him, bending over so he could see her perky breasts beneath her blouse. Her freckled cheeks and long, fiery red hair brushed against his mouth as she moved closer still and flicked out her tongue in his left ear.

"The last two years you've been the highlight of my Memorial Day weekend, Darci," Bentley offered in a raspy voice that clearly showed he was losing control.

"Well, Governor. Let's make sure nothing changes this year." With that, Darci unzipped the Governor's pants and began stroking his shaft to bring it to attention. While doing so, she took Bentley's right hand and placed it on her crotch.

Bentley thought to himself. "Lord Jesus, thank you for allowing me to still function."

With the moves of someone who'd done the deed at least a few times before, the 21-year-old "townie" tore open a Trojan wrapper, placed the rubber in her mouth, bent down and slipped the protection on Bentley's now hardened member while taking in all of its considerable length.

The elderly Wellington was amazed she remembered from one year to the next exactly how he liked it. Was it the $300 "contribution" to her Lexington Community College tuition? Or did she simply come by it naturally? The slow, wet warmth of Darci's mouth moving up and down, accompanied by her swirling tongue and soft moans of encouragement, gave him such an amazing sensation. He felt like his eyeballs were going to pop out of their sockets.

Then Darci was sitting on top of him, driving him deep into her and using her seemingly endless legs to move herself up and down his pole. He still couldn't get over how his lower extremities felt absolutely nothing while his manhood made him feel so alive.

"Give it to me hard!... Piledrive me!... Ahhhhhhh!" And then it was over. The sexual fireworks he'd just experienced set a really high bar for the pyrotechnics to come outside.

Darci cleaned up quickly. She removed the rubber and wrapper; used a tissue to wipe Bentley's groin; placed the rubber, wrapper and tissue in a second tissue and tossed it in the waste basket under the desk.

"Wallet's over there," Bentley managed while still breathing quite heavily. Without skipping a beat, she opened the Governor's wallet, removed three, crisp $100 bills, folded them twice and placed them in her oval squeeze mini-coin purse. She then rolled the serving cart into the far corner of the room. Looking over her shoulder as she left the office, she said: "My pleasure, Governor. Enjoy the food, and happy Memorial Day!" Bentley was already feeding his face, famished after his escapade.

Walking briskly down the hallway, she passed by an expectant Abigail Prescott Wellington. "Did you satisfy him, Darci?"

"Pretty sure, Mrs. Wellington. The Governor couldn't wait to dive into his hors d'oeuvres."

Pleased to hear of her performance, the Wellington family matriarch waited until Darci was out of sight before returning to the crowd of guests who were about to witness the long day's final event.

Back in the office, Bentley Wellington removed a fifth of 101 proof Bourbonesque from the nearby liquor cabinet, gave himself a two-ounce pour and washed down a couple of mini quiches he'd just popped in his mouth. "They really are exquisite," he said to himself.

A couple of minutes later, he felt his lips, tongue and then throat begin to swell, almost imperceptibly at first but then rapidly worsening. Now having difficulty breathing and then convulsing, he felt a sharp pain coursing through his left arm and shoulder before losing consciousness.

At that moment Darci, having left her coin purse on the serving cart in Bentley's study, returned to retrieve it. Seeing him slumped over the desk and motionless, she panicked. Picking up her purse, she rushed from the study, walking quickly down the hallway and out the front door. With the pyrotechnics just then starting, the young redhead left the Wellington estate in her powder blue 1975 VW Beetle without anyone noticing her hasty departure.

Her head spinning, Darci stopped 15 minutes down the road at a payphone located by a gas station. Fearing the worst, Darci called 911 and quickly told the dispatcher on duty that she believed former Kentucky Governor Bentley Wellington "had suffered a medical setback" at his residence and urged the dispatcher to have an ambulance sent immediately to the Lexington estate. Not waiting for questions, she hung up the receiver, returned to her car and made her way to I-64 West. She didn't stop until reaching Louisville where she found a pub near the University of Louisville campus.

Taking a seat at a swivel chair toward the back of the bar, Darci downed three large drafts along with far too many beer nuts. When the pub closed at 2:00 a.m., she stumbled out, found her vehicle near the back of the parking lot and fell asleep at the wheel of her car before starting the engine, not wanting to think about what the morning might bring.

Meanwhile, the former two-term Governor of the Commonwealth of Kentucky, current chief executive of Bourbonesque LLC and patriarch of Kentucky's "first family" hadn't survived long enough to see his last fireworks show, although he certainly experienced one of life's great pleasures before passing on.

Chapter 47 – More Questions than Answers

With the 45-minute fireworks show almost over, Abigail was approached by Woodrow, the Wellingtons' long-time butler. Now 70, the stately black gentleman had been in the family's employ since just before Bentley Wellington's second term as governor. He was trembling as he described what had transpired over the past 20 minutes.

A phone call had come from the Fayette County sheriff's department at about 10:15 p.m. The officer at the other end of the line explained to Woodrow that a 911 dispatcher received an anonymous but urgent call from an obviously distressed individual indicating Bentley Wellington had "suffered a medical setback." Could he check on the former governor's condition and call him back on his direct line? Meanwhile, an ambulance from the University of Kentucky Hospital was on its way.

Heading to the study where he knew the Governor typically retreated to watch the fireworks, Woodrow had found Bentley slumped over the desk and motionless. Within minutes, the ambulance had made its way up the long drive leading to the Wellington estate.

Woodrow met the team at the front door and guided them to the study. Paramedic Jonathan Jackson examined Bentley Wellington, looked up at the butler and shook his head. "He's gone." Jackson told Woodrow to find Mrs. Wellington while he called the officer at the Fayette County Sheriff's Department to give him an update.

Given the high public profile of the deceased, the large number of visitors whose whereabouts could not be established at any specific point in time, the anonymous call and the obscure information provided to the dispatcher, the officer decided a detective and CSI officer should head to the Wellington estate and instructed Jackson to make sure nobody entered the study.

By 11:30, virtually all of the Memorial Day crowd had left the grounds. A few of the departing guests asked about the ambulance parked in front of the mansion. Woodrow told those folks the ambulance was there in case anyone was injured by the evening's pyrotechnics.

Moments later, Detective Galen Grauman of the Lexington Bureau of Investigation and Carly Selman, senior investigator with the City's Crime Scene Investigation Group, arrived on the scene.

Grauman stepped from his 1978 Chevy Impala dressed in a well-worn medium brown sports jacket, beige khaki pants and brown penny loafers. Selman emerged from a white van marked "Lexington CSI," wearing a CSI jacket and light blue cotton pants, carrying a large bag stocked with everything she could possibly need: consent/search forms, graph paper and pencils; crime scene barricade tape; index cards, spray paint and other markers to place by noted evidence items; a camera and extra film; a flashlight with extra batteries and footwear casting materials; a small ruler, measuring wheel and tape measures; a latent print kit, bodily fluid collection kit, disposable tweezers, evidence seals/tape and paper bags, and personal protective equipment (e.g., gloves, booties, hair covering, overalls and mask).

Abigail, who had returned to her residence after sending the last of the Wellingtons' departing guests on their way, met the two law enforcement officers at the door. Detective Grauman and Officer Selman introduced themselves and offered condolences for her loss. Abigail asked the detective and CSI officer if they would like coffee. "We'll need some time in the study, Mrs. Wellington," the detective replied. "Then I'll need to ask you a few questions. Coffee would be fine at that time."

Selman then handed Abigail a consent/search form, explaining that Kentucky law required her signature to enable the Lexington CSI Group to examine the study and gather evidence. Seeing her apprehension, Grauman added: "Given the 911 dispatch call from someone who clearly did not want to be identified but was apparently aware something had gone wrong, we need to do everything possible to preserve the scene of your husband's death. We're not saying a crime was committed, but we certainly want to determine cause of death."

Nodding her understanding and signing the form, Abigail then called into the kitchen: "Edna. Would you please brew us a pot of coffee?" She then asked Woodrow to escort her "guests" to the study. "I have to find my son, Beau, to let him know about his father. If you'll excuse me."

Entering the study, Grauman thanked Woodrow for his assistance, the tone of his voice clearly indicating he and his colleague from CSI were to be left alone to comb the room and examine the body.

Donning booties, gloves, hair covering and mask, Selman began by taking photographs of the body from multiple angles. Upon close inspection, she noticed what appeared to be traces of vomit in the deceased's mouth and on the desk near his face. Reaching for her bodily fluid collection kit, the CSI officer carefully captured the residue for evaluation by the crime lab.

Grauman, gloves and booties now on his hands and feet to make sure he wouldn't contaminate the area, was focusing on the uneaten food items remaining in trays still sitting atop the Sterno burners. He noted that decidedly fewer quiches remained than the number of other appetizers.

"Carly, when you have a moment would you come over here and place the remaining hors d'oeuvres in sealed plastic bags, separating each food type in its own bag?" Then looking down at the waste basket to the left of the desk, he added: "And you might want to use your tweezers to retrieve the contents of the trash can. I suspect the crime lab will need to examine all of these items. We'll want to check for finger prints."

After the detective and CSI officer finished the bulk of their work in the study, Grauman instructed the paramedic to transport the body to the University of Kentucky Hospital for examination by a physician, who was licensed to officially pronounce the body "DOA" (dead on arrival). Selman would follow the ambulance to the hospital and talk with the physician responsible for examining the deceased while Grauman interviewed the widow.

Carly Selman's final tasks were to mark and document the deceased's position and cordon off the study with yellow crime-scene tape.

***

Abigail rejoined Detective Grauman in the living room and was accompanied by her son, Beauregard, who was disoriented from a combination of alcohol and the news of his father's death.

Motioning for the detective to make himself comfortable on the sofa, she and Beau sat on easy chairs directly across from Grauman. Edna emerged from the kitchen with a porcelain pot of coffee, three cups and saucers, a creamer and condiments set on a silver tray, which she placed on a coffee table situated between Grauman and the two Wellingtons.

"How do you take your coffee, sir?" inquired Edna. Galen Grauman took his black with Sweet'n'Low. The housekeeper poured a second cup for Abigail and a third for Beau. Both took their caffeine with cream and sugar.

Detective Grauman pulled a small pad and ball-point pen from the inside pocket of his sports jacket and began to ask questions:

"When was the last time you saw your husband alive, Mrs. Wellington?" Grauman began.

"Let me think for a minute," said Abigail as she paused to consider what had transpired over the course of a long and very busy day. "It was either during the M*A*S*H episode viewing in our barn or during the Michael Jackson tribute. With so many guests, Bentley, Beau and I seldom see each other and almost never spend time together. In fact, we always have a pre-event logistics meeting to go over roles and responsibilities. Given my husband's mobility issues, our butler Woodrow typically moves him from place to place."

"So," the detective asked, "would it be safe to say that Woodrow knows the approximate time your husband was wheeled into the study?"

Abigail nodded affirmatively, asking if the detective would like to have Woodrow come in to answer that question. Grauman agreed, thinking he could always follow up at another time if additional questions for the butler proved necessary. Extremely competent and used to working for a family that was highly organized and lived by a timetable, Woodrow quickly established for the detective a window between 7:45 and 8:00 p.m. as the approximate time the deceased had been wheeled into the study.

With Abigail, Beauregard and Woodrow all together, the detective then asked: "Do you know of anyone who might have visited Mr. Wellington between the time he'd been brought to the study and the time the Fayette County sheriff's department called to ask that someone to check on him?"

Grauman watched intently as Beau and Woodrow exchanged uneasy glances and then turned expectantly toward Abigail. Looking a bit uncomfortable, she began a rather lengthy explanation of what had turned into an annual Memorial Day ritual in the years following the 1980 hunting accident and stroke that had left her husband paralyzed in his lower extremities.

"Bentley and I hadn't been intimate for quite some time. But he periodically complained about still having 'urges' and longed for a woman to service him." Galen Grauman tried desperately to keep a poker face while listening to Abigail struggle to find the proper words to describe the situation. Beau was having his own difficulties in processing this apparently new information about his late father – particularly coming from the lips of his mother...in response to a detective's questioning...and in front of the family butler.

Abigail continued: "Bentley knew from, uh...personal experience that he could, er...still function. She then interrupted her narrative. "Detective, this is so very difficult!" With that, tears began to trickle down her cheeks.

"Take your time, Mrs. Wellington. I understand how challenging this must be," Galen said in a reassuring voice.

"One of the barn hands here at our stables is a rather attractive young lady who comes from poor folks. She'd been saving money to put herself through community college. A few years back, she asked if we had any additional work available so she could earn some extra money. She had a bit of a reputation as a fast girl, so I broached the subject of satisfying my husband."

Beauregard's jaw dropped as his mother continued. Woodrow, who didn't seem at all surprised by the unfolding story, simply stood nearby...motionless.

Abigail finished her story by detailing the skit as a "full-service" member of the wait staff that Darci McDougal first played on Memorial Day of 1981 as a then-18-year-old barn hand and part-time college student. It was a role she would reprise the following year and for a third time earlier that evening.

"To answer your question, detective: Yes, I saw Darci McDougal coming down the hallway from the study where Bentley had been waiting for the fireworks to begin. I asked Darci if the Governor enjoyed himself. She said he had and noted he'd worked up a pretty good appetite in the process. I don't recall her *exact* words."

"Just a couple more questions for now, Mrs. Wellington." Detective Grauman was going over his notes and then looked up. "Do you know what time you and Darci exchanged words?"

"As a matter of fact, I do," Abigail said quickly. "Darci was supposed to finish with Bentley shortly before the fireworks show was to begin at 10 p.m. Not wanting to interfere with what I knew was going on in the study, I waited about halfway down the hallway. I wanted to check with her before heading outside to the grandstand to announce the start of our grand finale. It was 9:45."

"Last question, Mrs. Wellington. The skit…with Darci dressed as a member of the wait staff, wheeling in the hors d'oeuvres, beginning to describe them and carrying out the subsequent seduction scene. Whose idea was that?"

Detective Galen Grauman's trained eyes witnessed a subtle change in Abigail's body language as the widow swallowed before answering: "Darci seemed to think that creating the illusion of seduction by a stranger would heighten and hasten my husband's sexual arousal. To my way of thinking, dressing like one of the servers made it easier for Darci to move from the food prep area to the study without attracting attention."

Listening to Mrs. Wellington's explanation, Grauman concluded aloud: "So it was a collaboration."

"Yes, I guess you could say that," agreed Abigail.

Closing his note pad, the detective rose and thanked Abigail, Beauregard and Woodrow for their time and cooperation "after a long day and under the most difficult of circumstances." Grauman informed the Wellingtons they'd be hearing from the Fayette County Coroner's Office about the cause of death.

"If I have further questions, I'll call. We'll likely need to speak with Darci McDougal tomorrow." With that, Woodrow escorted Galen Grauman to the door. A few minutes later, the detective was headed to the hospital where he would be reconnecting with Carly Selman. All Galen could do was sigh at the prospect of another "all-nighter."

Chapter 48 – AuTopsy-Turvy

Now approaching one o'clock in the morning, Galen Grauman quickly found Carly Selman in the office of the examining physician. Dr. Francis Fitzgerald had completed his exam and was preparing documents confirming what Galen, Carly and the deceased's wife and son already knew: Bentley Wellington would be declared "dead on arrival." Additionally, Dr. Fitzgerald would also establish an official time of death.

As soon as Selman had arrived at the hospital, she'd called Alex White at his home in Georgetown, about 15 miles north of downtown Lexington. White was in charge of the Fayette County Medical Examiner & Coroner's Office. When learning of Bentley Wellington's death and what Selman's initial inspection of the Wellington study had uncovered, he told the CSI officer he'd be at his office within the hour and would do his level best to have a senior colleague, Evelyn Proctor, join them.

"As soon as the physician on duty makes his pronouncement, he should order the body sent to our office," White told Selman who, in turn, relayed the directive to Dr. Fitzgerald. That would be an easy task inasmuch as the hospital's location was less than two miles from the coroner's office.

One significant factor made investigation into the probable cause of death of Bentley Wellington a bit less time-consuming. Given his status as a former governor of the Commonwealth, two major health-related incidents had been extensively reported by the state's media outlets and were a matter of public record – his near-death experience back in the '50s due to a severe allergic reaction to ingesting Maryland blue crab at the annual Governors Conference in Baltimore, and the more recent hunting accident in Tennessee and subsequent stroke he suffered in 1980.

"I have some rather interesting items we'll need to run through the State Police Crime Lab in Frankfort," Selman told White. "Detective Grauman and I will be at your office within the next hour or two. The detective will be able to provide you with some context."

Shortly thereafter, Galen Grauman joined Selman at the hospital. Pleased with the progress and knowing it would be awhile before Alex White would be ready to see them, Grauman suggested to Carly they head over to the Waffle House for a very early breakfast and some coffee.

"Guess you missed your opportunity for caffeine back at the Wellington estate. It may not be in your job description, but I'd like to get your opinion on the info provided by Mrs. Wellington. I usually get to play "good cop-bad cop" with my partner, Al Trowbridge, who's not at all shy about second-guessing me. He won't be back from vacation until Wednesday, so I'm hoping you'll fill in – unofficially of course."

Hesitating, Grauman then removed some folded bills from his right pants pocket to take stock of money on-hand and added with a slight chuckle: "Yep, I got it...Breakfast is on me!"

"You said the magic words," said Carly. Ten minutes later, their vehicles parked in front of the bright yellow sign with black lettering, Galen recounted his interview with Abigail Prescott Wellington over a couple of pots of hot coffee, cheese n' eggs, Jimmy Dean sausage and grits.

***

Now on his third cup of joe, Detective Grauman was listening to Carly Selman's take on the Wellington interview:

"As I go over the evening's chronology, one thing doesn't seem to fit," Carly said as she reached once again for her half-full coffee mug that had been annoyingly lukewarm for the past 10 minutes. "Abigail made it clear she wanted to check on Darci's progress before re-joining her guests for the fireworks. She indicated the two had exchanged words, which included a comment by Darci on Bentley Wellington's post-coitus appetite." Selman paused and asked rhetorically: "If this was the third rendition of 'Darci-Bentley,' why did Mrs. Wellington need to check in ... particularly in the midst of such a hectic agenda? Wouldn't it have been just as easy to wait 15 or 20 minutes longer and see how her husband was doing after the fireworks show had begun?"

Grauman rubbed his chin while contemplating the CSI officer's question: "Maybe she wanted to be with her guests during the finale," the detective said. "Or given the great lengths the 'Missus' had gone to in arranging this, oh what would you call it...this annual 'treat,' she wanted to make sure hubby got his money's worth."

"It's so weird, I guess just about anything's possible," Selman paused momentarily. "From an overall perspective, resorting to paid sex seems to support the rumors that the Wellington marriage had long ago become an arrangement of convenience."

Looking up at the clock behind the counter, Grauman slid from the cramped booth and headed to the cash register to pay the bill. Carly asked the waitress for a cup of coffee to go. It was just past three in the morning. By 3:30, they'd be going over the evening's events with Alex White at the Fayette County Medical Examiner & Coroner's office.

***

Some 90 minutes after arriving, Galen Grauman and Carly Selman had given Alex White, director of the Medical Examiner & Coroner's Office, and Evelyn Proctor, the chief medical examiner and licensed forensic pathologist, all the details surrounding the demise of Bentley Wellington. Having listened intently, White paused before offering his thoughts.

"From what you describe and with the information we thus far have available, our emerging theory has us focusing on two internal events – a hemorrhagic stroke and severe case of anaphylaxis. These events may have taken place simultaneously." Dr. Proctor will explain further.

"A hemorrhagic stroke occurs when blood vessels in the brain rupture, causing blood to accumulate in the surrounding brain tissue and placing pressure on the brain. It can leave part of the brain deprived of blood and oxygen. Physical inactivity, heavy alcohol use, smoking, poor dietary habits and drug use are among factors that increase the risk of stroke."

Dr. Proctor paused to allow this initial information to sink in before continuing.

"Anaphylaxis is a serious systemic allergic reaction that is rapid in onset and may cause death. It typically results in the following symptoms that manifest themselves over hours, if not minutes, in an itchy rash, throat or tongue swelling, shortness of breath, vomiting, lightheadedness and low blood pressure. Common causes include insect bites and stings, foods and medications. Other causes include latex exposure.

"Although not common, some people develop anaphylaxis from aerobic exercise, such as jogging, or even less intense physical activity, such as walking. Eating certain foods before exercise or exercising when the weather is hot, cold or humid also has been linked to anaphylaxis in some people.

"Obviously, our hypothesis is supported by Governor Wellington's medical history," Alex White chimed in. "A report from the crime lab confirming the content of the food items gathered from the study and identifying any finger prints from the items retrieved from the waste basket will be helpful. But an autopsy is critical in enabling us to confirm the cause of death," he added.

"When can we expect the lab reports?" asked Grauman. "With the circumstances surrounding the Governor's death, we're certainly in a position to order an autopsy without seeking permission from family members." The detective stopped talking to consider another option. "But maybe we should present the prospect of an autopsy to Mrs. Wellington to get her reaction. If she balks, might it be because she has something to hide?"

With a rush placed on receiving the results, White expected to have the report by the end of business that day. Dr. Proctor said she could perform the autopsy as soon as she had an opportunity to read the report.

"Well," concluded Detective Grauman, "that leaves me to question Darci McDougal; the manager of *Bluegrass Gas*, the firm that handled the Wellington family's Memorial Day bash; and Beauregard Wellington, who clearly had consumed a significant amount of alcohol and seemed to be in shock as a result of his father's sudden death. After I speak with them, I'll have another go at Mrs. Wellington. By tomorrow evening, I'm hoping we'll be in a better position to judge whether the Governor's demise was an unfortunate set of circumstances or due to actions of a more sinister nature. If it's the latter, it all boils down to the same old formula: Who had motive, opportunity and means?"

Chapter 49 – Acquisition Target

Marci Davis Jeffries had built a solid career at Steinberg Stavros Rogers & Co. The midtown-Manhattan global asset management firm was a perfect fit for her, given her expertise in the energy and transportation sectors.

In recent years, Marci had taken on additional responsibilities as a global analyst and policy advisor to the automotive industry, concentrating specifically on supply-chain management. Only a few months earlier at the annual Society of Automotive Engineers (SAE) convention in Detroit, she delivered a well-received paper on the need to streamline communications and operational relationships between OEMs (original equipment manufacturers) and Tiered suppliers.

Companies supplying OEMs with sub-assemblies, components and materials are classified by tiers reflecting their relative commercial distance (i.e., level of direct access and accountability) to the OEM. Tier I suppliers provide their products directly to the manufacturer, while Tier II and III suppliers provide their products to the supplier at the next higher level in the chain.

It wasn't out of the ordinary for Marci's firm to field the occasional call from a mergers & acquisitions firm looking for industry research that might portend changes in the dynamics of a particular business sector.

On this Tuesday morning, the day after Memorial Day, Marci received a call from a young research associate in the Dublin office of Collins, Connell & O'Brien. Shea O'Halloran was looking for information on emerging technologies and supply chain efficiencies for a cash-rich U.K.-based Tier I supplier to the automotive industry. Specifically, Ms. O'Halloran was tasked with determining the pros and cons of acquiring well-run small to mid-sized companies at the Tier II and Tier III levels.

About 10 minutes into the conversation, the researcher popped a question that caught Marci a bit off guard: "And off the top of your head, would you know of any businesses that might see themselves as an acquisition candidate?"

Marci thought for a minute and remembering her son's good

friend, Jorge, she answered: "As a matter of fact I do. There's a firm in Wuppertal, a small town near Düsseldorf, that might prove to be low-hanging fruit. The founder, Gretchen Weiß Hauptmann, still owns the company. GWH GmbH."

Using her department's somewhat antiquated telecopier, Marci sent her research paper and some market analyses to Ms. O'Halloran, who was grateful for not having to wait for an international delivery. Before ending the call, Marci suggested Ms. O'Halloran act promptly on the information related to the powder metal parts producer.

"The P/M industry is at the early stages of a big consolidation trend. As owners of Mom & Pop shops look to cash in on their lifetime investments, they'll be snapped up by large companies that can afford the R&D funds necessary to develop robust processes, increase reliability and improve operating efficiencies. Additionally, they'll be acquiring existing contracts with OEMs and Tier I suppliers who would likely welcome greater stability in the supply chain."

In Ireland, Shea O'Halloran was busy taking notes and printed in bold lettering **GWH GmbH/Wuppertal, Germany/Gretchen Weiß Hauptmann**. O'Halloran now underlined with her ball-point pen – twice for emphasis – the information and scribbled "Steinberg Stavros analyst recommends quick action." Then in all caps the research associate added the words: "ACQUISITION TARGET!"

Chapter 50 – Reflections Interrupted

It was approaching half past nine as Calvin Thomas stood over a ribeye he was pan-frying for dinner. Calvin had taken it from the freezer moments ago and simply dumped it into the pan, seasoned it and turned up the burner to begin the process of converting the meat from its frozen state to a perfectly prepared medium rare. After years of repetition, he'd mastered the ability to by-pass defrosting – a situation necessitated by far too many late-night meals following long hours logged as a Brooklyn detective. Having spent the entire day and part of the evening negotiating Memorial Day traffic, Calvin was craving red meat and mashed potatoes... and lots of both.

Calvin reflected on the day's events. He'd started at nine that morning in Atlantic City when he picked up Connie Pett for her return trip to Manhattan's West side. Traffic had become increasingly congested as he and his passenger moved north on the Garden State Parkway until transferring to the New Jersey Turnpike before crossing the Raritan River. From that point to the George Washington Bridge, vehicles were crawling.

It wasn't until four in the afternoon that he'd exited the West Side Highway at the 79th Street Boat Basin and pulled in front of Consuela's apartment building at the corner of West End Avenue and W. 79th Street.

Carrying her luggage to the elevator, he suddenly realized how comfortable he'd become in Connie's presence. Between the Saturday evening gathering at the Molly Pitcher Inn and the drive back to the City, Calvin had come to learn about Consuela Parks Pettiford, her legal career and the family tragedy that resulted in her trip to A.C. As a detective, he had an inkling about the nature of the newly formed relationship between Connie and Jasmine. It was one of the few topics he refused to explore.

Calvin hadn't been alone in thinking about the Memorial Day weekend. While the pair waited for the elevator to reach the lobby, Consuela was struck by the realization that she'd be alone in her apartment after spending so much time over the past five days in the company of others.

Friday and Saturday evenings with Jasmine had been what?... Adventurous? Exhilarating? Both, to be sure. Had she learned anything about her own sexuality? She appeared to be comfortable with another woman. Or was it the person rather than the gender? And what *were* her feelings toward Jasmine?...Love? No, it was way too early for that. But in the aftermath of two extraordinary evenings of physical indulgence, what stayed with her most was... yes, a growing friendship!

And what about the gentleman standing alongside her? She'd found him physically attractive at first glance. He was self-assured, intelligent, worldly...and he projected a sense of serenity and security. Were those traits she longed for in a partner? Or was it the circumstances surrounding the recent death of her parents that made those qualities particularly desirable at this time?

As the elevator door opened, Consuela was struck with a sudden sense of urgency: "Calvin, would you like to join me for a drink? You must be incredibly tired from all that driving."

As the detective flipped over his ribeye and added butter and milk to the pot of instant mashed potato flakes, the lines in his forehead crinkled as he recalled his response: "Appreciate the invitation, Consuela. But the sooner I get back on the road, the sooner I'll be home."

With that, Consuela reached up and gave him a kiss on his left cheek, her lips remaining there for a good few seconds. "Thanks for the tour on Thursday, Calvin. You have my business card and home phone number." She took her suitcase, garment bag and tote from Calvin, stepped inside the elevator and waved as the door closed.

***

Alternately downing chunks of steak and swallowing mouthfuls of mashed potatoes (with an occasional swig of Coke to wash everything down), Calvin Thomas was carefully considering the number of days he should wait before calling Consuela. He finally decided on Thursday evening, allowing two full days to pass but not waiting any longer. He wouldn't presume she'd be home at the start of a weekend.

Calvin's raging internal debate was suddenly halted by the ring of his telephone. Reaching for the wall-mounted unit by the kitchen table at which he was seated, he wondered who'd be calling just after midnight following the long holiday weekend.

"Calvin Thomas? This is FBI field agent Madison Meriwether in Lexington – Matts to those in the Bureau who know me."

Barely able to acknowledge that Meriwether was indeed speaking to the person he'd been seeking, Matts continued: "I've been assigned to continue monitoring activities of the Wellington family here in Kentucky, which includes maintaining electronic surveillance of their Lexington estate. I believe you were the person who installed that equipment?"

"Yes, that's right," answered Calvin, wondering where this conversation was headed. "Can I help you with something?"

"Well, sir. I've been unable to get in touch with Sammy Eisenstat, the FBI field officer up your way who's in charge of the current investigation. So I'm reaching out to you," Meriwether said and then paused. "It seems we have a situation on our hands."

About 20 minutes later and with Meriwether's update completed, Calvin Thomas asked: "Can you play the pertinent section of the tape for me?"

FBI field agent Madison Meriwether obliged:

Bentley Wellington: "What do we have here, young lady? And what's your name?"

Darci McDougal: "My name is Darci. *(Pause with noise of a first tray being placed on a Sterno burner.)* "These mushrooms are baked and stuffed with goat cheese and bread crumbs.

Darci McDougal: *(Pause with noise of a second tray being placed on a Sterno burner.)* "These mini spinach and cheese pizza rolls consist of pizza sauce, wilted spinach and parmesan cheese rolled into whole wheat pizza dough and then baked until golden brown and gooey.

Darci McDougal: *(Pause with noise of a third tray being placed on a Sterno burner.)* "These are buttermilk fried chicken fingers, which we prepare by flattening chicken breasts, slicing them into large strips and placing them in a large bowl. Then we completely cover the strips with buttermilk and refrigerate for about five hours. Before frying, we fill pie plates with flour and season with salt and pepper. We then heat skillets with about a half inch of oil and simultaneously coat the chicken fingers with the seasoned flour. It takes 10 to 12 minutes to fry each batch."

Darci McDougal: *(Pause with noise of a fourth tray being placed on a Sterno burner.)* "These are incredibly sumptuous. The insides have salmon with spinach and mild cheddar cheese that will melt in your mouth."

Darci McDougal: *(pause with noise of last tray being placed on a Sterno burner.)* "You know what these are, Governor...Pigs in a blanket. Remind you of anything?"

Bentley Wellington: "The last two years, you've been the highlight of my Memorial Day weekend, Darci."

Darci McDougal: "Well, Governor. Let's make sure nothing changes this year." *(Sound of pants being unzipped.)*

Bentley Wellington: *(moaning and panting)*

(Sound of a wrapper being torn followed soon thereafter by slurping sounds. Another pause is followed by wheelchair movement.)

Bentley Wellington: "Give it to me hard!... Piledrive me!... Ahhhhhhh!"

(Sound of something being tossed into a waste basket)

Bentley Wellington: "Wallet's over there." *Heavy breathing followed by sound of crisp bills being counted and then a service cart being rolled across the room.)*

Darci McDougal: "My pleasure, Governor. Enjoy the food and happy Memorial Day!" *(Sound of Darci exiting the room.)*

(Sounds of a person eating food from the trays and then opening a cabinet and pouring a drink from a bottle.)

The balance of the tape included a thud and wretched gasps for air. A minute or two of silence was followed by the sound of footsteps entering the room. A pause was followed by the same footsteps hastily exiting the room.

Calvin Thomas whistled softly after listening to the tape. Then to FBI field agent Meriwether: "One way or another, Matts, I'll get ahold of Sammy Eisenstat within the next couple of hours. I'm sure Sammy will call you directly."

Chapter 51 – Let's Go to the Audio Tapes

Did the 3 a.m. meal at Waffle House constitute a very early breakfast or a very late dinner? In either case, Galen Grauman felt the need to start his "official" Tuesday workday with coffee and something solid to eat.

Just leaving was the overnight waitress who recognized him from the wee hours of the morning. "Back again so soon?" she said. "You must lead one hell of an interesting life."

"Don't worry, sugar. I'll take care of your man!" A rather attractive brunette sauntered over to that section of the counter where Galen was seated. "Whatever Dixie served you last night, I guarantee *Pixie's* food will taste a whole lot better."

"Is this an act the two of you have? Now don't tell me, your compadre over there is Mr. Jinks!"

"No, this is Sam Sellers. Be nice to him or you might find shells in your scrambled eggs." Clearly, Pixie had taken the detective's comment literally and didn't catch his reference to the trio of Hanna-Barbera cartoon characters and Mr. Jinks' signature line: "I hate you meeces to pieces!"

Rather than explain himself, Galen simply asked for a hard roll and butter with his coffee. He had too much on his mind and far too little sleep to deal with this much-too-perky personality. More to shut off further discourse than to read the latest news, he stepped outside the door and bought a copy of the *Courier-Journal* from the newspaper vending rack.

Returning to his counter swivel stool, the detective opened to the sports section and the Triple-A American Association baseball standings. A long-time fan of the St. Louis Cardinals, he was pleased to see the Louisville Redbirds, the Cards' top Minor League affiliate, in first place. He wondered when Todd Worrell, the Cards' first-round selection in the 1982 Amateur Entry Draft, would be promoted from the Double-A Arkansas Travelers to Louisville. Galen had seen him pitch the previous summer while vacationing in Erie, PA, and thought Worrell had the arm to make it to the Majors. He'd love to see him on the mound at Cardinal Stadium, which seemed to be on pace to draw one million fans – a feat that had never been accomplished in the Minors.

"Need a top-off?" Pixie asked while reaching for his partially filled coffee mug before he had a chance to answer. One of Galen's pet peeves was the dreaded (at least in his mind) "top-off" because he then had to add a fraction of a packet of artificial sweetener to achieve his precisely desired taste. This wasn't working out well at all. Abruptly rising, he asked as politely as he could muster: "Never mind, Pixie. If you could just get me a cup to go...black with one Sweet'n Low."

"Sure, sugar," she said while heading over to the to-go cups and lids. Galen thought to quip: "No, not sugar...Sweet'n Low!" but thought better of it.

Looking at his watch as he opened the door to his Impala, Detective Grauman was pleased he'd be headed away from downtown Lexington and the post-Memorial Day morning rush-hour traffic. With the just-concluded holiday festivities, too many drivers wouldn't be focused on getting safely from point A to point B.

Arriving at the Wellington estate at 9:30, Grauman was greeted at the front door by Woodrow. Asked where he could find Darci, the butler pointed at the crest of a hill off to the west and told him she'd be at the Triple-B Racing Stables main barn about a quarter mile away. "Shall I ask Mrs. Wellington to join you?" he asked. The detective said he needed to have a one-on-one conversation with Ms. McDougal and returned to his car for the short drive over the hill.

***

Darci McDougal had been startled by knocking on the windshield of her car. Now with a splitting headache, she rolled down her window and asked the City of Louisville police officer for the time. Informed that it was 5:30 in the morning, Darci told him she'd had a bit too much to drink and rather than risk the 90-minute drive back to Lexington, she opted for a few hours of sleep in the parking lot next to the pub before heading safely back home. After checking her license and registration, the officer said he'd be returning in about 20 minutes and suggested she be on her way.

Some two hours later, Darci was driving her VW Beetle over the winding dirt road toward the main barn of Triple-B Racing Stables. She'd tuned in to WBKY 91.3 FM, the University of Kentucky's NPR station, to see if there were any news about Governor Wellington. Hearing nothing germane from the morning news, she decided against stopping by the main house to pick up her usual breakfast of biscuits and gravy from Edna. Darci knew a full day's chores awaited her and she was almost an hour behind schedule already. She needed to take a hot shower, make a pot of coffee and start her work, no matter how tired she might be. She'd learn soon enough if "the worst" had occurred late last night.

***

Grauman parked his Impala next to a powder blue VW Beetle. Ordinarily there'd be at least a half dozen vehicles in the lot, but this was the week Beauregard Wellington was shipping several horses to Churchill Downs, and many of Beau's employees were already in Louisville. After reviewing notes from the previous evening's discussion with Mrs. Wellington, he emerged from his vehicle and entered the main barn.

A few stalls from the entrance was a tall, slender woman with fiery red hair who could only be Darci McDougal. Country music blaring from her radio masked Galen's approach as the barn hand had opened the sliding door to the stall and was attaching buckets of grain and water to the stall's bars. Coming out to grab a flake of hay to complete her task, a somewhat startled Darci came face-to-face with the detective.

"Who are *you*?" she asked, although judging from the man's appearance and demeanor, Darci figured he was law enforcement.

"I'm Galen Grauman, detective with the Lexington Bureau of Investigation," he answered while showing his badge and providing Darci with his business card. "Is the Governor, uh...?" Visibly shaken and beginning to sob, Grauman finished the sentence she was unable to complete: "Dead?...Yes, Ms. McDougal." The detective waited until Darci had regained some composure and then added: "Suppose you tell me what went on last night."

Some 20 minutes later, the young barn hand had completed her story, starting with her agreement three years ago to service Bentley Wellington on Memorial Day and including every detail of the previous evening.

So let me get this straight: "Mrs. Wellington provided you with the same outfit worn by the other members of the *Bluegrass Gas* servers?"

"Yes, Detective Grauman."

"And Mrs. Wellington instructed you to pick up a cart from the caterer's prep area a little before 9 p.m. and load hors d'oeuvres from the main buffet table into five empty steel trays?"

"Yes sir."

"Did she mention any specific items you should include in the trays?"

"No," Darci stated hesitantly as she thought back to the previous evening. "But Mrs. Wellington *did* tell me *not* to give the Governor any of the mini quiches stuffed with crab."

Grauman hesitated before asking the next question: "Did she say *why* you shouldn't include them?"

"I remember her specific words, detective. She said, 'Crab and the Governor's stomach don't get along too well with each other,'" Darci answered. "So I was extra careful not to include hors d'oeuvres from the tray marked 'crab-stuffed quiche.'"

The detective continued his questioning: "And why would you describe in detail the content of and manner in which each hors d'oeuvre was prepared?"

"The Governor didn't just like – he *loved* – his hors d'oeuvres. I moved down the line, describing each item, saving the pigs in blankets for last...of course, for the obvious reason. It was all foreplay. You know, building anticipation."

Shifting the interrogation, Grauman asked: "When you returned to retrieve your purse, why didn't you say something to somebody when you saw the Governor slumped over the desk?"

"I panicked, thinking he might've had a heart attack after our sex. All I wanted to do is get as far away as possible...as quickly as possible," Darci said as tears once more welled up in her eyes. "But as I drove away, I knew I couldn't simply leave him there, so I stopped at a gas station with a pay phone outside and called the 911 dispatcher."

"Okay, Darci. I believe you. Relax and hang tight. Don't leave town. We may have additional questions. If you have anything else to tell me, call my direct number. If I'm not at the office, leave a number for me to call and I'll be in touch as soon as possible."

With that, Galen left the barn and headed back to his office to pick up messages and to arrange an early afternoon meeting with Laurie Van Zant at her *Bluegrass Gas* office.

***

Toward the end of the morning rush hour, area radio stations began to report on Bentley Wellington's passing at the family estate, although cause of death had not yet been determined. The only other detail was that the Governor's death had occurred shortly after the annual Memorial Day gala at the Wellington estate.

Listening on his car radio, Grauman was pleased with the paucity of information offered by the UK Hospital spokesperson. He knew the Fayette County Medical Examiner & Coroner's Office would not be adding anything of substance until Dr. Proctor was able to speak with him.

Awaiting Galen at his office was Madison Meriwether, the Lexington-based FBI field agent. The two knew each other professionally, having worked together on a few cross-jurisdictional investigations over the years, and socially, having faced each other in the local 30-and-over recreational softball league during the past couple of summers.

After exchanging pleasantries, Grauman asked the obvious question: "So what brings you to my neck of the woods, Matts?"

"Well, it just so happens – for reasons I won't get into – that we have a recording of the activities in Bentley Wellington's study last night...and I figured you'd want to hear it. Let's find ourselves a conference room with a speakerphone. Then we can patch in one of our techies to play the tape."

"Give me a sec. I need to nail down an early afternoon appointment with Laurie Van Zant, the event manager for yesterday's big bash." Grauman felt the adrenalin rush coursing through his body and could hear it in his voice.

The detective called the main number at *Bluegrass Gas* and

asked to speak with Van Zant. He was told she wouldn't be in until 2 p.m. because of a late-night clean-up at the Wellington family's Memorial Day event.

"This is Detective Galen Grauman of the Lexington Bureau of Investigation, ma'am. It's imperative I speak with Miss Van Zant as soon as possible. It's in connection with the death of Governor Wellington last night."

"Oh dear," the receptionist replied in a somewhat distressed tone. "Let me patch you through to her personal assistant." A minute later, Grauman had an appointment to meet with Laurie Van Zant at 2:30 p.m.

Grauman then led Matts Meriwether to the conference room at the far end of the office where the two Lexington-based law enforcement officers listened to the sex skit performed by Darci McDougal for Bentley Wellington.

"It's exactly as she told me," Galen told Matts after the two listened to the tape. "And I suspect we'll be able to match the recording of the anonymous call taken by our 911 dispatcher with Darci's voice."

Matts then summarized the findings of the FBI's months-long investigation into the Wellington family, starting with circumstances surrounding the 1980 hunting incident that left the Governor paralyzed, continuing with Beauregard Wellington's gambling addiction and its impact on a pending IPO for Thoroughbred Bs Farm, and ending with Abigail chafing at her husband's tight grip on Bourbonesque's purse strings and at his new connections to a right-wing Neo-Nazi organization in Germany.

"Now you'll have a better perspective on the subject matter of the following tapes," added Meriwether. He then asked the FBI technician on the other end of the line to first play the 4 p.m. meeting involving Abigail, Bentley and Beauregard Wellington, and then play the 2:30 p.m. conversation between father and son that preceded the Memorial Day planning session.

"That's it," the techie said at the end of the second tape.

"Thanks," Matts responded. "That'll be all for now."

"Well," said Galen. We have a seriously troubled family involved in some seriously questionable activities. Activities that could certainly provide a motive if foul play turns out to be involved. One member of that family just paid for those complexities with his life. The rest of the day just became a whole lot more interesting."

"Keep me in the loop, Galen. This investigation appears to be sprouting tentacles and we have multiple jurisdictions involved."

***

As dusk settled on the Wellington's sprawling Thoroughbred Bs Farm less than 24 hours after her family's annual Memorial Day shindig, Abigail Prescott Wellington's brain was working overtime. Given the circumstances, she was not eager to leave for Bardstown the next day to address operational issues at Bourbonesque and receive monthly projections as was her practice on the first business day of each month. Her mind was on anything but the distillery.

But she'd just heard from a Dr. Proctor of the Fayette County Medical Examiner & Coroner's Office. In discussing cause of death, Proctor had explained there were two factors that led to Bentley Wellington's death – a hemorrhagic stroke and anaphylactic shock. "The devil is in the details," Abigail thought to herself in recalling a rather cogent part of Dr. Proctor's analysis:

"The anaphylaxis might very well have contributed to the stroke. We know from an examination of the food in the study and the food particles found inside your husband's mouth that, apparently, the quiche included crab meat. Of course, we are aware of the Governor's history of acute allergic reaction to crab. We'd need his medical records to review the specifics of his adverse reaction to crab during the Governors' Conference in Maryland back in the '50s if we're going to be more specific about cause and effect.

"Given the circumstances surrounding your husband's death, I'd ask if you'd like us to perform an autopsy?"

Abigail asked Dr. Proctor for some time to mull it over. She'd want to see what her son, Beauregard, thought about an autopsy. They both likely needed some time to think about it.

Now Abigail began to fret about the interviews Detective Galen Grauman had conducted earlier in the day with that red-headed minx Darci McDougal; her event manager, Laurie Van Zant, and Beau. Suddenly, a trip to Bardstown and a return to routine business tasks had some appeal.

Chapter 52 – Prep for the Tremont Stakes

The day after Memorial Day was a busy one for a pair of horsemen whose paths were destined to cross on consecutive weekends. Beauregard Wellington and TJ Cutter were preparing to ship horses from their home-based stables for a weekend stakes race. This time, the venue would be Belmont Park in Elmont, NY. The race was the Grade III Tremont Stakes, one of the key early tests for two-year-old colts to be run at six furlongs on Saturday, June 4th.

From stalls on the backstretch of both Churchill Downs and Monmouth Park, two promising colts – Wellington's *B 4-Warned* and Cutter's unraced *Cut Me A Break* – had been loaded into their vans for the trip to Elmont, an unincorporated community in Hempstead, Nassau County, Long Island.

B 4-Warned had raced once, winning a 5-furlong Maiden Special Weight race at Churchill Downs the Saturday after Derby weekend. Andy Delaney had given the two-year-old colt a heady ride in a crowded field of 10, made particularly challenging by the horse's outside post position. Delaney thought enough of the horse to commit to riding him again. His agent was working on securing at least a couple of additional mounts, if for no other reason than to give his jockey some races over the course.

Cut Me A Break was unraced, but had worked brilliantly at Monmouth under Angel Barrera, who'd be riding him on Saturday. Cutter typically didn't throw his horses into stakes races prematurely, but none of the youngsters entered in the Tremont had raced more than three times. With a fast track, he felt confident his horse would be competitive.

In Oceanport early that morning, Cutter oversaw workouts for his 5-year-old mare, *Classy C'ville Lassie*, and 3-year-old colt, *It Cuts Too Deep*. TJ's plans for the mare included the Grade III Eatontown Stakes, a 1 1/16-mile turf race scheduled for late June, and the Grade II Molly Pitcher Stakes, a race on the main track at the same distance slated for the end of August. Both races were for fillies and mares 3-years-old and up.

The Leesburg, VA native had bigger aspirations for his colt. Not far enough along from a development standpoint to participate in the Triple Crown races, *It Cuts Too Deep* had broken his maiden at first asking, winning a 5½ furlong race at south Florida's Calder Race Course in early May. Cutter's plan called for his 3-year-old charge to gradually stretch out at Monmouth Park, running first in a 7-furlong allowance race in early June and then, three weeks later, in the Salvator Mile Handicap for 3-year-olds and up. At that point, Cutter would take a look at the field for the meet's richest and most prestigious race, the Haskell Invitational, a Grade I Stakes for 3-year-olds run at a mile-and-an-eighth. An invitation-only race, the Haskell was a realistic objective if the colt was successful in the 7-furlong allowance and Salvator Mile.

Monmouth Park's directors set up the Haskell as an invitational handicap, seeking to attract those horses that had performed best in the Kentucky Derby, Preakness and Belmont. The race was strategically scheduled to enable trainers to freshen their thoroughbreds from the rigors of competing in the Triple Crown races. The purse, quite naturally, was the largest offered at the meet, sufficient to entice the connections of the best thoroughbreds in training.

Following the workouts, Cutter headed back to the barn and prepared *Cut Me A Break* for the relatively short trip to Belmont.

***

Tuesday was busy for Beauregard Wellington as well. His duties as owner and trainer of Triple-B Racing Stables would be bracketed by a conversation with his mother that morning regarding a list of "to dos" in preparing for his father's funeral, and a late afternoon appointment with Galen Grauman of the Fayette County Bureau of Investigation.

Beau had to make his way over to Louisville to oversee loading his 3-year-old colt, *B 4-Warned*, for the 12+ hour trip to Belmont Park. His assistant trainer, Ian Snelling, a native Brit who'd spent the last dozen years in the employ of Thoroughbred Bs Farm and then Triple-B Racing Stables, was accompanying the colt to New York. In addition, Beau wanted to have a preliminary conversation with jockey Andy Delaney about how his colt stacked up against the field for the upcoming Tremont Stakes. Grauman was set to meet with him at the Wellington estate at 4:30 p.m.

Finally, there was a small matter of depositing the $150,000 check his now-deceased father had given him on Sunday to take care of his most recent gambling debt. The more Beau thought about it, the more concerned he became about bank policies surrounding payee access to funds in the immediate aftermath of a payor's death and how funds under his control were structured.

Beau had three bank accounts – the two business accounts covering Triple-B Racing Stables and Thoroughbred Bs Farm and a personal account. With an IPO pending and the associated scrutiny of regulatory agencies, he dared not undertake any unusual activity in the business accounts. Unfortunately, the balance in his personal account was insufficient to cover the check, in which case he might require approval from his mother for immediate access. Bentley had always made it clear their father-son debt-related arrangements were not to be made known to Abigail, who already knew of Beau's gambling habit – just not its full extent.

The last couple of times he owed his Jersey-based bookmaker, Beau had been late in squaring his account. Because of his family's wealth, he'd been forgiven his tardiness the first go-around; the second time he was obliged to pay the "vig," which amounted to 20 percent of his $50,000 wager.

Now his total debt had reached just over a quarter-million dollars. His current payment consisted of $125,000 plus the vig of $25,000 for a total of $150K. Beau knew he'd see the bookie's area runner in his Churchill Downs stables at their predetermined, post-wager transaction time of 1:30 p.m. It was always on the first business day following a bet. Beau had a phone number with a Cincinnati area code to call at least 24 hours in advance if he couldn't make a meeting because he was out of state.

Arriving in Louisville, he tended to the departure of *B 4-Warned* and his assistant trainer, then spoke with his Tremont Stakes jockey. Settling into a wooden chair at a desk in a sparsely furnished makeshift office toward the back of the barn, Beau waited for the arrival of a stocky, middle-aged Irishman he knew only as "Squints."

Legs up on the desk while reading *The Courier-Journal* sports section and listening to Louisville's WHAS News Radio, Beauregard Wellington suddenly realized how much of a physical and mental toll the Memorial Day weekend had taken on him. He reflected on the exasperating loss at Monmouth Park (the race as well as the wager), the Sunday family meetings including what turned out to be the last conversation he'd ever have with his dad, the long day of celebration at which he constantly had to be "on" and the traumatic end to the evening. He checked his watch, which read 1:25. And now, with the heavy-set figure suddenly appearing in the doorway to his office, he'd have to deal with Squints.

"Afternoon, Mr. Wellington," Squints said with a cordial tone that belied the reason for his visit. "I believe we have a transaction to consummate."

Beau looked up from his newspaper, turned off the radio and stared at the runner for a moment or two before responding: "I guess you haven't heard the news? Governor Wellington died late last night."

"Your daddy?... I'm terribly sorry, Mr. Wellington." Squints paused as if for effect. "But I'm not paying a condolence call. Now do you have a package for me?"

A bit flustered, Beau reached into his right pants pocket and pulled out the $150,000 check and showed it to Squints. The runner took it from Beau and examined it for a few seconds.

"I have no doubt the check is good, Mr. Wellington. But as you know from the rules we established when opening an account for you, we are a cash-only enterprise. This check isn't worth the paper it's written on – at least not to our people." Another pause, then in a tone Beau found somewhat intimidating: "We're in quite the predicament. Your recent track record on timely payments has my superiors running short on patience."

Returning the check to the now ashen-faced horseman, Squints then sent Beau a very clear message. "I'll be back here this evening at nine o'clock sharp. I'll expect the cash at that time." As he handed over the check, the runner slowly squeezed Beau's fingers together and held them in a vice-like grip as Wellington unsuccessfully attempted to free himself.

"Do we understand, Mr. Wellington?" Tears of pain forming in his eyes, all the rattled young horseman could do was shake his head in acknowledgement.

Chapter 53 – A "FUBAR" Moment

It was approaching 5:45 p.m. on Tuesday. Sammy Eisenstat had just employed an acronym he hadn't used for quite some time. The FBI field agent in charge of what seemed to be an ever-expanding, multi-faceted investigation had just finished listening to Calvin Thomas, who ran through details of Bentley Wellington's death late the previous night. His parting comment to the former Brooklyn detective, current limo driver and part-time FBI contractor?..."This investigation has now achieved FUBAR status. For the time being, let's make sure we touch base with each other at least once a day."

Eisenstat, banking on Marcus McQueen still being in his Louisville office the day after a long holiday weekend, called to get his take on what had transpired at the Wellington estate. He also wanted to listen to both family-meeting tapes and the Bentley Wellington-Darci McDougal tape, all of which Calvin had described in great detail.

"Well, what say you?" Eisenstat asked after he and McQueen finished listening. The telephone line was silent for several seconds before McQueen spoke.

IIe began by stating thc obvious: "So many questions and not much by way of answers at this juncture. But let's start with the most fundamental question of whether the factors contributing to Bentley Wellington's death were mere happenstance or well planned."

McQueen then filled in Eisenstat on the autopsy report he and Galen Grauman had just received from the Fayette County Medical Examiner & Coroner's office. The report listed the cause of death as a fatal stroke triggered by anaphylactic shock – most likely brought on by ingesting significant amounts of crab quiche. He also read the last sentence: "There is no evidence to suggest that sexual activity played a part in the deceased's death."

McQueen then told Eisenstat that his Lexington field agent, Madison Meriwether, was keeping tabs on Detective Galen Grauman's progress with interviewing persons of interest. "I believe Grauman was scheduled to question Darci McDougal this morning; Laurie Van Zant, the Wellingtons' Memorial Day event coordinator, early this afternoon, and Beau Wellington toward the end of the day. I should be hearing from Matts shortly."

***

Galen Grauman had four takeaways from his meeting with Laurie Van Zant. *First*, the manager of *Bluegrass Gas* was incredibly organized and a stickler for detail as evidenced by her ability to quickly retrieve records of the 1982 and 1981 Wellington events and to determine that crab in any form had not been on the menu.

Second, she was a control freak and had a hand in every single aspect of the Wellington event, not the least of which were the menu items, serving times, layouts and wait staff assignments.

Third, Ms. Van Zant, counter to everything else concerning her management of the event, had no knowledge of the pre-fireworks escapade engineered by Abigail Wellington for her husband – neither Darci McDougal's use of a wait-staff outfit...nor her hijacking of a serving cart, steel trays and Sterno burners.

Fourth, the event manager – likely owing to a combination of her relatively young age and residence in southern California until 12 years ago – was not aware of Bentley Wellington's allergic reaction to crab. More important, Abigail Wellington did not alert her to that fact even while suggesting crab quiche as an hors d'oeuvre...and even while adding salmon quiche as an additional offering.

Armed with this information, Grauman had gone over to the Wellington estate for his appointment with Beau. Afterwards, he'd go to the coroner's office to pick up the report Alex White and Dr. Evelyn Proctor promised would be ready by the end of the business day.

***

Galen was met at the front door by Woodrow, the family butler, who ushered the detective into the parlor where a clearly distraught Beauregard Wellington was waiting.

"I realize what a difficult time this has been for you, Mr. Wellington," Grauman said in mustering his most compassionate tone. "Would later this evening be a better time for you to answer a few questions?" he added, suspecting Beauregard wanted this interview to be over and done with as quickly as possible.

"No, I'm fine," answered Beau. "Fire away."

Grauman couldn't help but ask about the ice pack Wellington was holding to the back of his right hand. "How'd you hurt yourself?"

Beau answered rather sheepishly: "Had some trouble loading one of our thoroughbreds into the van in Louisville this afternoon. We're running in the Tremont Stakes on Saturday at Belmont."

Having listened to the FBI tape of Beau and Bentley discussing the $150,000 check to help pay off his gambling debt, the Lexington detective suspected Beau might have been hurt in some other fashion. An unpleasant encounter with an undesirable visitor while at the stables at Churchill Downs was his educated guess.

"Goes along with the territory, right?" Galen didn't wait for a response, but simply followed the remark with his questions.

"Tell me, Mr. Wellington. How much are you involved in the details of your family's Memorial Day event?"

"Quite honestly, I pretty much take marching orders from mom. She asks *Bluegrass Gas* to come up with an overall theme. The firm's owner, Laurie Van Zant, then develops proposals for entertainment, staging, food and such, and the two hash out the details. This year was a bit different for me. With our pending IPO, I was responsible for developing a presentation to fellow Kentucky horsemen so we could get their take on our plans."

The detective had taken out his pad and was diligently writing. Once Beau finished, Galen followed up with an abruptness and change of tone that startled Wellington: "How well do you know Darci McDougal?"

"Where do I begin?" Beau thought to himself and proceeded to commit a cardinal sin by answering the question with another, one that hinted there was a story to tell. "Professionally or personally?" he asked.

Galen immediately picked up the scent of something that didn't smell quite right. "Well, let's start with Ms. McDougal's job at Triple-B Racing Stables. How long has she worked here? What are her responsibilities? Has she been a good employee? Does she have plans other than continuing to work here?"

Somewhat at ease with the initial series of questions, Beau became quite talkative – even expansive in his responses. Then

Grauman hit him with a change of pace: "And did you and Ms. McDougal have any kind of personal relationship?"

After uttering: "Well, that's easy. We have none," Beauregard Wellington saw his three-year history with Darci McDougal flash across his mind's eye – her initial job interview at Triple-B Racing Stables, an encounter that at once left him breathless with her physical beauty and intrigued by a maturity well beyond her years; Darci's early rebuffs of his efforts to engage her socially, and finally, albeit reluctantly, yielding to his persistent requests for a date, which had eventually led to an intimate and closely guarded involvement over the past 18 months.

Unsure of what this detective knew but confident that Darci wouldn't have divulged anything of their relationship, Beau opted for the quite simple but hugely untruthful answer.

Everything about Beauregard Wellington's answer – the immediate terse response, tone of voice and facial expression – told the veteran detective Beau was lying. For his part, Beau believed he'd done a reasonable job in responding to the detective's question.

His interview completed, Galen Grauman asked what plans Beau had for the remainder of the day in case he had any further questions. "I have to make a stop to do some banking and then head back to Louisville to tend to some business," Beau said. "I'll be home late tonight."

Woodrow escorted the detective to the front door. Before leaving, Galen turned to the butler and said: "I may need to ask you a few questions, Woodrow. Is there a time when it would be easy for the two of us to talk alone?" Woodrow explained that Mrs. Wellington was scheduled to be in Bardstown to take care of some business at Bourbonesque, so "tomorrow at about 10:30 a.m. should be fine."

***

Galen drove into Lexington, heading for the coroner's office and a meeting with Alex White and Dr. Evelyn Proctor. After scanning the promised report, Galen asked Alex if he could use a private line. Escorting the detective into a vacant conference room and pointing to a button on the phone, the ME left the room and closed the door behind him.

Grauman dialed the number for Madison Meriwether. Still at his desk, Matts listened intently as his counterpart went through the report and filled him in on his interviews with Darci McDougal and Beauregard Wellington, including the ice pack Beau had been applying to his right hand.

"I gotta tell ya' Matts. I don't like the way ..."

The FBI field agent interrupted: "I'm a step ahead of you, Galen. I'm on my way over to Churchill Downs."

Chapter 54 – Destination Düsseldorf

Sammy Eisenstat had seen his investigation rapidly expand from New Jersey and Kentucky to include law enforcement agencies in Canada and Germany. He was in the midst of arranging a meeting in Düsseldorf with Gustav Zimmermann, officer in charge of the North Rhine-Westphalia (NRW) Police Force inspection team; LKA NRW Investigation Bureau Officer Bertram Krieger; Jakob Seidel of the NRW Exchange Supervisory Authority; the Mossad's David Katzman, and Cam Connors of the RCMP.

Katzman was already in Düsseldorf, having met with Krieger, Zimmermann and Seidel on Monday. Connors arranged to fly from Ottawa to Düsseldorf by way of Toronto on Thursday for a Friday morning arrival. Eisenstat would take off from JFK in New York on Thursday evening, arriving a half hour earlier than the RCMP officer. They'd meet after passing through Customs and share a taxi to the offices of the North Rhine-Westphalia's State Investigation Bureau.

There would actually be two meetings that Friday – a group session at 11 a.m. and a late-afternoon meeting with Gretchen Weiß Hauptmann. Jakob Seidel was responsible for ensuring Frau Hauptmann's appearance.

Having directed Calvin Thomas to keep a watchful eye on Jürgen Hauptmann because of the situation in Wuppertal, Eisenstat now knew there'd been a second suspicious death within the past 48 hours. Local law enforcement's investigation into the death of former Kentucky Governor Bentley Wellington had focused on Wellington's son and wife as well as a young female employed by Triple-B Racing Stables.

Following a hunch, Eisenstat then called Marcus McQueen, head of FBI Field Ops in Kentucky, to suggest McQueen's team check the guest list to see if anyone had ties to a German organization, Munich-based Deutsche und amerikanische Führungskräfte für bilaterale Beziehungen,

"The English translation, German and American Leaders for Bilateral Relations, sounds innocent enough," said Eisenstat, "but the organization shares a building in Munich with Die

Nationaldemokratische Partei Deutschlands." He went on to explain that a small group of the NDP had a history of rogue 'seek-and-destroy' missions aimed at removing those Germans who'd sympathized with Jews during World War II.

"Let's cover all the bases and be certain these people aren't involved in Wellington's death."

Chapter 55 – Lighter in the Wallet

Perspiration – no, beads of sweat was more accurate – formed at Beau's hairline and ran down his forehead as he walked into Central Bank, the Wellington family's primary banking institution since its founding as the Southern Industrial Loan Company back in 1938. The bottom line was that he needed to leave the bank with $150,000 in cash, an amount that would bring him up-to-date with his bookie and leave him owing just over $100K. Beau would be able to cover the balance by the end of the two-week period he'd been given in order to "be made whole." He'd be meeting with Squints at his assigned stables at Churchill Downs at 9:00 p.m.

It wasn't so much that Beau wouldn't be able to convert his late dad's check into cash; it was the timing, coming on the heels of his dad's death, and his belief that Dowling Chism, first vice president of the Lexington branch and the Wellingtons' relationship banker, would likely mention the transaction to Abigail the next time the two met. He couldn't very well ask him *not* to say anything to his mom, a move that would set off alarm bells with Mr. Chism.

"Please extend my most heartfelt condolences to Abigail," Chism said as he rose from his chair and extended his hand. "The Commonwealth has lost one of its greatest treasures. Give this authorization to Ms. Bryant. She'll have your funds prepared."

"I'd shake, but my right hand was at the wrong end of one of our horses we were loading for a trip to New York," said Beau. "But thanks for your help. I'll give mom your message."

Beau headed for Ms. Bryant's desk and handed the AVP a black briefcase. She disappeared for a couple of minutes and then returned with it now filled with 15 banded stacks of hundred-dollar bills. "Would you like to count it Mr. Wellington?" Bryant offered.

"No, that won't be necessary. Thanks for the quick turnaround." With that, Beau headed out the revolving door to the bank's parking lot and his red 1982 Ford F150 Pickup. Looking at his wristwatch, he noted there was time for a bite to eat and decided to stop at the KFC location just before the

Lexington entrance to I-64 West. He'd have ample time before his appointment with Squints.

Beau was well aware of the tenuous situation in which he'd placed himself with his gambling. He was all-too-familiar with the Kentucky Statute in effect as of March 1977 – *Horse races, messenger betting prohibited*– which read, in part:

"Any person who, either for himself or as agent or employee of another, wagers money or anything of value on a horse race run or about to be run or advertised, posted or reported as being run at any race track in or out of this state, or who engages in the occupation of receiving, making, transmitting or negotiating, either in person or by messenger, telephone or telegraph, wagers on horse races run or about to be run or advertised, posted or reported as being run or about to be run at any race track in or out of the state, shall, except in the case of wagers made within the enclosure of a race track licensed by the Kentucky Horse Racing Commission during an authorized race meeting at that track, or an enclosure during regular meetings in which running, trotting or pacing races are being conducted by associations regularly organized for that purpose, be guilty of a Class A misdemeanor."

It wasn't the penalty, itself, that was of paramount concern, although discovery surely would result in suspension of his trainer's license. It was the risk of an abrupt end to his plans for raising funds for Thoroughbred Bs Farm through an IPO.

If Wellington had thought further about the individuals with whom he was transacting business, he would know his activity would leave him prone to extortion, bribery, and pressure to participate in race fixing and a host of other white-collar crimes once Thoroughbred Bs Farm was a publicly traded entity. Considering he'd come from a family with a long history of public service to residents of both the Commonwealth, Beau was remarkably devoid of a sense of responsibility to his current and future constituencies.

Beau arrived at his Churchill Downs stables about half-an-hour before his scheduled appointment with Squints. Unbeknownst to the young Kentucky horseman, Matts Meriwether and three other FBI agents had already taken positions in a horse trailer from which they'd be able to record and photograph the meeting, as well as in an adjacent stable where they could intervene if the meeting turned ugly.

By 9:30 p.m., three things were certain: Squints had his organization's money, Beau had possession of the cancelled marker indicating his account had been credited for the $150K payment... and the FBI had the evidence it needed to ensure there would be no SEC approval for a publicly traded TBF, Inc.

Chapter 56 – Woodrow

There was virtually nothing that had escaped the watchful eye of Woodrow Abraham Jefferson over the course of his decades-long tenure as butler at the Wellington residence. Hired after the Second World War, Woodrow had served as a cook for the Tuskegee Airmen at Moton Field, the training ground for the famed African-American military pilots located near Tuskegee, Alabama. He'd been recommended for employment to Senator Buff Wellington by a senior staffer from the office of Sen. J. Archibald Guilford (D-AL) who, along with Woodrow, was a native of Montgomery, Alabama.

With service as a member of the support staff to the U.S. military, Woodrow had long ago learned the importance of the phrase that became famous during World War II: "Loose lips sink ships." He continued to adhere to this directive during his tenure with the Commonwealth's first family. Given Buford's and Bentley's high profiles in federal and state politics, to mention nothing of what Abigail Prescott's addition to the family brought to the table, Woodrow had certainly been within earshot of more private discussions and plans in the pipeline than he cared to recount.

Regardless of the topic, irrespective of family members' personal opinions and despite individuals occasionally pushing against the boundaries of sound ethical judgment or legal behavior, Woodrow Abraham Jefferson maintained his silence and remained loyal to his employer.

Over the years, the Wellington family butler had honed an ability to remember the minutia while keeping sight of the overall picture. He also had an uncanny knack for observing without being observed. In short, Woodrow not only knew *where* all the family skeletons were hidden, but *how* and *why* they were hidden as well.

On the evening before his morning interview with Detective Grauman, Woodrow Abraham Jefferson already had gone over in his mind the weekend's events as well as those observations he'd stored in his memory bank from the past several years. He knew what he was going to say...and perhaps more importantly, what he *wasn't* prepared to reveal.

Chapter 57 – Reflect and Recalibrate

For Gretchen Weiß Hauptmann, Wednesday morning had been emotionally draining, having given the eulogy for the late Hanna Schröder at memorial services. Returning to her Hückeswagen home in a rented Mercedes, she was having serious reservations about the process she'd devised for deciding the future direction of her now 25-year-old business.

"Was this my way of providing colleagues with information and asking them to formulate and articulate their own opinions? Or is it that I've lost the burning desire to lead, a desire that fueled the business's growth for the past quarter of a century?"

Wahrheit gesagt (Truth be told), the loss of Hanna, together with Jorge's recent call regarding his nightmare about Fabian, had left Gretchen feeling very lonely and vulnerable. As an empty-nester with her only son an ocean away and a husband long gone, Gretchen had come to the realization she was mentally exhausted… in fact, burned out. The more she thought about it, the more she longed for a simpler life – or at least as normal a life as one who'd long kept the deepest and darkest of secrets could maintain.

Opening the front door, she was greeted by Pulver, who was very happy to see her, very hungry and very much in need of a brief trip outside – the last two not necessarily in that order. Having taken care of her German Shepherd's needs, Gretchen walked into the study to unload her briefcase. No sooner had she made herself comfortable behind the desk than the telephone rang. It was her business line.

Picking up, she was greeted by a young woman with an Irish accent:

"Is Ms. Hauptmann available?"

"Yes, I'm Gretchen Weiß Hauptmann. How might I help you?"

"My name is Shea O'Halloran. I'm a research associate with the Dublin office of Collins, Connell & O'Brien. We are M&A specialists with a particular emphasis on the transportation sector. One of our clients, a U.K.-based Tier 1 supplier to automotive OEMs, is quite interested in P/M technologies. We understand you might be amenable to a transaction."

Ms. O'Halloran was waiting for a response. Gretchen felt like she was living in a dream world. Not one to believe in stars aligning, it seemed as though that was precisely what had happened – particularly in light of her train of thought driving home from Hanna Schröder's services. Clearly, she wasn't prepared to offer any kind of response. But just as clearly, she didn't want to dismiss what could be a fortuitous turn of events.

"I've just returned from a memorial service. My long-time administrative assistant recently died in an automobile accident. Will you give me your direct dial so I can call you later this afternoon?"

"Of course, Ms. Hauptmann. I am so sorry for your loss."

"Just one question if I might. Who provided you with information about my company?"

Shea O'Halloran saw no reason to withhold the information. "It was a Ms. Jeffries – Marci Davis Jeffries – with the New York firm of Steinberg Stavros Rogers & Co., Inc. It's a global asset management firm specializing in the energy and transportation industries."

"Thank you, Ms. O'Halloran. I will call you back this afternoon," after which Gretchen slowly returned the receiver to its cradle and sat there stunned. From across the Atlantic Ocean at precisely the right time, Marci Davis Jeffries – the mother of the young man who'd arranged for her son's summer job at Monmouth Park – had offered up a potentially life-changing solution to a despondent soul in need of a lifeline.

About 90 minutes later, Gretchen was back on the phone with Collins, Connell & O'Brien, prepared to begin discussions on a potential sale of GWH GmbH to Manchester Automotive Suppliers International. By the end of the call, die Vorsitzende had agreed to meet with representatives of Collins, Connell & O'Brien. Shea O'Halloran and Aiden O'Brien would be flying into Düsseldorf the next morning for an early afternoon tour of GWH GmbH, followed by a preliminary sit-down discussion. Realizing she'd need to assemble a team with the legal and management expertise to represent her interests, Gretchen decided to reach out to the person who suggested GWH as an acquisition target, Marci Davis Jeffries.

The desk clock read 5:30 p.m. locally, indicating folks were heading home from their jobs. But in Manhattan the work day -- six hours younger – was in full swing. Gretchen called the general number for Steinberg Stavros Rogers & Co. and asked the operator for Marci Davis Jeffries. Hauptmann felt her pulse racing as she hoped against hope that Jeffries was at her desk and would be willing and able to arrange for appropriate professional resources to be at a meeting in Europe on such incredibly short notice. In her favor? Ms. Jeffries was evidently very knowledgeable about the P/M industry in general and had done her homework on GWH GmbH in particular.

Gretchen's good fortune continued as Marci was just returning to her office from a departmental meeting. Ironic that two women whose only sons were linked by friendship should have their first conversation as key players in a potential international business transaction.

After exchanging pleasantries, Gretchen recounted the call from Shea O'Halloran and her agreement to meet with members of Collins, Connell & O'Brien the very next day. She then brought Marci up to speed on events of the past several days – the Advisory Board's weekend retreat to discuss whether GWH GmbH should become a public company or continue as a private firm, and the untimely death of her administrative assistant that brought the pending decision to an immediate halt. What Hauptmann didn't include were the details surrounding the auto accident and the growing possibility that the intended victim of that accident was Gretchen, herself.

"There are a host of questions with respect to transitioning operations that any prospective buyer will want you to address," explained Marci as she began setting the table for issues Gretchen should consider.

"Are there any other owners of the firm apart from you? What is the status of contracts involving key management positions? Are there any golden parachutes in the event of a sale? Would you be willing to play an advisory role to the acquiring company to ensure a smooth transition?"

"These are all issues I've contemplated over the past few years, but would need to reconsider in light of my current state of mind regarding my own future," answered Gretchen. "What I require most at this point is a team to represent me and my firm's interests at tomorrow's meeting. Is there any possibility you could make this happen?"

One of the key reasons Marci Davis Jeffries' star at Steinberg Stavros had risen over the years had been her uncanny ability to anticipate the actions of clients, prospects and other players within the business sectors Marci had spent so much time studying. While she didn't expect a call to come this quickly and hadn't known whether it would be someone from the Dublin M&A firm or the German P/M parts producer, Ms. Jeffries had already set wheels in motion for her firm's potential involvement.

"I have a standard international contract we can fax to you. You can review the terms this evening. If you have questions, you can call me at home. Don't worry about the time."

Ms. Jeffries continued: "Often times we partner with the law firm of Stratton-Oakes. I've taken the liberty of speaking with Charles Janovsky here in New York. He indicated he could assign one of his associates should an engagement materialize. I'll reach out to Mr. Janovsky and explain the immediate need."

Then came the final piece: "As it happens, our firm has an office in Frankfurt, and I'm certain we can have someone in Wuppertal tomorrow. I suspect the speed with which a team has been assembled will underscore to Collins, Connell & O'Brien your seriousness in considering any offer that might come from that firm's client."

A few more details along with the mutual promise to tell their sons about the chance encounter and the conversation was over. For Marci Davis Jeffries, there were calls to be made in order to finalize the joint participation of both her firm and Stratton-Oakes. For Gretchen Weiß Hauptmann, a faxed contract was shortly available for her review. Making a copy and scribbling a few notes in the margins during a first read, Hauptmann suddenly felt fatigued but strangely calm. She retreated to the bedroom and soon fell asleep.

***

Her second day back in the saddle at Stratton-Oakes after her eventful Memorial Day weekend, Consuela Parks Pettiford felt...what exactly? Liberated?...emotionally drained?...confused? Perhaps a little bit of each but better off for the experience.

Consuela was reacquainting herself with *U.S. v. NatAgriCo*, the case she'd been researching when the world came crashing down around her. As would happen all-too-often over the next weeks and months, her thoughts returned to NYPD Detective Mark Makowski's call telling her that her parents had been found murdered, victims in an armed robbery at the *A.M. Bagels/P.M. Burgers* restaurant.

Unsure when his bright young associate would be returning, Charles Janovsky had considered transferring her work on *U.S. v. NatAgriCo* to another associate, a move that would enable Consuela to hit the reset button following her personal tragedy. Coincidentally, the call from Marci Davis Jeffries at Steinberg Stavros provided him with just such an opportunity.

From the door of his corner office, Janovsky asked his administrative assistant, Janice Jensen, to locate Ms. Pettiford. "I believe she's in the library downstairs. Have her join me in my office ASAP. Thanks."

Five minutes later, Ms. Jensen reappeared with Consuela, who took a seat as Janovsky waved her in while continuing to leaf through the contents of a manila file folder already labeled GWH GmbH/Steinberg Stavros. "Please close the door behind you, Janice."

Not knowing what to expect, Consuela felt a bit uneasy. Janovsky, a senior partner with more than 30 years at Stratton-Oakes – five of which were spent in Tokyo and another 10 in The Hague – saw his prize associate seemed a bit out of sorts. His first words were designed to put her at ease.

"How are you doing this week, Consuela?" the tone of the veteran attorney's voice clearly conveying a mix of compassion and concern.

"I'm still a bit unsettled, Mr. Janovsky. But I gave myself a long weekend down the Jersey shore, met some interesting folks and came back Monday evening determined to move forward," explained Consuela. "It's what my parents would have wanted."

"I see you've quickly picked up on the lingo," Janovsky said in noting the young associate's use of the phrase, 'down the Jersey shore.' "I've had a home in the Hamptons for the past several years," Janovsky said. "Something quite soothing about the sand, the salt and the Sound." Consuela thought about recounting Jasmine's factoid about the origins of the ocean's salty air, but thought better of it.

"Moving on to the business at hand: I have an out-of-town assignment for you," her boss said as he handed Pettiford the file.

"Ms. Jensen has asked Travel to book you on tonight's early evening Lufthansa flight from JFK to Düsseldorf. You'll be flying business class with Ms. Marci Davis Jeffries of Steinberg Stavros Rogers & Co. Our firm has partnered with them on several M&A transactions over the years."

It was all Consuela could do to keep her jaw from dropping as Janovsky revealed her travel companion. She then remembered the words spoken by FBI agent Sammy Eisenstat only last Saturday:

"One of you is a practicing attorney. Another is close to completing a legal education and taking a Bar exam. Two others have spent their careers in law enforcement and have taken oaths of service. You have ethical and, in all likelihood, legal obligations to follow the FBI's aforementioned directive. We will periodically check on each of you to ask whether you are complying. I needn't remind you that it is a crime to lie to the FBI."

There was little doubt in her mind that Marci Davis Jeffries was related to Sean Davis Jeffries. Was she an older sister?...or even Sean's mother? And might this assignment in some way be tangentially related to the FBI/Sean Davis Jeffries probe into the Wellington family in Kentucky?

No matter. She was bound to secrecy – ethically, legally and more specifically for the sake of her future as an attorney.

As Janovsky escorted Consuela to the door, he said in almost a fatherly tone: "You'd better head home and pack for a week because we won't know if this preliminary meeting will result in more serious discussions. Be sure to take your passport and Stratton-Oakes American Express card. On your way downstairs, stop by Petty Cash and complete a requisition form for five-hundred dollars in U.S. currency. Right now, the dollar is worth about 2.5 Deutsche Marks. Ms. Jensen should have your airline ticket at her desk. We'll be arranging for room reservations in Wuppertal through GWH.

"Ms. Jeffries is highly competent, incredibly organized and extremely well-versed in the transportation and energy sectors as well as in supply-chain management," Janovsky continued. "By the time you land, I expect you'll be up to speed. If you're not sure of something, don't hesitate to ask. Remember, the mark of a good business advisor is not so much having the answers, but asking the proper questions."

With that piece of advice, Janovsky wished Consuela Parks Pettiford good luck and safe travels.

Chapter 58 – Means to an End...or Just an End

Wolfgang Becker, CEO of GWH GmbH, sat across a small table from Advisory Board member Dieter Hartmann. They had agreed to meet at an out-of-the-way pub in Bergisch Gladbach, 43 kilometers south of Wuppertal.

The two men arrived in separate cars, with Becker having rented the oldest and most unassuming vehicle he could find at a used-car lot in nearby Köln (Cologne). They came dressed in jeans. well-worn cotton shirts and beat-up shoes, further looking the part of local blue-collar grunts by going unshaven for the past 24 hours. They'd taken every conceivable precaution to guard against somebody noticing they were meeting alone in the aftermath of the untimely death of Hanna Schröder.

Becker had spent the past eight years as Gretchen Weiß Hauptmann's personal choice for chief executive officer of GWH GmbH. Initially, he was grateful for the opportunity to join his former Pulver-Metall Lüdenscheid colleague. The performance incentive clause in his contract was the means by which he could secure an appreciable financial interest in a company whose P/M processes held many technical and cost advantages over more traditional production techniques such as casting, forging and stamping.

Yet Becker had grown increasingly frustrated by his boss's plodding and risk-averse leadership style. In eight years, he'd realized only half of his potential ownership interest in GWH GmbH and strongly believed Frau Hauptmann was the primary hinderance. Over the past several months, he became bolder in speaking favorably – and often – to members of his management team as well as those on the Advisory Board about the benefits of taking their P/M parts manufacturing business public.

Apart from his track record of aggressive management, Becker had become bullish on the place of corporate Germany in an increasingly international business environment. His views had been largely colored by his growing involvement with the far-right Nationaldemokratische Partei Deutschlands (NDP). His desire to expand his influence abroad was perhaps best reflected in his recruitment of corporate executives in the United States, including Bourbonesque's Bentley Wellington, for membership in the German and American Business Executives for Bilateral Relations.

Further emboldened by Frau Hauptmann's long-overdue decision to seek the advice of her peers within the GWH family on financing options to accelerate growth, he dared to skew the five-year operational assumptions and financial projections for both a publicly traded GWH AG in the aftermath of equity financing and for a still privately owned GWH GmbH following debt financing via the bond market. Aggressive assumptions were built into the former while conservative assumptions were presented in the latter.

Becker was playing a "long game," looking to capitalize on his projected position of power in a fast-growing and publicly traded business. He would make decisions that skirted or even crossed the bounds of legality as situations presented themselves, depending upon the extent of financial gain for both himself and the political party with which he was aligned.

Dieter Hartmann had lived for decades in deep despondency and with suppressed rage over the loss of his two young children, Luka and Emil, in the closing months of the war and the subsequent loss of his wife, Monika, soon after. Yet the rise in recent years of the NDP and its radical neo-Nazi militant wing had given him a renewed sense of purpose.

Hartmann found the British and, in particular, the Americans hypocritical and sanctimonious, speaking of Nazi atrocities when during their race across Germany they'd thrown women and children in cages and allowed them to die slow deaths from illness and lack of food.

And so the long-time resident of Wuppertal learned to endure life for the sole purpose of exacting revenge on those he felt were responsible for the deaths of his wife and children. He would Extrahieren Sie sein persönliches Pfund Fleisch (extract his personal pound of flesh) from the English, from the Americans and, in particular, from the Jews. Dismayed at what the post-war government had done to remove Nazism from German society, he would happily help others commit white-collar crimes that disrupted the government's increasingly capitalistic system.

Listening to his fellow NDP sympathizer provide updates on activities locally and across the Atlantic in Kentucky, Hartmann was not at all pleased. First, a year spent cultivating the wealthy American chief executive, former Kentucky governor and high-profile thoroughbred horseman Bentley Wellington for membership in the *German and American Business Executives for Bilateral Relations* had apparently been for naught.

"Our contact in Cincinnati told me Wellington passed away on the eve of his family's annual Memorial Day extravaganza," said Becker, "with the cause of death under investigation."

Second, and even more concerning, the LKA NRW was assuming the lead investigative role in the death of Hanna Schröder. It was a clear indication the authorities believed a serious crime had been committed. "My understanding is that Eine Mitteilung über Datum und Uhrzeit zur Befragung erscheinen (a notice of date and time to appear for questioning) at the LKA NRW headquarters in Düsseldorf is in the mail to each person who attended our weekend meeting," the GWH chief executive said. "I expect this to take place in short order."

"So within 48 hours we lose a major potential U.S.-based donor and have our plans to convert GWH GmbH to a publicly traded company come to an abrupt halt because our founder's dog needs to be fed and let out of the house before our vote the following morning?" Hartmann responded out of sheer frustration. "Es ist genug, um mich krank zu machen!" ("It's enough to make me sick!")

"At this point, we need to lay low. We neither heard nor saw anything out of the ordinary that night. I see this as simply a temporary setback. The best we can do is give die Vorsitzende time to recover emotionally," urged Becker. "This situation may actually play favorably into our public offering narrative. A GWH AG," he rationalized, "wouldn't be so vulnerable to unanticipated events having negative consequences for a single majority owner and hence, the company as a whole."

While Hartmann appeared to acquiesce, his thoughts were heading in a far different direction. He was concerned about the interviews the LKA NRW would be conducting. What if anything might his fellow Advisory Board member Barnard Scholz say about the abrupt end to a decades-long friendship? And upon a more thorough check into his and Wolfgang Becker's activities in connection with Bentley Wellington, might investigators somehow link these deaths? He still didn't know the cause of the Bourbonesque chief executive's passing.

Looking at the situation in a rare moment of clarity, Hartmann saw Wolfgang Becker's plan had gone horribly awry and believed there was little chance the overly aggressive chief executive would survive the fallout. He wouldn't for a moment consider turning in Becker to the authorities, even if he *had* been the primary architect of a plan to turn GWH into an instrument for ill-gotten gains with Becker and the NDP as the two main beneficiaries.

No, Dieter Hartmann would simply act on his own...swiftly and with finality.

"Are you with me, Dieter?" asked Becker.

"Ja, eindeutig." ("Yes, absolutely.")

"Es ist dann geregelt. Lass uns unser Bier trinken und gehen." ("It's settled then. Let's finish our beer and leave.")

Chapter 59 – Facts Versus Truths

Abigail Prescott Wellington was well on her way to Bourbonesque's offices in Bardstown for her Wednesday, June 1st business meeting when Galen Grauman pulled onto the lengthy access road that led to the Wellington family residence. Woodrow Abraham Jefferson was waiting outside the front door.

Pointing to a full-grown Southern Magnolia tree about 50 yards off the south wing of the mansion, Woodrow opened the conversation: "Morning detective. Let's head over to the wooden chairs beneath the magnolia," he suggested. There was a warm, pleasant and continuing breeze blowing from west to east. The butler added: "Over here with the shade and breeze, we can talk comfortably and without the electronic surveillance picking up our conversation."

Grauman was surprised, but not shocked. He'd done his homework on Woodrow and knew of his background dating back to his days at the Tuskegee Air Field in Alabama. He imagined that very little escaped this man's attention, hence the reason this morning's interview was so important.

"You don't mind if I take notes," asked Grauman as he took a small pad and pen from his inside jacket pocket. "I could start with some specific questions, Mr. Jefferson," the detective began by according the butler a measure of respect in using his surname, "but I suspect I'm far better off allowing you to tell me a story." Grauman thought for a minute, then added: "I'm *always* interested in facts, Mr. Jefferson. But if you're the kind of person I believe you to be, then I'll settle for the truth."

Woodrow began with his observations from the time he'd wheeled Bentley Wellington into the study until the time he discovered the Governor's body slumped over his desk. He had seen not one, but two switches of the cardboard placards labeled "Salmon Quiche" and "Crab-stuffed Quiche" – the first switch had been made by Beau and the second by Abigail.

"If the placards were switched twice," Detective Grauman began...

"...the actions would have negated each other," Woodrow

finished his thought.

The detective picked up the trail of logic: "There could have been a *third* change of the placards in question, or an event staffer might have misplaced the two quiche placards when the serving trays were initially set up, or yet another person might have brought crab-stuffed quiche into the study."

"Let me move from facts to truths, detective," whereupon Woodrow set out to explain the actions and motives of each member of the Wellington family. He'd wind up using each finger on his right hand to emphasize his points:

"First, Missus Wellington never forgave her husband for the incident in San Francisco and its aftermath – the rape of a well-educated, attractive African-American senior aide, a non-disclosure agreement with the victim, and the birth of a child.

"Second, Mistah Bentley had long suspected his wife was behind the hunting 'accident' that resulted in his stroke and paralysis. He knew too much about guns to have been so reckless, and no one other than the Missus had access to the locked storage area in the guest house.

"Third, Missus Wellington had grown incredibly frustrated at Mistah Bentley's refusal to invest in growing the distillery, particularly when she had to pick up the slack after her husband's stroke and paralysis. The company operations had been a source of ongoing arguments that became more frequent and more intense. In fact, the Missus sold her part of her daddy's coal-mining business so she'd have cash available to compensate for her men folks' poor decisions.

"Fourth, Mastah Beauregard and Miss McDougal have been seeing each other for quite some time, and things recently had become serious. There is nothing in the young man's life that he is more passionate about than Darci, and that includes thoroughbred racing. When she told Beau about her annual Memorial Day 'appointment' with his dad – including Missus Wellington's role in arranging it so Darci could make some extra money to pay for her schooling – Mastah Beau was some kinda mad. He couldn't believe his mother would take advantage of a teenager who'd do just about anything to make ends meet. And he was furious that his daddy was abusing yet another employee when he could have gone elsewhere for the same service, if you know what I mean.

"Fifth, Mastah Beau had become increasingly angry at the way his daddy spoke down to him when it came to his gambling. He saw the Governor as incredibly hypocritical given his own history when it came to drinking and lecherous behavior. You see, Mastah Beau had known for quite some time about the 'incident' and blamed his father for creating their dysfunctional family.

"Mistah Wellington," Woodrow summed up, "was lonely, weary and deeply frustrated with his life. He'd long felt unloved and unappreciated by wife and son. As I wheeled him into the study this past Monday evening, he said he wished his life would finally come to an end.

"Now I have to tell you, Detective Grauman. In the aftermath of his hunting accident, I'd listened to the Governor complain about his 'miserable existence' and 'wretched situation' on more than a few occasions, so his comment didn't cause me undue alarm – particularly since he was about to experience one of his few pleasures.

"Given how the Missus and Mastah Beauregard felt about the Governor, it's fitting that both tried to do away with him." Woodrow paused and then added: "And ain't it ironic that neither actually *caused* his death? He must have asked somebody to bring him the crab quiche…although I didn't see anyone entering the study."

Galen Grauman closed his note pad and rubbed his chin while carefully considering what to say. "You don't know how the Governor came by the crab-stuffed quiche, do you?"

"What I can tell you is that I did not provide the Governor with crab quiche," answered Woodrow in a matter-of-fact tone.

"And even if you *did* know, you wouldn't be telling me, would you?" the detective hazarded a guess.

"All I know, detective, is that Mister Wellington had ample opportunity to take crab-stuffed quiche from the hors d'oeuvre table, from a few hours before the evening meal was served to just before I wheeled the Governor into his study."

With that, Galen Grauman rose from his chair beneath the magnolia tree, shook Woodrow's hand and thanked him for his candor. As he returned to his vehicle for the trip back to his Lexington office, he was pretty much convinced that Bentley Wellington had intentionally eaten crab-stuffed quiche in a successful attempt to take his own life.

But what to do about Woodrow's account of the attempts by Abigail and Beauregard to take the Governor's life? It wasn't Galen Grauman's job to make the case. That was up to the Fayette County Prosecutor's Office – and that department's decision on whether a grand jury should be assembled to review the evidence.

Chapter 60 – Agreement in Sight...But a Snag!

Reiner Huber of Stratton-Oakes' European headquarters office in Frankfurt had been alerted by his New York City-based partner Charles Janovsky, who briefed him on an opportunity that had just come in over the transom thru the international asset management firm of Steinberg Stavros Rogers & Co. Herr Huber indicated he had nothing on his agenda for the next day. In fact, he was scheduled to begin summer holidays in a couple of weeks and had begun assigning case work to his associates.

Holder of the L.L.M. in Corporate Restructuring from prestigious Ruprecht-Karls-Universität Heidelberg, Huber was one of Germany's preeminent corporate attorneys and said he'd be delighted to meet Frau Hauptmann at GWH GmbH um elf Uhr (at 11 a.m.). Going the extra mile (or kilometer, in this case), Reiner added he would travel to Düsseldorf after work and stay overnight at one of the airport hotels in order to meet Marci Davis Jeffries and Consuela Parks Pettiford when they cleared customs the next morning. That would allow them time to talk during the limo ride to Wuppertal before getting together with their client.

"I'm very confident in the abilities of Ms. Jeffries and Ms. Pettiford," Janovsky felt almost obligated to state, "but we really appreciate your willingness to anchor the effort for these two, ah, how would you say "Löwinnen?"

"Yes, Lionesses!" acknowledged Huber. "I haven't had any *business* dealings with Collins, Connell & O'Brien, but I once spoke at a symposium on intra-European business transactions at the Dublin Business School. The invitation came from one of the firm's founders, Aidan O'Brien, who was then serving on the school's board of visitors. We will do just fine, Charles."

Herr Huber's words proved prescient. By the time Lufthansa's overnight flight from JFK to Düsseldorf was "wheels up," Marci had brought Consuela up to speed on the state of the P/M industry and its current place in the supply chain, GWH GmbH's operations and financial performance, and the corporate culture Gretchen Weiß Hauptmann had instilled in the organization.

Marci then spent the first hour of the flight discussing what additional information and insights they'd want to glean from Frau Hauptmann, outlining how the client's answers would form the underpinning of their strategy in the initial discussion with Collins, Connell & O'Brien, and providing an overview of prospective purchaser Manchester Automotive Suppliers International.

By the time the Stratton-Oakes/Steinberg Stavros team arrived at GWH, Reiner Huber was so confident in his "Löwinnen" that he believed his role would be little more than adding a couple of cogent questions or seasoned insights to the conversation. In fact, he was slightly more concerned about showing their potential client he wasn't simply window dressing.

Jeffries, Pettiford and Huber met with Gretchen for a little over an hour in the main conference room before Shea O'Halloran and Aiden O'Brien arrived. Marci noted with relief that the client's responses to the team's questions had been very much in line with her previous day's initial conversation and appeared to underscore her serious commitment to selling the business.

As the names of the visitors were announced over the intercom by the receptionist in the lobby, Rainer remarked quietly: "O'Brien attending is a good sign. It likely means this potential transaction is a high priority."

After an exchange of pleasantries and business cards, O'Brien and O'Halloran sat attentively as Marci Davis Jeffries set the stage by providing an overview of the P/M industry and the advantages of P/M-related technologies over more traditional parts manufacturing processes. Consuela Parks Pettiford followed by offering a few prime examples of industries other than the automotive sector that were experiencing their first successful applications of powder metallurgy, along with recent and more robust processes that were improving operating efficiencies as well as production standards.

Gretchen then presented her firm's operations overview for the next five years including two sets of financial projections – an aggressive set which she pointedly indicated had been developed by her management team for an internal meeting held just last week and her own more conservative set provided especially for the current meeting.

Finally, Rainer Huber offered an assessment from 30,000 feet of the regulatory climate for intra-European corporate transactions and how he expected the business community to move from internationalism to globalization. His message?... There was no better time than the present to be acquiring a firm like GWH GmbH.

For lunch, Gretchen arranged for a local caterer to deliver meat and cheese platters consisting of Rauchschinken (dark smoked ham), Westfaelischer Schinken (Westfalian ham) and Fleischwurst (bologna), along with Jarlsberg, Limburger and Butterkäse (butter cheese); an assortment of breads that included Bauernbrot (Farmer Bread), Black Bread, Pumpernickel and Dark Rye, and a choice of Beck's, Paulaner München, Veltins Pilsener or kohlensäurehaltiges Wasser (sparkling water). Herr Huber subtly nodded his approval in Gretchen's direction.

As the mid-day meal was concluding, Rainer Huber and Aiden O'Brien had moved toward the other end of the conference room where they were locked in discussion. Closing in on the two o'clock hour, Marci suggested a 15-minute break to allow everyone time to catch up on calls and retrieve messages from their offices. When they reconvened, the group would be taken on a 45-minute tour of GWH's P/M presses, machining operations and research & testing lab.

Gretchen had her shift manager, Bernt Lenhardt, conduct the tour. Well-spoken with a wry sense of humor, the 12-year GWH vet showcased his ability to be entertaining as well as informative. He didn't get bogged down in unnecessary details, handling questions from Shea O'Halloran and Aiden O'Brien easily, thoroughly yet succinctly. Die Vorsitzende was quite pleased with her decision to delegate the task to this particular member of her staff.

Upon the group's return to the conference room, it was Aiden O'Brien who spoke: "It's quite evident from what we've heard and seen today that GWH would be a good fit for our client, Manchester Automotive Suppliers International. I've spoken to the company's president, Alton Bahnsen, who is very keen to meet with you and your advisors. Inasmuch as Ms. Jeffries and Ms. Pettiford are here from New York and Herr Huber has traveled from Frankfurt, we are hoping you might be available to meet with Mr. Bahnsen tomorrow morning. He's willing to fly over this evening so we can get an early start on discussions."

All eyes turned to Gretchen Weiß Hauptmann. "As it so happens, I am clear until about 1500 hours. The NRW has asked me to meet with its investigative team regarding the auto accident that took the life of my administrative assistant. I suppose we could get started as early as 0700 hours. We can have a working breakfast and go from there." Marci, Consuela and Rainer all nodded affirmatively.

"It's settled then," beamed the senior partner of Collins, Connell & O'Brien. "I'll notify Mr. Bahnsen." O'Brien paused for a couple of moments, taking a deep breath. "Of course, there will be numerous issues to resolve other than sale price – status of your contracts with customers, retention and/or termination of members of management, employee compensation.

"As you are likely aware," he continued, "our client has been quite active over the past few years in adding to the company's product portfolio via acquisition. It's been our policy, whenever possible, to retain the services of the acquired firm's chief executive as a consultant for a two-year period. 'MASI,' as the company is often called, finds it helps transition the new business into the overall operating environment."

Injecting himself quickly into the conversation before Gretchen had an opportunity to respond, Reiner said his team would evaluate the request and confer with Frau Hauptmann. "This will be one of many pieces to the negotiating puzzle. In the end, we hope to put all the pieces together."

***

At meeting's end, Shea O'Halloran and Aiden O'Brien made their way back to the Sheraton Düsseldorf Airport Hotel where they'd have a late dinner with MASI's Alton Bahnsen to discuss strategy for the next day's negotiations.

Back at GWH, the Stratton-Oakes/Steinberg Stavros team had their own strategy session with Gretchen Weiß Hauptmann. Sale price, oddly enough, took less than five minutes to discuss. The major challenge was coming to grips with a response to MASI's request to have the GWH founder and majority owner to stay on as a consultant.

Her bottom line was fairly straightforward, and she shared her sentiments with members of her team: "If I sell the business, I want a clean break." She then lapsed into silence.

What Gretchen had come to realize is that her willingness to transition GWH from a private firm to a publicly traded company actually would have been the first move toward eventually stepping completely away. Hanna Schröder's death over the past weekend had provided that moment of clarity.

But Gretchen dreaded the thought of remaining close to the daily decision-making process for a company she would no longer own. Deep in thought, she was startled to hear a youthful voice call out: "Frau Hauptmann." Then louder when she didn't answer immediately: "Frau Hauptmann!"

"I apologize. I was lost in thought, Ms. Pettiford. Yes, what is it?"

"Do you have anyone on your management team or on your advisory board who might be capable of filling a two-year commitment to counseling MASI?"

"Oh, mein Gott!" Gretchen exclaimed as a smile crossed her face. "Of course – Barnard Scholz!" She proceeded to give Consuela, Marci Davis Jeffries and Reiner Huber a quick profile.

"And Barnard currently sits on our seven-member Advisory Board," Hauptmann concluded.

"This may well be a solution," Reiner said in a manner designed to bring die Vorsitzende down to earth. "But this is where we want the negotiation on this point to *end*...not where we want it to *begin*. It may very well be that in order to get what we want when it comes to your post-transaction role, Gretchen, we have to concede on some other point that is equally important to Alton Bahnsen."

"Well, if it's at all possible," chimed in Marci, "you ought to have this discussion with Barnard Scholz. It won't do any good to negotiate something you can't deliver. While he sounds the part, the bigger question is whether he'd be interested."

Gretchen wouldn't need to call Barnard in DuBois, PA. What had begun as a weekend retreat in Wuppertal to decide the future of GWH GmbH, had turned into a weeklong stay in Germany due to the death of Gretchen's assistant and the subsequent investigation by the LKA-NRW. Scholz, along with the other members of the company's Advisory Board and management team, were scheduled to appear for questioning on Friday at the North Rhine-Westphalia criminal investigation unit in Düsseldorf.

In the meantime, Barnard was marking time by reacquainting himself with the latest developments coming out of GWH's research lab. The GWH founder simply asked her receptionist to arrange dinner for two at a local restaurant.

At the same time, hotel reservations were made through the weekend at the Park Villa for Ms. Pettiford and Ms. Jeffries, both of whom were in sore need of some serious shuteye. Reiner Huber called back to the Stratton-Oakes office in Frankfurt to ask his administrative assistant to extend his room at the Sheraton Düsseldorf Airport Hotel (coincidentally the same hotel at which Alton Bahnsen and his M&A team were staying) for that evening only, figuring he wouldn't need to be in Wuppertal beyond Saturday.

***

Gretchen and her colleague on the Advisory Board, Barnard Scholz, had their respective reasons for the rather uncomfortable silence that dominated the 15-minute drive from GWH GmbH to Villa Scarpati Restaurant & Hotel. Still new to the idea of using Barnard Scholz's involvement as a negotiating tool for the sale of GWH to MASI, Gretchen was going over in her mind exactly how and when during their meal she should broach the topic with Barnard.

For Scholz, the past several days had been agonizing, from the unwanted, uncalled for and totally irrational behavior of his fellow Advisory Board member Dieter Hartmann, to Hanna Schröder's untimely death and the LKA NRW investigation now underway. He hadn't spoken a word to anyone about Hartmann's behavior, but had the nagging feeling that somehow the two were linked.

With a comfortable late spring evening at hand, Gretchen and Barnard took advantage and requested seating at the far end of the terrace. Gretchen ordered a bottle of Red Bordeaux, Chateau de Goëlane 1975. The two toasted, with Scholz whole-heartedly agreeing to the appropriateness of her words: "Es kommen bessere Zeiten." ("Better times are coming.")

"I have something extremely important to discuss with you, Barnard – something that will be followed by a business proposition," Gretchen said as she emptied her first glass. "So let's order now because what I have to say will take some time." With that, the two opened their menus. Gretchen quickly decided on Scaloppini di Vitello (Veal Scaloppini); Barnard took a bit more time before choosing Zuppa di Pesci (Italian Fish & Seafood Stew).

For the next hour, Barnard Scholz sat mesmerized by Gretchen's candor in how she'd decided to neither maintain GWH GmbH as a private firm nor transition the business to a publicly traded company...but rather sell the business to a firm based in the United Kingdom. If the long-time veteran of the P/M industry had been surprised by die Vorsitzende's revelation, he was shocked by the proposal that followed.

Gretchen explained MASI's policy of retaining the chief executive of an acquired business as a consultant for two years whenever possible to facilitate a smooth transition of business operations. She then repeated what she'd told members of her transaction team earlier in the day – that she dreaded the thought of remaining close to the daily decision-making process for a company she would no longer own.

"One of the Stratton-Oakes associates asked if there was a member of our management team or Advisory Board who might be capable of taking on this role." Gretchen paused and continued: "It didn't take me long to figure on a short list of one, Barnard. That's you." At that point, Gretchen stopped, poured herself a second glass of wine and took a healthy albeit uncharacteristic swig.

Gretchen had talked through the opening salads and finished as the main course arrived. The two ate in silence as Scholz digested her proposal. It was a big ask – geographic relocation across the Atlantic from a stateside residence to which he'd become accustomed; a departure from academe and a return to the business world; a radically different daily routine followed by a huge unknown after 24 months...and all at the age of 68. The myriad details to be worked out were mind-numbing.

Yet...the compensation would provide him with a level of financial security that would enhance his quality of life just two years down the road. And then there was the challenge of taking on a role in which he could truly make a difference in people's lives and in the industry to which he'd devoted his entire professional career. Finally, there was certainty in the knowledge that should he turn away from the offer, he'd always wonder what might have been.

There was no asking the timeframe for providing an answer. Barnard Scholz simply announced to Gretchen: "Lassen Sie uns einen Blick darauf haben." ("Let's have a go at it!")

***

Since Monday's initial planning session, Bertram Krieger, the officer in charge of the State Investigation Bureau in Düsseldorf (LKA NRW), had had his team of inspectors working round-the-clock in conducting deep background checks on each person attending the GWH GmbH weekend retreat at the Hotel Park Villa in Wuppertal.

With painstaking detail, inspectors had combed thru the personal and professional lives of each individual. By Wednesday morning, the LKA NRW was able to clear seven persons – Elina Lang-Haas, Mia Mangels, Harald Schneider and Eckhardt Vogt of GWH's Advisory Board, as well as Engel Fischer, Garrick Imhoff and Dedrick Walter of the Management team. An LKA NRW inspector was stationed outside the Basilika St. Laurentius and notified the seven that they no longer were persons of interest and would not be required to appear for questioning on Friday.

The other individuals – Barnard Scholz, Dieter Hartmann, Wilhelm Fuchs and Wolfgang Becker – were not so fortunate. Hartmann's appointment was at 1000 hours, Fuchs was to be interviewed at 1130 hours, Becker at 1300 hours and Scholz slated for 1430 hours. Gretchen Weiß Hauptmann was scheduled to arrive at 1600 hours.

As a precaution, Krieger assigned one of his inspectors, Gunther Böhm, to patrol Frau Hauptmann's residence to ensure her security. Inspector Böhm's assignment would begin am Donnerstagabend (on Thursday evening).

Chapter 61 – What to File? What to File?

Sitting down at his desk to begin paperwork on the investigation into the death of Bentley Wellington, Detective Galen Grauman thought...thought again...and thought some more.

Woodrow Jefferson, the Wellingtons' long-time butler, had been nothing if not honest. Years of interviewing witnesses, persons of interest and suspects told Grauman as much. From all Woodrow had said about his time in the Wellingtons' employ, he clearly had an uncanny ability to meld into the background in the midst of a crowd. Lastly, he had a wise man's sense of justice.

Woodrow's account had given the Lexington Bureau of Investigation detective a uniquely objective perspective on the multi-layered relationships between father and son, mother and son and husband and wife. These relationships never really involved the entire family unit. It had always been two of them, with the third left out of the working equation. Even when Bentley, Abigail and Beauregard gathered in the run-up to the Wellingtons' annual Memorial Day extravaganza, there had been no detailed discussion among the three. Abigail ruled the roost, so to speak, with Bentley and Beau clearly in subservient roles.

How long had this dynamic existed? Detective Grauman suspected it had been present ever since Beau came into Abigail's and Bentley's world, but mushroomed in the aftermath of Bentley's hunting accident.

After notifying the Fayette County Medical Examiner & Coroner's Office that an autopsy wouldn't be necessary, Grauman began typing. Based on the available evidence, eye-witness accounts and interviews with persons of interest, the detective believed the "real" cause of death was suicide. Grauman's extensive interview notes would become part of the report and shared with the Fayette County Prosecutor's Office.

Given the expansive reach of the case, Grauman immediately shared the latest information with FBI field agent Matts Meriwether and FBI Director of Kentucky Operations Marcus McQueen. They, in turn, informed Grauman of the money exchange between Beauregard Wellington and Squints.

By day's end the FBI lead agent on the case, Sammy Eisenstat, was apprised of all the latest developments. Given the pace of events taking place in Kentucky, Canada and Germany, timely communication was more critical than ever. After hearing from Marcus McQueen, Eisenstat touched base with Calvin Thomas, who'd been keeping an eye on Jorge Hauptmann as the recent Seton Hall University grad continued his car-jockey duties at Monmouth Park. All quiet down the Jersey shore, he sent a fax to the LKA NRW office in Düsseldorf to update Herr Krieger and the Mossad's David Katzman on the safety of Gretchen Weiß Hauptmann's only son.

Chapter 62 – Conflagration & Pulverization

At 26 years old, Gunther Böhm was new to the LKA NRW. Married for two years, he and his wife, Mia, had recently learned they were expecting their first child. Living in a small apartment in the city of Solingen, the couple had begun to look at small houses in the city's outskirts. Böhm wanted to make a good impression on his boss, Bertram Krieger, the officer in charge of the State Investigation Bureau. The pay for members of the criminal unit was higher than in other NRW units.

Before heading off to his security assignment at the Hückeswagen home of Gretchen Weiß Hauptmann, Gunther telephoned Mia to tell her they'd likely need to pass on weekend house hunting because of the special duty he'd pulled. Mia, curious as always when it came to his job, was disappointed her husband couldn't offer details other than it involved overnight work that would begin just before dark that evening. He wouldn't be home until Freitag morgens (Friday, mid-morning).

***

As a member of the Mossad and not formally attached to any official German law enforcement unit, David Katzman had the ability to operate without the usual legal constraints. The only caveat had been a mutual understanding that any illegal activities, if discovered, would be met with a swift disavowal by the governments of Germany and Israel.

By the time Wolfgang Becker and Dieter Hartmann set their Wednesday evening meeting, the LKA NRW had already narrowed its list of suspects. From the moment Becker, Fuchs and Hartmann left Hanna Schröder's service in Wuppertal, Katzman had made it his business to tail Hartmann. Experience told him if there were any "dirty work" in the offing, it would be coming from the low-level grunt Hartmann – not the current head of GWH GmbH's management team or its director of strategic planning. His hunch paid off in spades when Becker and Hartmann met at a roadside pub in Bergisch Gladbach.

Heading into the pub shortly after Hartmann, the Mossad agent took a seat at the bar close enough to overhear fragments of the discussion between the two Germans.

Katzman was aware Krieger had assigned security to Frau Hauptmann. But despite a busy night ahead of preparing for the next day's interviews, he decided to do a couple of passes by Hauptmann's home just to make sure all was copacetic.

***

Gretchen and Barnard finished their main course, were sipping kaffee and talking casually about various aspects of the GWH operation – the need for equipment upgrades, developments in more robust production processes, the importance of materials handling and ideas for efficiencies in managing levels of inventory.

Suddenly, Barnard remembered he had wanted to tell die Vorsitzende about Dieter Hartmann's abrupt attitude change and his sense that Dieter's irrational behavior was somehow connected to the unfortunate event that halted the retreat. He also noted that Wolfgang Becker's projections seemed somewhat overly optimistic for a publicly traded GWH AG and minimized the administrative costs of a range of shareholder-related activities.

Hauptmann was pleased on two levels: first, Scholz had shown a greater depth of understanding in the firm's operations than she'd previously attributed to him, and second, she'd correctly perceived a rift of sorts between Hartmann and Scholz.

At the same time, Gretchen was a bit unnerved listening to Barnard confirm her observations on the relationship between the two Advisory Board members and, in the next breath, hearing Scholz's comments on Becker's numbers. Among so many thoughts about events over the past several days, there was an emerging feeling that there might be a connection between Hartmann's erratic behavior; Becker's projections (which she, herself, had modified for her meeting earlier that day), and the auto accident that may, indeed, have been meant for her.

Then, as if a consequential puzzle piece had been dropped suddenly into place, everything clicked. Gretchen went through her reasoning with Scholz: "What if the accident didn't occur until I was driving home from the retreat, with a vote already having taken place to what...take the firm public? Nobody knew I would be sending Hanna back to her home in the middle of the night to tend to Pulver. And nobody could have foreseen me telling Hanna *not* to use her own vehicle."

Gretchen then offered her thoughts on Wolfgang Becker's time with the company. Over the past couple of years, she knew the CEO had become increasingly restless with the incremental financial gains of the business at a time when many competitors were becoming more aggressive. He'd certainly been a more outspoken proponent of taking the company public. And, of course, there was the clause in his contract that tied an increased ownership interest to bottom-line performance.

Shivers ran up and down her spine at the possibility multiple individuals could have been playing a dangerous high-stakes game. Her train of thought had been sobering to Scholz as well.

Taking the napkin from her lap and placing it on the table, Gretchen said: "We both have busy days tomorrow, Barnard. Let's call it an evening." The pair walked through the restaurant, down the steps and toward the back of the parking lot. Both Hauptmann and Scholz were using rented vehicles – Gretchen for obvious reasons and Scholz because he preferred the flexibility a vehicle afforded him during his now extended stay in the Düsseldorf area.

As Gretchen went to unlock the driver's side door, she heard a whisper coming from the slightly opened rear window: "Steigen Sie ins Auto und sagen Sie Herrn Scholz, dass er neben Ihnen sitzen soll...Schnell!" ("Get in the car and tell Mr. Scholz to sit next to you...Quickly!") As Gretchen turned toward the back window, she stared at the tip of a Heckler & Koch P7 semi-automatic pistol pointing directly at her head. The voice belonged to Dieter Hartmann.

After the two shocked dinner companions made their way into the front of the automobile, Hartmann ordered Gretchen to drive to her home. On the way, he unloaded the loathing that had been festering for the better part of four decades, giving Gretchen and Barnard a very dark picture of where Dieter Hartmann had been – and quite alarmingly, where he was headed.

Hartmann hissed: "Die quälende Reise, die ich für euch beide im Sinn habe, verblasst im Vergleich zu dem, was meine Familie ertragen musste. ("The torturous journey I have in mind for the two of you pales compared with what my family had to endure.")

"How dare the Americans and British speak of Jews as victims of Nazi atrocities. Caging women and children to let them die?!? Such hypocrits! And now our government is taking steps to purge Nazism from the country and its culture?!? Adolf Hitler should be lionized as a national hero, not ridiculed as a war-time criminal. Where the Third Reich fell short, due in no small part to traitors like you two, the NDP will succeed."

He continued: "Warum haben Sie Hanna Schröder mitten in der Nacht zu Ihnen nach Hause geschickt?" ("Why did you send Hanna Schröder to your house in the middle of the night?")

It was a rhetorical question, but for some reason Gretchen felt compelled to answer: "Weil mein Hund gefüttert und aus dem Haus gelassen werden musste." ("Because my dog needed to be fed and let out of the house.")

"Barnard, you have been brainwashed by your time in the United States. Listening to you carry on about Americans, I take it you actually believe in their 'unique experiment' in democracy. Greater nations than theirs have fallen. Their time of reckoning will soon arrive.

"And you, Frau Hauptmann, a person who once *served* the Third Reich by helping to transport Jews to our camps. For *you* to marry a Jew? Someone who aided in their travel to Palestine? What a disgrace!"

With Dieter Hartmann's last words, tears welled up in Gretchen's eyes. He knew. How many others knew? And if Dieter Hartmann had knowledge of her secret, was his information about Fabian true as well?

From time to time, she'd suspected her husband might be a Jew. The gaps in information on time spent during the war. An occasional awkward silence when the two had been discussing certain topics. The realization that they'd both kept deep secrets from each other.

And then another thought: Did Fabian know about *her* wartime activities? Is that what precipitated his sudden departure?

They were now approaching Hückeswagen and her home, with the car having fallen eerily silent. Coming to a stop in the driveway, Hartmann ordered Hauptmann and Scholz out of the car and toward the front door. At just past 10:30 p.m., dusk was rapidly turning into the darkness of night. With twin floor lamps on in the living room, Hartmann could see inside the house and noticed a large German Shepherd wagging his tail in anticipation of his companion opening the door.

"Open the door and tell your dog to sit between the love seat and sofa," Dieter commanded, adding: "...otherwise I'll shoot him first." He stood back as Gretchen followed his orders. "Now both of you, on the love seat," he barked, motioning his gun to the far end of the living room.

Noticing a light dimmer next to the living room entrance, he moved the lever ever so slightly upward, which provided just enough light from the overhead chandelier to see any movement by his captives. He then moved toward the floor lamps and turned them off.

Hartmann stood facing Gretchen and Barnard, removed a small can of lighter fluid from his inside right jacket pocket and began squirting the liquid on the sofa and across the wood flooring. After it was empty, he returned the can to his jacket pocket and removed a cigarette lighter from the left pocket of his pants.

Gretchen started to sob. Barnard pleaded with his former friend to reconsider the cold-blooded murder of two innocent colleagues.

Then came a succession of events that in the aggregate took place within a span of less than a minute:

Gunther Böhm, arriving for his overnight assignment, didn't have the luxury of a formal introduction. Seeing a man turning off lights with two others seated together nearby (unusual for the Hauptmann residence at that time of night), he jumped out of his unmarkiertes Polizeiauto (unmarked police car) and walked briskly toward the front door. By the time Inspector Böhm was halfway there, a fire had been started and was spreading rapidly, indicating to Gunther that an accelerant had been used. Now certain about the presence of a home invader, he rapidly changed course and literally leapt through the adjacent living room window.

Dieter Hartmann, reacting to the window shattering, turned to see a large man scrambling to his feet. He turned and got off three rounds from his semi-automatic, missing his target with the first shot but grazing Gunther's right leg and piercing his right arm with the second and third shots. The force of the bullets and close proximity of the shooter dropped the LKA NRW officer in his tracks.

That Hartmann didn't continue the assault was due to Pulver. The 11-year-old guide-dog-turned-guard-dog instinctively reacted to the gunfire, closed the distance to the shooter in a fraction of a second and felled Hartman and knocked the gun from his hand. Pulver's attack was mercilessly efficient, the guard dog ripping at Hartmann's throat for a good 20 seconds until the attacker briefly convulsed and then lay motionless on the carpet with massive amounts of blood pooling on the dark brown wood floor.

With flames spreading and smoke quickly filling the front part of the house, Barnard and Gretchen dragged Gunther out the front door to the base of a giant oak tree about 40 yards from the front of the house. Pulver followed closely behind them. As they attempted to stanch the bleeding from Böhm's wounds, the officer introduced himself.

At that moment, David Katzman arrived at the blazing home, quickly exited his rented vehicle and identified himself as "additional assistance" sent by Bertram Krieger of the LKA NRW. Seeing as no harm had come to either Hauptmann or Scholz, he quickly asked Böhm where he'd been wounded and whether he could manage the dozen steps to his car with help. Nodding in the affirmative, Katzman loaded the officer into his vehicle.

He then ordered Gretchen and Barnard to take Pulver and drive directly to the LKA NRW office in Düsseldorf. He'd be taking Böhm to a hospital in Remscheid, about 15 kilometers to the west.

"The hospital is only 20 minutes from here," Katzman said in a calm and reassuring voice. "By the time you arrive at the LKA NRW office – it should take you about an hour – I will have placed our officer friend in good hands and will have called the staff in Düsseldorf to tell them what happened here and to expect you in short order."

On the way to the hospital, Katzman passed right by the Hückeswagen Feuerwehr (fire station). He stopped just long enough to alert the person on duty to the fire at the Hauptmann home just a couple of minutes up the road.

"There won't be much left of the place," said Katzman.

Chapter 63 – A Reckoning

Wednesday had already been a long day for Abigail Prescott Wellington. While in Bardstown, she called the Governor's office to go over details for her late husband to lie in state on Sunday at the State Capitol Building in Frankfort. The corpse would then be returned to the Wellington residence for a private ceremony on Monday, after which he'd be buried in the family plot at the eastern end of Thoroughbred Bs Farm.

Returning home, Abigail was met at the front door by Woodrow, who asked when she would be ready to receive the day's messages.

"I have a splitting headache, Woodrow. If you would bring me two Tylenol and a tall glass of Coke with ice, you can give me the day's news – good, bad or indifferent." With that, Abigail flopped in the sitting room recliner to await his return.

"Almost all of the messages have been condolence calls from friends, public officials and business associates," said Woodrow.

"Oh, and make sure the Tylenol is in the *new* packaging," added Abigail in a subtle reference to last September's Tylenol cyanide crisis that resulted in one of the first major product recalls in American history.

Given events of the past week, Woodrow wondered for a split second if the Widow Wellington wasn't tempting fate. "Well, at least I don't have to worry about Mrs. Wellington's state of mind," the butler thought to himself after handing Abigail her Coke along with a pair of Tylenol gelcaps in a small porcelain dish.

"Then there was a call from Dowling Chism," the butler added. "He wants you to give him a call at his home any time between 7 and 9 p.m."

Chism, first vice president at the Lexington branch of Central Bank, had been the family banker since Bentley left politics in December of 1955. Dowling had become quite friendly with Abigail over the years and proudly noted to anyone who'd listen that he'd grown the Lexington branch's assets by adding the Bowling, Claywell, Prescott & Trivette Coal Co. to its portfolio of business accounts.

For many years a frequent visitor to Central Bank, Abigail

almost always brought little Beauregard with her. Chism made it a point to have a Tootsie Roll pop for the boy. And for the year-end holiday season as well as on Beau's birthday, the bank officer always had a special gift for him, ranging from a beginner's model railroad set and toy ice-cream maker to an Adolph Rupp autographed basketball. And "Uncle Dow" helped Beau open his first Christmas savings account when he was eight years old.

Dutifully, Abigail called Dowling after she'd inhaled a Swanson's TV Dinner of turkey with gravy and dressing, peas & carrots in seasoned sauce, whipped potatoes and apple-cranberry cake cobbler. It was one of Abigail's favorite comfort meals when she'd been short on time and long on stress.

"What's up, Dow?" asked Abigail as the banker answered the call on the first ring. She wondered if he'd been waiting near his telephone for her call.

After the briefest of sorry-for-your-loss statements, Chism cut right to the chase: "I'm really concerned about Beau, Abigail. I've known him since he was knee-high to a grasshopper, and I can tell you straightaway that something's very wrong." Dowling then recounted her son's visit to the bank earlier in the day and Beauregard cashing a check from Bentley's personal checking account for $150,000, a transaction made noteworthy because of beads of sweat rolling down Beau's forehead and the young man's apparent need to conduct business quickly.

"When I went to shake his hand, Beau declined and volunteered he'd injured it while loading a horse into his van," Chism explained, "except the tone of his voice left me unconvinced that was how it happened.

"Not that it's ever my business," the Central Bank officer offered, "but he never mentioned why he needed that kind of cash. It *is* highly unusual."

Abigail feared the worst, but didn't want anyone – in particular the family's personal banker – even *considering* something untoward was occurring. So she invented a fabrication: "Oh, that. We've decided to give all of our employees at Triple-B Racing Stables and Thoroughbred Bs Farm cash bonuses this year." As soon as the words left her mouth, she knew how implausible it must have sounded to Dowling. First, there was the tax-reporting requirements for employees as well as the bookkeeping documentation for the employer. Second, the banker knew the practice was completely foreign to any of the Wellingtons' businesses – even Beau's. Well, she'd have to live with what she'd blurted out, Abigail thought as she thanked Chism for the heads-up and his condolences.

This latest episode in her son's financial irregularities convinced her more than ever of the actions she'd been considering for the past couple of weeks. She would sit Beau down tomorrow morning for a "come-to-Jesus" conversation in which "Mama Wellington" would tell her son exactly how things would go down.

Chapter 64 – Hit Pause and Reconsider

The telephone rang Friday morning at the ungodly hour of 0500 in the hotel room of Aiden O'Brien, senior partner at Collins, Connell & O'Brien. It was Reiner Huber of Stratton-Oakes/Frankfurt, who began by simply stating: "There have been some unforeseen developments overnight involving the LKA NRW's investigation into last weekend's auto accident, Mr. O'Brien. Today's meeting is critically important. Is it possible for members of our team to meet with your people at a conference room at the Sheraton where you're staying, say at 1200 hours?"

"Under the circumstances, I'm sure that would be acceptable to Mr. Bahnsen," O'Brien answered. "I'll have Shea O'Halloran make the arrangements."

Seated with Bertram Krieger and David Katzman at LKA NRW headquarters, Gretchen Weiß Hauptmann and Barnard Scholz were asked once again to recount details of their harrowing experience. Gretchen described their dinner at Scarpati's, Dieter Hartmann's ambush from the back seat of her rental car in the restaurant parking lot, and the traumatic drive to her home – made more so by Hartmann's crazed monologue.

Barnard picked up the details from that point, telling of the rapid succession of events that started with Hartmann setting Hauptmann's house ablaze, Gunther Böhm's timely crash through the front window, Hartmann shooting the LKA NRW officer, Pulver's attack and their subsequent escape.

✳✳✳

By 0900, Krieger's meeting included "a cast of thousands," David Katzman thought to himself. Exaggeration notwithstanding, at least a half-dozen additional characters were involved – Jakob Seidel, case officer for the NRW Exchange Supervisory Authority; members of the GWH GmbH transaction team, including Reiner Huber, Marci Davis Jeffries and Consuela Parks Pettiford, and the recently arrived Sammy Eisenstat of the FBI and Cameron Connors of the RCMP.

Gustav Zimmermann, the officer-in-charge of the NRW team that had investigated Hanna Schröder's fatal accident, was currently gathering evidence at the Hauptmann residence crime scene.

Krieger and Katzman fully briefed Eisenstat and Connors on what had transpired, from Wednesday's funeral service and the clandestine meeting between Dieter Hartmann and Wolfgang Becker that night to events the following evening. When Krieger then introduced members of the GWH GmbH transaction team to the American and Canadian law enforcement representatives, Eisenstat shot a glance at Consuela Parks Pettiford. When Krieger finished, the FBI agent asked if he could have a minute with Ms. Pettiford.

Stepping into the hallway corridor and in response to Eisenstat's simple question, "What are you doing here?" Consuela quickly briefed Eisenstat on the Steinberg Stavros/Stratton-Oakes relationship and her boss, Charles Janovsky, assigning her to the GWH GmbH transaction team. The FBI agent kept the tie between the current situation and the Wellington family investigation he was leading back in the States to himself.

Consuela, figuring there probably *was* some sort of link between the case Eisenstat had warned her away from and the situation here in Germany, recalled the line made famous by Sergeant Schultz in the TV series *Hogan's Heroes*: "I know nothing!" The young attorney, also thinking back to Eisenstat's cautionary words at the Molly Pitcher Inn in New Jersey, decided to not even theorize on the matter.

Then there was Marci Davis Jeffries' involvement. Eisenstat suspected Sean was smart enough not to discuss his investigation into the Wellington family with his mother. While his FBI training and experience told him coincidences rarely happen, his gut told him this might be an exception. Sean and Jorge Hauptmann were close friends, so it stood to reason Marci would know of Jorge's mom's business. And that would certainly explain her recommendation to the Dublin-based M&A firm to pursue GWH GmbH as a potential acquisition. "What are the odds?" he said to himself.

***

Having met his father and learning about his wartime activities, Jürgen Hauptmann had become increasingly concerned over his mother's safety. He now figured his mother had been the true target of the crash that killed Hanna Schröder, making him increasingly anxious to hear from David Katzman.

By Friday morning, Jorge decided he'd had enough waiting and contacted David's father, Irv, at his Seaside Heights arcade. The retired Brooklyn cop immediately called his buddy, Calvin Thomas, who he knew was keeping an eye on Jorge. Calvin had already been alerted by Sammy Eisenstat at "zero-dark-thirty" about the previous evening's attempt on Gretchen's life.

"You should assure Jorge that his mom is safe and in the good hands of the LKA NRW," the FBI agent explained. "Tell him both he *and* you should move to one of our FBI safe houses and await further instructions. We still have a pair of suspects we know to be at-large and until those individuals are located and questioned, the authorities can't be sure whether others are involved."

Within hours, Calvin Thomas and Jürgen Hauptmann were safely inside an old bungalow in the north Jersey shore town of Keansburg.

Chapter 65 – The Incredible Occurs at Elmont

On Thursday morning, June 2nd, Abigail Wellington drew a line in the sand. Confronting her only child with what she knew had been the latest episode in a habit that would inevitably lead to his ruin, "Abby" laid out the map she'd outlined in her mind for Beau only recently and whose finer points she was still completing as she spoke. That map included details not only for his business career but for his personal life as well. At the end of their conversation, one that provided Beau with little opportunity for input, she would present two options so stark in their likely outcomes that Beau literally had no choice.

At the conclusion of their meeting, Beau simply said, "I see what you're getting at, ma'am. I understand."

Abigail Prescott Wellington thought to herself: "What's that they say about leading a horse to water, but not being able to make it drink?... Well, scratch that one from the Prescott vernacular."

***

It was a spectacular Saturday afternoon in Elmont, NY, home of Belmont Park Race Track. A warm breeze blew in from the southwest and Jamaica Bay on an 82-degree day with almost no humidity. A few clusters of fluffy cumulus clouds passed slowly from west to east.

TJ Cutter was pleased to have both his kid sister, Jasmine, and newfound acquaintance, Sean Davis Jeffries, accompany him to Belmont Park for *Cut Me A Break's* maiden voyage. Was it just his imagination?...or was there something a bit out of the ordinary in the way Jasmine's eyes locked onto Sean when they were first introduced this past Saturday?

TJ certainly noticed the bond his sister seemed to have developed with the young attorney, Consuela Parks Pettiford, and thought the prospect of having young friends with promising futures augured well for a young woman who'd experienced more than her fair share of life's hard knocks.

It would be a few hours before he would head downstairs to await his groom to deliver *Cut Me A Break* from an assigned stable behind the backstretch to his paddock stall. Unlike most race days at Monmouth Park, he had no other duties save for preparing his entry for the Tremont Stakes. TJ took the time to chat with Sean and Jasmine, getting to better know the Seton Hall Law School student and reacquainting himself with an apparently reborn and upbeat sister. And yet while TJ enjoyed his conversation with them, he was happy to yield to the apparent connection developing between Jasmine and Sean.

Not far from the VIP seats occupied by the Cutter party were Abigail Prescott Wellington and Ian Snelling, Triple-B Racing Stables' assistant trainer. The Widow Wellington hadn't seen one of the family's thoroughbreds race since *Wanna B Yours* captured the Grade I Central Bank Ashland Oaks in 1979 at Keeneland Race Course in Lexington. The three-year-old filly, now a broodmare, covered the 8½ furlongs on dirt (1.0625 miles to be exact) in a track-record 1:35 flat. Today, she'd be watching *B 4-Warned* attempt to extend his undefeated streak to a pair of races.

Abigail had met Snelling just a couple of times during his entire tenure as Beau's assistant. Both were preoccupied with thoughts of business they'd be conducting later in the day. Snelling was assessing the track conditions and their potential impact on race strategy, considering whether front-runners would be able to hold their speed through the stretch or if the rail held any advantage over lanes toward the middle of the track. Abigail, on the other hand, was contemplating a possible meeting with TJ Cutter. She suspected the best opportunity to make that happen would be after the stakes race, since Cutting Edge Stables had an entry in the Tremont Stakes as well. In fact, TJ Cutter's presence at Belmont Park had been the only reason for Abigail's trip north.

***

In the jockeys' room that morning, Angel Barrera and his agent, Chris McCardle, went over pre-race strategy with TJ Cutter a second time. They'd spoken earlier in the week at Monmouth Park. Back then, Cutter shared what Barrera already knew: this race was a handicapper's nightmare.

Having ridden in several of these stakes races with mostly unproven and inexperienced thoroughbreds, Barrera knew he'd be facing a large field consisting of a few first-time starters and additional entries coming off their maiden wins. Several of the thoroughbreds had shipped in from tracks across the country. Finally, a pair of entries had reached the winner's circle twice, with both of them having won at two different race courses.

The field for the six-furlong Tremont Stakes consisted of 10 two-year-old colts. Barrera and McCardle each had the day's Belmont Park program, along with a copy of *The Daily Racing Form*.

As best the Cutter-Barrera-McCardle triumvirate could determine based on the limited number of races their competition had run, the race looked to shape up as a cavalry charge. Most of the entries had either wired (i.e., led from start to finish) a Maiden field or set very fast fractions on the lead and then faltered in roughly the last furlong (220 yards).

When push came to shove, however, TJ Cutter identified three entries as the principal adversaries for *Cut Me A Break*, carrying 116 lbs., most of which would be Angel Barrera.

The first was *Brooklyn-Manhattan Transit*, who won at first asking in early March at 5½ furlongs in a Maiden Special Weight race during Aqueduct's winter meet. Owned by Finger Lakes Farm, the gray colt finished second in a five-furlong allowance race at "the Big A" two weeks later.

Never to be confused with a front-runner, *Brooklyn-Manhattan Transit* never-the-less made a last-to-first move that began as the two-year-old colt headed into the turn and ended with a monster run straightening for home. At 5½ furlongs, the Gary Greene-trained horse got up in the last strides to win. With a half-furlong less real estate to negotiate in his second start, he lost by a half-length.

Running for the third time in allowance company, *Brooklyn-Manhattan Transit* buried an eight-horse field comprised of New York State bred colts at his Finger Lakes "home" track in Farmington, NY (about 25 miles southeast of Rochester). By now referred to as *BMT*, the gray colt cruised to victory in the six-furlong race that Greene viewed as the thoroughbred's final prep before the Tremont Stakes. Belmont's 1½-mile oval would be more to the late closer's liking than the tighter turns experienced at Aqueduct and

277

Finger Lakes. His jockey, veteran rider Julio Castro, aboard for all three of his prior races, would again have the mount. *BMT* was one of two entries carrying high weight of 121 lbs.

The second entry that was cause for concern, according to Cutter, was an Ohio-bred brown colt named *Buckeye Bully*. The two-year old finished as runner-up in his first effort while entered for a $45,000 price tag in a five-furlong Maiden Claiming race the first week of May at Arlington Park in Illinois. *The Daily Racing Form's* observation was that the first-time starter had "raced greenly."

One week later in a six-furlong Maiden Special Weight tilt at Ak-sar-ben in Omaha, the Larry Lester-owned-and-trained colt entered the winner's circle after demolishing a field of seven by eight lengths on a sloppy track. The horse completed six furlongs in what racegoers typically call a "boat race" because of the snail-like winning time of 1:15.3.

Heading east to Delaware Park and back on a fast track, *Buckeye Bully* then won an allowance race the third week of May. Underscoring his sterling effort, the horse stretched out his speed for the 6½-furlong race, wiring a field of nine in a fast time of 1:14.3.

Starting three times inside of a month at three different race tracks while showing marked improvement with each outing, *Buckeye Bully* would now be attempting to continue his success while taking a big step up in class. Cutting back a half furlong off his 6½ furlong victory in Stanton, DE, seemed to mark Larry Lester's charge as a horse to watch. A winner of two races, the horse had been assigned co-high weight of 121 lbs.

After looking at his three races, Cutter could only marvel at the horse's versatility. "The colt evidently isn't bothered by the travel. He's run well at multiple tracks, so not having a race over the course wouldn't seem to be an obstacle. And the horse has been successful on an off track as well as a fast one," TJ said out loud. He wouldn't say it in front of Barrera or McCardle, but Larry Lester had picked up the services of the red-hot Stevie Thorn for today's assignment which, to Cutter's way of thinking, was an added advantage. He'd run at 116 lbs., five pounds less than his originally assigned weight.

Cutter's third labeled threat was Beau Wellington's *B 4-Warned*, a big chestnut colt who scored a very impressive win over a highly regarded group of eight colts in his debut on opening day at Churchill Downs. There had been two leaders setting torrid early fractions of

0:21.3 and 0:44.4 in the five-furlong tilt. *B 4-Warned*, with Andy Delaney aboard, stalked the pace-setters and saved ground by tucking in along the rail. After a half-mile, Delaney shifted leads and moved his mount to the outside where the colt kicked it into another gear and won by a length in a brisk time of 0:58.3.

With a month before his second start at the Tremont Stakes, Wellington had been gradually working his horse up to the six-furlong Tremont distance. Each time, *B 4 Warned* was clocked with the fastest morning work at his distance – three furlongs breezing at 34.3 on May 7th, four furlongs breezing at 45.2 on May 14th, and five furlongs handily at 59.4 before galloping out an additional furlong on May 21st.

***

Knowing Triple-B Racing Stables was to be represented by *B 4-Warned* in the Tremont Stakes, Sean Davis Jeffries wondered if Beauregard Wellington would travel to Belmont Park for the race. With Governor Wellington's recent death and understanding what was involved in arranging services for a former public official, Sean wasn't so sure Beau would make the trip. He also hadn't fully processed his feelings now that the object of his years-long obsession was no longer alive. For the first time, Sean had begun to think of Beau as a fellow victim of his father's actions, not to mention that he was his half-brother.

He was grateful for Jasmine Cutter's presence, which gave him something to keep his mind from dwelling on the matter. Really more than grateful, Sean was intrigued by the attractive young woman who was apparently quite comfortable in her own skin.

Jasmine was pleased TJ had invited her to accompany him to Belmont Park. She'd always loved the races and caught herself thinking back to younger and simpler days at Cutter Farms just north of Leesburg, before the death of their father and the accident that had left their mother paralyzed from the neck down. Listening to Sean talk about his tentative plans upon finishing law school at Seton Hall, Jasmine wondered if her brother might be trying to play matchmaker.

Brother's motives aside, Jasmine was questioning her sexuality

279

after the electric weekend with Connie. Should Memorial Day weekend be filed under one-time experience? Or life-changing event? Only time would tell.

Knowing there was a decent chance *Cut Me A Break* might find his way to the winner's circle, TJ told Sean and Jasmine earlier in the week to "dress nicely" in case their picture would be taken at Elmont. Cutter, bringing an element of superstition to his actions in and around the races, didn't come right out and mention exactly why they'd find themselves in a photograph, but both got the message.

Sean was wearing stonewashed khaki pants with a blue-and-white checked button-down shirt, navy blazer and black penny loafers. Jasmine, having taken a recent liking to black-and-yellow clothes combinations, chose form-fitting mustard-yellow slacks and a black button-down three-quarters-sleeve blouse opened perhaps one button more than necessary revealing the "work" of her yellow push-up bra. She finished off her outfit with comfy black-leather flats.

TJ Cutter glanced over at his two guests, noting how good they looked as a couple. He then returned to a conversation he was having with Vernon and Cecelia Bouquet, owners of Finger Lakes Farm and *Brooklyn-Manhattan Transit*. The Virginia horseman learned the couple had entered thoroughbred racing rather late in life.

Both born and raised in Staten Island, the two had been married in their early 20s. Neither were college educated, but worked in a succession of corporate accounting and clerical positions in Manhattan. For years they would escape oppressive summer heat by taking a two-week vacation in Skaneateles, NY, and would break up the cold winter months by heading to Las Vegas for a long weekend.

On one unforgettable February night in 1981 at the Sands Hotel & Casino, Vernon and Cecelia rode an incredible streak playing craps (Vernon) and silver-dollar one-armed bandits (Cecelia) to became multi-millionaires. That spring, the two purchased a small farm just north of Skaneateles in Onondaga County. The Bouquets renamed the former equestrian center Finger Lakes Farm and hired a fellow New Dorp High School alumnus, Gary Greene, to spend up to $250,000 in acquiring and training a pair of thoroughbred yearlings.

Heading to the Fasig-Tipton Auction held in Saratoga Springs,

NY, Greene purchased a gray colt and bay filly. The colt, *Brooklyn-Manhattan Transit*, was sired by *Spectacular Bid* out of the broodmare *Moon Glitter*, a Kentucky bred who'd been shipped to Milfer Farm in Unadilla, NY (about 42 miles northeast of Binghamton), where the 1979 Kentucky Derby and Preakness winner was standing at stud.

"Vernon...Cecelia, I'd like to introduce you to my sister, Jasmine Cutter, and a business associate of mine, Sean Davis Jeffries. Jasmine, Sean. These are the Bouquets, owners of *Brooklyn-Manhattan Transit*."

Introductions performed, TJ reached out to Vernon Bouquet, placing his left hand on the right shoulder of *BMT's* co-owner while extending his right hand in friendship. With a nod to Cecelia Bouquet, he slowly moved away. "Well, good luck to both of you. I'm sure we'll meet again. I have to be heading down to the paddock. It's just about that time."

***

TJ Cutter stood alongside Angel Barrera, offering his assessment and very specific instructions for his jockey's trip aboard *Cut Me A Break* (#4):

"If the race plays out as I envision it, Stevie Thorn will have *Buckeye Bully* breaking fast to take the lead from his #2 post position. Honestly, I cannot see this two-year-old colt wiring a field of this quality when this race is his fourth within the past month. If the trainer thought the horse was this good, he'd never risk losing him in a Maiden claiming race for a $45,000 price tag.

"Knowing Beau Wellington, *Be 4-Warned*, from the #6 post, is likely to tuck in behind the early leader and lay just off the pace where he can either go for it after four furlongs or, if the pace is too slow – let's say the half is in 0:45.3 or slower – move to the lead a bit earlier. He's trained exceptionally well leading up to this race, so we're dealing with a top-flight horse in peak condition.

"But this is where you have to thread the needle. Julio Castro will have *Brooklyn-Manhattan Transit* (#7) making a big late charge. We need to have our colt close enough to Delaney to overtake *B 4-Warned* in the last furlong, but have enough horse left to withstand a fast-closing *BMT*. It's all about the clock in your head, Angel."

Cutter returned to his box just in time to join Jasmine and Sean for the race.

"They're at post" ...followed by "The flag is up"...and then "They're off!"

As if TJ Cutter had license to author the script, *Buckeye Bully* was alert from the gate and grabbed the lead along the rail. Pressing Stevie Thorn from the get-go was another first-time starter, *The Sheck By A Neck*, a brown colt whose sire, *Shecky Greene*, was the 1973 Eclipse Award Sprint Champion and famously led the Kentucky Derby for seven furlongs before Secretariat captured the first of his Triple Crown-winning races.

Meanwhile Andy Delaney placed *B 4-Warned* third behind the two pace setters through an initial quarter of 0:21.4 and the half in 0:44.3. Barrera, sensing extremely fast opening fractions, had a tight grip on *Cut Me A Break* who was full of run. Barrera looked over his right shoulder to see *Brooklyn-Manhattan Transit* beginning to make his move about 10 lengths back of his horse. At the same time *Buckeye Bully* began to fade although *The Sheck By A Neck* maintained a one-length lead.

With five furlongs in a sizzling 0:57.1, both Barrera and Delaney, on their respective mounts, switched leads and passed a game but finally tiring *The Sheck By A Neck*. In the final furlong, the only question was whether *BMT*, closing like a freight train on the outside, would get up in time to catch the new co-leaders.

As three horses hit the wire, the race was too close to call, with *B 4-Warned* closest to the rail, *Brooklyn-Manhattan Transit* on the far outside and *Cut Me A Break* between horses. The final time was an extraordinary 1:08.4. Amazingly, all three thoroughbreds crossed the finish line with heads down, each maximizing their reach.

Jasmine was hoarse by the time the race was over. Sean had rarely seen such an exciting finish, reminding him of the 10 times during the 1977 and 1978 seasons that *Affirmed* and *Alydar* had dueled as two- and three-year-old colts. *Affirmed's* winning margin in five of his seven victories ranged from a half-length to a pair of necks, a head and a nose.

When the numbers were finally posted, there was momentary

confusion. The number 6, representing *B 4-Warned,* appeared in the top position, followed by the number 4, *Cut Me A Break.* Number 7, *Brooklyn-Manhattan Transit,* was listed third. But the first two numbers, 6 and 4, were flashing simultaneously. Without a simultaneous red INQUIRY or OBJECTION sign displayed, the two flashing numbers meant the photo revealed both horses had hit the finish line at the same time. Meanwhile, the same photo showed *BMT* finishing third, just a neck behind the co-winners.

For only the second time in the history of the Tremont Stakes, first run in 1887, the race ended in a dead heat. In 1970 Cragwood Stables' *Raise Your Glass,* ridden by Jorge Velasquez, and Gedney Farms' *Tamtent,* with Eddie Belmonte in the saddle, shared the winner's circle.

Now TJ, Jasmine and Sean made their way toward the winner's circle, as did Abigail Prescott Wellington and assistant trainer Ian Snelling. It took a few minutes for both winning horses to be positioned for the track photographer, during which TJ introduced himself, his sister and his "associate" to Abigail and Ian. At that point, the photographer snapped multiple shots of the Tremont Stakes trophy presentation, the hardware held jointly by Cutter and Wellington. Snelling stood to the right of Abigail, while Jasmine and Sean stood to the left of TJ.

With horses on their way back to the barn, TJ was about to suggest to Sean and Jasmine that they head over to valet parking and decide where to have dinner when he heard Mrs. Wellington's voice call his name:

"Mr. Cutter...Mr. Cutter! Do you have a moment? Forgive me for being so bold, but my son Beau recounted the conversation he had with you last week regarding the IPO he'd been planning for Thoroughbred Bs Farm."

It wasn't lost on Cutter that Abigail Wellington used the past-perfect tense when referring to her son's planned IPO.

"Might I invite you and your guests to dine with us?" offered Abigail. "We're planning on going to Peter Luger's in Brooklyn. Perhaps the two of us might spend some time at the bar before joining the others for dinner. I'd like to give you an update on what has been a rapidly changing situation for our family and...well, I have a proposition I'd like you to consider."

For the second consecutive weekend, TJ Cutter had been

approached by a member of the Wellington family to consider a business proposal. And for the second time, he'd follow his long-standing rule of never saying no before listening.

"Sure, Mrs. Wellington. We'd be happy to join you." With that, TJ, Jasmine and Sean departed for the valet parking area. With a hoard of racing fans exiting Belmont Park in addition to the typical Saturday evening traffic heading into the City, the 28-mile journey to Peter Luger's took about 90 minutes.

On the way to Brooklyn, it was Sean who spoke first: "This has been quite a week. Bentley Wellington kicks the bucket in Lexington on Monday. And today I'm standing face-to-face with his widow in the winner's circle at Belmont Park." Then Sean asked: "Mr. Cutter. Do you think Mrs. Wellington recognized my middle name?"

"It wouldn't surprise me at all, Sean," TJ answered. "But I'm sure she'll do her level best not to let on if she's connected the dots."

Sean then realized that Jasmine may not have been aware of his connection with the Wellington family, although he suspected TJ might have explained the story to his sister in the aftermath of their dinner at the Molly Pitcher Inn. For the time being, he decided to let the matter rest.

Sean offered Jasmine the front seat so she could easily talk with her brother, but she declined and said it would be easier to "catch a few zees" stretched out in the back alone.

"That gray colt, *Brooklyn-Manhattan Transit*, was pretty impressive," said Sean after several minutes of silence. "I'll bet his best races are ahead of him, particularly when he competes at a mile or longer."

"Do you think I should contact the Bouquets to see if they'd be willing to sell?" asked TJ. "Or maybe ask if they'd be interested in syndicating the horse?"

Expecting to listen to Sean's considered opinion, TJ instead heard his sister chime in from the back seat: "Off the colt's first three races, *BMT* has certainly shown consistent late run. And his daddy certainly showed what he could do at the Derby distance."

"Go on, Jasmine," prodded her brother.

"The Bouquets are not from money, but it's certainly evident from their story that they love the sport. I'm not sure they'd be willing to do an outright sale of *BMT*, which would be emotionally difficult, to my way of thinking. But selling a share – possibly even a *majority* interest in the two-year-old – might be a way of accelerating their involvement in thoroughbred racing while maintaining their connection to the horse that brought them their first success. Sort of like having your cake and eating it too."

The two young men in the car were stunned into momentary silence. TJ hadn't thought Jasmine was within earshot of his conversation with the Bouquets, while Sean had missed the entirety of the exchange between TJ and the owners of *Brooklyn-Manhattan Transit.*

Jasmine's off-the-cuff take on her brother's hypothetical business proposition for two individuals she'd seen for the first time was spot-on and showed the kind of insightful business analysis he would expect from someone who...well, had been in the thoroughbred business for years. All TJ could think of was the old saying: "...out of the mouths of babes."

Looking back, Sean Davis Jeffries might very well have pointed to Jasmine's cogent remark from the back seat of her brother's car as the moment he became smitten.

***

Sitting at a table for six, Triple-B Racing Stables' assistant trainer Ian Snelling, Jasmine Cutter and Sean Davis Jeffries shared an awkward silence amid the loud and sometimes boisterous Saturday evening diners and ongoing bustle of wait staff at one of the world's most famous steak houses. Snelling made an attempt at small talk, first asking Sean about his experience in thoroughbred racing and then turning to Jasmine to inquire whether she'd made the trip from Leesburg, VA, specifically for the Tremont Stakes. Sean wondered how long Snelling had been working with the Wellington family's thoroughbred operation and whether it was his first stateside gig. All three would be feeling so much better when TJ and Abigail finished their business conversation at the bar and joined them for dinner.

What had seemed like a long 20 minutes later, Jasmine saw her brother approaching their table. TJ went directly to Snelling and bent over to whisper something in his ear. Abruptly, Snelling rose from his chair, said it had been a pleasure to meet their acquaintance and left the dining room.

Jasmine and Sean both looked inquisitively in TJ's direction. Cutter simply called over a waiter and ordered for all of them: "We'll have three of your best Filet Mignons, medium, with Bearnaise Sauce, baked potatoes with butter and sour cream and asparagus. And if you'll please bring us three bottles of St. Pauli Girl."

Then turning to his two rather startled companions, he said in a very matter-of-fact voice: "As you know, last week Beau Wellington asked if I'd be willing to combine our family's thoroughbred operation with his as part of a mega IPO. Just now, Abigail Wellington told me recent events have caused them to go in a completely different direction." TJ then removed a #10 envelope from his inside jacket pocket and handed it to Sean.

"The details are right here. Why don't you take a first shot at reviewing what they have in mind, Sean?" Then he looked at his sister: "And Jasmine, how about giving some more thought to what we should offer the Bouquets for *Brooklyn-Manhattan Transit*." Pausing a moment to allow Sean and Jasmine to regain their equilibrium, he added: "Let's enjoy the meal. We have a lot to discuss on our way back to Jersey.

Chapter 66 – The Stand-In...and an Extraction

It was a few minutes before 1200 hours when Barnard Scholz, accompanied by Reiner Huber, Consuela Parks Pettiford, Marci Davis Jeffries and Jakob Seidel, entered the second-floor conference room at the Sheraton Airport Hotel for the follow-up transaction meeting with Alton Bahnsen, chief executive of Manchester Automotive Suppliers International, and his M&A representatives from Collins, Connell & O'Brien.

"Where is Frau Hauptmann?" asked Aiden O'Brien.

As agreed in their meeting at LKA NRW headquarters earlier that morning, response to the anticipated opening question was handled by Seidel in his capacity as case officer for the NRW Exchange Supervisory Authority:

"I regret to inform you that last night, there was a successful attempt to take the life of GWH GmbH founder and chairperson Gretchen Weiß Hauptmann." After audible gasps from MASI's Alton Bahnsen and both representatives of Collins, Connell & O'Brien, Seidel continued.

"Dieter Hartmann, a disgruntled and disturbed member of the firm's Advisory Board, kidnapped at gunpoint both Frau Hauptmann and Barnard Scholz, who is here today, as they left an area restaurant after a dinner meeting. He forced them to drive to Hauptmann's residence and then set the Hauptmann home ablaze. An LKA NRW officer was shot by the assailant while attempting to save Frau Hauptmann and Herr Scholz. The officer was able to pull himself and Herr Scholz to safety, but he could not rescue Frau Hauptmann or the attacker. The victim's German Shepherd is missing and is presumed to have perished in the fire as well.

"As you're likely aware from preliminary conversations between Ms. O'Halloran and Frau Hauptmann as well as from yesterday's meeting, GWH GmbH had been considering whether to undertake an initial public offering of stock or, in the alternative, to seek debt financing for an aggressive expansion of its operations. An earlier attempt on die Vorsitzende's life resulted in the death of her long-time administrative assistant, Hanna Schröder. That, along with

Collins, Connell & O'Brien's timely inquiry, were transformative in the founder's decision to pursue an outright sale.

"At this point, Barnard Scholz, a member of the GWH GmbH Advisory Board who has spent his entire professional career in the P/M industry, both here in Germany and in the United States, will provide you with a status on the organization's ownership and daily operations moving forward."

Rising from his chair, Barnard Scholz continued with the prepared narrative:

"As is the case with most businesses, there has been a succession plan in place at GWH GmbH when it comes to ownership, overall management and daily operational control.

"*First*, dealing with ownership: The death of Frau Hauptmann has left controlling interest and, effectively, sole ownership in the hands of her only child, Jürgen Hauptmann. Now residing in the United States, he just completed his bachelor's degree in business administration from Seton Hall University and had planned to return to Germany for his M.Sc. in Automotive Engineering at RWTH Aachen University. We don't yet know what impact the current situation might have on this plan, but Jürgen has indicated he is committed to the sale of GWH GmbH.

"There is a small minority stake that had been held by Wolfgang Becker. As of this morning, Mr. Becker has been dismissed as chief executive of the firm and, under terms of his contract, has forfeited the right to any shares in the company earned to date.

"*Second*, on daily operations: With the exception of Herr Becker, the entire management team remains in place. The firm's succession plan, given the death of our founder and departure of the chief executive, calls for me to assume the dual roles of der Vorsitzender (the chairman) of the Advisory Board and der Hauptgeschäftsführer (the chief executive) of the management team. We'll need to identify candidates to fill two Advisory Board vacancies – mine and that of Dieter Hartmann.

"With stable ownership and operations, it is our intention to pursue the sale of GWH GmbH. To speak more on this issue, I'll turn things over to Marci Davis Jeffries."

"It would be unrealistic of us to expect your organization to purchase GWH under current circumstances. Thus, we have the bare bones of a proposal consisting of four major points for you and your M&A advisors to consider:

First, GWH GmbH is prepared to continue operating under the leadership of Barnard Scholz for the next 12 months with MASI retaining right of first refusal to acquire the firm.

Second, Herr Scholz will make himself available to MASI as a consultant for up to 24 months if a sale is consummated, thereby adhering to MASI's stated preference for using top management of an acquired firm to facilitate a transition to MASI operations and corporate culture.

Third, GWH GmbH will accept a MASI-designated candidate to fill one of the vacancies on its Advisory Board.

Fourth, both parties will continue negotiating in good faith on a final purchase price, proceeds of any sale to be directed to a U.S. bank account designated by Jürgen Hauptmann.

"We'd ask that you take the next 10 business days to consider this proposal, at which time representatives from your M&A firm, Collins, Connell & O'Brien, can let me know whether MASI would like to proceed."

An awkward moment of silence followed the conclusion of the early afternoon presentation. There was a brief exchange of whispers between Aiden O'Brien and Alton Bahnsen, after which O'Brien spoke: "First, let me extend my deepest sympathies to the entire GWH family, from Jürgen Hauptmann and the family members of Hanna Schröder, to all of the firm's employees. I can only imagine the incredibly difficult time you've all been through over the past several days and the challenges you face in the days, weeks and months to come.

"I know I speak for Alton Bahnsen and members of his management team when I say that Manchester Automotive Suppliers International remains deeply interested in pursuing the acquisition of your business. We all truly believe your P/M operation and those you employ would have a bright future within the MASI organization. Let's continue to talk. We'll send a couple of our senior managers to Wuppertal next week to tour the facility and start asking questions."

With that, meeting participants rose from their chairs and gathered toward the front entrance of the meeting room. Good-byes were exchanged and scheduled follow-up calls were agreed upon. Fairly quickly, people exited. After all, it was Friday afternoon, the weekend beckoned and people had international flights to catch.

***

At about the same time Barnard Scholz was addressing MASI Chief Executive Alton Bahnsen and his M&A team, "Gretta Schoener" was making her way toward the Air Canada gate at Düsseldorf Airport, accompanied by her German Shepherd guide dog, RCMP Senior Field Officer Cameron Connors and the Mossad's David Katzman. She would be boarding an Air Canada DC-8 with non-stop service to Toronto.

The Government of Canada had quickly prepared Gretta's work visa and had gone so far as to arrange a mid-level managerial position with a Ford Motor Company of Canada production plant in St. Thomas, Ontario, about 140 kilometers west of Hamilton. Her Majesty's Government in Ottawa arranged for Schoener to rent a two-bedroom home in the small town of Woodstock that had been in its safe-house inventory. Halfway between St. Thomas and Hamilton, the location would be a comfortable drive to both cities. The plant would also provide Gretta with a 1981 Ford Escort so Gretta could negotiate the daily commute.

Cam Connors had described the easier part of her new life – the name, the employment, the home and car – in the early morning hours back in Düsseldorf. The tougher part – her husband's current life in Hamilton, the reason he disappeared so abruptly without a trace all those years ago, and the fact she'd soon be headed for a reunion – was left for David Katzman to explain during the flight across the Atlantic.

Of course, there were no guarantees that Brian Harper and Gretta Schoener would want to reunite. Hence, the reason for placing the rental agreement for the home in Gretta's name. David Katzman, who'd played a key role in reuniting Jorge and Fabian (Brian), had a gut feeling the son would play a significant role in bringing his parents together again.

***

Bertram Krieger had three tasks remaining on Friday. First, he called Mia Böhm to let her know that her husband, Gunther, was resting comfortably in a Remscheid hospital and in stable condition. He gave her the direct dial to his room and told her one of his inspectors was standing guard simply as a security precaution. Yes, she was free to visit any time.

Next, Krieger dispatched two inspectors to GWH GmbH in Wuppertal, where they arrested Wolfgang Becker for conspiracy to commit murder, "with additional charges pending."

Finally, the LKA NRW director met with his head of public affairs to devise a cover story and communication rollout plan regarding the "death" of Gretchen Weiß Hauptmann and her guard dog, Pulver.

It would be left to Barnard Scholz to handle announcements to employees, customers and the local business community regarding what had transpired, so long as they were consistent with the LKA NRW communications.

***

At the departure gates designated for Lufthansa international flights, Sammy Eisenstat called a special desk at the FBI office in Trenton. The staffer on duty connected him to the Keansburg safe house where Calvin Thomas and Jorge Hauptmann were holed up.

"Calvin. Sammy Eisenstat here. "The 'package' is in transit to Toronto with Cam Connors of the RCMP and David Katzman. Take Jorge and make your way up to Hamilton. One of John Edgerton's RCMP Security Service officers will have specific instructions for you at the Buffalo/Peace Bridge crossing once you arrive on the Fort Erie side."

Chapter 67 – A Waste of Taxpayer Dollars

Galen Grauman turned over his paperwork on Bentley Wellington's death to the Fayette Commonwealth Attorney's Office in the City of Lexington. It would be up to Fayette Commonwealth Attorney Barton Wysocki to ask the Fayette County Grand Jury to determine whether there was sufficient evidence of a crime to warrant a trial.

In all his years, the Fayette Commonwealth Attorney had never reviewed a more bizarre set of circumstances surrounding an individual's death, let alone that of a former Kentucky governor.

If Woodrow Jefferson's eye-witness account was to be believed, Abigail Prescott Wellington and Beauregard Wellington, the deceased's wife and son, had *both* attempted to murder Bentley Wellington. But because they'd both done so in the exact same manner (i.e., switching a salmon quiche placard with a crab quiche placard), both attempts failed by cancelling out each other.

In the end, it hadn't mattered because the victim, himself, had committed suicide by intentionally eating the crab quiche. The investigating detective's questioning of the family butler revealed that the deceased told him he wanted to end his own life that very day.

The Wellington family continued to be known as "the Commonwealth's first family" long after Bentley Wellington left office. The thoroughbreds Beau Wellington raced at Churchill Downs, Keeneland and Turfway Park were highly popular among Kentuckians, as was the bourbon that Bourbonesque produced out of Bardstown. The family's annual Memorial Day extravaganza had been one of the biggest events on the state's social calendar. And the family had been employing dozens of the Commonwealth's citizens for decades.

"What was there to gain," Barton Wysocki asked himself, "by placing two high-profile individuals on trial for attempting to murder a crippled old man who wanted to die anyway and wound up committing suicide?

"No," Wysocki reasoned, "such a move would be immensely unpopular and a huge waste of taxpayer dollars." At the end of the day, the evidence gathered by Galen Grauman that pointed to criminal behavior by Abigail and Beauregard Wellington went no further than the "circular file" of the Fayette Commonwealth Attorney.

Chapter 68 – Departures...and an Arrival

Abigail was the sole member of the immediate family inside the Commonwealth's Capitol Building in Frankfort on Sunday. By her side was Woodrow Jefferson. They were among thousands, including some distant cousins from both the Prescott and Wellington sides of the family, to pay their respects as the former two-time Governor of Kentucky had been lying in state. Noticeably absent was Beauregard Wellington, a fact that hadn't escaped the media's attention and was a topic of much conjecture in the days to follow.

Beau had some unfinished business in Louisville that day, making a final payment of $100,000 to the runner Squints and closing his account with the Jersey bookmaking operation. The money, provided to him by Abigail, was part of a far-reaching and all-encompassing mother-and-son agreement that would change both of their lives.

Darci McDougal accompanied Beau on his trip to Louisville, although she had been deposited at a local Waffle House to wait for him to wrap up the unseemly portion of the day's business. Beau said his farewell to Squints without incident, and soon he and Darci were having breakfast together.

Afterward, the two made their way to the Louisville office of Sotheby's to meet with Tammy Sinclair, a representative specializing in international properties. Miss Sinclair agreed to open her office on Sunday especially for Beau and Darci and had prepared a binder at Abigail Wellington's behest that featured a half dozen available properties in Ireland. After much debate, the two decided upon Crokershill Castle (Cnoc an Chrócaraigh in Irish) in County Kilkenny, a bit west of the City of Kilkenny. Beau negotiated a final price of one million Irish pounds, or 1.232 million U.S. dollars. A fixer-upper, Beau figured it would cost another 400,000 Irish pounds to renovate the castle to accommodate their lifestyle.

Rising on Monday morning back in Lexington to uncommonly cool and rainy weather, Beau and Darci headed down the stairs to the first floor of the guest house. They'd already placed travel bags containing their summer wardrobes in the F-150 pick-up the previous evening, protecting them under canvas because of the weather. They were now saying their farewells to barn hands before driving to the main residence to see Woodrow, Edna and lastly Abigail.

"Thanks for all you've done, Mrs. Wellington," Darci offered as she unabashedly embraced Abigail.

Disengaging, the widow responded: "Darci McDougal, you take care of my son. As you're well aware, he needs strong handling." With a smile rarely seen from Abigail in recent weeks, she added: "You may even need to go to the whip." Both women chuckled at the appropriateness of the thoroughbred industry turn of phrase. Finally, she told Darci: "After today, please call me Abigail...And, by the way, I'm dropping the 'Wellington'. I'll be 'Abigail Prescott' now."

Turning to her son, Abigail spoke sternly: "I've laid out a sizable amount of capital to make sure you get off on the right foot. You'll return the deposit to me once Bentley's last will and testament has been reviewed by our family attorney and the appropriate documents reach Uncle Dow's desk at Central Bank."

Then some words of caution: "You have the talent to succeed if you have the will to put your demons permanently to rest. Don't let me down. More importantly, don't let Darci or yourself down. Remember what Branch Rickey once said – 'Luck is the residue of hard work.'"

Beau found it strange his mom would use a phrase from the thoroughbred business and a quote from a baseball luminary in her parting words, as she hadn't been much of a fan of either horse racing or baseball.

"Take it easy, Abby. And let me know what you hear from Cutter." Always using his mom's first name when talking business.

***

While migrant barn hands were burying Bentley Wellington later that day at the family plot on Thoroughbred Bs Farm in Lexington, Beau and Darci were back at Sotheby's exchanging paperwork to acquire Cnoc an Chrócaraigh Castle. A 20 percent deposit was made from a recently opened Central Bank money market account held by Abigail Prescott Wellington, another element of the mother-son pact. Money market accounts had only recently been introduced to U.S. banks, courtesy of the Garn–St. Germain Depository Institutions Act of 1982.

As the couple left Sotheby's, Beau thought ahead to the next few days and how Darci would likely experience more of the world in that short period of time than in her previous 21 years. He was thankful that Darci already had a U.S. passport, which he'd asked her to secure several months ago when he'd been planning a getaway weekend to the Bahamas.

The Wellington family's private jet was waiting for them at the airport in Louisville for a short flight to Chicago's O'Hare. They spent Monday evening at one of Chicago's classic hotels, Palmer House, and shopped the Magnificent Mile on Tuesday. Taking a limo back to O'Hare, Beau and Darci then boarded an Aer Lingus flight to Ireland that evening, landing in Dublin the following morning.

Beau had arranged for a five-night stay at The Clarence, located in Dublin City Centre on the River Liffey. But first was a 10-minute taxi ride to Sotheby's local office to pick up keys to their new residence and to ask the local agent, Anne Sheehy, for recommendations for an architect, an interior designer and a residential construction crew. The professionals were likely to have their practices in Dublin. The labor end of their project – from carpentry and masonry to plumbing and electrical – would be hired locally.

While Beau had originally planned on giving Darci responsibility for interviewing candidates for the interior design work, he was pleasantly surprised at how organized she was and wound up asking her to handle the masonry and plumbing hires as well. The couple spent Thursday and Friday interviewing in Dublin and Saturday meeting contractor candidates in Kilkenny. On Sunday they took a deep breath and booked a double-decker bus tour in the morning and a boat tour on the Liffey in the late afternoon.

One additional task Beau and Darci undertook during their Kilkenny visit was locking down a three-month rental unit, a modest one-bedroom/one-bathroom furnished stone cottage. From there, Darci took over the lion's share of supervising construction contractors once the work of the architect and interior designer had been completed.

And remembering Abby's last words, Beauregard made sure to

frequently compliment Darci on the "great work" she was doing. After all, her efforts enabled Beau to focus on their future, which was central to the arrangement Abigail had presented to him and he had felt obligated to accept.

***

Working with the Irish Development Authority (IDA), the agency responsible for attracting and retaining inward foreign direct investment into Ireland, Beauregard Wellington began work on a two-phase plan to launch Bourbonesque International (BI).

Phase one would have BI functioning as a distributor of bourbon products imported from Bourbonesque LLC of Bardstown, KY, replete with distribution channels, business-to-business marketing and a consumer advertising campaign.

Phase two would be far more challenging because it involved producing bourbon – which, in turn, requires corn. To quote from Shakespeare's *Hamlet*: "And therein lies the rub."

For the longest time, sweet corn had been regarded as a "no-grow" in Ireland. Many gardeners had viewed it as a semi-tropical vegetable, one requiring intense sunlight and heat to crop and ripen. The traditional varieties of sweet corn took a long time in the sun to mature and thus were virtually guaranteed to disappoint over the *Irish "summer"* (a misnomer if ever there was one). This had all changed in 1916 with the introduction of the double-cross hybrid seed.

Extremely short on land used to grow crops but long on the use of barley and oats to produce Irish whiskey and other blended whiskeys, Ireland had not been a producer of *any* consequence when it came to corn and therefore bourbon. It was Abigail Prescott's goal to first introduce to the Irish marketplace Bourbonesque's imported bourbon, and then to gradually loosen the stranglehold whiskey enjoyed on Ireland's hard liquor-consuming public.

Abigail had mixed feelings about one other piece of culture that continued to be central to Ireland – its long history of gambling, with all forms *legal* throughout the country. Should her son fall victim to his demons once again, at least he'd find it difficult to run afoul of the law.

Traditionally unregulated, Ireland finally issued the 1926 Betting Act with revisions a decade later that stipulated anyone taking bets on a sporting event was required to carry a license from the government.

The Gaming and Lotteries Act of 1956 made casino gambling illegal, but loopholes in the law allowed for private, members-only "gambling clubs" to emerge in their place. This satisfied the needs of bettors who, through the '60s, '70s and early '80s regularly flocked to hundreds of betting shops across Ireland to wager on all sporting events, in particular both horse and dog racing.

Surprisingly, it was Darci whose interest had been piqued by the "quaint neighborhood betting parlors" as she liked to call them. Not too long after Beau and Darci moved into the just-completed Crokershill Castle, the youthful American redhead blurted out over dinner: "I've done a lot of reading about the licensing requirements for operating one of those cute, local shops where you can bet on the thoroughbreds. Once the bourbon distributorship is up and running, I'd love to start my own business."

Almost as an afterthought, Darci added: "Did you know that gambling debts in Ireland are not enforceable?"

Chapter 69 – Eigentümerwechsel?

The mood at the King Street East Tim Horton's in the City of Hamilton – the one where Mossad agent David Katzman had first contacted Brian Harper (a.k.a., Fabian Hauptman) – had shifted from initial disbelief...to a mixture of joy and relief. Seemingly countless questions and difficult answers ended with the sobering realization by a husband and wife who'd been separated for 17 years through extraordinary circumstances that minds and hearts couldn't quite overcome the distance between them.

Fabian Hauptman (one 'n') and Gretchen Hauptmann (two 'n's) would no longer be husband and wife. Brian Harper and Gretta Schoener would be close friends with the strongest link possible – a son, Jürgen, a young man with a lifetime of promise and dreams ahead of him who they both loved unconditionally.

After an early Friday evening arrival in Toronto and an expedited inspection at customs, the travel party of Gretta Schoener, David Katzman, Cam Connors and Pulver had driven to Hamilton where rooms at the Royal Connaught Hotel were waiting. Meanwhile Calvin Thomas, with Jorge Hauptmann in tow, had stopped at one of the chain motels off the QEW just north of Fort Erie. They'd been told to wait until late Saturday morning before heading to Hamilton and the King Street East Tim Horton's. That would give Brian and Gretta an opportunity to get reacquainted and be ready to have their son join what likely would be a complicated three-way discussion.

It was early afternoon before Calvin Thomas delivered Jorge into the waiting arms of Gretta and the strong handshake of Brian. Thomas then joined Cam Connors and David Katzman for lunch at the Capri Restaurant, a nearby local Italian eatery.

"What do you place the odds of Brian, Gretta and Jorge coming out of Tim Horton's as a traditional family unit?" Connors asked aloud although he wasn't really expecting an answer.

"Well, 17 years is a long time for two people to live apart. And we know the sordid details behind Fabian's – I mean Brian's – sudden departure," added Katzman. "After all, Brian wasn't just *any* German Jew..." the Mossad agent began. "And Gretta wasn't just *any* German working for Hitler's Nazi Party," Thomas finished.

At Tim Horton's, Gretta was describing for her son the broad strokes of the life the Government of Canada had arranged for her: the house in Woodstock, the managerial position at the Ford of Canada production plant in St. Thomas and the car that enabled her to commute to work, to visit Jorge in New Jersey and to be close to Hamilton where his dad lived.

"So, you two aren't getting back together?" Jorge asked.

There was a long pause before Jorge's dad spoke: "It's not as simple as you might think, restarting a marriage after such a long time apart." Searching for an appropriate analogy, Brian added: "It's like a car that has traveled a lot of miles and then finds itself in freezing temperatures for months. There's a good chance the engine won't turn over with the first twist of the ignition key.

"I don't think either of us are closing the door completely, Jorge."

"More than anything," Gretta picked up, "we need time to adjust to our changed lives. I suspect we'll always be friends. More importantly, we want to be the best mom and the best dad we can be."

Jorge sat there for a moment, rose from the table and asked, "Would anyone like another donut or two?" Gretta and Brian looked at each other and nodded.

When he returned, Jorge's spirits seemed to have lifted: "I get it, guys. It's sort of like when parents agree to a separation but don't finalize a divorce. The two of you need time to adjust, to process. I'm just grateful to know the two of you are safe and living in a place where we can see each other just about any time we want."

With that, mother, father and son finished their donuts and coffee in silence. "Jorge. Why don't the two of us head over to your mom's new home, help her unpack, see what furnishings she might want to buy and go food shopping?"

"That would be great, Brian," said Gretta. One group hug later, the three left Tim Horton's, immediately running into Calvin Thomas, Cam Connors and David Katzman.

"We're going to be just fine," said Brian. "Gretta will fill you in on our collective thinking moving forward."

Over the next few days, Cam Connors would make the necessary introductions at Gretta Harper's new place of employment and brief Gretta on what she needed to do to establish permanent residency and apply for Canadian citizenship. A representative of the RCMP Security Service would handle any questions from immigration officials.

Additionally, Gretta was told to avoid any and all communication with individuals and/or organizations in Germany or persons and/or institutions in *any* country involved in the GWH GmbH-MASI negotiations. After all, she was now under "deep cover."

Updates on the discussions between Barnard Scholz and his Steinberg Stavros/Stratton-Oakes transaction team and Alton Bahnsen of MASI and his Collins, Connell & O'Brien/M&A advisors would come to her through the RCMP. Her son would need to make himself available to sign documents and have an appropriate U.S. bank account opened to receive funds if the negotiations were successful.

After two attempts on her life, Gretta realized yet again the enormous psychological damage, massive death and incalculable destruction the Third Reich had inflicted on her nation, its citizens, the Jewish people and the world as a whole. All these years later, Nazi sympathizers were at it again.

Through the selfless efforts of the Mossad agent – and for that matter the heroic actions of her husband during World War II – she had begun to contemplate yet another major change in her life.

About two weeks after her arrival in Canada, she began a weekly Sunday morning trek to Toronto. Her destination was Temple Hebron, whose members practiced Reform Judaism and where she began a program that, when completed, would enable her to join the Jewish faith. Whether this might have any impact on her relationship with Brian was not the point. As she learned more and more about the Jewish people – their history, their religion, their culture – Gretta had become more and more convinced she was headed in the right direction.

July turned to August and on the morning of the 11th, a Thursday, the RCMP's John Edgerton called to inform Gretta negotiations for the sale of GWH had been completed. All that remained in order to finalize the transaction was Jürgen's signature on several legal documents. That took place the following morning, after which a wire transfer of 71.220 million Deutsche Marks or 30 million U.S. Dollars, was made to Jorge's money market account at Citibank's branch in Newark, NJ.

While Gretta could take great comfort in the fact that the financial fruits of her labor in Wuppertal had finally been realized, it was the pre-conversion lessons at Temple Hebron in Toronto that seemed to have brought her a peace of mind she hadn't experienced since... well, that she actually had never experienced before. And if Gretta Schoener was able to listen to herself when she went to bed each night, the woman formerly known as Gretchen Weiß Hauptmann would notice she no longer talked in her sleep.

Chapter 70 – What Are the Odds, Y'all?

Abigail Prescott and her family attorney, Dax Baxter, were well prepared for their meeting with Thomas Jefferson Cutter III, set for 10:00 a.m. on this Sunday morning, June 19th. Baxter had not been the Wellington family's lawyer; he had spent a good part of his career representing the business and family interests of Abigail's daddy, Ezekiel ("Zeke") Prescott.

A native of Fairmont, West Virginia, Baxter was a Mountaineer through and through. He'd earned both his undergraduate and law degrees in Morgantown at West Virginia University and passed the Kentucky, Virginia and West Virginia Bars when it became apparent clients in the coal industry were where his bread would be buttered. He'd represented Zeke Prescott from the earliest days of his involvement with coal, and had moved to Frankfort at about the time Abigail married Governor Bentley Wellington.

Now 78, Dax only took on the occasional client. When Abigail called to tell him what she had in mind, Baxter agreed to handle the matter and decided this work would be a perfect way to culminate his legal career. It was the product of Abigail's and Dax's thinking that had gone into the content of the #10 envelope the Widow Wellington gave to TJ Cutter after the Tremont Stakes dead heat 15 days ago.

On a morning where temperatures had already reached into the mid-80s by 10 o'clock, folks in and around Lexington were preparing for a scorcher. At the main house on Thoroughbred Bs Farm, the overhead fans were running on high as Abigail and Dax waited for Cutter and his associates to arrive.

On Saturday evening, "the day before" as TJ liked to say, his party of six checked into The Galt House in Louisville, an 11-year-old hotel on 4th Street. Named for the nearby historic hotel that had been erected in 1835 and demolished in 1921, The Galt House was the city's only hotel on the Ohio River.

Over breakfast on Sunday morning, Cutter and his team had gone over their respective roles. Like Abigail Prescott and Dax Baxter, TJ Cutter's team was ready. They'd hop in a limo for the 90-minute drive to Thoroughbred Bs Farm.

***

Dinner at Peter Luger's in Brooklyn 15 days ago had certainly been a relaxing way to end a successful day at Belmont Park. But TJ Cutter was not looking forward to driving late into the evening. He had stops in Jersey City to drop off Sean Davis Jeffries at his mom's home and to the Seaside Heights boardwalk bungalow he'd purchased for his kid sister.

Thinking further, he had a thought: "Hey, Jasmine. How about spending the night with me in Deal? I'll take you the rest of the way in the morning. We can stop and have breakfast along the way."

Shocked but pleased with the offer, Jasmine jumped at the opportunity. "Thanks. Don't mind if I do. Besides, I'd love to see how the other half lives," she quipped. TJ's kid sister suspected the Deal home her brother was using while his UVA buddy, Dan Steffan, was in Europe would expose her to a whole new level of opulence.

By the time they reached the Holland Tunnel, Sean had digested the outline of Abigail Prescott Wellington's bold and expansive proposal. The frustrating part for both members of the Cutter family had been listening to Jeffries' cryptic comments while he was reading, but having *absolutely no idea* how those comments played into the content.

"So, here are four key points," Sean finally said as he finished reading. Scanning the outline, he continued:

"First, all thoroughbred horses competing under Triple-B Racing Stables will be sold to Cutting Edge Stables, along with barns, stables and equipment that includes but is not necessarily limited to riding gear, feed, transportation vans and any other property associated with proper upkeep. The value of individual horses shall be negotiated between the parties. If agreement on sale price cannot be reached, a mutually acceptable arbiter shall be chosen to make final determinations.

"Second, all broodmares and stallions currently under the ownership of Thoroughbred Bs Farm shall be sold to Cutter Farms, along with barns, stables and equipment that includes but is not necessarily limited to medical supplies, feed, transportation vans, and any other property associated with proper upkeep. The value of individual stallions and broodmares shall be negotiated between the parties. If agreement on sale price cannot be reached a mutually acceptable arbiter shall be chosen to make final determinations.

"Third, with the exception of the family plot, the Wellington property in Lexington, consisting of approximately 740 acres of land, the family residence and guest house, barns and stables as heretofore mentioned, as well as the training track, shall be included in a 50-year land lease which then reverts to Beauregard Wellington or his named beneficiaries. The annual lease will be set at an amount to be negotiated between the parties, with a mutually acceptable arbiter chosen to make a final determination as to fee if the parties cannot come to an agreement.

"Fourth, all current employees of Triple-B Racing Stables and Thoroughbred Bs Farm, as well as the staff working at the Wellington mansion and guest house will be retained for a minimum of 12 months. Exceptions include anyone directly involved with the racing and/or breeding performance of thoroughbred horses purchased as part of this agreement."

Jasmine's reaction was immediate and straight to the point: "Why in the world would we want to enter into *any* kind of agreement if the land reverts to Beau Wellington or his named beneficiaries 50 years down the road? If the Widow Wellington wants to cash in the family's 'thoroughbred chips,' she should be all in. Damn it, let her keep the property and simply sell us the horses currently competing, along with their fucking stallions and broodmares. And yes, pun definitely intended. Hell, we have a thousand acres and can simply move the horses to Virginia."

"I tend to agree, Mr. Cutter," Sean added. "I can't see leasing land for a quarter million dollars a year for 50 years, only to have the property pulled out from under you. Having spent time studying the Wellingtons' properties, I should think that an offer of $15,000 per acre, or $11 million plus for 740 acres, may be overpaying by today's Fayette County land values but should be more than sufficient for an outright sale. Let's say you throw in another $3 million for the mansion, guest house, barns, stables and training track."

Sean felt funny casually throwing out dollar figures in the millions when the money wasn't his. But the notion of a land lease seemed to be a non-starter, to him as well as to Jasmine.

"What do *you* think, TJ?" asked Jasmine.

"I agree with both of you when it comes to a land lease," answered Cutter. "If our family is going to shell out millions of dollars, it's not going to be for leasing property – whether it's 10 years, 50 years or 99 years. But even if we can persuade Abigail Prescott Wellington to sell, I still have two significant concerns and they revolve around care for mom and our lack of management depth when it comes to people resources. If we're going to do this, I need to bring in individuals who can do the job and in whom I have complete trust."

By Sunday, the 12th, after several back-and-forth volleys by phone, TJ Cutter had resolved the land lease versus sale issue with Abigail Prescott, agreeing on a purchase price of $16 million for the Wellington family's sprawling thoroughbred horse farm in Lexington and all structures located on the land.

Once again it had been Jasmine's "big picture" thinking that placed the matter in proper perspective. "Look at what Abigail Prescott Wellington has had to deal with over the past few years...a paralyzed husband who didn't allow her to make the investments necessary to move his distillery forward and a son who attempted to undertake an IPO while gambling with illegal bookmakers. The husband then chooses the family's biggest party of the year to off himself, which had to be embarrassing for the matriarch of the Commonwealth's 'first family.'

"I'm telling you, TJ, this lady wants out," Jasmine stated forcefully. "And if we offer her a shade more than a fair shake moneywise, she'll fold."

Cutter had done some serious thinking about how he might apply trusted resources to manage a pair of breeding operations and two racing outfits in locations separated by a 485-mile, 9½ hour westward drive through the mountains of West Virginia and Eastern Kentucky.

His first call was to his older sister, Judith, and her husband,

Rex Reston. Judith, always a horse lover, had earned her degree in equine science while at Texas A&M. The couple lived on the Reston family ranch north of Denton and had spent the past several years breeding quarter horses and racing them at New Mexico tracks.

Recently, Judith and Rex had been discussing the possibility of heading east. Judith wanted to be closer to her family and Rex was interested in expanding into the thoroughbred business, based on his exposure to the mixed programs of quarter-horse and thoroughbred racing at Ruidoso Downs and the Downs at Albuquerque. The problem had been an inability financially to start a thoroughbred business from scratch. Younger brother TJ was now presenting a way in which such an expansion could take place.

After two conversations with TJ, the two agreed to a six-month transition period during which they'd van a few of their quarter horses from New Mexico to a farm and training facility near Rixeyville, VA, about 50 miles south of Leesburg. Maintaining a limited interest in the quarter-horse business, they planned to race at River Downs in Cincinnati from the beginning of July to the beginning of September starting with the 1984 season. Meanwhile, Judith would oversee Cutter Farms while helping to care for Hannah Gordon-Cutter. Rex would live in the Cutter family home.

The next step might have been a tad more challenging, simply because TJ knew the backgrounds of the individuals he'd be looking to bring together. He'd start by contacting his former college roomie, FBI field agent Sammy Eisenstat, to bring him up-to-speed with the Abigail Prescott proposal, get his feedback on the status of the federal and local investigations into the Wellington family and whether he had a green light to proceed with a transaction.

"It would have been better had you told me about this as soon as the Widow Wellington presented you with the proposal," Eisenstat said a bit too sternly for TJ's comfort.

"Well, I first wanted to know if we had serious interest in pursuing a deal," answered Cutter "...and if Prescott hadn't been flexible in the outright sale of Thoroughbred Bs Farm versus a land lease, it would have been a non-starter.

"By the way, Abigail insisted I use her maiden name, Prescott," added TJ. "She's not very subtle about her distaste for the Wellington name. Can't say I blame her, given what she's put up with all these years."

307

"Recent events have all worked in your favor, roomie," Sammy explained. "The Fayette Commonwealth Attorney, Barton Wysocki, refused to even submit evidence to the Grand Jury for consideration on whether any criminal charges should be brought. When he spoke with our Kentucky director of field ops, Marcus McQueen, Wysocki told him submitting evidence to a Grand Jury would be a waste of taxpayer dollars, particularly with Governor Wellington's death having been declared a suicide."

Cutter recounted his subsequent conversation with Abigail, during which she mentioned her role in getting Beau out from under his gambling debt with illegal bookmakers and her generous proposal, contingent upon divesting himself of the Wellingtons' thoroughbred breeding and racing businesses, to finance a new start for her son and his intended, Darci McDougal – *in Ireland, of all places.*

"Well, that certainly squares with our eyewitness account of Beau making a payment in Louisville to a runner for the Jersey bookmaker's operation. It saves us the time and expense of pursuing a prosecution. Not only that," the FBI agent added, "but we currently don't have an extradition treaty with Ireland, although my understanding is that may soon change. I suspect Ms. Prescott knew that when she planned all this and shipped Beau off to Dublin. If the current Administration in D.C. wants to test a new extradition agreement, I doubt it would be for something as inconsequential as this."

Cutter told his fellow UVA alum what he had in mind. Hearing Eisenstat indicate that the FBI "should have no issue with you pursuing the transaction," Cutter began to make calls to "guests" for a "celebratory dinner gathering." Given the topic of his hidden agenda, TJ decided the Molly Pitcher Inn would be the perfect place and hoped Friday evening, June 17th – five days' advance notice – would be acceptable. Promising there would be no FBI agents attending, he was able to convince each invitee to attend.

His last call had gone to Denton Dandridge. Before answering in the affirmative, Dandridge wanted Cutter to know he'd recently begun seeing Marci Davis Jeffries. Dandridge knew Marci's son, Sean, had recently been in touch with the Virginia horseman.

"Thank you for the heads up, Denton. Small world, you know. Sean will be another of my dinner guests on Friday evening."

"Well, alright then," Dandridge said in accepting TJ's invitation. "I'll send you some background information on my practice. If you have material for me to review in advance of Friday's meeting, send it via overnight to my attention at the Rusk Center in Athens."

"Let me be clear, Denton. The Cutters have a family attorney who's handled business for Cutter Farms and Cutting Edge Stables," Cutter said and then added: "We're retaining your services for the transaction we hope to consummate with Abigail Prescott. If all goes well, however, I envision you handling all subsequent activities in connection with any acquired assets."

There were six place settings in the private room at the Molly Pitcher Inn. For three of TJ Cutter's invitees, the mezzanine-level Tea Room was an all-too-familiar scene. Shrimp cocktail and a charcuterie board of various meats, cheeses and duck pâté with crackers were served as appetizers. Guests were given a choice of baked Virginia ham or broiled flounder for dinner.

Since each guest knew at least two others in the small party of six, talk came easily. For TJ and the two attorneys, it had been easy to stay away from the main topic to be discussed. Jasmine, Calvin and Sean kept their conversations casual.

When dinner plates were cleared TJ, seated at the head of the table, clanked his glass with a dessert spoon, waited a few seconds and then began:

> "All of you know each other, if not prior to this evening then certainly with the banter going back and forth throughout our meal. We're here to celebrate what I suspect will be the purchase by Cutter Farms of the Lexington, KY-based Thoroughbred Bs Farm and Triple-B Racing Stables. A price for the outright sale of these two entities has been reached after several lengthy conversations with Abigail Prescott. For all of you, the Widow Wellington has made it clear her preferred name moving forward is 'Abigail Prescott.' Please make note of that point.

> "Back to our gathering this evening. Mr. Dandridge, here, a fellow native Virginian, has been retained to represent Cutter Farms in this transaction. As our family attorney, James A.

Grey – Jim to all of you from this moment forward – is here to assist Denton inasmuch as he knows the legal history of our businesses and has knowledge of what skeletons are hidden in the family closet.

"For my three guests, I've asked you here to offer each of you an opportunity. I apologize for keeping my agenda a secret, but I didn't want you speculating on specifics before this evening. Now you'll have a chance to ask questions and to talk amongst yourselves."

Before turning to the opportunities he'd be presenting to Calvin Thomas, Sean Davis Jeffries and to his younger sister, Jasmine, Cutter brought the group up-to-date on the duties his older sister, Judith, and her husband Rex Reston would be filling at Cutter Farms:

"Judith and Rex coming east to Leesburg will give me the flexibility to take on some additional responsibilities in overseeing our Kentucky operations in addition to what we do at Cutting Edge Stables. I use the word '*some*' additional responsibilities when referring to the Kentucky businesses because I would like to hand off day-to-day supervision to the three of you."

The facial expressions on Sean and Jasmine showed they'd been completely surprised. To say it wasn't the first rodeo for Calvin Thomas would be quite the understatement. He sat expressionless, waiting to learn the substance of what Cutter had to offer.

"Calvin, you've had the advantage of spending a few months in part-time positions at Bourbonesque in Bardstown and Thoroughbred Bs Farm in Lexington, gathering information about business operations and, well...other matters. I'd like to put your experience to work by asking you to take on the position of Director of Facilities. You'd be responsible for maintaining and upgrading the stables, barns, training track, main residence and guest house. You'll set annual objectives, be given a budget to meet those objectives and report directly to me. Your initial contract will be for two years, so you have enough time to familiarize yourself with the financial and human resources you'll need to be effective and efficient. There will be a base salary plus bonus and one-year anniversary raise based on how well you do as an individual and how well the organization as a whole performs. I don't believe an individual's compensation should be anyone else's business, so you and I can meet immediately after this meeting to discuss numbers." Then, after hesitating: "Oh yes. You'll need to regrow your mustache and add a beard and afro – at least initially. We don't want anyone to connect you with Carson Tobias."

With that last requirement Calvin Thomas slipped, allowing an ever-so-small upward curl in his lips. In truth, he'd been wondering about the next chapter in his life. He was getting a bit too long in the tooth for all the town car driving plus the odd work as either a detective for private clients or the even more seldom contract work from the FBI.

"Sean, I've been impressed by your integrity as well as your knowledge of the thoroughbred industry. I'd like to offer you a position as the Cutting Edge Stables attorney in charge of negotiating contracts with jockey's agents. After you graduate Seton Hall Law, I recommend you take the Bar Exams in Kentucky and Virginia in addition to New Jersey. Jim, here, will be retiring in another year or two, and I'd like you to transition into his role as our family attorney. We can talk tomorrow morning about compensation packages. We're likely looking at an initial signing bonus, payment on a per-contract basis while you're still completing your law degree, and then a salary for your first year as an attorney. I expect you'll find my offer competitive with first-year law school graduates employed in the New York metropolitan area."

Sean Davis Jeffries could not conceal his smile. "Thank you, Mr. Cutter," he said with possibly a bit too much gratitude – at least for someone who'd have to play his share of poker when sitting across from jockeys' agents. "I'll look forward to talking with you in the morning."

"Jasmine. You've displayed some remarkable insights over the past week or so, and I sense you've turned a corner in your personal growth. I would like you to consider becoming Supervisor of Thoroughbred Development & Training. In this role, you and any assistants reporting to you will be responsible for feeding, exercising and training our young thoroughbreds until they're ready to compete at the nation's race tracks as two- and three-year-old colts and fillies. I'm talking about putting together an optimal program for all of our horses and then tailoring protocols based on an individual horse's specific needs. You, too, will have an annual budget and, as is the case with Calvin, I'm offering you a two-year contract with the same performance bonus structure. We can talk tomorrow afternoon about the specifics."

Looking around the room, the Virginia horseman who, seemingly only yesterday, had been asked to become part of a mega-IPO involving the vast thoroughbred business of "the Commonwealth's First Family," now found himself on the cusp of finalizing a transaction that would place Thoroughbred Bs Farm and Triple-B Racing Stables under the Cutter family's silks.

As if reading the minds of the three individuals who collectively would determine whether this monumental transaction moved forward, Cutter clinked his glass again to bring the small group to attention:

"I'm a great believer in how businesses in Europe treat employees' vacation time, which is to have workers disappear 'on holiday' for up to a month each summer and return ready to work. I'm prepared to give each of you four weeks of paid time off between the Memorial Day and Labor Day weekends, as long as you coordinate your vacations so at least one of you remains at our as-yet-to-be-named farm in Lexington.

"Additionally, we will have a five-day retreat between Thanksgiving Day and the end-of-year holidays during which we'll review our performance for the year about to be completed and plan for the new year about to begin. We'll choose a fun venue where we can work hard and play hard. You'll each be able to invite a guest and Cutter Farms will pay for all travel, lodging, food and entertainment expenses."

Now, with an additional reason to celebrate, the party of six was ready for dessert – crème brûlée because, as Jasmine said, "Life is sooooo sweet!"

***

The meeting at Abigail Prescott's home in Lexington had been surprisingly cordial at the outset, with introductions made and sweet tea prepared for all.

With the sale price of the farm itself having been agreed upon ahead of time, much of the day's discussion centered around the specifics of employment agreements for those who'd been working on the Wellington payroll.

Additional time was spent reviewing the seller's contracts that were still in force. A Lexington veterinarian, jockeys based at Triple-B Racing Stables' home track of Churchill Downs, racetrack stables at the Louisville track and an out-of-town transportation company were among such contracts.

The bulk of the day, however, was given to negotiating the value of Abigail Prescott's thoroughbreds. A few days prior to their meeting, Dax Baxter and Ian Snelling had sent three distinct lists to Cutter for review – one for thoroughbreds racing or in training; a second for stallions and broodmares in the breeding program, and a third for "companion" ponies (used for support and friendship) and "stable" or "lead" ponies (used for training thoroughbreds on the farm or at the track on race day).

A complete biography for each horse in the first and second groups was included: for those racing or in training - lineage, unpublished as well as published workouts, past performances and earnings; for stallions and broodmares - lineage, career performances and career earnings along with similar info for their offspring/foals. Multiple photos of each horse were provided as well.

Cutter was expected to come to the meeting with opening offers to purchase while Prescott would have opening offers to sell. The parties would negotiate from that point. The Virginia horseman could inspect each horse before a final agreement was consummated. Anticipating a sale following her ultimatum to Beau, Abigail made sure all thoroughbreds currently racing and breeding under her ownership were either on the Lexington farm or stabled at Keeneland.

It was at this point that Sean Davis Jeffries requested a copy of both parties' lists that included their respective opening offers. Abigail locked eyes with TJ Cutter's young African-American associate. Pausing a bit, Prescott called for Woodrow and asked him to "make an additional copy for Mr. Davis."

While Sean had been introduced as "Sean Davis Jeffries," there was no doubt in his mind the lady sitting across from him had intentionally referred to him by his mother's last name. Was this some sort of intimidation tactic? He returned the stare.

If other members of the Cutter contingent caught Ms. Prescott's "slip of the tongue," they weren't showing any outward signs. Inwardly seething, Sean kept his cool, took the copied lists from the butler, reached in his briefcase for a solar-powered hand-held calculator and spent the next several minutes developing a pair of computations while Denton Dandridge and Dax Baxter discussed the relative merits of career earnings versus in-the-money percentage. Upon finishing his calculations and jotting down some notes on a lined yellow legal pad, Sean pushed it to the left so TJ Cutter could look at his work.

After reviewing Sean's notes, Cutter asked if he could have a minute or two to confer with his associates. Nodding, Abigail rose from her chair and suggested that Ian and Dax adjourn with her to the kitchen where they could refill their glasses with sweet tea.

TJ then showed Denton, Jim and Jasmine Sean's notes and followed with his thoughts on how to proceed. The attorneys looked at each other and gave their admittedly tepid approval. Jasmine, ever the firebrand and rather annoyed at what she perceived as Abigail Prescott's intentional faux pas, simply said, "Damn straight, TJ. She needs us a helluva lot more than we need her!"

When seller, attorney and trainer returned from the kitchen, TJ spoke in an assertive tone that Jasmine had rarely heard from her older brother:

"My colleague, Mr. *Jeffries* (TJ looked directly at Abigail when he emphasized 'Jeffries'), has calculated the difference between our offers to purchase, in the aggregate, and your offers to sell, in the aggregate, is $4 million. We've been negotiating on the value of individual thoroughbreds for the better part of three hours now. And while I'm prepared to continue in this fashion for however long it takes to go through the entire list of colts, fillies, geldings, mares, stallions, broodmares and for that matter, even stable ponies that might be pulling the morning milk trucks here in Lexington, I'd like to suggest we simply split the difference between the two numbers to arrive at a final negotiated value.

"What say you, Mr. Baxter...Mr. Snelling...Ms. Prescott?"

By 4:30 in the afternoon, all the i's were dotted and t's were crossed. Signatures had been affixed to contracts of sale, a payment schedule for Ms. Prescott's horses had been agreed upon, and Denton Dandridge had given to Dax Baxter an initial check from Cutter Farms in the amount of $16 million made payable to Abigail Prescott.

Not one to waste time, Abigail had already purchased five acres of land in Bardstown near Bourbonesque and retained an architect to design and oversee construction of an 8,000 square foot home. Meanwhile, the management team of Calvin Thomas, Jasmine Cutter and Sean Davis Jeffries would be heading back to Lexington immediately after Labor Day.

With both parties exiting the mansion that would soon belong to the Cutter family, Denton Dandridge and Jim Grey shook hands with Dax Baxter as the three attorneys gathered for some last-minute shop talk. Meanwhile, TJ and Ian Snelling were huddling to speak about specific horses already committed to participate in races through the end of August.

Woodrow, standing next to Calvin Thomas, remarked, "It'll be a pleasure working for you as well as Mr. Cutter and the others."

"Not *for* us, Mr. Jefferson," answered Calvin. "You'll be working *with* us.

Extending his hand, Woodrow said: "Thank you for that. Have a safe trip home, Mistah *Carson*." Never surprised, Calvin smiled and gave the butler a wink and a nod while walking toward Cutter and his lawyers.

315

Searching for small talk outside the front door, Jasmine and Sean were with Abigail: "With the Derby and all, Ms. Prescott, you're probably up on fashion at Churchill Downs. What do you think about me dyeing my hair red for next year's event?" With a look of disdain, the now former owner of Thoroughbred Bs Farm and Triple-B Racing Stables didn't answer. Not knowing about Darci McDougal, TJ's kid sister couldn't understand the reason for Abigail's facial expression.

Sean, taking advantage of the silent reaction to Jasmine's question, looked Abigail straight in the eyes and simply said: "Yes, I *am* her son, Mrs. *Wellington*."

And with that, Sean Davis Jeffries took Jasmine's arm and escorted her to the stretch limo that would be taking the Cutter team to the Louisville Airport and their flight back to New Jersey.

The only son of Marci Davis Jeffries didn't look back, although he had the distinct feeling he wouldn't be seeing the last of Miss Prescott.

###

CPSIA information can be obtained
at www.ICGtesting.com
Printed in the USA
FSHW021223181119
64231FS